END OF TRACK

Books by F. VAN WYCK MASON

END OF TRACK

By

F. VAN WYCK MASON

THE BOOK CLUB
121, CHARING CROSS ROAD
LONDON, W.C.2

THIS EDITION 1946

To my old and valued friend
JOHN ALAN MAXWELL
May his hand never falter nor
his colours grow dim

BOOK
PRODUCTION
WAR ECONOMY
STANDARD

THIS BOOK IS PRODUCED
IN COMPLETE CONFORMITY
WITH THE AUTHORIZED ECONOMY STANDARD

MADE AND PRINTED IN GREAT BRITAIN BY PURNELL AND SONS, LTD.,
PAULTON (SOMSERET) AND LONDON

END OF TRACK

CHAPTER I

HALF revealed by the yellow-white glare of the approaching headlight, two men sprawled beside the right-of-way; a road-bed so
freshly laid that the rails still showed the gleam of their original
polish.

"Looks like a freight," panted the shorter of the two. "But
will yon train stop?"

"Hope so, Mac," responded the other briefly. "Those Cheyenne
Dogs ain't far behind. It'll be taps pronto if this string of cars
runs by us."

As the train approached, the taller of the two men bent and
hastily struck a match. A crumpled piece of paper burst into flame
making a glare in the blue-blackness of the Nebraska night. The
tongue of flame flared into being just long enough to throw into
bold perspective a rugged, perspiring face so gaunt that, at first
glance, it might have been taken for an Indian's. However, the tall
man's fringed buckskin shirt, the sombrero of unmistakably Mexican
design and the wide, elaborately silver-decorated belt proved that
this was no redskin.

"If they dinna stop, Bob," asked the second man, "what'll we
do?"

The taller man shrugged his lean shoulders.

"Guess that's a case of fightin' it out with the Dogs, Mac," he
said. "Reckon the Cheyennes are mighty mean to prisoners—
leastwise, they were when I was a kid back in Kansas."

The whistle of the train screeched, half drowning out the grumbling complaint of the shorter of the two lying beside the track.

"Goddam those red de'ils," said the Scotchman. "Nobody
shoots a good horse like that. I hated to lose ours."

"Maybe you'd rather lose your scalp, Colin," snapped the other.

He patted a bulging army haversack that slanted over his left
hip, partially obscuring the red stripe that ran down the side of his
breeches.

"Or this," he said.

The Scotchman turned, glanced at the haversack and shook his
head.

"Not that, laddie! Yon siller should buy us a good night's
sleep with the brawest lass in Kearney—but, losh, I'm forgetting
you're almost a married mon!"

5

Robert Burton, late captain of the Eighth Kentucky Cavalry, C.S.A., stood upright and waved the flaming piece of paper back and forth as the train bore down on him. Moving to the middle of the tracks, he appeared to dare the locomotive to run him down. There was the whistling of brakes and, clattering, clanking and panting like a winded elephant, the balloon-stacked engine ground to a stop, its cow-catcher not fifty feet from Burton. The man in the fringed shirt raised his hands as a yell came from the cab of the locomotive.

"Don't shoot!" he called. "We're friends!"

As Colin scrambled up beside him, his hands upraised, a pair of hard-faced trainmen jumped down from the cab of the puffing locomotive, each levelling a carbine on the men standing on the tracks.

The foremost, a bearded giant, squinted down the barrel of his Remington and growled.

"Keep 'em up, you two, and what the hell do you want?"

"Got jumped by Injuns awhile back," Burton explained. "They're probably right behind us. Pick us up and let's get movin'."

"Cheyennes?" asked the bearded man.

"Yeah, Dog Warriors. They jumped us in that divide up west of here and shot our hosses out from under us. We were lucky to make the train line, I——"

The big man with the beard turned to his companion.

"Gee!" he exclaimed. "Them Cheyennes are bustin' loose again!"

The smaller of the two trainmen, a pudgy figure with a greasy cap pushed askew on the back of a mop of yellow hair, frowned.

"Injuns are always scarin' tenderfeet," he said. "Every time somebody from the East sees an Injun, they yell 'Cheyenne!' Like as not, it was a bunch of Pawnees, goin' into Julesburg to get drunk."

"Y'dom idiot!" Colin MacKaye shouted. "We know Pawnees and we know Cheyennes! We know Arapahoes and Sioux and—we know every goddam tribe in the country! Get us aboard your train and get us the hell out of here, before they come down on us!"

"Aw," said the bearded man, "you're tryin' to git a free ride, huh?"

Burton's lean face flushed in the darkness as he walked toward the bearded rifleman.

"My partner and I have been fightin' most of the afternoon," he said quietly. "I'm tired of fightin' but if I have to, I think I can take you on."

The man he addressed peered through the gloom.

"You look like you been winged," he said. "What got you—arrer or a bullet?"

"Arrow," Burton replied briefly. "Just a graze."

"That's good—arrer wounds ain't no joke—damn Comanche plugged me in the leg this spring."

"Shake a foot, you fellers," the engineer called down from his cab. "We gotta get rollin' if we're goin' to put Number 15 into Willer Creek on time."

Robert Burton paused. "You got any soldiers aboard?" he asked. "These hills are crawlin' with Cheyennes and a sprinklin' of Brule Sioux."

The engineer spat into the darkness.

"Nary a trooper aboard," he said, "but to hell with them red sons a'bitches! I'll git my train through."

He sent a rush of steam roaring up to make the low bare hills resound.

"They's a passenger car tacked onto the end," he continued. "Jed'll take your fare if you got any money—and you better have, if you want to ride this train."

He blew off steam again while the fireman fed logs to the loco-motive's hungry maw. Sparks showered up from the funnel and went whirling madly off to the east.

"Better hurry," the second fireman said as he passed his carbine up to the engineer and swung aboard. "And don't you worry about Injuns, boys. They pop at us sometimes and once in a while some crazy buck tries to rope the smokestack but that's all they do."

Burton, with long, quick strides, led Colin MacKaye toward the dim glow of lighted car windows far to the rear of the long train, the thrums of his hunting shirt softly tapping on wide, weather-beaten shoulders.

'Union Pacific Railroad'—ghostly white, the words glimmered on a long succession of cars.

Ever scanning the velvet blackness beyond the Platte, the two men passed a stock car in which horses stamped and squealed, destined for the End o' Track. Next, they hurried past flat cars heaped with precious ties, each slab of wood worth three dollars in this treeless prairie country.

A brakeman perched on a boxcar's roof waved a warning as he yelled, "Better shake a leg, boys. We ain't waitin' long in these parts."

Over his shoulder, Burton glimpsed the glare of flames licking up from the smokestack to tinge the locomotive's thick plume of smoke a furious scarlet. Number 15's whistle screeched impatiently, then the trucks of the one passenger car, coupled on just before the train's chunky caboose, retched and the two men swung lightly up onto the car's steps as the freight commenced its westward journey.

When Captain Robert Burton opened the door of the coach, he

found himself looking at as oddly assorted a company as he had seen since, as a gangling stripling, he had left his father's Kansas farm to join Bedford Forrest's hard riding, ever hungry troopers. Lord, how much water had spilled over the dam since then!

Four smoky lamps were shedding an amber glare on the car's interior and just barely revealing shadowed details. Near the door, a couple of sunburned soldiers on furlough lolled on their seat, ignoring the eyes of the others in the car. They frankly fondled two painted trollops who, in gay, too frilly dresses, promptly fixed their eyes on Burton and Colin. The harlots' eyes were appraising, then languishing, as they took in the height and breadth of the Captain so effectively framed in the coach doorway.

When MacKaye closed the door behind him, a hard-faced passenger looked up from a poker game that was in progress, a suitcase serving as a table, and briefly studied the newcomers.

"Heyo," he drawled, shooting his none-too-clean celluloid cuffs. "Like to join us, brother?"

Burton shook his head as he continued down the aisle.

"Never played poker in my life with fellows I met on a train or a steamboat."

"Say, listen," growled the gambler, "do you mean——"

He half rose from his seat before Burton's level eyes fixed themselves squarely on his face. Then the hard-faced man sank back into his seat and picked up his cards.

Followed by Colin MacKaye, late of Her Britannic Majesty's Household Cavalry, Burton strode on.

The greater number of passengers in the car were men—alike only in their alertness and the need of soap and water. Among them Burton recognized clerks, contractors, soldiers, labourers and surveyors; all headed for the roaring mushroom railroad towns further west. Not a man in the car but was armed somehow. Several soft-spoken, long-moustached individuals were veritable walking arsenals with two guns slung at their hips and an assortment of derringers, knives and daggers in their belts. Most of the men had a carbine or rifle of some kind propped close to him. Even the handful of painted, shrill-voiced whores carried pearl-handled derringers in their handbags. The two being manhandled by the soldiers brazenly dangled their deadly little pistols at the ends of the bright ribbons made fast to their rattlesnake skin belts.

The two men made their way toward an unoccupied seat in the rear of the car. Burton, hampered by his heavy haversack, struggled to keep his balance in the lurching car as he climbed over the mounds of baggage stacked in the aisle. Then, as the train swayed sharply, the Captain caught one of his elaborate steel and gold spurs in a carpetbag. He staggered and half fell into the lap of a young woman who, heavily veiled, was dozing amid the luggage piled about her. Burton's hand encountered the sleeper's knee and perforce he clutched its round softness to recover himself.

The results were astonishing and immediate.

"Oh! You—you—— !"

The girl's hand flashed up and dealt Burton a ringing slap beside the mouth. As the Captain straightened, blood rushed furiously into a long scar that ran from above his left ear to the line of his black hair.

"Why—why, ma'am," Burton fumbled, "I didn't mean—I——"

A pair of outraged brown eyes surveyed him icily.

"I know," the girl snapped. "You lost your balance and didn't mean to—to clutch me. Three other *gentlemen* have done the same thing !"

"But, ma'am——"

A chorus of jeering laughs rose through the car as the other occupants craned their necks in the direction of Burton and the girl. The young lady's cheeks flamed with embarrassment and she jerked her head to look out the window at the passing blackness.

"I apologize, ma'am," Burton said meekly, "but if three other gents have done the same thing, you must be plumb magnetic."

The girl's head swung back toward him, her eyes furious.

"Why, I—of all the impertinent—how dare you——"

"Leave be, Bob," advised Colin, gently pushing Burton toward the empty seat. "Ye'd best catch some rest, m'lad, or your braw lass will think it's a scarecrow come home to roost."

Grinning, Captain Robert Burton, late of Forrest's cavalry and more recently of the army of Emperor Maximilian of Mexico, touched his wide sombrero and moved on. The lamplight glinted on the handle of a curiously long-bladed knife he wore just back of the holstered revolver on his right hip. The same light picked out the red stripe on his dark blue breeches. As he seated himself beside Colin, a hail came from across the aisle.

"Settle us a bet," called a gaunt individual in a blue flannel shirt. "My pardner, Joe here, allows by them blue pants you must be a Yank. I say you talk Secesh."

Burton smiled briefly, his white teeth flashing.

"Collect your bet, stranger," he said. "These blue pants were made in Tampico. Durin' the last war I was a Reb."

The blue-shirted man nodded eagerly.

"Mister, so was I. Fought all through in Longstreet's Corps, Army o' No'thern Virginny. Shake."

Burton clasped the grimy outstretched hand.

"I was with Forrest," he said. "Never met up with Longstreet's Corps but they did some mighty fine fightin', from what I hear."

"Forrest didn't do bad, either," responded the man in the blue shirt. "And, listen. Better tell your pardner to sit further away from the window after we pass Willow Creek."

"Why ?"

The Virginian bit off a chew of tobacco from a plug, then tendered it to his seat companion who boasted an enormous set of ginger-coloured whiskers.

"Account of them damn Injuns take a pot shot every once in a while," he explained. "By the law of averages, even a redskin cain't miss *all* the time."

Burton nodded as he placed the haversack on the floor between his feet. He eased the big Colt onto his lap, twisted his sheath knife into a comfortable position and, while Colin fell off into an instantaneous sleep, surveyed the other passengers.

Most of these unshaven, red-faced men wore fragments of blue or grey uniforms. Three seats forward and across the aisle from Burton sat a grizzled cavalry sergeant engaged in a noisy game of rondo cooloo with a pair of privates and man whose flashy dress labelled him a 'drummer.' The two soldiers and their trollops in the front of the car appeared to have settled down to nap. The girl whose knee he had encountered and whose palm his face had encountered sat rigidly erect with lasting indignation written in every line of her head and her slight, softly rounded shoulders.

The man across the aisle, noticing Burton's interested observation, leaned over and yowled a would-be whisper into the Captain's ear over the clatter of the car wheels.

"Touchy little Yank, ain't she ?" the Virginian asked. "She sho' gave you a mean clip on the jaw."

"She's right pretty," Burton replied uneasily. "I didn't mean to bother her."

"Aw hell, she's one of them spoiled high-and-mighty gals from N'Yawk or somewhere like that," grunted the ginger-whiskered Joe, beside the veteran of Longstreet's Corps. "Ever since she got on the train at Omaha she's been orderin' everybody around like they was niggers. Sho' has got a big surprise comin' to her when she gets to where she's goin'. Out at the End o' Track they don't care who you was back where you come from. It's what you are when you get there."

"Who is she ?" Burton asked.

As he asked the question Burton swore at himself. What did he care who this girl might be when, waiting for him, was Enid Culver ? How wonderfully patient Enid had been—always sure that he'd come, as he now was coming, to claim her.

"She's a Miss Valcour, the conductor told me," said the man in the blue shirt. "Her pappy's a Senator, no less—one of the railroad backers, I guess."

"Queer he'd let her travel alone like that."

"She ain't alone, exactly. She's got a maidservant with her but the maid's scared stiff of Injuns so she's hidin' out in the baggage compartment. But, speakin' of Injuns, how-come you got that arrer hole in your sleeve?"

Burton glanced down at the puncture in the buckskin hunting shirt and shrugged.

"Nothin' but a scratch," he said almost apologetically. "My pardner and I got chased by a bunch of Cheyennes and along about sundown they caught up with us. Killed our hosses about a mile from the railroad but we managed to fight 'em off and get away after dark."

The Captain's voice was casual but it electrified those in the passenger car. Heads turned, including the oval face of Mistress Valcour, to stare at the long-legged figure lounging in his seat.

"Did you say Injuns?" somebody asked from the other end of the car.

"Yeah," drawled Burton. "Southern Cheyennes. Seemed right mean, too."

A gaunt, sad-eyed cattleman in a gaudy pair of breeches tucked into high-heeled boots suddenly jerked himself out of his doze and stood up. Without a word he pulled a Spencer carbine down from the luggage rack and tested the action of the gun's lever experimentally, spilling a cartridge out into the aisle. The man shoved the cartridge back into the magazine, eyed the gun for a moment and then leaned it beside his seat. Then he sank back and resumed his nap.

That was the signal for a general check-up on the train's armament. The trollops with the soldiers examined their tiny derringers; the soldiers grasped their muskets, the gamblers swung their guns into a more handy position.

The veteran of Longstreet's Division rubbed his chin with a speculative thumb.

"Reckon that 'ud be Turkey Leg's bunch—goddam 'em! Been raisin' hell around these parts for some time. Cavalry from Fort McPherson's been chasin' 'em so I reckon they'll be headin' back to the Republican River by now."

"Huh!" grunted the ginger-whiskered companion of the Virginian. "Effen you think Turkey Leg's gonna be scared back to his own diggin's by a bunch of pip-squeak cavalry like is comin' out of McPherson, you're dead wrong. That Injun can outride and outguess any Yank cavalry that ever tried to tell one end of the hoss from the other."

"Ugh!" grunted a voice in emphatic endorsement.

Burton turned to look at an Indian who sat on the floor at the far end of the car, wrapped in a glaring scarlet blanket. A Pawnee and obviously drunk.

"'Horse soljer never ketchum Dog Soljer," mumbled the Pawnee, nodding gravely. "Only North Scout ketchum. I North Scout one time. Kill plenty Dog Soljer. Kill hundred-two hundred, think-be."

"Go on!" scoffed Ginger-Beard. "You ain't killed nothin' but a hundred jugs of red-eye!"

The Pawnee eyed the bearded man steadily for a time, then snorted and pulled his blanket closer about him, shutting his eyes and seeming to doze instantly. The train rattled on through the night, swaying, clanking, squeaking.

"Ain't nothin' to worry about," the Longstreet veteran told Burton. "Them redskins ain't never bothered a train yet. Think they're dragons or somethin', I guess."

A man in the uniform of an infantry corporal twisted in his seat and called down toward the Virginian.

"Mebbe they ain't wrecked none," he volunteered, "but they're sure shot at plenty of trains. Killed five passengers last week alone——"

"In that case," Burton suggested, "maybe the ladies had better go up to the baggage car."

"Sure thing," somebody ahead agreed. "Gals are a sight too scarce in this country for us to let 'em get hurt by any lousy Cheyennes!"

The suggestion voiced by Bob Burton was relayed forward. First to leave their seats were the two Cyprians in the front of the car who apparently seized on the recommendation as an excuse to get away from the fumbling pawings of the soldiers. Three or four other women, obviously of the same profession, caught up their skirts, and, simpering and giggling, went swaying toward the door leading to the baggage car. As they passed, lurching with the motion of the train, several male hands went out to steady them— hands that inevitably seemed to clutch a leg, a thigh or some other interesting part of the girls' anatomy.

"Quit it!" shrilled one of the girls, slapping viciously at the mahogany-coloured hand of a man that reached for her with an especially daring clutch. "In Julesburg it'll cost you five bucks to do that!"

"Okay, Honeybird," the man replied. "Remind me when we git there and mebbe I'll buy you a bottle of bubbly at the King o' the Hills Bar. Iffen you're nice to me, that is."

The girl showed uneven teeth between carmine lips as she grinned.

"That's a date," she said. "And there ain't a girl in this part of the country that can be half as nice to you as I can—if I'm full of champagne, that is."

A few moments later, the only woman left in the passenger car was the girl in blue whose palm had stung Captain Bob Burton's cheek. When one of the men seated next to her leaned over, urging the girl to follow the others into the baggage car, she shook her head disdainfully. Burton, watching, grinned. Not a chance that a little aristocrat like that would deign to use the same shelter that harboured a group of whores.

"Give you five to one we pull into North Platte without even a window busted," a gambler called. Finding no takers, the card shark spat into the aisle and returned to his game of poker.

The drunken Pawnee began to snore and Burton slumped further down in the bumpy seat, composing himself to think of Enid—Enid ! No longer was she half a continent away but a scant hundred miles distant. Wait till she saw the contents of that heavy haversack ! There was music in every *clickety-clack* of the rails, sounding a song that made Burton's heart grow lighter with each passing moment. How worthwhile it had been to go on fighting. They'd buy a spread, of course, and then——

The car wheels had commenced to grind on a curve when the locomotive's whistle screamed like a great beast in agony. Viciously the train bucked twice, hurling the passengers about, sending them sprawling into the aisles or doubling them up over the seats ahead. Then the car shot sickeningly into space, tilting upward. It crashed down again amid a horrid crackling of splintered wood and tinkling glass. Howls, screams and curses sounded up ahead as the front of the passenger car jammed into the rear of the baggage car, crushing the vehicle into kindling.

The kerosene lamps had blinked out with the first jar of the impact. Burton felt himself being hurled through blackness while debris rained down on him. His head banged against something sharp and he saw more lights than he had seen since the siege of Fort Donelson.

CHAPTER II

IT was a macabre, distorted scene worthy of the brush of Gustave Doré which gradually materialized in Robert Burton's dazed vision. A queer flickering light enabled him to make out a double row of seats leaning drunkenly above him. About him arms, legs and hands beat at the air from beneath the wreckage that covered the bodies. As he desperately lashed consciousness back into his benumbed body, a grey streamer of acrid wood smoke stung his nostrils. Fire !

He battled to free himself of the timbers that pinioned him and, as he fought, he heard a sound that chilled his spine. Over the cries of the injured came the hideous screeching "*Ah who-o-wah !*" that marked the war cry of the Southern Cheyennes.

The Captain found that he was pinned by debris lying on the roof of the coach which in its death agonies must have turned completely over. Painfully he pulled free as the smoke grew thicker and the flicker of hungry flames burst through the shattered front of the car.

"MacKaye !" he yelled in frenzy. "Colin ! Where are you ?"

"Aiblins in hell," came a muffled voice. Then a groping hand struck Burton's shoulder. "Dinna think I'm hurt. Are you ?"

"No, let's get out of here !"

His eyes blinded by the billowing smoke, the ex-Confederate frantically felt for his guns. One of them had fallen from its holster but the other still was in place.

"This way !" yelled a bull-like voice. "Come this way ! Hyars a big hole fer you to climb through."

Slowly, the two men crawled over piles of luggage, car seats that had been ripped loose and bodies which proved at one glance to be past help. The glare of the flames mounted higher outside the coach, illuminating a scene that made even Burton shudder—and Burton had witnessed the massacres after the capture of Queretaro.

The soldier of fortune fought back a panicky surge as a puff of hot smoke and a tongue of flame reached out for him.

"Keep your head," he told himself. "You've got to get out ! You've got to get back to Enid Culver ! Enid ! "

He gulped gratefully as a blast of fresh air told him that he must be nearing a hole in the side of the shattered coach. Just as he was about to fling himself out of this maelstrom of heat and flame and death, he paused. His fingers had encountered something smoothly soft among the jagged splinters and shattered glass. The fire roared up again and Burton found his fingers clutching the skirt of the Valcour girl. It was impossible to tell whether Senator Valcour's daughter was dead or alive but he instinctively reached to gather the girl into his arms. Her head lolled limply and a dark trickle crept down from the corner of her mouth to mar the pallor of her chin.

Other survivors, like grotesque caricatures of humans amid the ruddy-tinted smoke, were crawling by him, bumping and floundering into him, whimpering, cursing and making animal noises of stark fear. Hotter grew the bitter smoke as the flames crackled over the wooden cars with horrible speed. Screams made an ear-splitting hell of the wrecked coach as luckless wretches, hopelessly pinned in the debris, watched the inexorable advance of the fire moving toward them.

Somehow Captain Robert Burton managed to stagger to his feet, to follow Colin MacKaye's big figure out through a hole in the side of the car. Tears streaming down his cheeks, coughing, and grinding broken glass underfoot, Bedford Forrest's ex-Captain suddenly lurched into fresh air that was sweeter than the headiest wine. His ears were filled with a howling clamour and he half lowered, half dropped the girl to the ground and strained his smoke-blinded eyes to see what was going on. He wiped his streaming eyes again and again before he saw what was happening.

Blazing coals from the locomotive's firebox had set fire to the wooden cars, furnishing light for a horde of half naked, hideously daubed Cheyennes who were swarming over the wrecked train, seeming impervious to the smoke and flames. Close at hand, five or six passengers were crouched half dazed on the road-bed embankment, rubbing their eyes and coughing. Two others, bleeding from ugly splinter wounds, lay watching the fire-lit saturnalia, panting like hurt animals.

Burton caught his breath with a groan of dismay. At any minute, he knew, those Cheyennes would be turning to other and grimmer amusements than looting the burning freight cars. More survivors of the passenger car came crawling and squirming out of the wreck but most of them, Burton saw at a glance, carried no weapons.

"Who's got guns?" he yelled to the men nearest him.

"I got a rifle. I got a Wesson——"

"That all? Then somebody's got to get back in that car and get guns! MacKaye!"

"Aye, Rob?" The gaunt Scot crawled up to Burton's side, the weird light of the flames revealing a long cut across his chin. Burton's eyes moved swiftly, surveying the terrain. About fifty yards to the right he saw a low hillock.

"Colin," he called over the roar of the fire and the insane screeching of the Cheyennes, "take the men up to the knoll. Carry this girl, too. Might make a stand there."

"Aye." The Scot nodded and turned to the survivors. "Any of ye ken how to fight a skirmish?"

"Reckon so," panted a surveyor in the remnants of a grey uniform. "Had four years o' practice. Where you-all goin'?"

"After guns," Burton called back as two more retching men, their clothing smouldering, came staggering out of the inferno of the burning train. Shouldering these men aside, Burton and the ginger-whiskered Virginian, who had appeared out of nowhere, shielded their faces from the heat and plunged back into the shambles. Burton felt about in the debris for guns, any kind of guns. As he worked frantically, he was struck by the bitter irony of his situation. What if he died to-night, with Enid so close to him after all these years?

Then, for the first time since the coach had made its mad plunge to destruction, Burton remembered his haversack. A pang of despair shot through him. The hard-earned fruits of two years of desperate fighting down in Mexico were bound up in that haversack and now they were about to vanish in smoke and flame ! That bag meant everything to their future—his and Enid's.

He fought down the impulse to forget his quest for rifles in a search for that precious knapsack.   He recalled the helpless survivors of the train wreck outside, practically unarmed, and he began digging through the wreckage again in his hunt for guns.

Four rifles and a pair of revolvers were all he could find before the flames, sweeping down the length of the car, drove him toward the hole in the side of the burning vehicle.   There, close to the opening, he met the ginger-whiskered man, singed and blistered, crawling through the orange-hued murk.

"I got five carbines and a pin-fire," he yelled.   "C'mon, boy, we gotta go—them Injuns will be gettin' hep any minute."

"Get me out ! I'm burning !"

"For God's sake, kill me.   I can't stand it !"

Burton's heart was sickened by the frenzied screams of those who were beyond help.   To try to aid any of those crushed beneath the flaming wreckage was senseless suicide, Burton knew, while unarmed men were waiting for the guns he was carrying—men whose scalps would dangle from the belts of the Dog Soldiers within a few minutes unless he brought help to them.   Shutting his ears to the shrieks and wails from the victims of the wreck, the ex-Confederate fought his way toward the hole that led to the outside.

As Burton lurched toward the great wound in the coach's side, his foot caught in something that tangled itself in his spurs when he tried to kick it loose.   He stooped awkwardly, holding the guns in one arm, and tried to disentangle the straps that were wrapped around his foot.   His fingers, as they pried at the straps, slid over a familiar stamped leather surface and he yelped instinctively.   His haversack !

He dropped the guns and used his long knife to slash through the sling strap that seemed to be caught on a splintered beam.   Then, hoisting the guns again, he picked up the case and plunged toward the makeshift exit.

Swaying, his hunting shirt blackened and smoking in half a dozen places, Robert Burton stumbled down into the ditch beside the right-of-way.   His tear-stung eyes made out three survivors of the wreck limping toward the summit of the little knoll Burton had directed Colin to use.   Already from the top of the diminutive hill brief spurts of flame were beginning to mark the first feeble defiance to a rain of arrows that whispered through the smoke-filled night, like soft-voiced messengers of doom.

Higher flared the flames from the burning train, lighting the whole Platte valley.   From inside the blazing passenger coach sounded a shot, another shot.

"Poor devils," Burton panted as he laboured up the hill. "Reckon I'd do the same myself."

"Hurry up ! " yelled the man with the ginger-coloured whiskers from ahead of Burton.

"They comin' ? "

"Yeah. Shake a leg or the swines will cut us off."

Only a few yards behind the two men and half screened by smoke lurked a handful of swift, shadowy figures. The ex-Confederate raced up beside his companion.

"We won't make it this way," he gasped. "Grab these rifles. I'll try to stand them off awhile."

"Like hell you will, Rebel—I'm a-staying too," the other yapped.

"Listen," Burton snarled. "They need those rifles up at the top. Get 'em up there ! This bag, too ! "

The ring of authority in Burton's voice forced obedience from the other. He took the haversack and firearms from the Captain and went scurrying up the sandy slope.

Luridly outlined by the flaming wreck, Burton knelt and swiftly adjusted the sights of a salvaged Spencer carbine he had kept. He felt a thrill of savage joy as he cradled the gun to his cheek—the same kind of unholy glee that had swept him in the midst of those deadly little skirmishes which had flickered up and down the Mississippi Valley and, later, the big-scale battles that had raged in Mexico.

"Seven shots," he said aloud. "Just enough to turn the trick —maybe."

Behind him the boots of the running man sounded loud, but louder still was the eerie whine of bullets passing overhead.

"*Wah-wah! Hoo——*"

A ragged line of dismounted Cheyennes broke through the smoke pall hanging over the right-of-way and headed toward Burton. In the van of the savages ran a copper-coloured giant who held a dripping long-haired scalp between his teeth as he waved a rifle he had picked up.

Dropping on one knee, Burton threw his sights on the leader. The Spencer's recoil jarred his shoulder as the gun spoke. The big Cheyenne threw his hands up, spun halfway around and fell heavily, the scalp still clutched in his teeth.

Burton knew that he was doomed unless the guns he had sent on ahead could reach the knoll in time and, if they did get there, those on the hill would have sense enough to cover his retreat. Jaws tight-locked, he drew down his sights on a crude yellow cross splashed across the breast of a Cheyenne who wore a wolf mask headdress. Again there was that welcome jar at his shoulder and the savage sprawled, headfirst. Burton pumped the carbine, sending an empty cartridge case tinkling to the ground.

Five shots left. The attackers came in faster now, utterly oblivious to all danger, drunk with blood-lust. Burton shifted his aim and with all the skill of an experienced skirmisher selected the closest of the screeching savages as his target.

Another and still another shot slammed out. Still the Cheyennes came on, their sweaty, near-naked bodies gleaming in the light of the fire. An arrow sighed past Burton's head, missing by inches. Another shaft thudded into the ground beside his black boots.

The nearest Indian was only ten yards away when he sent home his fifth shot almost in the face of the fantastically painted Cheyenne.

Had the bearded man with the guns been hit? Had he bolted? Why didn't those men on the knoll open fire? A few seconds more and it would be too late. A chill sweat sprang out on Burton's forehead.

"For God's sake," he yelled, "let 'em have it! Fire, you damn fools!"

Only one or two shots answered his appeal. Too bad. No Enid now. He decided to shoot up to the last minute, then break for the top of the knoll. Not that he would ever get there, but a man had to fight as long as he could.

His sixth shot was sent home at point-blank range. Then the Indians were leaping at him. Talon-fingered hands reached him. There were howls in his ears. Burton managed to fire his last shot into the face of a towering chief who wore four tall *coup* feathers twisted into his braided scalp lock.

He gave ground in order to reverse his gun, using the butt as a club. He swung the gun in an arc and felt it land. He stepped back a few more paces and swung the gun again. Wildly, he looked about him for an opening through which he might make a break for the knoll. The red glare revealed a ring of faces about him, each one more hideous than its neighbour. Snarling like wolves, thrusting with lances decorated with feathers and scalps, the Dog Soldiers closed in. The carbine swung again, knocking aside a questing spear and smashing the skull of its carrier. Burton dodged a flailing war axe, wheeled and heaved his heavy boot to the groin of an onrushing savage. That gave him time to swing the carbine again.

He knew he was but postponing the inevitable. He knew it was but a question of time before the Indians buried him in their charge. Still he fought on, teeth bared, eyes blazing.

And as he swung the carbine, certain vivid memories flashed through his mind. He glimpsed a perfect picture of a wild cavalry charge before Corinth; of a Yankee officer's sabre cutting at him and missing. He saw Enid in his arms, her eyes half closed, her mouth warm and pulsating beneath his. He saw again the canals of Xochimilco with perfumed romance.

He swung his carbine doggedly. Hands clawed at him from the night, clutched him, jerked him this way and that. Knives glittered and Bob Burton set his teeth, awaiting the first sting of the steel.

Then, from the hill-top came rolling a steady volley of rifle shots. The ex-Confederate heard the familiar sound of bullets smacking into human flesh. One Indian howled like a crippled dog and went rolling away, clutching his middle. Others dropped noiselessly. Another volley roared down from the knoll.

Captain Burton never knew how he escaped the hail of lead that smashed into the Indians about him. He watched the Indians drop while others abruptly fled. Soon the crowd of savages had evaporated to only four braves who, ignoring the shots from the hill, still hacked and thrust at the ex-Confederate officer. Another volley crashed out and more writhing shapes dotted the slope. Two Indians were left to dodge Burton's swinging carbine.

The beleaguered Captain retreated a few steps, then clubbed with his gun to beat down the guard of a brave who wore a coyote headdress. Howling, the Cheyenne fell back, his shattered left arm dangling limply, and staggered away. The remaining warrior raised a hatchet and leaped in on the breathless, sweat-blinded white man.

Burton gave ground again when he found that his last blow had splintered the carbine's stock. The struggle on the slope became a duel. Burton tried to swing his assailant around so as to give some rifleman from above a clear shot at the brave, but the wily Cheyenne used him for a shield until, as Burton's heel turned on a loose stone and he staggered, the brave raised his glittering hatchet and sprang.

The soldier of fortune kicked out with all his failing strength. The Indian, twisting, caught the kick on his thigh and grunted. Then, with a howl of fury and triumph, the Indian swung his hatchet to send the deadly blade hissing past Burton's shoulder. The white man wrenched his body out of the path of the hatchet and grabbed at his holster. The gun was gone !

Dimly conscious of the shouts from the top of the knoll and the chorus of screams from the Indians crouched behind the road-bed, the adventurer's hand flashed to the back of his wide silver-mounted belt to close on the rawhide-wrapped handle of the bowie knife. The ten inches of steel blade flashed free as the Cheyenne's war hatchet smashed at his head again.

The Indian leaped forward as he struck. Burton, at the same time, dived in at the Cheyenne, his whole sinewy frame bunched behind his knife hand. There was a thudding jar which shook Burton as he closed with the slippery body of the savage, stinking with its rancid sweat. The knife struck some bone that held for a split second and then the blade slid home. Burton's knife hand was drenched by a hot flood. Expertly, he jammed down on the knife handle before jerking out the long blade. The Cheyenne squalled once. Then, as Burton swung away, the Indian dropped forward on his face, the fire-illuminated feathers of his war bonnet standing out at grotesque angles.

As the brave dropped there came a shout from the handful of survivors at the top of the knoll; a howl of rage from the Indians below. The Cheyennes tried another rush at Burton but a withering volley from the hilltop drove them to cover again. The ex-Confederate, gasping and stumbling, ran to the top of the hill and threw himself among the white men who waited for him.

There were fourteen men—and the girl. Fourteen men with only a few guns and less ammunition. Burton looked about him and bit back a groan.

"God damme," said Colin MacKaye, crouched beside Burton. "That makes a fair bid to do us in proper!"

He pointed and Burton raised his head to see a swarm of Indians, mounted on their rugged ponies, come galloping around the end of the blazing train. Apparently, this new group had been attracted by the glare of the fire and had galloped up to join in the looting and scalping. The dismounted Dog Soldiers greeted their tribesmen with wild screams, gesturing toward the knoll. Then, mounted and dismounted, the savages made a new assault on the hill.

CHAPTER III

"AMMUNITION'S verra near oot," growled Colin, sighting down the barrel of a Spencer and picking a brave off his pony's back.

"Save it then!" Burton commanded. "This snipin' won't get us anywhere."

His gaunt face bleak, Burton caught up a rifle and adjusted its sights with trembling, bloodstained fingers. Two of the men on the knoll lay motionless, one with an arrow in his throat and another with a musket ball in his forehead. The girl, Burton saw, still lay unconscious with a long blue-gartered leg showing where her voluminous skirt had been rumpled.

"Nobody fire till I give the order," the ex-Confederate snapped. "Close up the circle."

The mounted Cheyennes had begun their inevitable tactics of riding around the hill in a slowly tightening circle, the braves hanging themselves over on the far sides of their ponies. At the foot of the hill and too far distant to make fair targets in the flickering light from the burning train, the dismounted savages waited as grimly patient as wolves.

"Ain't got but ten shots," said one of the men sprawled in a shallow hollow near Burton. "How many you got, Virginny?"

"About fifteen," said the man who had fought with Longstreet. "Savin' the last one for myself, too, if them Cheyennes bust our ring. Savin' two—one for the gal, yonder."

"Keep your sights low," Burton said. "We're shootin' down hill. Try volleys and count three between each one. Seems like our only chance is to give 'em enough hell that they'll haul out of here".

It was a strange group that fought off the Cheyennes that night on that unnamed hilltop. No two men were dressed alike. Some were flashily clothed, others wore the roughest of patched garments. Cowboys, soldiers, gamblers, trainmen and merchants, they waited for the commands of the gaunt young man with the quick grey eyes.

Nor were the weapons of the doomed handful less varied. Nine of them were lucky enough to carry Spencer repeating carbines. In addition, there was a sprinkling of obsolete Sharp's carbines— clumsy single shot affairs just a shade more efficient than old muzzle loaders. A brakeman with the broken shaft of an arrow sprouting from one shoulder clutched a long-barrelled pin-fire gun of the type furnished Union Pacific train crews. The rest had revolvers, derringers and—in one instance—a duelling pistol with a beautifully chased barrel.

"We cain't stand 'em off," sobbed a wild-eyed youth. "There must be a couple of thousand of them red swines!"

"Ye're daft, laddie," corrected Colin MacKaye in his measured, grave voice. "Not more'n a hundred, if that. We can lick 'em. It's been done plenty o' times by men not half so braw as you and me."

The boy clamped his teeth over a quivering lower lip and turned away. Burton watched him with sympathetic eyes. Maybe, he thought, the kid had a girl waiting for him, too. Maybe he was on his way to a girl with soft white arms and warm full lips, like Enid's.

On hands and knees, he scrambled toward the unconscious girl who lay mercifully unknowing of the doom that threatened her. His hand straightened her skirt before he raised a limp arm to feel the Valcour girl's pulse. It beat faintly but steadily. Easily, he lowered the arm, then looked down at the revolver he held in his hand.

Should he do it now? Later, when the ammunition was gone, it might be too late. In the heat of beating off a concerted rush by the Indians, there might not be time—the last shot might be fired with the girl still alive.

Because there was no doubt in his mind that this girl from the East would rather a thousand times be shot than be captured—that is, if she had the least idea of what lay in store for a white woman captured by Indians. There would be rape, of course, and torture later. He still retained a vivid picture of his glimpse of a young Mormon girl who had been captured by Comanches—the hardwood coals that the Indians had heaped on her stomach as she lay, staked out naked on the plains.

There was a mounting screech from the encircling Indians. Burton scrambled back to the firing line.

"Steady, men," he said in a voice that showed no quaver. "Here they come!"

He surveyed his dwindling force and felt a glow of pride. The battle light was shining in Colin MacKaye's eyes as he cuddled a Spencer stock to his cheek. A cavalry sergeant was singing a ribald song as one of his heavy black moustaches drooped over the lock of his rifle. In one place crouched a wounded brakeman, cursing steadily as he held his revolver ready, pausing in his oaths only enough to vomit blood.

A swelling thunder of hoofs told Burton that the mounted Cheyennes were getting ready to ride in, converge and overwhelm the survivors. They offered tempting targets as they grouped for the charge, but not a man on the hilltop pulled a trigger as Burton gave sharp commands to hold fire.

"*Wah-wah! Wah!*"

The Indians bunched and began thundering up the slope. A big savage on a white pony rode out ahead, brandishing a heavy carbine, motioning to each side of him.

Although Captain Robert Burton had felt Death's cold breath many times during the past six years, he came closer to being unnerved then than ever before. There was something peculiarly awesome in the vista of the painted rider, the swaying lances, the tossing war bonnets. Burton's forefinger crept through the trigger guard of his Spencer. He decided to wait until the foremost horseman passed the still body of the Indian he had killed with his knife and then——

A lifetime dragged by. Louder swelled the infernal clamour of the savages. They came closer—closer.

"Now!"

The volley thundered out, smothering the top of the knoll with acrid powder smoke.

"One!" As he peered through the smoke he began to count, snapping forward the ejector lever of his rifle. "Two!" He sent the empty cartridge spinning away. "Three!" Through a gap in the smoke he caught in the sights a daubed chief flourishing a lance. He squeezed the trigger, then cursed bitterly as an over-eager young warrior rode in front of the chief at the last second and went whirling off his pony, killed by the shot intended for the chief.

When the echoes of the second volley rumbled back from among the barren hills across the Platte, there rose the shrieks of wounded horses and howls of stricken savages. Still the Cheyenne attack pressed on.

A third volley crashed out into the distorted faces of the Indians not fifty feet away. The carbine at Burton's shoulder was growing hot now and the ex-Confederate's ears buzzed from the concussion of the shots about him. The whole world seemed filled with tossing feathers, streaks of gunfire, rearing horses, painted faces that belonged in a horrid nightmare.

Rising on one knee, Burton, MacKaye and the cavalry sergeant formed a nucleus about which the others gathered. Then the youngster whose nerves had almost snapped before the charge gave a wild scream and jumped over the rim of the knoll. Hands reached out to grab him but he slipped away and ran shrieking down the slope. He had not travelled twenty feet before a Cheyenne lance caught him between the shoulder blades and he pitched forward.

The fourth volley was delivered at point-blank range, ripping great holes in the ranks of Indians. An incredible number of savages went down before the fire. Close packed as they were, the Cheyennes provided a target that gave the heavy carbine slugs the chance to tear through as many as three bodies before their force was spent.

The Indians recoiled, then came on again. Burton's head whirled with the confusion of the mad battle. Was it time to kill the girl? Could he reload? Were the Cheyennes breaking through? He blinked and coughed in the swirling powder smoke.

Now the Cheyennes were coming up over the hilltop. No time now for volleys. It was every man for himself and God help those taken alive. Burton fired into the ochre and red painted chest of a brave at whose saddlebow hung a pair of fresh scalps shedding gruesome red drops onto the pony's forelegs.

Up, up, towered the Indian as the pony reared, directly over Burton, Then the horse dropped over on its haunches. The soldier of fortune bent to snatch up a revolver from a fallen white man. As he cocked the gun, a shot banged in his face and singed away one of his eyebrows, Half dazed, he snapped a shot into a redskinned face and then looked around for another target, He gaped in amazement as he found the top of the knoll deserted of all live Cheyennes. Close at hand stood MacKaye and the bareheaded cavalry sergeant. Streaked with powder, both men were frantically searching their pockets for ammunition.

Burton had heard that it was a curious characteristic of the Indians to quit an attack just as victory was within their grasp, and now he was seeing proof of that freak habit.

"Beat 'em off, by God ! " roared a black-bearded trapper, drunk with triumph. "Blew the swines off'n the hill! By God, I'll git me a souvernir!"

With a ghastly grin he whipped out a skinning knife and seized the braids of the nearest dead Indian. As Burton watched, disgusted, the trapper slid his knife under the skin above the Cheyenne's left ear and made a quick, circular motion which freed the grisly trophy. The bearded man straightened and shook the scalp in the direction of the fleeing Cheyennes.

"That!" he yelled. "Look at that, ye damn butchers! That's a napper I got—afore ye git mine."

"Your napper's all right this time," called the wounded brakeman. "They won't be comin' back."

"The hell they won't," panted the cavalry sergeant, looking up from the makeshift bandage he was clumsily adjusting to his right forearm. "They'll be comin' and they'll get us next time. There ain't but eight of us now with not enough ammunition to stick in your ear."

Burton looked down the slope of the knoll to witness a scene that must have given pause to even such ferocious Cheyenne warriors as the Red Shields, the Elk Horn Scrapers and the Dog Soldiers. Those few minutes of frenzied battle had virtually carpeted the slope with dead men and horses. Here and there a wounded horse lashed out with its hoofs and there was a sprinkling of wounded men who writhed and twisted grotesquely in their pain. Warriors on foot had already begun dragging away some of the less exposed dead and wounded, as was their invariable custom.

Captain Robert Burton turned to look at his own little band. Six of the fifteen men who had begun the fight now lay sprawled in tragically distorted positions. Across the circle lay a gambler, his gay red silk waistcoat dyed a deeper crimson, doubled up with a Kit Fox arrow in his neck. The Confederate veteran who had fought with Longstreet had come at last to the end of his battles. A hideous abdominal wound from which poured incredible quantities of bright blood had sent him to join the comrades who had fallen beside him in the Civil War.

"How many cartridges left?" asked Burton, dreading the answer.

"Two."

"Ain't got any."

"I got three."

"I got four .38's. I'll divvy up with somebody."

Burton bit his lip to keep his face from reflecting the dismay that threatened to swamp him. An average of three shots apiece left. And at the foot of the hill there still swarmed an army of Cheyennes, building up their rage with war whoops, preparing to rush the hill again. Surely the next attack would give the Cheyennes red scalping knives.

"Any chance of getting cartridges off those dead Indians?" Bob asked the cavalry sergeant. The soldier shook his head gloomily.

"Not much," he said. "Ain't no Injuns got modern guns exceptin' maybe some Sioux. Damn traders ain't watched so close up in the Black Hills and they slip some guns to the redskins, but not around these parts."

"Hell," drawled the black-bearded trapper. "What's the use of foolin' ourselves? We ain't goin' to last longer'n a snowball in hell. Lucky I had my fun in Julesburg last week. I guess Kansas Kate can hunt herself up a new sweetie to-morrow and I bet he ain't half the man I was."

Burton shook his buzzing head to clear it. It was ironic that he had survived some of the worst battles of the Civil War and had come through a dozen murderous clashes between Emperor Maximilian's mercenaries and the fiendishly cruel Indians of Juarez and Diaz, only to die in a historically insignificant skirmish beside a wrecked train.

'Think!' urged an inward voice. 'You've got to think! There must be some way out of this!'

He started as a voice came from the bottom of the hill—a voice which spoke guttural English!

"Hey, you up thar'! Ef you surrenders peaceable, Turkey Leg swears to let ye keep yore hair!"

"Who in hell is that?" Burton demanded of the cavalry sergeant.

"Must be one of the Bent brothers," growled the soldier. "They're a pair of renegades livin' with the Cheyennes."

"Can we believe yon clapperclaw?" asked Colin MacKaye.

"Hell, no!" exploded the trapper. "George Bent would be one of the first to spill your guts onto your feet."

"No!" cried the brakeman, his mouth trembling. "Let's bargain! We're sure to be killed if they rush us again."

"Better be killed by our own guns than let the squaws do it," a lanky cattleman said. "I ain't trustin' no Cheyenne."

"Me neither——"

Burton cupped his hands and called down the hill.

"Tell Turkey Leg we'll fight it out," he yelled. "There's twenty-five of us with plenty of ammunition. Come on up and we'll give you a dose like the first one."

"Twenty-five hell!" came the gruff reply from below contemptuously. "We know you ain't got more'n a half dozen left and ye're out of ammunition. I'm a white man and I'm tryin' to do you a favour."

"White man!" jeered the trapper. "Your mother got kicked out of the Comanche tribe because she laid up with a stinkin' Ute."

"I'll git yore scalp for that," grated Bent. "I give you yore chance and ye wouldn't take it."

Suddenly a plan flashed into Burton's mind. Lowering his voice, he gathered his little band and explained.

"This may cost us our necks but we haven't got much to lose," he said. "Are you game?"

"Aye," promptly agreed Colin MacKaye. "I've never yet gone agley on Rob Burton's say-so."

"What's the idea again?" asked the trapper.

"We'll fire some shots in the air," Burton said. "That'll convince 'em that we've plenty of ammunition."

"For God's sake, no!" quavered the brakeman. "They know we're done for and we'd be helpless without even the little ammunition we've still got."

"Don't be a damn fool!" Burton said in a fierce undertone. "This is the only chance we've got—to hold them off until help gets here. I'm in command here. Follow your orders."

He raised his voice to a shout.

"Go to hell, you lousy renegade! We've got ammunition to burn. Listen to this!" Then, in a breathless whisper, "Everybody fire!"

Every man on the hilltop knew that by wasting that shot he might be shortening his life just that much, but all, except the brakeman and one other, raised their weapons toward the sky and sent a salvo up into the blackness of the night.

"Another!"

Grim-jawed, Burton wheeled and levelled his Colt full at the brakeman's twitching face. "You too, damn you!"

The trainman obeyed and a second volley roared out. From below came amazed yells from the Indians. Burton sprang upright. Hatless, his fringed shirt and red-striped breeches fouled and bloody, he stood against the purple-black background of the sky and waved defiance with his empty Spencer.

"How's that?" he yelled. "Maybe you'll believe us now!"

"Like hell," came back the taunting voice of the renegade. "We're a-comin' for you in a minute and then you'll wish to Gawd you'd listened to me."

"Now, you crazy fool," groaned the wounded brakeman, "I hope you're satisfied."

"'Twas a braw try, Rob," said Colin MacKaye, shaking his head slowly, "but it looks like we lost the gamble."

CHAPTER IV

THE minutes dragged by while the tiny band at the top of the knoll watched the Indians swarm over the unburnt cars of the train, intent on plunder. Twice groups of horsemen collected and Burton felt an icy fist squeeze his heart. Each time the counter-attraction of a new lot of plunder postponed the charge that was sure to come. The marauders emptied the freight cars of cases of tinned food, bolts of cloth, kegs of liquor and the rest of the myriad assortment of goods which had been destined for the roaring towns that were mushrooming along the line of the westward-reaching Union Pacific.

Burton saw a hulking, half drunken Dog Soldier leap off his war pony, knot one end of a bolt of silk to the tail of his mount and then, leaping astride again, go careening off over the prairies with the precious stuff unrolling behind him. Delighted howls greeted the idea and others copied the scheme until soon the whole flame-tinted plain was alive with screeching, galloping warriors weaving a fantastic pattern. Other savages were smashing cases of lamp chimneys, hacking through new harness with their knives and dressing themselves in women's garments.

"When's the next freight due?" Burton asked the brakeman.

"Number Three's due along in an hour," came the trainman's surly response. "But the glare of that fire prob'ly will scare them off."

"Likely to be any soldiers on it?"

"Hell, I don't know," said the brakeman. "At Kearney they said there were some replacements due for the Second Cavalry and they'll soon be goin' up to Fort Sedgwick. I don't know what train they'll be on. I don't run the U.P."

"Why not clear out of here and try to meet Number Three on the other side of the curve?" someone suggested. "The train ought to be warned. They might think it was just a regular wreck and get right into the middle of those Injuns before they find out different."

"Naw," said the cavalry sergeant. "We'd never make it. They'd be on top of us in a minute."

"Hey, listen," the trapper said. "That sounds pretty good to me. I'll go. I think I can find a way. I know this prairie same's I do the seat of my pants."

"If you can find a route to get down off this hill," Burton said, "we can slip away, one at a time. Maybe we can fool 'em."

The trapper was gone, cautiously backing out of the shallow pit he had scooped out of the dirt on the hilltop, before Burton had finished speaking. The ex-Confederate wriggled into the place and slanted one of the useless rifles over the edge of the knoll. Next he placed across the breach an abandoned hat, making a dummy that might—just might—be convincing in the uncertain light.

The bearded trapper was back in a few minutes.

"Found a way," he said hoarsely. "One at a time now and not too close together. I'll drag a gun butt along so you can follow my trail. First man that loses his head and tries to run for it gets my last bullet in the belly."

Breathless and well aware that a false move meant an unpleasant death, the defenders of the knoll one by one crawled off into the darkness to follow the trail made by the trapper. As each man left, Burton arranged a dummy to take his place. After five minutes only the stiffening dead, Colin MacKaye, Burton and the unconscious girl remained on the hill.

"All right. Out with you, Mac——"

"No, I'll not leave ye." The Scot's ruddy features contracted stubbornly. "Ye'll be needin' help wi' the lass."

"Go ahead, Mac," the soldier of fortune said sharply. "If I don't get away it'll be up to you to tell Enid that—that I loved her. And it'll be up to you, too, to take care of her."

The Scottish adventurer's angular jaw tightened as he nodded.

"As ye wish. But you're an unco' fine mon, Robbie—I'll never meet a finer. I—I ken ye want me to carry the knapsack?"

"Right, Mac. And get through! You've got to get through!"

"I'll do it, laddie. I promise ye that!"

He slipped away into the darkness and Burton was left alone with the motionless girl on the knoll top. From below came the sound of quarrelsome Cheyennes as the Indians grew drunker and more belligerent. It was fortunate, Burton told himself, that no Indian could hold liquor. Unless the chiefs stayed sober the savages might drink themselves sodden and forget that they had a score to settle with the white men on the hill.

He crawled to the side of the Valcour girl and placed his lips close to her ear.

"Miss Valcour," he muttered. "Rouse yourself for God's sake!"

No motion came to the long black eyelashes that rested on her cheek like tiny black feathers fallen on a white silk cushion. Perhaps she was dead. He placed his ear to the girl's bosom. The thickness of her clothes plus the clamour of the marauders below made it impossible for him to hear anything. He tested the pulse but could feel no stir of the blood in her wrist.

"No use gettin' scragged for a corpse—even a pretty one," he muttered, looking around.

The neck of a pint bottle protruded from the dead gambler's coat and he snatched it up. He tried to pour some of the liquor between the girl's teeth but the malodorous raw whisky trickled out of the corner of her mouth.

'She's gone,' Burton thought. His hand felt beneath one rounded breast but the thick silk muffled any beat that might be there. Burton sat back on his haunches and reached for his long knife.

'You sure would raise hell if you were conscious,' he mused, 'but I've got to find out if you're alive or not. Beggin' your pardon, ma'am."

The knife flashed, slitting through the silk at the girl's throat, cutting downward ruthlessly. Twin mounds of rosebud-dotted flesh burst from their confines as though grateful for their release. Burton instinctively eyed their beauty for a moment before he bent to press his ear to the smooth warm flesh beneath the girl's left breast.

"Ah," he breathed. "So you're still alive, eh?"

He raised the whisky bottle again, lifted the unconscious girl's head to one knee and pried upon the teeth that were as white and regular as moonstones on a necklace.

"C'mon," he said. "Have a drink on me."

This time, the girl swallowed and the beat of her heart beneath the ex-Confederate's fingers seemed to go stronger. Still holding the Valcour girl in a half upright position, Burton reached for the knife again, and cut lower, snapping corset strings. The rounded breasts lifted as the girl's lungs reached for air.

'Some day,' Burton reflected, 'women are goin' to get dressed in some kind of clothes that'll let 'em breathe.'

A rising howl came from below and Burton lowered the Senator's daughter to the sandy ground while he crawled to the rim of the knoll to look down at the Cheyennes. The horsemen were bunching again. He scrambled back to Mistress Valcour. More whisky trickled down the girl's throat and her eyes fluttered, then slid open.

"—I—what? Oh, get away! Go away!"

Burton clamped a hand over the girl's mouth and winced as her teeth bit into a finger.

"Shut up!" he hissed. "Cheyennes—Indians—all around us!"

Her eyes probed his with a frightened glare. Then the girl's lids began to flutter again. Burton snatched his hand away and proffered the whisky bottle.

"Don't faint again!" he ordered. "Drink this and keep quiet if you want to save your hair."

He raised the bottle to her lips and fed her the fiery fluid until she coughed and gagged. While she caught her breath, Burton raised the whisky to his own mouth and took a long pull. The liquor warmed his veins, seeming to give him fresh strength for the grim task that lay ahead. When he lowered the flask, he found the girl staring at him. Critically, he viewed the voluminous skirts she wore and shook his head.

"You couldn't run in a Sibley tent like that," he said. "Take it off."

"Why—what—*ohhhh!*"

For the first time since she had regained consciousness, the girl became aware of the fact that she was being regarded by a man while she was virtually nude from her throat to waist. She sat erect, clutching the slashed dress about her bosom.

"You—you did this?" she demanded.

B

"Had to," said Burton briefly. "You couldn't breathe. Wait a minute and for God's sake don't stand up."

He crawled over to a dead body that lay nearby.

"Get rid of those skirts," he ordered over his shoulder. "I'll throw you some pants. Hurry up."

Jessica Valcour started to protest then caught the savage glance the soldier of fortune cast in her direction. She shivered and began to fumble with hooks and buttons. Burton laboured at his task of dragging off a slain teamster's buckskin breeches, half conscious of the whimpering sound behind him as the girl pulled off her skirt.

The pants finally came off and he turned to crawl back. The girl was huddled against a tuft of sage, her arms crossed over her breasts, her slim legs showing beneath the brief shift she wore. As he crawled toward Jessica Valcour, Burton saw the girl's mouth open preparatory to a scream.

"You yell and I'll slap you," he snapped. "Listen, ma'am. I could have gone with the others but I stuck around to take care of you. And I've seen plenty of women so I know how they're made. If you think I'm romantically inclined here with a couple of hundred drunken Cheyennes gettin' ready to rush this hill, you're wrong. Now put on these pants and do it quick."

Still sobbing, the girl awkwardly began to pull on the breeches. Burton turned away to peer down over the rim of the knoll at the Indians. They still were milling about, made uncertain by the liquor and wine they had swilled. He crawled back and with ungentle hands hauled the pants up over the girl's rear. She gasped and struck at his hands but before she could open her mouth in protest there came a howling scream from below.

Again Burton left the girl, to crawl to his vantage point. Were the Cheyennes massing for the attack? No, they were pelting furiously down the track toward the bend, ki-yi-ing and brandishing their lances.

"Some poor devil sighted, probably," the ex-Confederate told himself. "But it gives us a chance."

He squirmed back to the girl and grabbed her arm.

"Follow me!" he ordered. "Quick!"

He caught the girl's hand and held it tightly as they raced down the slope of the knoll between the tumbled corpses of men and horses. A veteran soldier, Burton knew that the departure of that detail of mounted Cheyennes toward the bend in the railroad meant that to follow the path made by the other fugitives from the hilltop would more than likely lead him and the girl into the clutch of the raiders. He veered away from the line of retreat used by the others, encouraged to see that Mistress Valcour could run. She seemed to be gaining strength with each stride, half pulled along by the lean-muscled ex-Confederate.

"I only hope," Burton was telling himself, "that whoever those redskins saw wasn't Colin ! But knowing Mac, it's a good bet that it wasn't."

The soldier of fortune and his stumbling charge gained the momentary protection offered by a thick clump of willows bordering a dry gully. His own breath was whistling in his throat and the girl was virtually sobbing with exhaustion. Burton suddenly dug in his heels and motioned violently to the woman. From a point close by, further up the gully, came a muted noise.

"Stay here," he hissed at the girl. He dropped Jessica Valcour's hand and drew from his belt that shining knife that had served him in such good stead, both in stopping the breathing of a Cheyenne who was too much alive and starting the breathing of a girl whom he had thought dead.

Burton began creeping forward through the underbrush. He froze to immobility when, ahead of him, he saw a pair of ponies standing. On one of the tough little mounts sat an Indian, swaying as he clutched the mane of his horse.

"A wounded Cheyenne, by God ! "

A few second's observation proved to Captain Robert Burton that the man on the lead pony was a Cheyenne Red Shield warrior who had been hit hard in the side by one of the slugs fired from the knoll during the brief and furious battle. He was still astride his war pony with his 'travel pony' secured by a rawhide hackamore. All Cheyennes of the mounted military societies travelled with two mounts ; the 'travel pony' for covering distance and the 'battle pony' used only in a fight.

The brave whom Burton watched climbed down from the back of the horse that had carried him into battle and had brought him out, sorely wounded. The Indian staggered as his feet struck the ground and he put up a hand on the horse to steady himself. If the man had been anything but a Cheyenne brave, the ex-Confederate would have given him more of a chance. But, as the vision of the white men and women who had fallen captives to the Cheyennes rose before Bob's eyes, the soldier of fortune leaped, his long knife gleaming dully.

The razor-sharp blade jammed down into the hollow between the shoulder joint and the collar bone as Burton clutched the brave. The Red Shield collapsed instantly with a bubbly sigh.

The 'battle pony' lunged frantically but, thanks to a Cheyenne custom, the loose end of the horse's hackamore was tied to the belt of the warrior. The dead weight of the slain brave acted as a stone halter on the rearing mount.

After soothing the frightened buckskin, Burton shortened the hackamore that secured the 'travel pony.' Under the ex-Confederate's soothing tones, both mounts quieted and began to crop at the willow leaves about them. Hurriedly, Burton converted the travel pony's single lead line into a rude sort of bridle. Even if the Valcour girl could ride, he knew she never would be able to manage this half-trained brute with a one-handed rawhide rein. That done, he risked leaving the ponies untended while he ran back to the daughter of Senator Valcour.

"Can you ride?" he demanded. "If you can't, I reckon I'd better lash your ankles under the belly of the hoss I've got for you."

"I—I can ride."

"Come on, then."

When he got the girl to the horses, he knelt and made a hand-step into which she expertly placed her foot. He swung her aboard the black and white 'travel pony' and watched approvingly as Mistress Valcour clenched her knees to give herself balance. Captain Burton had ridden bareback before and it was an experience he would not wish on his worst enemy. But in this instance it had to be bareback—or death.

The Cheyennes could ride these unsaddled horses all day and all night without flinching but for anyone not used to it from childhood it was torture. The Indian ponies were hard-bitted, half starved mounts with a backbone like the ridgepole of a steeply-pitched shed. After a minute's riding on a Cheyenne pony, one's *derrière* felt as though it were going to split in halves. After two minutes' ride, the imaginary split usually reached the base of one's skull.

Burton expertly vaulted to the top of the 'battle pony' and turned the animal's head with a twist of the feather-decorated hackamore. The beast shied a bit at the feel of boots along his sides but the ex-Confederate's low voice and commanding hand soon brought the horse down to a quivering standstill. Carefully, Burton began walking the pony out of the gully, looking back over his shoulder to see that Jessica Valcour was following on her more docile mount. Once he saw that the girl could handle the makeshift bridle, Captain Bob kicked his horse into a gallop. Willow branches whipped his face as the ' battle pony ' bunched and stretched its way along the stone-scattered floor of the gulch. Burton hauled on his hackamore long enough to let the trailing horse catch up with him. Then, careful of his raking spurs, he gave the pony its head again.

The Eastern girl was a good rider. Soon after they emerged from the gully she was alongside him. He reached out and grabbed the rawhide bit, fastened behind the pony's jaw teeth, to lead the animal.

"You're doin' fine, ma'am," he encouraged. "Now pull yourself together because we've got to ride mighty hard from now on."

Clinging to the reins Burton had fashioned, Mistress Valcour had no opportunity to guard the slashed front of her dress. With the night air blowing strongly, sending the shredded pieces of silk fluttering outward to reveal her white body, she looked to the soldier of fortune like some kind of Valkyrie. The girl's eyes caught Burton's with an angry glare and he looked away.

"Hang on," he counselled. "Here we go!"

The two horses burst out of the willows with the suddenness of a brace of stags roused by coursing hounds. The Indian ponies stretched themselves into a race with each other. The girl hunched over the mane of her mount as Burton clung to the bit of the 'travel pony.' The two horses thundered up the rise of a ridge and down the other side into darkness that was blissfully empty of the sound of the Indian howls that had rent the night about the wrecked train.

Burton reined in his horse to a canter and shot out a hand to steady the lurching shoulders of the girl he had saved. He hauled back on the hackamore suddenly and brought both horses to a stop as Jessica Valcour half toppled over the neck of her mount.

"Listen," Burton breathed.

From somewhere behind them sounded the angry wail of a locomotive's whistle.

"That must be Number Three," Burton said. "That either means we're safe or we're in more trouble than before. If the Cheyennes run, they may run this way. If they fight—well, in either case we've got to start ridin' and ridin' hard, sister!"

CHAPTER V

THEY rode on through a vast stillness broken only by the querulous complaint of a prairie owl or the nocturnal hymn of a coyote.

"Ohhh! Please stop!" came the girl's faint plea. "My—I simply can't ride any further."

"You've got to," came Burton's blunt retort. "I know how you feel, ma'am, but you'd feel a hell—you'd feel a lot worse if a Dog Soldier caught up with us. Nobody knows whether they've come this way after that other train came down the line. We can't stop. Not short of the south fork of Dismal River. It's not so far away. Come on—you can do it!"

He steeled himself against the tears which streamed from the girl's eyes as she shifted herself from one side to the other, trying to find an impossibly comfortable position.

"You're doin' mighty well," he encouraged. "Just a little longer. If they're chasin' us they'd never go beyond the Dismal. Beyond, there's Sioux country and even a Cheyenne is afraid of a Sioux."

A half hour passed with the Indian ponies trotting steadily. Then the Valcour girl crumpled over the neck of her horse.

"For heaven's sake, stop!" she implored. "My—my limbs are raw."

"Better than the torture stake! You've no idea what a Cheyenne squaw likes to do to a captive white woman."

"Oh, I hate you!"

"Lot of people have hated me, ma'am. I'm used to it. Keep ridin'."

The horses' hoofs drummed steadily on over the level sagebrush-dotted plain while the stars swung higher in the heavens. From far behind, the two riders heard the faint sound of rifle shots and then silence. Burton wondered about the fate of the fugitives who had slipped away from the knoll beside the tracks. MacKaye—had he gotten away?

At length they came to an alder-fringed creek. The two hard-ridden ponies, blowing mightily, splashed into the water and lowered their muzzles gratefully. It was then that the girl slid off her pony and landed with a splash in the water. Burton dismounted, knowing that the horses would not bolt with all that water at hand. He dredged up Mistress Valcour from the creek, a dripping, unlovely thing.

"Come on," the ex-Confederate urged. "You can't let go like this!"

"Go on and leave me! I—I don't care if the Indians do come. I won't ride any further."

"Rest awhile," Burton said, as he lowered the girl to the bank of the creek. "I'll get the ponies. Better drink a little water if you haven't swallowed too much and stretch out for a few minutes. And button those pants the right way so you won't chafe so much. Here, let me show you how those waist laces go."

He stretched out a hand. The girl shrank away, her eyes ablaze despite her exhaustion.

"Let me alone! Don't touch me!"

Burton dropped his hand and stepped back.

"Lady," he said carefully, "you're almighty unreasonable. Out this way folks gen'rally are grateful for havin' their lives saved. What you need to cure you of the way you're carryin' on would be a damn good spankin'."

Jessica Valcour summoned up enough strength to get to her feet, forgetting the condition of her slashed blouse. Her breasts heaved wildly as she confronted Burton, chin up, her legs wavering with weariness.

"Spank me?" she demanded. "Do you know who I am?"

Burton cast her one brief look of disgust and then turned away.

"Cover yourself up, ma'am," he said brutally.

From behind him came the girl's infuriated voice.

"You—you——" she stammered. "I guess this is what I should

expect from one of those dreadful Rebels who tried to ruin our country. I suppose you're one of those typical Southern gentlemen."

Burton turned with a grin as she clutched the tattered remnants of her blouse to her. The girl's anger, he reasoned, would give her new strength and strength was what she needed.

"And you," he said, "are a No'thern aristocrat, I reckon? Well, when the story of that war is written proper you'll read where the aristocrats up No'th had as much to do with that war as the young bloods in South Ca'lina."

"My father—my father will have you punished for this!" stormed the girl.

"Punished for exactly what?" inquired Burton calmly. "For savin' your life?"

"For treating me like a body servant, for pawing me while I was unconscious! No gentleman would do a thing like that."

The ex-Confederate slipped his long knife from its scabbard and jammed it into the gritty soil of the creek bank. The two ponies still drank. Burton looked up at the girl from under lowering eyebrows.

"Listen, ma'am," the soldier of fortune said. "If I didn't paw you, as you call it, that pretty hair of yours would be decorating a Dog Soldier's lance by now. And I don't paw unconscious women. I like 'em a little livelier than that. Y'see, I don't come from Boston, ma'am."

He examined the blade of his knife and found it clean enough. Replacing it in its scabbard, he continued.

"Let's understand each other. I think you're useless! You're one of those whimperin', soft-handed doll women who set themselves up to sneer at girls who have the heart and guts enough to come out here into the wilderness and work and fight for the men they love. To put it frankly, ma'am, I despise your sort. I wouldn't touch you with a ten-foot pole to please myself. Your father don't rate acey-deucey with me till I meet him and find out if he's all right. His *dinero* or the title he's got don't matter a flea bite to me. If this was back East I'd ride off and let you find your own way home but since it ain't, I reckon I'll have to see you to North Platte. But don't keep accusin' me of tryin' to make love to you. I've got a girl waitin' for me that would make six of you."

He got up from his squatting position and moved down to the creek to bring in the horses. When he returned, the girl, still wavering, spoke in a stilted voice.

"I'm sorry I'm indebted to you," she said. "You'll be rewarded—well paid. But I'm not going to ride for another hour."

Burton grinned with an amiability that masked his grim purpose.

"You're goin' to mount now," he said, "if I have to tie you on."

"No."

He bent to pick the girl up in his arms. Her fist lashed out and tapped his hollow cheek. But even as he straightened in fury, she slumped forward against him quite unconscious. He looked down at her and his features softened.

"Poor little fool," he murmured as he splashed water onto her face. "Maybe I've driven her too hard. But we've got to get to North Platte."

The girl's eyelashes fluttered and then her eyes opened.

"I—I'm sorry," she mumbled. "I'll ride."

He helped her carefully to her feet and led her to her pony. She staggered as she walked and after Burton, with arms surprisingly gentle, lifted her to the pony's back she swayed in the saddle. Burton vaulted to his own horse's back and rode up alongside the girl.

"Now ma'am," he directed, "just you put one arm around my neck and hang on. It won't be so tough that way."

In a gesture of exhausted surrender the girl placed one slender arm around the ex-Confederate's neck as Burton put his arm around her waist. Then Jessica Valcour sank back into the comforting cradle made by the soldier of fortune's arm, her head tilted back and her patrician features reflecting the pale light of the stars.

Thus the two rode on over the prairie amid a silence broken only by the steady clump of hoofs and the snorting of the reined-in ponies. Burton's eyes roved from side to side on the alert for any untoward motion but there was nothing abroad in that region, apparently, save the prairie dogs and, on occasion, a slinking coyote. Dew had drenched both the long-legged rider and his sleeping burden before a curious milky glow invaded the purple black of the sky to herald the imminence of dawn.

Jessica Valcour slept on, slumped far over in her saddle, her rounded cheek pressed against the thrums of Burton's buckskin shirt. The adventurer held her on her jogging horse, regardless of the barbs of pain that were shooting through his arm. Eventually, when the burden of the position grew too much to stand, the ex-Confederate swept the girl up onto his own horse, placing her in front of him. The second Indian pony veered off as Mistress Valcour's other arm instinctively clasped about her rescuer. The Indian pony did not seem to mind the double burden. It jogged on steadily. A ' battle pony,' it had been trained to carry double weight, the Indian custom in battle being to have braves whose horses had been killed leap up in front of a mounted tribal brother.

Soon there began the eerie pre-dawn howling of wolves and coyotes. Then dense coveys of quail and sage hens commence to flush out of the parched buffalo grass and sagebrush. High overhead a single lark lifted a hymn to the new day. As the light increased the horizon moved continuously further away, revealing a vista of dun-hued prairies, terminated here and there by a row of pale hills—hills which might have been sandbanks unnumbered ages ago when the glacial waters of Lake Algonquin had covered this virtually treeless region.

Robert Burton's heart lifted at the clean immensity of this world and warmed to behold once more scenes so familiar to him. He grinned as he saw a herd of wild mustangs grazing about a mile away and lifted his rein hand in an involuntary salute to a band of shaggy buffalo that raised their blunt heads to watch him as he passed with his strange burden.

How far they had ridden during the night, Burton could only guess, but it must have been nearly forty miles. Every fibre of his tough body screamed its protest at his estimate, telling him that it was closer to four hundred.

"Reckon we can swing south now and head for North Platte," he said aloud. At the sound of his voice the girl in his arms stirred a trifle. He glanced down and studied her face, the perfect complexion, the narrowly-arched brows, the long up-slanting eyes and the tumbled red-brown curls that framed her face. Despite the dried blood, the dirt and the lines of exhaustion, Jessica Valcour still was a beautiful woman—of a beauty foreign to Enid Culver's solid, golden glory.

Enid! God willing, he was actually going to see her to-day, before yonder sun had set! Wonderful Enid, the thought of whom had steeled him in the dark hours and had made the bitter toil worth while. He never had told her that it was on her account alone that he had gone to Mexico as a mercenary to retrieve the fortune lost when the South had sunk to final defeat. Now he could tell her and explain why he had been so long away.

He planned the day, step by step.

In North Platte he would clean up, buy some clothes, before he boarded the next train to Julesburg. Once there—he thought of the heavy haversack that Colin had carried off the knoll. Colin would get through—he *had* to! For in that haversack were the emeralds he would drape around Enid's white throat, the pearls, the diamonds—enough, converted to cash, for the purchase of the ranch. But Colin would get through!

A noise, faint and distant, wrenched him free from his thoughts. He straightened in the saddle and shot his keen eyes toward the left. There, far away, was a rising puff of smoke—another. Indian signals? He reined in sharply, then relaxed. The rising sun's first rays flashed on a distant window and then another until the dotted welcoming signals formed a row of reflected lights.

That was North Platte, the dying and deserted base camp for the Union Pacific and the jumping-off place for the town's successor— wicked murderous Julesburg, the newest ' Hell on Wheels.' Each westernmost U.P. base camp was given that nickname and each one lived up to its name.

He kicked the pony into a faster trot, his heart high. Would it be smarter, he wondered, to take up ranching immediately or try for a job with the U.P. until the road was put through ? There were stories of big money to be made on the railroad. He was no engineer but he could qualify as a scout. The Cheyennes were no more wily or fierce than General Juarez's Yaquis and Mayarites whom he had outwitted and outfought down in Mexico on the scorching plains of Guanajuato.

Again his thoughts were interrupted when the girl's arms tightened about him. Drugged with sleep and obviously in the middle of some dream, she raised lips as soft and brightly red as though fashioned of scarlet satin.

"Darling," she murmured. "Kiss—kiss me——"

Burton looked down at the girl he had rescued and smiled. Then he bent and lightly touched his lips to hers.

"Anything to oblige, ma'am," he chuckled.

CHAPTER VI

THE passenger coach's wheels went *rickety-rack rickety-rack* over the rails toward Julesburg. It was a soothing rhythm Captain Robert Burton decided, as he sat beside Colin MacKaye in the seat of the coach, his heavy knapsack on his lap, discharged from his responsibility to the spoiled female from the East.

Colin had been waiting for Burton when the ex-Confederate had ridden into North Platte.

"How did you get here so fast ?" Burton had asked.

"Killed a brave, took his pony and came straight on, laddie," the Scot had replied calmly. "And here's your haversack. Aiblins I've worried m'sel' sick o'er it, mon. I think it was what brought me through, worrying about all that siller. I was domned determined the red de'ils would'na get it."

Bit by bit, Burton had learned the story of MacKaye's escape. The Scot had headed for the bend and then, hearing shots that bespoke Indian action against some of the fugitives, had cut off the trail and struck across country. A lone Cheyenne had blundered across his path and had dropped with a carbine bullet through his skull. That shot had brought other savages in pursuit and there had been a chase, interrupted when a detachment of the Second Cavalry had thundered up to disperse the Cheyennes in a pitched battle.

And now—*rickety-rack rickety-rack* with each turn of the wheels bringing Bob Burton closer to Enid. He leaned back in his seat and closed his eyes. It had been four years almost to the day since he had seen her. That had been after Vicksburg when he had been given an unexpected leave. That, he told himself, added up to one thousand four hundred and fifty-six days. No, add one for Leap Year.

The taurine bellow of the conductor could be heard in the next car. "Julesburg in ten minutes ! Julesburg in ten minutes !"

Chuckling, Colin MacKaye yawned and stretched before he stood up to take down a brown slouch hat from the luggage rack.

"What you so gleeful about ?" Burton asked.

"I'd hae given a lot to see ye lugging yon hoity-toity Valcour lass ! Domn ! And both of ye hating the other ! Or was that all a story ye both made up? Sure you two didn't cuddle a wee bit out there ?"

"Damn you, Colin," Burton snapped as he grinned. "You know how I feel about her. Thank God I won't be seein' her again."

"Dinna be so sure. I heard she was heading for Julesburg, too."

"She won't be bothered with me, anyway," Burton said. "Not with her father a big politician stock promoter for the railroad. Rich as Croesus, probably."

The Scot dodged the end of a huge duffle bag that swung past on a miner's shoulder and shrugged.

"He'll nae be so rich soon, I'm thinking," he remarked.

"Why not ?"

"In North Platte they were saying the U.P.'s nigh to bankruptcy," MacKaye said soberly. "'Tis rumoured Congress has refused more subsidies unless the line reaches Big Spring within the month. And they say it's near impossible to do that—what with the desert ahead and the Cheyennes, Sioux and Crows harrying the labourers. So your proud beauty might not be so proud come a month more."

"Who told you all this ?"

"Oh, the troopers and the station master in North Platte. He told me while I was waiting around for somebody to find your ugly carcass. He's so sure o' ruin he's looking around for a likely farm. 'Twas he that said old Senator Andrew Valcour has his last saxpence invested i' the road."

The engineer whistled stridently for brakes as the train clattered past a village of fifteen or twenty tepees around which squaws toiled in the brilliant sunshine and wolfish dogs scavenged. A short distance away on the prairie small naked boys watched a herd of grazing ponies. Rising straight from the blackened vents in the lodge tops came slender threads of blue smoke.

Clatter, clank ! The brakes were tightened and the train slowed down while rattling past an untidy collection of immigrant tents. Next, the train passed a siding on which rested dozens of battered dump cars. Another siding accommodated four or five big Rogers type locomotives and a pair of chunky little switching engines. All of them had tenders stacked high with firewood.

The couplings banged and rattled. Through the dust the passengers could make out a slow plodding 'bull train. The white tops of the freight wagons—the prairie schooners—glinted in the sun to mark the passage of a convoy headed for Julesburg or for Fort Sedgwick further down the South Platte River. The longhorned, brown and white oxen moved at a snail's pace as the dust rose in clouds about the wagons, almost obliterating the tail 'schooners' from view.

"Julesburg! All off! End o' line!" a brakesman yowled. "Julesburg! Beware of pickpockets!"

"And everything else!" came the roaring response from the passengers who had made this trip before and who had made a ritual of the addition to the brakeman's formal warning, demanded by regulations.

Burton peered out of the window before he jammed his way into the aisle.

"Julesburg!" Right outside this canvas and slab-board town lay the Culver ranch. And Enid! Enid!

He hefted the knapsack as he followed MacKaye down the narrow aisle to the platform and then to the station baking in the terrific noonday sun. He looked about him, inoculated instantly with the strange fever that prevailed. Everywhere there was the spirit of energy—vital, elemental—in the air. It was written in the sunburnt faces of the men about him, the free swing to their stride, the determined set to their shoulders. Everyone was vigorous, restless, rude, primitive—attuned to a momentum that swept the new arrival along in a mighty current.

"Losh, Rob," muttered Colin MacKaye. "Look at all the people. Are they not braw and lusty? And I thocht it was a wilderness oot here."

"I miscalculated, too," Burton admitted. "It seems we were both wrong, Mac."

For a moment the two men stood stockstill, staring at the scene before them. At least two thousand people were on hand to welcome the arrival of the noon train. Over the tracks and surrounding the train were soldiers off duty; dirty Indians in stained buckskins and gaudy blankets; pale-faced, well-dressed men who viewed the newcomers with chill and speculative eyes; shirt-sleeved railroad men; brawny Irish baggage smashers; and a host of loafers who gaped at the descending passengers as though they were from another world.

Burton tugged at the entranced MacKaye's elbow.

"Come on, Colin," he said. "Let's *andar* out of this mob 've got to find Enid. I suppose the postmaster——"

"Bide a wee," MacKaye protested. "Look. Ye'll be amused to watch this."

A file of sunburned soldiers, bayonets gleaming in the sun, were busy clearing a path to the last car on the train. Along this path came an infantry major in company with a grey-haired man who wore a tailored black coat and riding breeches. The two walked to the foot of the steps of the last car and waited. Then Jessica Valcour put in her appearance. She paused, looking over the heads of the wondering crowd, for all the world like an actress making an entrance. She was, Burton noted, more radiantly lovely than ever in a black costume that made the most of her creamy skin and slim-waisted figure.

"Losh," Colin said nudging Bob. "She had the whole car to hersel'. 'Tis evidently somewhat to be a politician's blue-eyed bairn."

"She's not blue-eyed," Burton corrected absently. "Her eyes are violet."

"Sooo?" asked Colin carefully. "And ye tell me ye didn't have a wee bit of snuggling out there——"

"Shut up," Burton said.

Burton saw Jessica Valcour throw herself into the grey-haired man's arms. The girl's clear voice came over the rumble of the crowd.

"Oh, Father, I hope that silly little accident we had didn't upset you?"

"Good God," said MacKaye in an awed whisper. "She calls last nicht's fight a silly little accident. She's daft."

Back down the aisle opened by the soldiers, Valcour led his daughter to a buggy drawn by two restless black thoroughbreds. A uniformed driver touched his hat as correctly as had ever a man-servant belonging to General the Honourable Sir Hubert MacKaye back in Edinburgh. Burton felt MacKaye wince as he watched that gesture. The ex-Confederate knew, as few men did, the life story of this uncommunicative Scot who stood beside him now on the platform of a frontier railroad station.

A roar of raucous laughter burst from the crowd as Senator Valcour handed his daughter into the carriage. The merriment became Homeric when a gambler assisting two handsome young whores into a buckboard whirled indignantly on the bearded loafer holding the reins.

"Touch your goddam hat!" he roared. "Can't you see their ladyships are comin' aboard?"

Blood rushed into Jessica Valcour's cheeks but neither the rail-road promoter nor the infantry major paid heed to the scene. The coachman flicked his whip and the buggy moved off. Burton said,

"Come on, Mac. Let's be getting on to the post office."

They found the place across a wide, dusty street opposite
Casement Brothers' big portable warehouse. The post office was
jammed and the impatient captain was forced to join a long line
leading to the small heavily-barred window. While he waited,
Burton absently scanned a flyblown collection of handbills adver-
tising the rates of Holloday's Overland Stage and the charges of
Messrs. Russel, Majors and Waddel, Freighters. There also were
notices posted by real estate sharks and a dozen 'Wanted, Dead or
Alive !' posters of the U.S. Marshal's office.

The line edged forward and Burton shifted from one foot to the
other, impatient to get to the window and learn of Enid's where-
abouts. A flushed, bottle-nosed individual with a sweeping moustache leaned across him to speak to the man behind the ex-
Confederate.

"You seen that new gal of Jack Smiley's ?"

"I shore did, Hank," responded the other. "By Gawd, she
shore is a purty piece of stuff. I ain't seen such yaller hair since I
was knee-high to a pra'rie dawg. I heard Smiley really married up
with her. That right ?"

"Jack, married ?" jeered the walrus-moustached one. "Are you
crazy ? Jack Smiley never gits married. He meets 'em, beds 'em
and leaves 'em. Shore wish I could afford same."

"Well, he can afford it—diff'rent one every night if he wants.
Heard say the King of the Hills is easy makin' him five thousand
a day."

The line shuffled a few inches nearer the window.

"Well, he shore picked a lulu this time. She's got class, this
one."

The two men yowled with laughter. Burton drew back as the
nauseous breath of the pair billowed up to his nose. The walrus-
moustached man ahead of him reached the window and turned
away. Burton looked through the bars at the collarless, squint-
eyed postmaster.

"Can you tell me how to get to the Culver ranch ?" he asked.

The postmaster scratched his ribs absently as his rheumy eyes
gazed off into space. Then the squint eyes switched back to Burton.

"Culver ?" he said. "I reckon you mean the feller that was
livin' in these parts before the railroad come. George Culver."

"That's the man."

"Well," said the postmaster carefully. "George Culver up
and died awhile back. Had a daughter, as I recollect, and she——"

"Miss Enid Culver," the ex-Confederate interrupted eagerly.
"That's the lady I want to locate."

The postmaster shifted an enormous chew of tobacco from one
side of his mouth to the other while his eyes tried to focus on Burton.

"Miss Culver, huh ?" he asked. "I—I reckon you're the feller

named Benton—no—Burton that used to send Miss Culver letters
with furrin stamps on them, ain't you?"

"Uh-huh. Where is she now?"

The postmaster blinked and picked up a package of letters.

"Why—uh—I reckon you might find her over to the Julesburg
House, mister," he said. "I—uh—*next!*"

Burton turned away from the window and found Colin MacKaye
waiting for him at the door.

"All right, Rob?" inquired the Scot.

"Right as a trivet. Come on, you old Chinchero!"

Captain Robert Burton saw nothing of the busy, restless crowds
as he paced along the street, seemingly paved with a velvet carpet
that was inches deep. It was only MacKaye's guiding hand at his
elbow that saved the ex-Confederate from being trampled by a
crowd of screeching, half-drunken cowboys who came galloping
recklessly down Julesburg's deep-rutted main street, waving bottles
as they rode.

"Losh, what a toon!" MacKaye grunted.

He tugged at Burton's elbow as he paused to look at the two
painted harlots who stood in a doorway, clad only in diaphanous
pink chemises. To every passer-by the bedaubed pair explained
their particular talents in easy-to-understand words. A few paces
further on down the splintered boardwalk, two dancehall harpies
sprang out and linked their arms through Burton's and Colin's,
screeching:

"In town for a good time, boys? Come on in and buy Mimi
and Alice a drink. Don't be shy, boys. Let's get acquainted.
We'll be nice to you. We're only young once!"

Energy! Even in its lowest strata the new West seethed with it.
There were no pale inhibitions, no strangling traditions here. Everything was for to-day and nothing for to-morrow. Yesterday was
buried in a nameless grave. To-morrow might never come.

The two soldiers of fortune had been accosted by no less than a
dozen clinging whores before they sighted the unpainted board
façade of the Julesburg House. As they passed the Golden Queen
Saloon they heard the staccato beat of shots and a hoarse scream of
mortal agony. This town, Burton thought, had certainly earned its
name of 'Hell on Wheels.' The stories he had heard of Julesburg
averaging one killing a day, apparently had not been exaggerated.

Swinging his precious haversack higher on his shoulder, Burton
passed the row of cavalry horses and cow ponies dozing at the
hitching rail and headed for the broad steps of the Julesburg House.
Enid—would she be there?

On the porch of the hotel set a few women, divided by an in-
visible marker that split the porch in half. On one side the sombrely-
clothed wives and mothers of freighters, ranchers and farmers rocked

sedately. On the opposite side were the gaily dressed Daughters of
Lilith in seductive poses. At the bottom of the steps, Colin MacKaye
turned and gently clapped his friend's shoulder.

"I'm thinking, Rob," he said, "that I'll e'en go and sample a
specimen o' the local whusky. You and the bonnie lassie will
ha'e somewhat to talk about. Ye'll find me at yon Blue Star."

The gallant, rawboned third son of The MacKaye of Glenkaye was
gone before Captain Robert Burton could utter a half-hearted protest.

With the same tingling sensation in his fingertips he had felt on
the eve of Corinth, the ex-Confederate automatically straightened
his newly purchased tie, brushed off the new sombrero and swung
up the steps into the gloom of the rudely furnished lobby. He
was about to cross to the desk when he glimpsed the back of a golden
head through a door leading off the lobby. Although the girl was
bent over a writing desk and had her back turned, Burton knew it was
Enid Culver. There was no mistaking the glorious silver-gold sheen
of her hair, the smoothness of the nape of her neck.

Burton crossed the gritty, carpetless floor of the lobby with his
heart drumming like partridge wings. He entered the stuffy little
writing room and still Enid did not look up. Her pen went on
scratching evenly across the paper.

"Enid !"

The girl's pen stumbled and then fell from her hand, leaving a
trail of blots across the paper.

"Enid ! Enid honey !"

Enid Culver twisted in her chair, eyes wide and mouth parted
in astonishment. For full ten seconds she stared at him and then
she sprang from the chair. Wordlessly, his hungry arms reached
for her, pulled her to him, enfolded her soft suppleness. He had
imagined this moment on so many nights when he had lain in bivouac
under the hot stars and cloudless skies of old Mexico. The fragrance
of her hair, the warmth of her full lips—they were as he had remembered them. Her body moulded itself to his for an instant and there
was a pounding pulse in Burton's brain. This ecstasy had been
worth waiting for.

A hand clamped itself on his shoulder and tore him out of Enid's
arms.

"Say you !"

Spun off balance, Burton swayed and staggered before he straightened. Confronting him was a tall man with a strong square face
that was dominated by pointed moustaches and small eyes, keen
as dagger points.

No puma could have struck faster or more devastatingly than
Robert Burton. One fist smashed into the stranger's jaw while
the other buried itself under his heart. The big man went back,
then surged in again.

Enid's wails came to Bob's ears as he hammered at the stranger's jaw. He was oblivious to the blows he was taking. He fought on with primitive viciousness until, at last, the big man went over backwards with a crash, taking the writing desk with him in his fall and splattering ink over the garish wallpaper.

The stranger lay unconscious, the skirts of his frock coat flung out to reveal the mother-of-pearl butts of two derringers protruding from the pockets of a flowered silk waistcoat.

"Get up, you !" Burton thundered.

The big man did not stir. The ex-Confederate stooped and snatched out the two derringers, stuffing them in his pockets. He turned to Enid.

"Sorry," he panted. "I couldn't help it."

"You fool !" she spat, her face suddenly lined and hard-angled. "He—he'll kill you. You don't know who he is !"

"Now, honey," Burton said soothingly. "Don't let a little fight upset you. He had it comin' to him. Who is he, anyway ?"

"He—he—oh, go away ! *Go away !*"

A glacial current seemed to have replaced the blood in Burton's veins. *Go away ?* No, he told himself, Enid Culver never would tell him to go away. He blinked and shook his head. The fellow, whoever he was, must have dazed him with some blow—this must be all a dreadful fantasy.

He looked at her and saw her bury her face in her hands. He stood before her, feet apart, with that heavy haversack still dragging at his shoulder.

"Go away ? Did you tell me to go away ?" he asked.

Her voice came muffled from between her fingers, hysterically unintelligible. Then she looked up at him, her face distorted with terror.

"You've got to go away," she gasped. "That—that is Jack Smiley—my—my husband !"

CHAPTER VII

"*Your husband !*"

It seemed as if a Minie ball had struck Captain Burton in the chest, blasting out his life, withering his stomach, shredding his bowels.

The girl made an attempt to meet his eyes. Then she looked away. Burton gave a harsh bark that might have been a laugh.

"Your husband," he snarled. "By God, that's good !"

"He—he—he's going to marry me soon, I mean."

To Burton's ears came the echo of the conversation of the men in line at the post office. "Jack Smiley married ? Are you crazy ? He meets 'em, beds 'em and leaves 'em."

He laughed again in that harsh, unnatural voice.

"So you're Jack Smiley's light o' love, his fancy woman. They're talkin' about you all over town, Enid, and how they'd like to bed you like Smiley's done."

Suddenly the girl blazed.

"It's all your fault," she rapped out. "C-can't you see? Father was killed by the Crows. I—I got tired of waiting and waiting—growing older—having no life, no love."

"Love!"

He swayed as he remembered the love he had borne for Enid Culver through those months of hell in Mexico.

"Jack was here; he was good to me."

She crossed the writing room in a wild flurry of grey skirts and caught up the big, handsomely brutal head of her lover to cradle it in her lap as she crouched. Over the still features of Smiley she glared at Burton.

"Oh you fool!" she cried. "You unutterable fool! Why did you leave and go off to Mexico like that? Do you think a girl grows younger, waiting for somebody who might be dead somewhere?"

"But——" his tongue seemed fashioned of thick cotton. "But you promised. I was getting money for you—for us." He made a stricken gesture toward the haversack. "I joined Maximilian—fought——"

"Fought!"

Savagely her voice rang out as she fixed her flaming eyes on Burton.

"Fought—yes, that's all you're good for, fighting. That's all you'll ever be—a down-at-the-heel soldier of fortune! I—I worked after Father was killed. Look at my hands—they'll prove it!"

She held out her hands but all that Burton could see were the flashing gems that Jack Smiley had placed there. As she bent forward, offering her hands in testimony, the ex-Confederate noticed that the grey dress she wore had been cut to Smiley's liking, too. He turned away, as though to stare were some sort of sacrilege, even knowing what Enid was now.

"I'm sick and tired of working," the girl said shrilly. "Now I'm going to enjoy myself. I'm happy—happy—happy!"

A strand of golden hair fell over one eye. She pushed it back with a trembling hand. Her lips drew back from her perfect teeth in an unlovely grimace.

"Get out, you fool!" she screamed. "Get out! Jack will kill you when he comes to. Get out, you poor romantic fool!"

From behind Burton came the trample of feet. In the door of the writing room appeared a thick-bodied man in shirt-sleeves, his hair slicked flat with bear's grease. Other faces, startled, incredulous, peered over his shoulders.

"My Gawd!" rapped the first man in awed tones. "Why—the damn fool's hit Jack !"

"What ? You mean somebody knocked out Jack Smiley ?"

Huddled on the floor, her lover's head in her lap, Enid Culver pointed a long arm at Captain Robert Burton.

"He did it !" she squalled. "He hit Jack from behind. He—he——"

The soldier of fortune's Colt .44 magically appeared in Burton's hand as there was a stir in the crowd at the doorway.

"Hold it !" he ordered. The slick-haired man's hand paused a few inches from the butt of his gun. "Hold it and keep it held. I used to be a pretty good shot. I still might be. Don't know. Like a little practice."

He walked slowly toward the door as the crowd fell back. Over his shoulder he called a parting.

"Glad to have met you, *Missus Smiley*. Reckon we both made a mistake. Only I've found out mine in time. Good luck to you."

Then, shoving the terrified slick-haired man aside, he marched out through the lobby of the hotel, pushing through the crowd that had gathered in the room. There was a babble of voices when he made his appearance in the lobby but a deathly stillness fell as the crowd parted to make a path for the hot-eyed young man in the red-striped blue breeches. The people of Julesburg knew Death when they saw it.

On the threshold of the Julesburg House, the Captain stopped. Laughing stridently he called out. "Come on, everybody ! Drinks are on me ! I'm invitin' you-all to the Blue Star and we'll drink— drink, by God, as none of you've ever drunk before !"

At each stride he made down the street the mad turmoil raging in Robert Burton's brain mounted like a brook fed by freshets from the melting snows. When he reached the Blue Star, his mind was a raging torrent of black despair, a flood-crest of hate and disillusionment.

In frenzied gaiety he threw wide the swinging doors of the Blue Star.

"Drinks !" he yelled. "Drinks for my friends ! Name your poison, friends, and drink to Captain Robert Burton of Forrest's outfit. Drink till it runs out of your ears. I aim to spend thirty thousand dollars before midnight."

A hand grabbed his arm and he looked down into the agonized eyes of Colin MacKaye.

"Nay, Rob !" the Scot pleaded. "I dinna ken what happened, but let's be done with this mob of scuts."

Burton flung off his friend's hand. His laugh rose again, eerie and harsh, as he walked away from MacKaye.

"Drinks!" he yelled in the voice that had marshalled so many Confederate battalions into line of battle. "Drink to a poor goddam fool!"

Roaring with delight they came; loafer, teamster, harlot, capper and section hand. Gamblers came to view this monied stranger and then drew away, forbidden liquor by their profession. Sweating, shouting and swearing joyously, they crowded in until the Blue Star could hold no more. Burton huddled over the bar pouring the raw red whisky down his throat and reaching into his haversack now and then to toss another magnificently flawless diamond onto the whisky-pooled slab.

"That ought to be enough," he said. "That ought to buy out this place with some to spare. There's plenty more where that came from."

"Oh, mon, mon!" pleaded MacKaye at Burton's elbow. "Dinna do this. There's no woman in the world worth such madness."

A ruffian with a bruised face shoved himself between Burton and the Scot and waggled a long-barrelled pistol under Colin's nose.

"Shut up, you!" the man ordered. "Let him spend. He's havin' a aces-up time for his *dinero*, ain't he?"

MacKaye's hand shot out and wrenched the pistol barrel upward toward the ceiling. The other hand doubled itself into a rock-knuckled fist and swung. There was a thud and the interloper landed on the floor. He looked at Colin in amazement and then scrabbled toward the door on hands and knees. The Scot laughed and tossed the gun he had wrested from the other's hand to the bartender. He cast a glance at Burton, then shrugged and turned away. He knew there was no holding the ex-Confederate when the man was in that black mood.

Cases of champagne fired volleys of corks up to the raw pine rafters, then sent their golden contents sparkling across the bar. The haversack was half empty when the last bottle of precious wine was drained.

"What? No more champagne?" Burton cried. He abandoned his work of tucking a thick cork into the beribboned garter of a staggering dancehall girl who could not have been out of her teens. "That's an outrage!"

The girl flung her arms around the ex-Confederate and hauled his head down to her mouth in a wet kiss.

"Come on over to the Prairie Belle," she slurred. "More room there. I'll treat you right, too, because you're handsome and you're a spender. After the Prairie Belle we'll go to my place."

"The saloon's a good idea," Burton agreed owlishly. "Let's go to the Prairie Belle."

He shoved his way toward the door, the girl clinging to his arm and Colin MacKaye ploughing through the crowd behind him. Outside the crowded, smoky saloon the fresh air hit him like a club. He sagged for a moment, then straightened with ludicrous dignity.

"This time yesterday," he announced gravely, "I thought I'd be married by now. Jus' a romantic fool, she called me. B'God she was right ! No more romance. No more foolishness."

Colin pushed the girl aside and threw an affectionate arm across the shoulders of the man under whom he had served through so many bitter campaigns in Mexico.

"Come, mon," he said. "Ha' done wi' your madness ! Dinna throw away the rest o' your siller. Come to bed, Rob, and to-morrow will be different."

"No bed for me, Mac. I'm going to make this day one I'll never forget. Carry on, MacKaye !"

The two men—the girl had dropped off at MacKaye's rude shove—were halfway across the wide street when a buggy pulled up in front of them and Captain Burton focused his wavering gaze on the face of Jessica Valcour. There was a uniformed Army corporal by her side. As she looked at the soldier of fortune, a puzzled twist came to her mouth.

"Captain Burton, I—I was looking for you."

The adventurer tried to bow from the waist and nearly toppled into the street before Colin's hand caught him. Burton straightened, his hat in hand, and grinned.

"Didn't mean to scare you," he announced. "Didn't have any idea of doin' anything but lettin' you breathe when I——"

"Corporal Shannon has a message from the Major at Fort Sedgwick and my father," the girl interrupted. "Corporal ?"

The Corporal, a youngster with the fuzz of a new beard on his cheeks, saluted and recited :

"Major Anderson's and Senator Valcour's compliments, sir, and would you do them the honour of having dinner at the fort to-morrow evening with Miss Valcour."

Captain Robert Burton drew himself erect, shunning MacKaye's steadying hold, and returned the corporal's salute as he had returned the salutes of better men than this boy would ever be; men who lay buried now along half the Mississippi Valley.

"Captain Burton's compliments to the Major and the Senator," he replied in a steady voice. "Captain Burton would be honoured to dine with Miss Valcour, her father and the commandant—if the invitation still is in effect to-morrow."

The girl stiffened and bit down a sharp retort. Passers-by were gathering on the boardwalk, making it necessary for her to keep her smile stiff on her face.

"We shall expect you then at seven to-morrow night, Captain. All right, Shannon."

Nettled by a flick of the corporal's whip, the blacks surged on and the buggy vanished around the stern of a lumbering Conestoga wagon. Burton watched it out of sight and then burst into strident laughter as he lurched on across the street. MacKaye started to follow, then stopped at a touch at his shoulder. He turned to find a lieutenant wearing soft brown sideburns and a worried expression.

"Get your friend out of town," the lieutenant warned.

"He'll no run away," Colin replied.

"He's *got* to run this time," said the officer grimly. "If you're his friend get him out of Julesburg, drunk or sober. Jack Smiley runs this town and your friend has made mincemeat out of Smiley. Get him away. It's his only chance."

Colin scowled as he pondered the earnest appeal of the lieutenant.

"Are there no law officers?" he asked. "Ha'e ye no sheriff or constables?"

The officer brushed his sideburns nervously.

"Hell," he ejaculated. "We've got a sheriff that Smiley owns and deputy sheriffs he owns and that's all. The soldiers have no jurisdiction in here. Smiley's got two or three hundred toughs in this town who owe him favours of one sort or another. Boot Hill is humpbacked with men who didn't do a tenth of what your friend did. Get him out!"

The friendly officer hurried away as MacKaye started for the Prairie Belle into which Burton had disappeared. He found the ex-Confederate at the bar, surrounded by a mob of hangers-on and dancehall girls. The Scot fought his way toward his friend. Burton laughed that shrill, unnatural laugh again and threw his arm over Colin's shoulder.

"Tryin' to keep me sober he is," the soldier of fortune jeered. "Won't lemme spend m'hard-earned money."

"Throw him out! Kill 'im! Get out of here, you——"

Burton's face suddenly lost its stupid grin. It became hard and deeply lined.

"First man that touches my friend," he announced, "has to gun me. And I'm pretty fast. Now everybody drink up and forget yesterday."

By now word had gone throughout Julesburg that some kind of madman was spilling diamonds on the bar to buy drinks for anyone who could lift a glass. A steady stream of men and women hurried to the Prairie Belle to join in the bacchanalia staged by the stranger who had knocked Jack Smiley unconscious. When the sun sank in its usual burst of breath-taking glory, and kerosene lamps began to shed their yellowish glare over the town, a swarm of hot and loud-voiced humans wallowed in the depths of a frontier mass spree. Hairy, red-faced men fought for no reason; others sang; still others staggered out into the street and pitched into the muck of the road. Painted, dishevelled women teetered on their high heels and led tottering drunks off to cribs and tent brothels picking their companions' pockets en route. Hard-eyed gamblers lured drunken celebrants into rooms where the poker and faro tables waited.

Slumped in a chair placed before the bar, haversack between his knees, sat Captain Robert Burton, presiding over the raucous carnival. His tongue might be thick, his feet unsteady, but his mind still was clear.

How well he remembered the diamond and pearl brooch he tossed onto the bar to be clutched by the avid fingers of the proprietor of the Prairie Belle. The Marquis of Ocampo had given it to him at Salvatierra in reward for leading a hopeless charge against the savage *encurados* of Jalisco. How often had he pictured that brooch gleaming beneath Enid's full throat.

That ruby ring that the redhead trollop was squeezing onto a finger? The betrayed and deluded Austrian, Maximilian himself, had given it to Burton for riding through the Republican Army with news of the victory of Camarones.

"To hell with 'em," the soldier of fortune mumbled. "They're no good now."

It was close to midnight when Captain Robert Burton's uncertain fingers scraped the bottom of the haversack and picked up but two pieces of jewellery. One was a jewelled comb that once had graced the head of a Mexican peeress. That, he tossed at the barkeeper. The other was the gem of the whole collection, a necklace of superb emeralds.

The ex-Confederate rose unsteadily to his feet and climbed upon the chair on which he had been sitting. From his long fingers swung the necklace of flashing emeralds.

"Here !" he yelled. "Look—you-all !"

A shout went up as those in the smoke-clouded Prairie Belle glimpsed the prize that Burton dangled before them.

"For the ladies !" shouted Bob. "Ladies forward !"

A roar of excitement sounded through the place. The throng surged forward, fascinated by the bits of solidified green fire that Burton held.

"Give it to me !" "No, give it to me !" "I'll do anything for you, honey !"

A swarm of cursing, pushing, scratching harlots and dancehall girls fought their way up to the chair where Burton stood. Hungrily they eyed the prize—pleaded for it, slobbered, whined and wheedled. Writhing fingers, brown, red and white, clawed upward toward the emeralds. Burton looked down at the crowd and laughed.

"I gave a li'l party," he said. "Everybody's had a good time. Now's my turn to have a good time. I got the right to pick the girl I'm gonna give this to."

Colin MacKaye's hands tore frantically at Burton's coat.

"Oh, Rob, Rob !" the Scot implored. "Dinna throw away yon bauble. 'Tis worth a gude ten thousand !"

"Gonna put it onna neck of a whore," Burton said with drunken insistence. "Was gonna put it onna neck of another whore but somebody a'ready owns her. Gonna pick my own now. Stand back, ladies, while I pick my bee-yoo-tious girl."

The girls dropped back from the chair, each one simpering and smiling in hopes of being the chosen one of the drunken stranger who threw away diamonds. Burton staggered down the aisle made by the trollops, searching each face with wavering eyes.

He reached the end of the line and turned to go back. As he revolved unsteadily, he saw a girl standing against the back wall of the saloon, taking no part in the saturnalia. She wore an abbreviated yellow dress, cut high on the thighs, and her slim, silk-covered knees were pressed tightly together. As Burton lurched up to her, the girl flinched and then, as though remembering what she was and where she was, she forced a dreadful mechanical smile to her painted face.

"Evenin', honey," she faltered. "Want a good time—I mean—I——"

Her voice died away as Bedford Forrest's captain clicked his heels and bowed. Burton's hand went out and instinctively the girl shrank back a half step.

"Don't be afraid," said Burton with drunken gravity. "I'm presentin' you with these. Ma'am—Miss——"

"Lulu Jameson," supplemented a hoarse voice. "Brand-new gal around here."

"In you, Miss Lulu, I pay honour to the whole of your lovely and fascinatin' sex," Burton mouthed.

Cheers hammered out, mingled with the snarls of the disappointed prostitutes as Burton clasped the emerald necklace about Lulu's neck. He pulled the girl's head around and planted a rough kiss on her mouth, then drew back to see the girl's lips quiver and her eyes fill with tears. He waggled a finger in front of her face.

"Never cry, Miss Lulu," he admonished, "when you get necklaces like that. Only cry when the man you love does you wrong."

The girl started to speak but her words were drowned out by a rising shout from the throng.

"King and Queen o' Julesburg ! King and Queen o' Julesburg ! Get 'em a coach. A buggy—anything !"

Now that the last of the jewels were gone, Burton's reserve cracked and he flung an arm around the waist of the girl in yellow.

"Come on, sweetheart!" he yelled. "You're my queen to-night! Let's show this town somethin'!"

Out onto the street poured the shaggy saturnalia, shouting, fighting, screaming, laughing. Shots were fired into the air. Somebody found a buggy and Burton and Lulu Jameson were bundled into it by rough men and painted women. The horses started up, led by a crowd of staggering celebrants while others clambered up onto the back and sides of the vehicle, the dancehall girls kicking high into the air and throwing kisses everywhere. Amid a fresh salvo of shots, the rout began to travel down the main street.

"By the great leapin' Moses, never was a night like this before!" bellowed a drunken prospector. "Ain't never drank champagne water before, neither."

"Ki-yi-yi," whooped a scarlet-faced cowboy. "I'm a lobo wolf from the Brazos and it's my night t'howl!"

"Never gonna see so much wine again," babbled a soldier from whose pockets protruded the long necks of three champagne bottles. "Hoo-ray for Bully Burton, the boy with the heart o' gold!"

The mad parade swayed on toward the prairie at the edge of town. Burton, laughing crazily, sat with one booted foot on the buggy's dashboard. One arm was around Lulu Jameson's waist and with his free hand he waved a whisky demijohn. From time to time he threw back his head to scream the "E-e-yah!" Rebel yell.

"Kiss me, Johnny Reb!" cried a dancehall girl as she threw herself across Burton's lap. "I'm from Geo'gia an' I hate Yanks!"

He planted a kiss on her hot wet mouth and then flung her from him. As she toppled out of the carriage, her dress caught on the buggy's whipsocket, ripping the flimsy stuff from one shoulder and exposing a flabby breast. The crowd whooped and the 'Geo'gia' girl smirked.

"Ah don' cayuh," she screeched. "Ah'm havin' sech a good time!"

Then, to Captain Robert Burton, C.S.A., the world began to revolve in dizzy circles. There was the crowd about him, kisses, whoops, drinks and more drinks, somebody's bare shoulder under his hand, momentary lull in the hullabaloo and a stern voice roaring:

"What's the meaning of this disgraceful scene?"

Burton's vision cleared a trifle then and he saw Senator Valcour standing on the front porch of his home, on the outskirts of Julesburg, a horse-pistol in his hand. He also made out the face of Jessica Valcour, peering over her father's shoulder, eyes wide with fright.

The ex-Confederate half roused himself in the seat of the buggy and waved a salute at the round-eyed girl.

"See you to-morra night!" he whooped.

Then he dropped back and there was a blank space. Next, it was dark and there was someone beside him on the bed. He reached out a hand and touched a warm body, pulled it close to him. The lips that met his were warm and full.

He saw the flaming train and heard the screams of the Cheyennes. He felt the ache of the long ride. He saw Enid Culver with her eyes wide as she stood up from the writing desk. He saw—he saw——

"Enid," he muttered. "Enid, is it you?"

"Yes," the girl answered. "It's Enid. Now go to sleep. Go to sleep."

Guiding arms pulled his head down to cushions of vibrant, pulsing flesh. It was a soft pillow and he closed his eyes.

"Sleep," the girl's voice counselled.

CHAPTER VIII

FIVE thousand imps beat on Robert Burton's temples with red-hot sledge hammers. His tongue was thicker and drier than it ever had been when he was lost in the desert of Sonora.

Bit by bit, a measure of confused consciousness returned and he opened his eyes, then shut them quickly as the sunlight stabbed at his eyeballs.

"Where in hell am I?" he asked himself. "Why's my head hurting so infernally? Why's that arrow wound in my arm giving me the devil?"

Gradually his vision cleared after he had opened his eyes a second time. He looked up at a fly-specked ceiling, then over at a wall on which hung a calendar. He turned his head, wincing at the pain and learned that he was lying on a bed.

He raised himself on an elbow and saw that he was undressed. He hastily pulled the sheet up about him.

"A hell of a mess," he muttered under his breath. "How'd I get mixed up in this?"

His nose wrinkled as he sniffed the perfume of the woman beside him. It was faint and fragrant. It came and went with each steady breath of the girl—a girl he never remembered having seen before.

He turned his head cautiously and looked at her. She lay facing him, lips half parted, lashes fringing her cheeks. Her face, despite the paint she wore, was childish and she slept with both hands doubled up close to her chin.

Innocent appearing though she might be, the paint on her face marked her. Captain Robert Burton winced with the realization that he had spent the night with one of the harlots of Julesburg.

It came back to him now. The scene in the hotel writing room. His insane eagerness to get rid of everything that might remind him of Enid and the wound she had dealt him. The super-spree he had staged. The ride through town. Then—oblivion.

He stirred experimentally and felt new throbbing pains drive through his skull.

"Better get moving," he told himself. "That man Smiley isn't the type to wait for the other fellow to make the first move. I'd better find Colin and get out of this place before I have to kill that man."

He swung his legs out of bed, stifling a groan, and sat up while his head revolved in a sickening lurch. He shook his black mane to clear his brain and stood up, a straight lean figure. With a backward glance at the sleeping girl, he climbed hastily into his clothes. He was dousing his face in the wash basin when he heard her stir. He turned, face dripping, and looked down at her. The girl's eyes were open, staring at him questioningly. Embarrassed, he turned away and reached for the crisp towel that hung on the rack.

"You—I hope you've been paid, ma'am," he muttered, keeping his face averted.

"Yes," came the small voice. "I——"

"Okay," Burton said. "I'll be gettin' out of here. Much obliged for everything."

He slung his pistol belt around his middle and fastened the buckle, still keeping his back to the bed. He took his sombrero from a hook on the door.

"Mister," came the voice from the bed. "You're forgetting something."

The ex-Confederate settled the wide-brimmed hat on his head carefully.

"You've already said that—that everything was paid up," he said. "What is it now?"

"I—I've got something for you."

He turned and looked at her, staring at him from the bed, the counterpane drawn up to her chin. A moment's revulsion swept through the rangy soldier of fortune. Women of her type, he told himself, were what they were. But this—this child!

He forced a grin as he touched the brim of his sombrero.

"You save it," he said with false heartiness. "I'll be back for it pretty soon. I'm in a hurry right now. But—but—well, thank you, ma'am."

He wrenched open the door of the little room, stepped over the two elaborately beribboned scarlet garters that drew tiny rings of colour on the floor and walked out into a narrow hallway. He found a steep stairway and cautiously descended into what appeared to be the back room of a small warehouse. Through an open door he could see the main storeroom piled high with stacks of dry goods, bales of blankets, rows of lanterns, horse collars, ready-made coats, boxes of shoes, boots and hats. There were sounds of activity in the front of the emporium although the sun was not up. Captain Burton turned to fumble for the back door of the place, pull the bolt and hurry outside.

After rubbing the red-hot marbles set into his skull—his eyes—he planned his course of action. He knew that he must find Colin MacKaye and get the Scot and himself out of town. To stay in Julesburg was to commit suicide, with Jack Smiley owning the town. However, he needed food—something to stay the queasy feeling in his stomach.

In the grey light of dawn, Julesburg had lost all semblance of the tawdry false pretence it had assumed during the hours of darkness. A jackass beyond the railroad began to bray just as the early riser started for a grubby little lunchroom near the freight depot where the mounds of railroad supplies loomed like man-made hills against the sky.

Mechanically he felt in his coat pockets. Nothing, He felt in other pockets. Nothing. Even the gold seal ring he wore which bore the crest brought from England by his cavalier ancestors was missing from his finger.

He turned back, then stopped.

"What the hell," he murmured to himself. "You asked for it, Burton. Man who makes a damn fool of himself has to expect that. Now you can start out again with the clothes you've got on and a pretty bad Colt .44. Meanwhile we've got to dig up Mac before we eat."

He looked about him and then set off down an alley that ran behind the buildings that formed Julesburg's main street. Here and there he came upon the snoring figures of his 'guests' of the night before. Once he carefully sidestepped a man who lay face down in the muck of the alley with a bloodstain crimsoning the back of his neck. No drunk he and, Burton knew at a glance, past help.

A boy of about thirteen came down the alley toward Burton and the ex-Confederate halted the lad. The freckled boy carried a milk pail over one arm and a battered stool dangled from the other hand.

"Gee, Mister," the boy said, "if you hurry you can see it !"

"See what ?"

"They's goin' to be a swell hangin' right soon. Wisht I could go but, goddam it, I gotta milk the old cow. Paw said he'd frale me plenty fervent if I didn't."

Burton stared at the boy.

"A hanging ?" he asked. "You ought to be glad you're going to miss it."

The boy stared up at Burton in amazement.

"Glad I'm missin' it ?" he asked. "Hell, mister, I seen easy twenty-five or thirty hangin's around this town and I ain't got my belly full yet. Ol' Jack Smiley's men know how to put on a mighty purty hangin' when they set their mind to it. Don't break the man's neck, y'see. Jest choke him easy so he'll wriggle 'round a little."

"What's this fellow done?" inquired the tall man in the red-striped blue breeches.

"Well," said the boy importantly, "this hombre was lookin' fer somebody—a stranger—and he went to a whore-house that a man name of Dirkin—he's a deputy sheriff—owns. Well, Dirkin's a right mean feller and when this man questions him Dirkin kicks him and they's a fight and this stranger hammers the guts out of Dirkin. So, naturally, Dirkin gets the sheriff and they gang up on this stranger and they say he's the feller that held up the U.P. back beyond Kearney last month and they took him off down the road to string him up."

"Tell me," Burton inquired, "have you seen or heard anything about a red-faced man, about my size, with blue eyes and a scar across one side of his face? A stranger?"

The boy's eyes widened.

"Y—you mean a feller wearin' one of them funny Greaser belts with silver and blue stones onto it?" he asked.

"That's the man," Burton said. "Where did you see him?"

The boy opened his mouth and fluttered his lips for a moment as he backed away from Burton. The soldier of fortune reached out and caught the youngster's ragged blue cotton shoulder.

"Where did you see him?" he demanded.

"Why—why, good Gawd, Mister," the boy blurted. "That's the feller they're fixin' to hang right now! Jack Smiley's boys probably got him dancin' on air by this time."

Drunk! howled Burton's brain. *Drunk and sleeping with a whore while Colin was looking for you and running up against Jack Smiley's crowd! And now he's being hanged because he was your friend!*

"Which way did they take him?" he asked in a dull voice. "Tell me, boy. Where did they take him?"

A grimy wart-speckled hand swung toward the east.

"Down 'long the track 'bout half a mile out o' town. They's a passel o' cottonwoods down there where most hangin's are done."

Burton whirled and ran down the alley to the first sidestreet, then onto the main street. He took the first horse he found, a black that was hitched to the rail outside a grain dealer's office. Behind him, as he rowelled his spurs deeply into the flanks of the outraged animal, he heard shouts and curses. One shot banged out. Leaning far over his mount's neck and with a hand caressing the black's muscle-bunched side, he rode at a furious pace past the Prairie Belle, past the Julesburg House and the rest of the shabby part of the town. Once along the track and heading east he jabbed the spurs again and again. The black laid his belly close to the ground in a furious burst of speed that made the wind tear at Burton's ears and set the thrums of his hunting shirt to fluttering like ragged battle flags in a breeze.

As he rode, he checked his gun. MacKaye ! Colin MacKaye !

"I'm comin', Mac," he panted. "Damn me, I'm late—but I'm comin' ! Hold out, old man. Hold out a minute longer. I've never let you down yet."

The black ripped through low clumps of dewy sagebrush, then skirted a rise that showed the yellow-green tops of cottonwoods standing beyond a bend in the dusty trail that followed the railroad. Instinctively Burton reined in and bent in the saddle to survey the ground. Fresh hoof prints on the dun-coloured earth proved that horsemen had passed by recently. He spurred the black again and reached for his old Colt.

Abruptly the trail swung out around a rise, then led under a low-swinging cottonwood branch. Eyes darting about from side to side. Burton's thumb drew back the hammer of his revolver. The black carried the soldier of fortune into the midst of the cottonwood grove with a rush, almost colliding with a pair of tethered broncos that stood among the grey-brown tree trunks. Near the horses stood two men, apparently arguing over an article they held between them. A red mist whirled before Burton's eyes as he recognized the turquoise and silver belt of Colin MacKaye.

The two men stiffened as Burton brought the black to its haunches with a powerful jerk on the reins. Sunlight gleamed briefly on steel as the nearest man whipped up a rifle and sent a bullet moaning past Burton's ear. A split second later the grey-faced horseman's Colt spat flame and the man with the stubby Wesson rifle screamed and staggered, clutching at the side of a dirty, red-checked shirt.

The black shied at the howling of the wounded man and a shot cracked out from the gun of the second man who had dived into the protective covering of a clump of sun-dried willows. Burton snapped a shot at this new enemy and, as the fellow stupidly left his cover to seek a better place, the ex-Confederate shot him down. The lumpish figure pitched forward and lay still.

Burton raised his voice in a cracked shout.

"Colin ! Colin ! For God's sake, where are you ?"

The soldier of fortune spurred his horse forward among the sun-dappled trees. Then he groaned as he brought the black to a halt.

He stared upward, his heart dying within him. There, dangling from a limb, was a hideously contorted figure—a figure at once familiar and weirdly strange. God ! Could the dreadful purplish face be that of Colin MacKaye, the gallant gentleman who had stood so sturdily beside Burton during three long years of war ?

His nerves close to the snapping point, the ex-Confederate forced his mount to approach the appalling object that swayed gently in the faint breeze. Colin's glassy eyes told Burton that there was no hope—the third son of The MacKaye of Glenkaye was dead.

Demonic voices dinned in Burton's ears, hammering at his reason.

'Your fault !' they screamed. 'You killed him ! You put that noose around his neck !'

He passed a shaking hand over his face and bowed in his saddle. Then he straightened and turned as voices came from behind him.

"Which way did he go ?"

"Right through there ! See his hoss's tracks ?"

Through a gap in the cottonwoods Burton caught a glimpse of Jack Smiley's cruelly handsome face agleam in the new sunlight as he headed a small group of riders that galloped toward him. Fury swept through Burton's soul at sight of the man. Twice within twenty-four hours Smiley had robbed him of people he had loved. The urge to kill swamped the ex-Confederate for a moment and he was beset by the blind impulse to charge straight at Julesburg's overlord. Then it was as if Colin spoke from above.

'Reason, laddie,' a phantom voice seemed to say. 'Ye'd do no good to either yerself or me were you to get yerself killed. Live to avenge me, Robbie. Live to avenge me !'

He turned the black's head away from the hanging tree as a new clamour arose behind him, telling the ex-Confederate that he had been sighted.

"Horse thief ! Horse thief ! Cut him off, you in there !"

The cold sweat standing out on his bronzed forehead, Burton wrenched the black around on its hind legs and dropped low over its neck as a rain of bullets came hissing through the branches. He could hear the slugs going *tacot! tchuk!* into the trunks of the cottonwoods. Ahead of him twigs and leaves came sailing down through the air as he rode headlong for a break in the trees.

Rowelling the black cruelly, Burton urged the powerful gelding into a surging gallop while behind him there arose a long-drawn yell that had sounded down through the ages; the dread hue and cry of men hunting a fellow human to his death.

Like a partridge flushed from a thicket the black gelding burst out of the willows fringing the cottonwood slump where Colin MacKaye had met his end. Lower over his horse's neck bent Robert Burton while more shots crackled out and puffs of dust sprang up from the sere brown grass roots about him.

Burton glanced over his shoulder to count some fifteen or twenty riders, whooping and yelling, coming out of the grove. In the van was Smiley, his long-skirted black coat whipping out behind him.

Gopher and prairie dog holes made treacherous going but the black seemed gifted with some sixth sense that enabled him to avoid the traps. Before two miles of the prairie had flashed by, the chase had been strung out in a long line with Smiley still leading the manhunters. A fierce hope filled Burton's heart. It might be possible that Smiley would gain a sufficient lead on his comrades to permit Burton to wheel quickly and then deal with MacKaye's murderer, Enid's paramour. Gradually he began to check the black as Smiley lengthened the distance between himself and his cronies.

Behind Smiley were three riders closely bunched and too close to give Burton the chance he was waiting for. Burton bided his time while a half mile more of dry prairie had flickered by. Then, when he saw that the other three riders had dropped back considerably, the ex-Confederate reined in sharply and turned the black to go for Smiley.

To his amazement, the overlord of Julesburg already had turned his own horse and was galloping back along the route he had come, quirting his bay madly. The other manhunters were turning, too, and joining in the retreat.

"What the hell?" Burton asked himself. "What made them do that?"

He looked about him and his heart leaped like a speared salmon. He saw the reason for the posse's about-face now. From a nearby gulch was pouring a disorderly column of Indians. The savages were too far off to recognize their tribe but, Burton estimated, they probably were Northern Cheyennes, Kiowas on the war path, or a band of Ogallalla Sioux raiding south of their regular stamping grounds. Cheyenne, Kiowa or Sioux, the Indians raised a longdrawn cry and turned their feather-decked ponies to head off the lone rider.

The Indians or Smiley? The grim-featured rider hesitated for only an instant, then began to lash his horse out onto the prairie, away from Julesburg. There was a chance that he might shake off the Indians but it meant certain death to turn back. A distant line of low hills seemed to offer some sort of refuge and he headed toward them. Purposefully, the Indians whipped their ponies and settled down to the chase.

CHAPTER IX

STINGING perspiration poured into Captain Robert Burton's bloodshot eyes as he urged his tiring horse into a faster gallop. Behind him came a dozen or more braves while the others in the column paced along at a slower rate, ominously confident that the chase would not last long.

The gelding was lathered with sweat as it thundered over the prairie, but the gallant horse was running a losing race. The Indians' ponies were fresh and the tough, hard-bitten little buckskins gained with every leap. Peering back over his shoulder, Burton could see the flash of red-tipped *coup* feathers flashing from lances, bridles and shields coming ever closer. The black stumbled, recovered and went on, but precious distance was lost in that moment's faltering break in the gelding's stride.

"It looks like it's over," Burton reflected bitterly. "And it's just as well, I reckon. Colin's gone, and Enid."

As the black horse's hoofs beat a frantic tattoo on the hard-baked earth, eerily reminiscent of the roll of a drum before a military execution, the soldier of fortune checked his gun. Two shots had been fired back among the cottonwoods. That left four still in the chamber.

"Reckon I can take a couple of those devils along with me for company," he said aloud.

His fatalistic planning came to an abrupt end when the black put a forefoot squarely into a gopher hole and went down with a sickening violence that pitched Burton over the gelding's head onto the dew-dampened ground. By a miracle the ex-Confederate landed rolling and, aside from having the wind driven out of him by the jar, suffered no injury.

He scrambled to his knees, cursing bitterly. Why couldn't he, he asked himself, have broken his neck in the fall and gone quickly to his death? Now, when his last bullet was gone, he would be at the tender mercies of Indians and their exquisite torture.

He tried to cock the .44 but the gun wavered as the whole sunlit plain rocked crazily. It was with difficulty that he made out the onrushing savages, screeching in their exultation. The foremost Indian was astride a piebald pony and wore a blue jacket of some kind. The second savage was clad in a scarlet breechcloth and leggings and brandished a spear.

Burton's vision cleared enough to let him glimpse a wolf device painted on the second Indian's feathered shield. Wolf! Then these riders were Pawnees—the Prussians of the Western plains—deadly enemies of the Sioux and Cheyenne.

Instantly he let his Colt thud to the ground and feebly made the Pawnee peace sign—holding the first two fingers of his right hand raised vertically toward his ear lobe, he then shoved them forward to arm's length and finally tilted the fingers forward in imitation of a wolf who scents danger.

The effect on the howling, copper-featured riders was instantaneous. The foremost Indian reined in on a regulation cavalry bridle while his companions jerked on rawhide hackamores. Clouds of dust swirled about, guttural voices called commands and hoofs thudded. From where he crouched half stunned on the ground, the Pawnees and their horses assumed incredible proportions to Burton's distorted vision. Their bright war feathers seemed to be yards long and their painted faces were masks of barbaric frightfulness.

"*Pa-ni I-ra-ri?* Pawnee brothers!" gasped the white man as long forgotten words came back out of the fogs of memory.

The ex-Confederate knew he was taking a fearful chance. That wolf sign on the shield might be a ruse such as was practised commonly among warring tribes. Quite possibly, Burton told himself grimly, these braves might be some of Turkey Leg's Cheyennes.

With lithe ease half a dozen smooth-limbed warriors vaulted off their battle ponies and came running toward Burton, the foremost levelling a carbine pistol-wise and the others raising their spears. The Indian in the blue jacket halted a few paces from Burton and cried,

"*Kets-i-ki-rurus-uks-ut-a?* Where have you been? Who are you?"

"Evil men pursued me, O my brothers," Burton panted. "By bad medicine these men in the stable of the Iron Horse slew a great warrior—my friend."

The leader of the group about the fallen officer nodded solemnly and a *coup* feather, stuck into the band of a cavalry Stetson, mimicked the nod.

"Buffalo Caller knows there are evil men in the stable of the Iron Horse."

Burton got to his feet and, surrounded by the fantastically garbed, evil-smelling Pawnees, limped over to view the black horse. The gallant beast lay stiff-legged, the victim of a broken neck.

"Pony dead," grunted a flat-faced brave. "I speak English. I Bleeding Fox. How, brother."

Burton soon got the idea that Bleeding Fox and Buffalo Caller were sub-chiefs and therefore he addressed them in the formal language due to leaders of the fighting Pawnees. Had the situation been different, the soldier of fortune would have found humour in the costumes that the warriors wore. Their dress was an incredible and grotesque mixture of cavalry uniforms and savage finery. Many of these hawk-eyed braves had cut the seat out of regular issue cavalry breeches so as to permit their muscular thighs and buttocks to retain their grip on the bare backs of their ponies.

Others wore blue jackets over their familiar blue or red breech-clouts while some sported black cavalry hats from which sprouted *coup* feathers or coyote brushes. Many wore issue boots with the vamps cut off. A few had strapped bright brass spurs to their naked feet.

Burton turned his aching head to eye a singular pair of figures who rode up at the head of a score or more of Skidi Pawnees. One

wore a complete cavalry officer's uniform except that he affected
leggings and moccasins instead of boots. The other and foremost
man was of medium height with a short grizzled beard and two of
the most piercingly black eyes Burton ever had seen on a white man.
He was clad in greasy fringed buckskins and wore a battered broad-
brimmed hat.

"Wal," he growled, "here's a pretty mess. Damn if the Major
and me knows whether we oughter take you back to 'Hell on
Wheels' or not."

"Reckon Jack Smiley will thank you if you do," Burton replied
heavily. "If you're a friend of his he'll give you plenty for my skin."

"Me ! A friend of that swine !" snorted the grey-bearded rider.
He sent a stream of tobacco juice arching toward the bleached skull
of a buffalo. "Wisht I could be sure you ain't one yourself."

"Well, Nick, from the looks of things I'm purty sure he ain't
a friend of Smiley's in good standin' right at the present."

It was the second white man who spoke. This soldierly individual
showed himself a man of the plains in every wrinkle of his face and
by his old rawhide complexion, his bleached hair. His keen grey
eyes ever busy, he sat a big half-breed hunter and the blue collar
of his uniform bore gold maple leaves.

"That was Smiley himself in the lead back there," the Major
continued, "and he didn't look like he was makin' to kiss this man
when he caught up with him. But, stranger, you'd better give an
account of yourself—and make it likely."

Briefly, Burton outlined the events of the day, omitting all refer-
ence to Enid Culver. When he had finished, the grizzled rider in
buckskins spat tobacco juice again, making a direct hit on a horned
toad that went hopping angrily away.

"So you dotted Boot Hill Jack !" he said. "Wal, sir, I shore
would enjoy shakin' the hand what punched him. The name's
Nick Janis—Dog Soldier Nick to my pardners. This here gent with
the 18-carat hair is Major Frank North. You'll have heard o'
North's Pawnee Scouts, I reckon ?"

When the three shook hands Burton read a cautious friendliness
in the Major's clear grey eyes.

"Where did you get the breeches ?" the Major asked after
Burton had drunk from a canteen and accepted the cold bacon and
hardtack that Janis proffered.

"Down in Mexico," Burton mumbled through his food. "Along
with a lot of other stuff I got rid of."

"What did you say you were aimin' to do in Julesburg ?"

What had he aimed to do in Julesburg ? A black tide of bitterness rolled over the adventurer's heart.

"Why—why I had reckoned on a deal there—a deal that meant
a lot. But—well, suh, it fell through and my last cent's gone. As

I told you, Smiley and his gang lynched my partner and—well, I don't know just what I'm going to do now."

Eyes narrowed, Major North passed a thoughtful hand over the square chin that jutted out from under his thin mouth.

"Too bad, Captain," he said. "Sounds like they handed you a regular Julesburg reception. That 'Hell on Wheels' is a cesspool of vice and murder. Wish Jack Casement——" His voice trailed off.

Burton straightened his sagging shoulders with an effort and forced some kind of a smile to his lips.

"Afraid I've taken up a lot of your time, Major, so I'll be on my way," he said. "Thanks for your help. Sorry I can't repay you, suh. Goodbye, Major. Goodbye, Nick."

He touched a salute to the brim of his hat and, spurred boots dragging wearily, started away from the ring of silent Pawnee scouts. His dark mood blackened as he limped past the dead gelding and caught the reproachful look in the glazed and lack-lustre eyes. Heedless of his course and aware only of the inescapable fact that Colin MacKaye was dead, he stumbled on.

"Hi, Cap'n!" came the thin, penetrating voice of Dog Soldier Nick. "Iffen you're right keen to part with your ha'r jest you keep on the way you're headed. Thar's a Cheyenne village o' forty lodges not ten miles in that direction."

A horseman came trotting up alongside Burton and the square brown face of Major North looked down at the soldier of fortune.

"Just where do you think you're goin'?" North demanded while the coppery Pawnees looked on in silence. "Not that it's any of my business."

"Why—why, it doesn't matter much," was Burton's stony reply. "And I'm afraid, suh, I'm delayin' you-all."

"Don't be a fool," said the Major brusquely. "You can't just quit, man."

He turned in his saddle and called out a string of commands, couched in guttural Pawnee. Within a moment, the dead gelding's saddle and bridle were placed on a bay pony and the horse led up to Burton.

"Mount up, Captain," Major North ordered, "and come along with us. You won't last long otherwise. Look back there."

Burton followed the direction in which the Major's lean finger pointed. On the top of a distant butte he made out several black specks. North eyed the figures through a pair of work-worn field glasses and then lowered them.

"Smiley," he said. "Persistent cuss, your friend."

"Friend! Friend? By God, Smiley is a friend, at that! That pretty-boy has given me something to live for. If it's the last thing I do, I'll kill him!"

"Plenty of men have said that," Nick Janis warned, "and they all wound up with lead in their back and dirt in their face. Boot Hill Jack's jest about king of these yere *mesas* so don't go sky-hootin' back into Julesburg less'n you've got plenty of hard shootin' *hombres* to back you up."

"I'm goin' back," Burton said slowly. "Smiley may be strong but I'll settle with him some day."

"Ugh," grunted the Pawnee sub-chief, Bleeding Fox. "Good. You do it, think-be."

He turned and grunted some words in Pawnee to Buffalo Caller. The other sub-chief nodded while the braves raised their lances and shook them in the air, whooping their approval. Vengeance was the first commandment of the Wolf Tribe.

Watched by the expressionless Pawnees, Robert Burton retrieved his revolver and cleaned it of dust and grit before making sure that his long knife was secure in its sheath. Then, with a face that might have been hewn out of brown marble, he swung up on the bay pony and sat it firmly while the buckskin, unaccustomed to the saddle and bridle, did its best to throw him in a wild series of vicious bucks and sunfish twists. A murmur of approval rose from the weirdly caparisoned detachment when the horse's rebellion ended with Burton still in the saddle.

"*Wagh !* Long Knife is a horseman !" Buffalo Caller grunted.

With a complete lack of confusion the scouting party got under way. Burton looked back over his shoulder to see the crows and magpies that had appeared out of nowhere settle in a cloud over the carcass of the black gelding that had served him so well.

At the end of three hours' ride the detachment was trotting along a trail which roughly paralleled the newly completed course of the Union Pacific.

"So you were in that wreck at Willow Creek," North was saying. "By God, it *is* a small world. I was up at End o' Track and gettin' set for a good meal of buffalo kidney when in runs a wild-eyed telegrapher.

"'Major North,' says he, 'Them damn red devils have gone and done it at last !'"

"'Done what ?' I asked."

"'Word's just come in from Kearney,' he says, 'that a bunch of massacreein' Cheyennes have derailed Number Fifteen and killed most of the passengers. Seems the fireman got scalped but he ran all the way to Clear Creek with the top of his head off and gave the word.'"

The Major paused to light a disreputable old pipe and sent acrid clouds of smoke scudding away behind him as he jogged along.

"Well, sir," he continued, "I got some hosses and Pawnee scouts aboard some flat cars and we broke all records down to Willow Island but all we found were a couple of drunken stragglers, the wreck and some odd pieces of train crew scattered around on the prairie. Of course the Dog Soldiers and the other Cheyennes had vamoosed."

The Chief of Scouts pointed with his pipe stem toward the grizzled man in fringed buckskins.

"By the way," he said, "Nick Janis's Injun name is Dog Soldier Killer but we all call him Dog Soldier Nick."

"How'd he get his name?" Burton asked arousing himself from a stupor of weariness and heartache.

"About twenty years ago the old fellow licked three Dog Soldiers single-handed. But to go back to Willow Creek, we found about sixty big blood spots—no Cheyenne bodies, of course—so you must have put up quite a fight."

Dog Soldier Nick, his bristly jaws busy on a new cud of tobacco, drew his sleek pony up alongside.

"Yes," he said, "and don't forget them chunks of meat what was poor Bully Brooks, the engineer, and Gregg Henshaw. They was some other whites on a little hilltop. All cut to kybobs, they was."

"They were dead before the Indians got them," Burton said.

"They were lucky," North continued. "Well, we've been lookin' for Turkey Leg's outfit ever since. They've scattered like they generally do after a raid and it makes it pretty hard to run 'em down."

A short silence reigned among the three whites and the *clip-clop* of their horses' hoofs sounded monotonously over the guttural talk of the Pawnees in the rear. Against the side of his carbine's worn scabbard, Major North tapped out his pipe ashes.

"What do you aim to do when we get to End o' Track?" he asked.

"Is that where you-all are headed?" returned Burton.

"Yes, we ought to get there towards sundown if we don't cut the trail of a war party. Any ideas on a job?"

"Why—why, I don't know. Haven't given the matter much thought. Reckon I'll head where there's fightin'. You see, suh, I've been skirmishin' around off and on durin' the most of the last six years so war's about the only trade I know."

"Soldier of fortune, eh?" asked Major North, wiping his sweaty face with a blue bandana that was knotted about his neck.

"Reckon that's about it."

Burton winced, remembering Enid Culver's blazing words. 'Down-at-the-heel soldier of fortune' was what she had called him. Well, she was right. He was sitting a borrowed horse with only his old Colt and the clothes he wore to call his own.

"Maybe I could land a job with some meat hunter's outfit," Burton added. "I heard somewhere that they make as high as five hundred dollars a month."

The Major snorted in genial derision.

"Thought you said you were a fightin' man," he jibed.

Blood leaped to Burton's cheekbones and dyed the long scar along the roots of his black hair.

"And who says I'm not?" he demanded.

"Not I," said North quickly. "You'd get plenty of excitement with the buffalo hunters but they're really only glorified butchers." North winked. "Don't repeat that to Dog Soldier Nick. He used to be one—still goes out on a hunt now and then when things are slack."

He shot Burton a keen look.

"What's wrong with the Pawnee Scouts?" he asked. "Why not join up with us. I'm needing another subordinate since"—the Chief of Scouts' face tightened—"since Tom Cummings was murdered in Julesburg last week."

"What rank?" asked Burton with faint interest showing in his sunken eyes.

"I expect I could get you a commission as captain of scouts," Major North replied. "Know any Injun?"

"Some," the ex-Confederate said. "I hail from east Kansas and besides Pawnee I can palaver along in Kiowa, Arapahoe and Sioux. Know the sign language, too, of course."

"You must have a good ear for languages."

"Tolerable, Major. Nothin' more."

Major North considered the proposition in silence, then said,

"We'll have a talk with General Casement when we reach End o' Track. Since it's excitement you want, Captain, I guess we can accommodate you and if you're handy with your weapons you may be of some use to both the U.P. and North's Pawnee Scouts."

"I reckon I've still a lot to learn," Burton admitted doubtfully, his hand wandering to the side of his belt, "but here's a sample of what I do know."

His hand flashed in an arc and a Pawnee riding close by let out a startled screech. The ten-inch knife had flashed by his ear and, narrowly missing two other Scouts, had neatly pinned to the ground an incautious prairie dog that had lingered too long in his inspection of the colourful cavalcade.

"*Wagh!*" A shout of excited approval arose from the Pawnee as the little animal gave a final kick and relaxed.

"Great leapin' Moses!" Dog Soldier Nick exclaimed delightedly, his yellow teeth exposed in a wide grin. "And ye allow ye've still things to l'arn?"

"Yes," Burton replied. "Down in Mexico a man isn't rated a real knife-thrower till he can nail a crow on the wing."

"A good touch, that knife play," North commented drily. "The Injuns will respect you now."

A Pawnee in a seatless pair of striped yellow pants bent from his pony to retrieve Burton's knife, then held it up. One by one the

bucks examined the bloodied blade, the handle of polished rawhide
and the knife's bright brass tang, fashioned in the shape of a wolf's
head. That tang seemed to bear a special significance to the Pawnee
braves.

"Knife throwin' comes in handy sometimes," Major North
said, "but around here you generally don't have time to get gay
with a knife. What can you do with that gun you're packin'?"

Burton hesitated and then shook his dusty head.

"I'm not so good with a gun, suh," he confessed. "And since
I'm kind of shaky now I reckon I'll wait till we fetch up where we're
goin' before I try to prove myself."

"That'll do, Captain. Too bad you're an ex-Reb."

"Why, suh?" asked Burton. "I've seen a lot of former Confederate soldiers around the U.P. And, besides, I took the oath
after Appomattox."

"Oh hell," Major North snorted. "There's not one man in a
hundred who gives a damn but that hundredth man happens to be
Colonel Barry. He just doesn't like Rebs. Came from Cham-
bersburg, Pennsylvania, and he still swears that the Rebs did a
lot of rapin' and lootin'."

"Well, by God, suh," said Burton heatedly, "if he can hold a
grudge like that ask him about Sherman's campaign and——"

"Easy, Captain," said Major North soothingly. "Take it
easy."

Burton relaxed in his saddle and lapsed into a miserable reverie.
He stared unseeingly at the ground sliding endlessly beneath his
pony's hoofs. He was, he told himself, the champion of lost
causes. First the War between the States, then Maximilian's campaign—and now he had lost his best friend and the girl he had
wanted to marry.

CHAPTER X

IT was close to sunset when Captain Burton, riding with Dog
Soldier Nick, first saw the pale blue columns of smoke rising from
beyond a high butte ahead.

"Wal, thar's your End o' Track," the buckskinned scout said.
"Damn shame we didn't come across a couple of dozen of Turkey
Leg's murderin' devils. Since they've got a taste for train wreckin'
we can figger on lockin' horns with them yet."

He eased his carbine back into the beautifully fringed and beaded
rawhide boot that hung at his saddle.

"Third squaw made it," he explained as he caught Burton's
admiring gaze. "Nice little Kiowa wench. Don't throw nothin'
but boy babies."

"How many children do you own, Nick?" the ex-Confederate asked curiously.

Dog Soldier Nick spat at a gopher hole.

"Hell," he said, "I don't know. I ain't been home for nigh onto five days!"

Burton saw a Pawnee brave ride up to Major North out on the right flank and converse briefly with the commander of the scouting force. Then the warrior flung up his arm. With a whoop the other Indian riders surged up and away toward the smoke columns that marked End o' Track. It was an impromptu race with each warrior bending low over his pony's neck, the bright red, yellow and blue blankets flung high in the air and the *coup* feathers threshing madly. The troop disappeared over the edge of a steep bluff and then re-appeared again in all their colourful madness.

"Ye can't stop 'em from doin' that," Janis explained. "They love to make a show when they come into camp. The Paddies and Micks like it, too. Sort of breaks up the monotony, so to speak."

He nodded his head toward the left and Burton, turning, saw that Buffalo Caller and Bleeding Fox had not joined the others. The two sub-chiefs held their position, proceeding at a placid gait.

"Them wise old bucks are *sabio*," the grizzled man explained. "They don't go in for them fool stunts like the young bloods. They know damn well some day thar's goin' to be a green camp guard on duty that'll cut loose fer general results into them playful Pawnees."

"And green troops," sighed Major North as he reined his horse in alongside Burton, "are all we've been gettin' lately. The few veterans we have are gettin' ready to pull out and go home-steadin'. When they're gone—God knows what will happen."

A moment later, the five riders paused on the crest of the butte to view an eye-filling panorama revealed, map-like, at their feet. Robert Burton blinked, aware once more of the same dynamic atmosphere that had prevailed in Julesburg. From the plain below arose a blend of noise that held the key of action. There was the clang of iron on steel, the thud of sledgehammers on wood, the throaty panting of locomotives, the creaking of axles—all contributing to the vital uproar.

End o' Track, to Burton, looked like a Union encampment of the war. The white cones of hundreds of Sibley tents were arranged in company streets. Closer to the tracks were dugouts similar to those he had seen at Vicksburg. 'Prairie Monitors,' North called them. Five locomotives idled on a siding, sending columns of blue-grey smoke twisting lazily up into the deep azure sky, seeming to brood over the dozens of flat cars which, laden with ties, stretched far back along the right-of-way.

A cracking of whips and the sound of groaning axles shifted Burton's attention to an old freighting and stagecoach road which skirted the bluff on which they stood. Along the narrow highway toiled an emigrant train which included more than a score of enormous Conestoga wagons and prairie schooners. The vehicles moved at a snail's pace on their ponderous wheels measuring six and eight feet across. Each wagon was drawn by at least six yoke of oxen. Amid a sifting, all-pervading cloud of dust they crept along, swaying tops dully agleam in the sunset. Alongside the caravan mounted men herded horses, milk cows, sheep and spare oxen.

Dog Soldier Nick slung a bowed leg around his saddle-horn and spat in the general direction of the wagon train.

"Quite a sight, ain't it?" he asked. "Another Mormon train headed fer old Brigham Young's colony. Ten to one they won't make it but you got to admire their guts. Them Mormons are right fine fighters, too. Found a batch of 'em one time and fer every Mormon man, woman or child we found they was at least ten Cheyennes—or the places where the Cheyennes had died, leastwise."

He rubbed his grey beard speculatively.

"Y'know," he said, "I've had a hankerin' to go out to Brigham Young's place and try that free love business. But, goddam it, my three wives don't let me git away!"

Burton smothered a smile as he looked about him, scanning the huge mounds of supplies piled beside the railroad tracks. There was bale on bale of hay which, according to Major North, cost thirty-four dollars a ton when delivered at End o' Track. Grain, North went on to say, was worth seven dollars a bushel; firewood, a mere hundred dollars a cord; and for each solid oak tie the directors of the Union Pacific were paying three dollars and a half.

"Yonder's the right-of-way, probably all built to-day," North said. "Looks like they've put up a fair stretch."

Beyond the camp and paralleling a stream called Lodge Pole Creek, a long embankment of freshly-turned earth lanced into the prairie for a distance of about three miles ahead of the last pair of gleaming rails. Further on stretched a line of telegraph poles with wires strung in place. The Major explained that the telegraph always kept ahead of the road gang to give warning of Indian raids.

It was the supper hour and throngs of the grading crew and construction gangmen were returning to camp, the former trundling in on four-horse supply carts, the latter on handcars. All of them were whooping and singing—the day's work done and food close at hand.

On the fringes of this encampment, Burton noticed, were the tents and pickets of the strategically disposed detachments of infantry and cavalry. His eyes singled out a familiar sight—a picket line with its horses kicking and biting at each other, as picketed troop horses always have and always will.

"It's a great sight," said Major North, "but we'll have to hurry if we're goin' to report to the General and still draw food and forage for to-night."

"Look at them damn idjits," grinned Dog Soldier Nick as he slapped a lean thigh.

Whooping and yelling, the Pawnee scouts now were galloping in a circle at the near side of the camp. Some stood on their ponies to fire their carbines and revolvers into the air. Others went through the most amazing feats of horsemanship that Burton ever had seen. One of the scouts slid beneath his buckskin's belly to reappear promptly on the other side of the animal. Another leaped off his pony, grabbed its tail and pulled himself up into position again. Watching the show was a cheering crowd of labourers.

"Casement's Irish love 'em," Janis said. "Them Micks are jest as wild as the Injuns. The Pawnees and the Micks git along like pups in a basket."

"You see, Captain," North explained as he put his horse to the 45-degree slope of the butte, "there's a practical reason, too. The Irish damned well know that if it weren't for my scouts a lot of 'em would lose their hair. In spite of all we could do, the Cheyennes and Sioux killed or captured more than thirty labourers last month. As I've already said, you've come at the right time—the showdown is due this summer."

"Showdown? I don't understand, suh."

"It's this way. The fighting tribes, Sioux, Blackfeet, Cheyennes and Arapahoes—to name a few—know that if the U.P. is built their huntin' grounds are sure to be ruined and"—his voice became deep with earnestness—"they're going to move heaven and hell to stop the railroad or force the U.P. to build further south. And the road will have to go south if President Johnson doesn't send more troops. The redskins are knockin' off surveyin' parties and supply trains almost every day. You can't blame the Injuns much, at that. When the buffalo and antelopes go they'll starve and go bare-assed. They know it and they're desperate."

"And if this route is abandoned to build south—what then?"

"Ruin! It'll mean the road can't go on. The Kansas Pacific is there already. Besides, the government wouldn't subsidize the Union Pacific on that route. As it is, Congress is yellin' like pigs under a gate at the cost of this road."

The small party presently rode down a gentle slope and crossed behind the immigrant train which was plodding on down the track known as Thirty Mile Ridge Road. After crossing a stretch of prairie the five horsemen reined in at a picket post where a quartet of cavalrymen in dust-stained blue stood to horse beside a pair of pup tents. A sergeant smartly presented sabre to Major North.

"Find any of them, sir?" he asked.

"Not this time, Sergeant," North called as they rode by. "But we'll get 'em soon."

Five minutes of trotting through the tented streets, as precisely laid out as those of any regiment, brought Burton and his guide to a large tent before which was posted a crudely painted sign: "Construction Division H.Q."

"Come along, Captain," North directed. "Nick will take the animals over to our camp."

Burton swung an aching leg out of the saddle and, like the veteran cavalryman he was, eased the cinch of his scrawny little Indian pony. The beast, astonished at such unprecedented consideration, snapped at him viciously.

The last golden sunbeams of this unforgettable day were striking almost horizontally through the big tent's doorway. Two orderlies sprang up and saluted as Major North entered. Inside, a captain and a grey-haired colonel in the uniforms of the Regular Army stood in deep conversation. They looked around expectantly as the Chief of Pawnee Scouts appeared, his moccasined feet padding the earthen floor.

"We were just talking about you, Major," said the captain. "Glad you're back—there's been hell to pay."

"That you, North?"

From behind a rough table at the far end of the headquarters tent rose a towering redheaded man in dusty civilian clothes. Hand outstretched in welcome, he skirted the table and came forward to greet the Chief of Scouts. Burton felt an instinctive liking for this big barrel-chested man with the flaming red beard and the facile features. On this man, too, was stamped the brand of those who strive and who are not easily turned aside.

"Yes, General. Sorry to have been gone so long."

"Well, North, did yez catch Turkey Leg?" the redheaded giant demanded.

"No, General," North replied, pulling off his fringed gauntlets. "He and his band got away too fast. We got a few stragglers."

"Then ye did get some?"

"Only about a half dozen scalps."

While the Indian fighter described his movements since leaving the wreck at Willow Creek, Robert Burton stood silent and uncomfortable, aware of a pair of searching eyes that belonged to a man in a colonel's uniform, still seated by the General's table. Conscious of the cold regard, the ex-Confederate pulled his aching body to attention and remained as rigidly erect as ever he had while standing before big, golden-bearded Jeb Stuart.

"And who might this be?" asked General Casement, levelling his penetrating blue eyes and a stubby brown forefinger at the straight figure in the Mexican belt and the red-striped breeches.

"Don't know much about Captain Burton," North said, "except he's handy with his weapons. He tells me he was in the Confederate Cavalry under Forrest's command durin' the late war and since then he's been fightin' for the Mexican Emperor. Smiley's crowd was chasin' him hell-for-leather out of Julesburg when we cut his trail."

The Contractor General of the Union Pacific Railroad lowered heavy red brows and addressed Burton.

"Stand easy," he directed. "Ye'll have been havin' a hard day. Is that true what Frank North tells me?"

"Yes suh. On my word."

"Then ye don't seem to have much skill in pickin' a winnin' side," came Casement's dry observation.

"No suh. I'm askin' for a job and a chance to get back at Smiley and his crowd."

The big Irishman stalked back to his chair and settled his bulk in its creaking confines.

"Ye are, are ye?" he asked. "And what were ye thinkin' of doin' now? Major North tells me you're stony broke."

"I—well, suh, I haven't any special ideas——"

"I'd thought of takin' him into the Pawnee Scouts," North broke in. "I need a new captain since Cummin's got his at Julesburg."

General Casement fumbled with his beard, frowning. Then he flashed a gleaming smile at Burton.

"If Frank wants ye," he said, "why, I guess that's all there is to it. All right, I'll——"

"Sorry, sir." Cold as the rasp of a skate blade on ice came the voice of the colonel who had been watching Burton so closely. "I regret that in my opinion this man is not acceptable for a commission in the United States Army."

"Now why in hell, Colonel Barry," demanded Casement, "is Captain Burton so decidedly unacceptable?"

Every head in the tent turned to face the harshly handsome officer who was in command of the troops assigned for the protection of the railroad builders.

"Because," came Colonel Barry's precise, inflectionless tones, "we already have too many Rebels in our ranks. I simply won't have any more."

He turned stiffly to confront the uncomfortable Constructor General.

"Please recall, sir, that I have spoken to you on this subject before and you agreed, so——"

"I object to that, Colonel," Major North cut in. "The Amnesty Decree makes objections on such grounds invalid."

"Legally, no doubt," replied the colonel as he flushed, "but it happens that I have heard of this man. Robert Burton was one of Bedford Forrest's most trusted lieutenants. No doubt he was a fit subordinate for that cowardly swine of a guerrilla."

His face gone grey, Burton surged forward. North clutched at him.

"You chinch!" he shouted. "Who are you to call General Forrest a guerrilla?"

"Maybe I *am* wrong," snapped back the colonel. "Maybe I should have called him a butcher. Perhaps you were there when Forrest's command murdered the negroes who surrendered at Fort Pillow."

North's hands tore at Burton's shoulders as the ex-Confederate surged forward again. The Chief of Scouts dragged the soldier of fortune back a moment before Burton's claw-like hands reached the colonel's throat.

"Steady!" North ordered. "Steady!"

"It's a goddam lie," Burton panted. "General Forrest was and is the best—the finest—the——"

His voice trailed off, strangled by emotion.

"You see?" came the frigid voice of Colonel Barry. "That's why I want no more Rebels on my force. They're hot-headed, insubordinate and quarrelsome."

"Faith," Casement muttered as his fingers drummed on the table top, "I know plenty of Yanks who'd have got red-headed, too, had ye said such things about Sheridan or Custer." He shrugged his shoulders. "But seein' you're in charge of the defence, I'll have to——"

"But really, General," Major North broke in, "I want Captain Burton. I'll vouch for his conduct."

"Sorry, Major," said Colonel Barry. "I won't recommend a commission for him and that's final."

He turned away from the two men in front of the table and pushed a paper toward General Casement.

"And now, General, about that forage for the advance guard. It's been scant and of abominable quality."

Seething with impotent rage, Burton followed Major North out of the tent. By the time they were in the company street, the ex-Confederate had mastered his fury and was able to muster a wan smile as he held out a hand to his rescuer.

"Thank you for your trouble, suh," he said, "and I'll never forget your kindness when I needed it most. Don't involve yourself further on my account. I'll make out, somehow."

"And some fine day," said the Chief of the Pawnee Scouts, "I'll have the pleasure of punchin' that sneering Barry *hombre* in the nose, court-martial or no court-martial. There's a typical West Point tin soldier for you. The goddam fool thinks he's still fightin' the Rebels. Why, he came within an ace of having two troops of the Seventh cut off and massacred by Sioux last spring."

He passed an arm through Burton's elbow.

"Come along," he urged as he waved a hand toward the outer edge of the camp where dozens of buffalo-hide tepees pointed their lodge poles and smoke-blackened vents toward the red and gold splendour of the twilight sky. "There'll be some supper for us yonder. We can talk further about this on a full belly. Did you ever notice, Captain, that few things seem quite so serious after a good meal?"

"You're mighty kind, suh," Burton protested, "but I owe you too much already. It would only complicate——"

He whirled, one hand going instinctively to his knife, as someone touched his shoulder from behind. He faced a hatchet-faced U.P. clerk in a brass-buttoned waistcoat.

"Cap'n Burton?" the messenger drawled. "General Casement says for you to come back and see him after supper."

CHAPTER XI

CAPTAIN ROBERT BURTON awoke at dawn after a night in which the memory of Colin MacKaye's body loomed with nightmarish insistence. Now he rolled over on his heap of soft buffalo calf robes and ran over again the conversation that had taken place in the headquarters tent on the previous night.

"For the time bein'," General Casement had said while he tugged at his full red beard, "we can use you as a meat hunter. It'll fill in the time while I—er—machinate a bit. Those damned redskins are harryin' the very divil out of our forage parties. No fresh meat in ten days. The pay will be four hundred a month and"—the sunburned Contractor General had added with a Celtic twinkle—"nary cent of it'll be paid 'less yez stay sober as a priest and bring in eight buffalo a day. 'Tis a hungry gang we have here, Captain, and maybe yez will have noticed at yer wars that nothin' starts trouble and disaffection quicker than yer slim rations. Now get along with yez and talk to Dog Soldier Nick. He'll equip yez at company expense—deductible from yer first pay."

"Dog Soldier Nick?" Burton had asked. "I thought he was one of the Pawnee Scouts."

"So he is, but first of all he's a buffalo hunter at heart. He gets sorrowful if he lacks a hunt once in a while."

Burton rolled out of his bed and delved into a greasy haversack to fish out a ration of army hardtack, beans and sow-belly. Just what had Casement meant by "for the time being"? And what did his parting phrase mean—"I'll be having a special use for yez later on if you've a stomach for such work."

Dawn was beginning to tint the starry fathomless sky when Dog Soldier Nick appeared, belching and yawning, from a nearby lodge in which lived his three Indian wives and his litter of halfbreed children. The step of the hunter's moccasined feet was soundless as he slouched up to Burton's side.

"Wal, at least ye ain't no slugabed," commented the frontiersman. "But you've got a lot to learn if yer to become a good buffler hunter. First off ye'd better get rid o' them highfalutin' bunion builders."

Contemptuously he indicated the thorn-scarred black boots that Burton held in his hand, ready to pull on.

"And as for them striped soljer pants, leave such giddy nonsense to the Yaller Legs and the Dough Boys. A half blind Injun boy could spot 'em a mile off. Hyar's a pair of buckskin britches good enough for a Ogallalla chief and these yere moccasins'll let yer board a pony a sight spryer than them there jack boots."

Among the valuable habits Burton had picked up during his years of campaigning was a willingness to listen and carefully consider all advice offered by those in whose country he lived. Flexibility—always flexibility—whether in customs, ethics or in manner of warfare, was his watchword. The ex-Confederate murmured a word of thanks and took off the expensive blue and red breeches fashioned for him by a voluble little tailor in Tampico. He pulled on the more pliant and nearly waterproof buckskin breeches, the thighs of which were liberally decorated with blue and white beadwork.

"They're right comfortable," he said with a faint note of his old light-heartedness in his voice. "When I have something to give them, I'll make your wives a present."

"Don't spoil 'em," grunted Dog Soldier Nick. "Them squaws feel plenty rewarded if I don't beat 'em more'n twice a week. Come on, Long Knife—that's what the Pawnees hev christened ye —we've got to mosey along and we're late as it is. There ain't been no meat in camp fer the last ten days. Ye see, Waters and his outfit shore got clipped o' their nappers by a passel o' Red Shields last Monday and less'n Apache Jack Ware and his boys show up this mornin' with some carcasses there'll be plenty o' empty bellies, sore heads and hell-to-pay in camp to-night."

"Hell-to-pay? Why? Haven't they ever gone hungry before?"

The grizzled frontiersman looked grave as he slung a sagging pouch of cartridges over his shoulder.

"Wal, ye see, Cap'n, that ain't all what's wrong."

"No?"

"No. Fer some reason nobody rightly understands, the Micks

and pick-swingers have been gettin' ugly. No fresh meat to-night would be like settin' the buffler grass afire; easy to start but hell to stop. These Irishmen are wild, I'm tellin' ye. That's why the Gen'ral asked Pa-ni Lesbar—Major North—to rig out a special buffler huntin' outfit and"—Dog Soldier Nick smirked modestly— "picked me to run it."

At the picket line at which the Pawnee scouts had hitched their nervous little ponies they found Buffalo Caller and a quartet of keen-eyed Pawnees waiting with blankets and hackamores already adjusted. Six Regular Army spring carts, each drawn by four horses and carrying a civilian teamster and one skinner, loomed in the background. Horses stamped and snuffled while Dog Soldier Nick silently dealt out to each Indian a heavy calibre, repeating Spencer carbine which could throw eight-ounce bullets with enough power to knock down the biggest bison—and also any man careless enough to fire it when off balance.

Mounts having been saddled and the gear gone over carefully, the buffalo hunters set off through the sleeping encampment. It was not until the party approached the line of pickets that they met anyone awake except the cooks already drowsily working at the task of preparing the morning meal for some three thousand men. At the outer line of infantry pickets, there was plenty of activity. Lanterns bobbed back and forth, voices were calling and the hoofs of horses tramped loudly.

"Somethin' up," Nick said tersely. "Come along; mebbe we'd better l'arn what's what."

He turned to the teamsters hunched on spring seats and sucking at their glowing pipes.

"You boys jest start out on the trail to Big Springs," he ordered. "Me and the Cap'n will jine ye in two shakes. Buffler Caller, you keep yer eyes on them spare ca'tridges."

A brief trot brought the two men to the picket line where, in the amber glow of lanterns, a group of stern-faced officers and men were busy at a forage wagon.

"Gawd !" panted a young private and reeled away to vomit. By kicking his horse forward Burton could see a quartet of troopers removing a red-stained canvas cover from the cart. A lantern was raised and a succession of chills went racing up and down the ex-Confederate's spine. He had seen ghastly sights before—far too many of them—but never had he beheld death in such a horrible guise. In the cart, with limbs rigid in odd postures, lay the bodies of four white men, all victims of studied savagery.

"Good God !" Burton choked despite himself.

All four men had been scalped, of course. The head of one had been skinned as well, leaving the musculature revealed as in a surgeon's anatomical plate. Another cadaver resembled some weird form of human porcupine, so thickly was it punctured with bright-feathered arrows. The other two were even more grossly mutilated. Fingers and hands had been cut off; empty eye sockets glared blackly upward; noses and ears had been severed; the pallid torsos had been slashed in horrible patterns. Burton's mustang, sniffing the sickish sweet odour of blood, reared and snorted.

Impassive, wooden-faced, Dog Soldier Nick looked down from his horse, pulled out his plug of tobacco and bit off an enormous chew. Then he gathered reins and turned his mount away.

"Wal, Long Knife," he said. "Thar's the handiwork o' our friends the Cheyennes. C'mon, 'pears like it's reely up to us to bring in some bufflers."

"Who—who were they?" Burton asked, wetting his lips.

"He was tol'rable cut up but that there one full o' arrers was Apache Jack Ware. Knew him by a bit o' tattooin' on his arm. Don't say nawthin' about this to them waggin fellers. They're scairt bad enough as it is."

"And that makes the second outfit this week?"

The grizzled buffalo hunter uttered a harsh laugh as the two men trotted to rejoin the little column.

"It's up to us to see we don't make the third," he grunted. "It'll be tech and go out thar to-day and I don't mind sayin' I'm plumb oneasy. Yessiree, we'll have to look mighty sharp."

With bridles jingling softly, the wagons rattled on over the pre-dawn greyness of the prairie. To Robert Burton, this struggle to build the Union Pacific was taking on a new significance. It was strange, he thought, how one could expect and reconcile himself to death in warfare and yet be revolted by the fact that men should have to die here so horribly. In order that a pair of steel rails might connect one coast of the continent with the other.

He wondered how many of the U.P.'s plump directors, secure in their comfortable offices back east, understood the incidental costs of their enterprise. How many greedy bondholders, clamouring for speed and more speed in the completion of the road, would insist on their demands if it had been their own sons or brothers who lay in the forage wagon back there beneath the flaring lanterns?

Gradually the morning song of the coyotes dwindled and larks, quail and a host of other birds began to call as if in a melodious effort to bring sanity back to a distracted world.

"Reckon our best bet's to head up Ash Hollow way," decided Dog Soldier Nick. "Thar's whar the Injuns is gen'rally thickest. So, I figgers, that's whar they won't be lookin' fer a meat party. Ever hunt bufflers before?"

"Yes," said Burton, rousing himself with an effort. "Years ago. Do you-all ring 'em hereabouts or gallop 'em?"

"Bufflers is a sight too scary to be ringed these days," replied the frontiersman, "so we'll have to gallop the critters. We'll have to take care not to run 'em too far and string out the carcasses. That's bad medicine in times like these."

Soon the hunters began to sight scattered groups of bison. In twos and threes the shaggy bearded brutes were browsing on the dew-heavy grass, but, lacking the mass courage of a herd, they dashed away at a ponderous gallop, snorting loudly and jerking their ridiculously tiny tails.

"Hope we don't scare any more o' them damn strays," Dog Soldier Nick muttered, craning his leathery neck. "Scairt strays is the surest warnin' to Injuns of a meat party. We'll have to make this trip mighty quick out and back."

Dawn was making a dazzling glory of the eastern sky and the draft horses drawing the spring wagons were well lathered when at last, the frontiersman's command brought the expedition to a halt. Robert Burton drew a deep breath as he looked up a wide valley which seemed to be covered by a vast brown carpet, segments of which varied in colour from tawny yellow to dark chocolate. Unbroken, but shifting, the pattern extended as far as the eye could reach.

"Gee!" cried a young teamster. "All them ain't buffaloes !"

"Sure," replied a long-whiskered driver. "What did you think they was—gophers ?"

"You're goin' to start at the upper end of the valley, aren't you ?" Burton asked as he slipped a handful of carbine cartridges into the front of his buckskin shirt.

"Yep." Dog Soldier Nick looked surprised. "But why did yer ask ?"

"Figured that if we ran the buffalo towards camp the teamsters can be skinnin' and cuttin' them up while headin' for home at the same time."

"You *have* hunted bufflers before."

Exposing his snaggled teeth in a grin, the frontiersman turned in his saddle and called a string of commands in Pawnee to the five silent Indians who sat with bright jet eyes ever studying the skyline. The Scouts, Burton noted, appeared to be as uneasy as Indians ever would permit themselves to be.

"Shake a leg about this, you gunners," said a veteran driver on the nearest team. "I ain't hankerin' to have my backside filled with arrers like pore Curly Waters."

Taking cover, Buffalo Caller, Burton and Nick, followed by the Pawnees, skirted the line of high bluffs forming the valley's western wall and then turned and rode out on the floor of the depression in a long single file. In uneasy silence the teamsters and skinners stayed where they were, watching the horsemen. Waiting for Nick's yell to start the drive, the hunters trotted toward the bison in line abreast.

Stationed on the right end of the line, Robert Burton felt his breath quicken. There must have been ten thousand buffaloes grazing in that valley. On the outskirts of the great herd were towering bulls standing guard. Every now and then these prairie monarchs stopped their grazing to lower massive heads and charge the wraith-like grey wolves that circled the herd in hopes of pulling down a straying calf or a sick beast.

Burton set his mustang to a quick trot. Off to the left Pawnee feathers were flashing in the new sun as they lifted their battle ponies to an easy gallop.

"Go git 'em! *Wagh! Ki-yi! Yip! Yip! Yip!*"

Dog Soldier Nick's long-drawn whoop echoed among the buttes. A few of the bison raised their heads and gazed stupidly about, then promptly resumed their cropping of the lush buffalo grass.

Despite the seven-mile trip out from camp, Burton's mustang proved as full of run as if it had freshly quitted the picket line. Like a thrown lance it skimmed past steaming piles of droppings, thundering down on the herd.

Burton told himself that he had six shots and each bullet should mean meat for the brawny crews at End o' Track. He wondered if he still had the old art of cutting out the tender young cows at a gallop. Could he still send a bullet thudding accurately home behind the left foreleg? The ex-Confederate singled out a young cow standing at the edge of the herd beside an enormous bull, as his first target. That bull, he knew, would be as tough as shoe leather, except for his hump.

The mustang's headlong run brought a cooling wind to fan Burton's face. Now bison on the nearer edge of the herd were at last beginning to show signs of alarm. Horned heads were jerking up, one by one. At length a sentry bull snorted, flicked up its tail and began to walk off along the edge of the herd. The cow Burton had selected moved unhurriedly away, licking her moist brown snout and mildly eyeing the approaching horse and rider.

Bang! Far off on the left of the line a Pawnee rifle split the stillness into a thousand resounding echoes. The whole herd awoke to its danger then and thousands of buffaloes got to their feet.

"Time to get busy! Get along, horse!"

The mustang, trained to this work, needed no guidance. Burton dropped his knotted reins and guided the brute with his knees as he whipped up the heavy Spencer, sighting just back of the cow's shoulder. The Spencer thundered, its recoil rattling the ex-Confederate's teeth. The cow stood still for an instant, shivering violently, then quietly collapsed with a bullet through her heart.

Now the herd was off in that rocking gallop so peculiar to the bison, which never trots. It was, as Burton had learned long ago, a most deceptive gait. It looked so slow and yet covered so much ground. Without urging, the pony quickened his gallop, hanging onto the edge of the herd. Another young cow lumbered along thirty yards away. Burton fired again and saw his target stumble and turn in a heavy somersault.

With the herd in full flight, the shooting was harder, and Burton's third shot clipped a shaggy monster that kept on for a good hundred yards before slowing. His blood warming, the ex-Confederate shot again and again.

It was slaughter, perhaps, but it had its dangers, too. Let the mustang put his foot in a hole as the black gelding had and the hundreds of thundering hoofs would flatten him to a bloody pulp within a few seconds. He also kept a sharp lookout for buffaloes that were running outside of him and the herd, knowing that scattered groups like those sometimes came rushing in with vicious charges.

An enormous bull from such a group came close to terminating the hunt for Burton when, with the speed of an express train, it came charging in from the right, head lowered and wicked, upturned horns lowered like lance heads to disembowel the mustang. The ex-Confederate dodged the bull's ponderous rush at the last split second when the clever mustang veered, then swung alongside the bison. Burton fired into the brute's shoulder and dropped it into the sagebrush, kicking furiously with its wool smouldering from the point-blank discharge.

Then came the difficult task of reloading the Spencer while riding at a full gallop and completely surrounded by buffalo. Some of the lumbering beasts were actually brushing his legs as he laboured at the job. To have reined in would have meant losing all chance to kill more bison within easy range of the skinners. He struggled and prayed that the mustang would keep its footing, alternately cursing the man who had designed the Spencer to load through its butt plate.

It was awkward business to wrench out the plunger and feed bullets snatched from his shirt front into a tiny aperture. However, it was not long before the carbine was reloaded and he was racing along, firing a lethal charge into the woolly side of a panic-stricken bison.

By the time he had emptied his magazine a second time he had accounted for ten bison. If the other hunters had done as well, he knew there had been enough meat killed to load the wagons. From now on, time would be doubly precious. The shots of the meat hunters would have warned every wandering war party within miles of what was going on.

He forced his way to the edge of the herd and headed back to finish off a brace of cripples. Panting from his exertions, he passed a small promontory projecting into the valley and automatically noted a trio of magpies furiously berating an unseen something. Then, when a quartet of black-eared jack-rabbits came bounding terror-stricken, down from the summit, Burton's brown-lidded eyes narrowed.

"What the hell !" he muttered.

His first impulse was to rein in and investigate, but when he glimpsed a faint but ominous gleam of metal among the sagebrush growing thick on the bluff top, he rode on with forced nonchalance. He dispatched the two cripples as methodically as if he and the meat party were the only humans in the valley. And, he knew, that was dangerously far from the case.

CHAPTER XII

WITH his heart pounding in his throat, Burton forced himself to ride leisurely back over the carcass-dotted valley floor to the point where the rest of the party now were occupied in cutting the throats of the fallen bison. The meat carts already had halted beside the first animals slain, the horses snorting and shying at the smell of hot blood.

"Um, so yer seen 'em, too," Dog Soldier Nick remarked calmly.

"Of course Long Knife, our brother, has seen," said Buffalo Caller, his eyes flickering toward that promontory that reared its bulk a scant quarter of a mile away. "But him good warrior so him not spread alarm like magpie."

"How did you know I saw them ?"

Before making a reply, the frontiersman stooped and skilfully cut out a cow's tongue, a prime delicacy of the plains, and slipped it into his saddlebag.

"Saw yer start to rein in," he explained. "Never do that again, Cap'n. I only hope them Injuns yonder didn't notice."

"What do you plan on doin' ?" Burton asked.

"Wal, when them others come in and git warned," the frontiersman drawled, "I figger our best stunt's to git back to the waggins mighty casual like and then, on the word, them teamsters and skinners can each grab a hoss and we'll all make a run fer it."

"Hold on, Nick." Burton, with a muscular hand reddened by the blood of the carcass he had begun to skin, beckoned the hunter aside. "We know the General wants this meat back at camp mighty bad. Maybe there's a way to save it. Listen, down in

Mexico I once worked a stunt when I was in a fix somethin' like this."

"Wal, spit it out. But the Pawnees and me ain't partin' with our nappers to fill no pick-swingers' bellies. *Sabe* that !"

Working all the while, Burton talked in rapid Pawnee to Nick and the copper-hued scouts.

"Now," he concluded, "we're not goin' to say anything to those teamsters for a while, anyway. Like as not they'd get upset and give the show away. Everybody work like there were no Cheyennes inside of fifty miles. Most likely the Injuns over yonder won't bother us right away, figurin' they can just as well kill us after we've skinned some meat for them."

The nearest Pawnee slapped himself on his bone and bead breastplate.

"*Wagh!*" he exclaimed. "It is good plan. Before the sun is much higher Proud Eagle will have counted plenty *coups*. Our brother, Captain Long Knife, puts the wisdom of an old dog wolf to shame."

For three hours the buffalo hunters and professional skinners toiled and sweated beneath a broiling sun while ravens and crows gathered in anticipation of the forthcoming banquet. Coyotes and wolves slunk impatiently back and forth at the mouths of distant *arroyos*. By ten o'clock all six forage wagons were filled and groaning beneath their butchered cargoes.

"By Gawd, that ought to hold them hollow-bellied Micks," panted a skinner who, red to the elbows, brushed a fly from his forehead and left a bloody streak across it.

"Yes, sir," another said, spitting into a heap of viscera, "them was mighty short rations last night. And boy, what I can do to a chunk of hump meat !"

"To hell with that, Jed," drawled a driver as he climbed up on the box and unwound his reins from a whipstock. "Come over to my tent. I got a couple of tongues stuck away."

"All right, boys." Burton's glance included all the sweaty brown faces of the civilians. "I've got a bit of news for you. Now don't act as if I'm sayin' anything out of the way. It may cost you all your lives if you act scared."

"Why ?" "What the hell ?" "What's goin' on ?"

"During the last three hours we've been workin' here," the ex-Confederate said with enforced calm, "there's been a bunch of Sioux and Cheyenne watchin' us from yonder hill."

"Holy God !" gasped the oldest teamster. "You don't mean there's a bunch of them red brutes hidin' over there !"

"That's right. We've got to play it pretty or—well, you-all know what's goin' to happen. Now, we've got to get this meat back or the boys'll go mighty hungry to-night; but first I reckon we've got to lock horns with those Cheyennes. It's time they were shown they can't always jump U.P. meat hunters and come out on top. Now listen to me."

He explained his plan as briefly as possible while a penetrating silence settled over the motley group of civilians in gory overalls, in buckskins, in faded blue and grey pantaloons. The meat party numbered about twenty-five men and they were a frightened looking lot when Burton finished talking.

"Aw, that idee'll never work," hotly protested one of the teamsters. "I'm all for gettin' aboard a hoss and ridin' for it."

"And so am I !" "Me too !"

"Don't be fools !" Burton's voice flicked out as staccato as a drover's lash. "These plugs in harness might be all right for haulin' carts but they wouldn't stand a ghost of a chance racin' against the Cheyenne war ponies."

"Cap'n Burton's right," Dog Soldier Nick cut in abruptly. "And jest one of you *hombres* try unhitchin' a hoss. Don't be damn fools ! Long Knife, the Pawnees and me c'n get away easy 'cause we're mounted right. So ye'd better listen to the Cap'n."

"This is a gamble," said Burton, raising his voice a trifle, "but I reckon the odds'll be even if you-all do your parts. This detail is goin' to form up like I said and ride along the base of that spur. We're goin' to ride so close under that ridge the Injuns are on that they won't be able to see what's goin' on without showin' themselves, which I reckon they don't want to do right yet. Now"— he pointed to the brown and red canvas covers such as had covered Apache Jack Ware's mutilated body—"rig those covers and the skinners in each cart get under the covers like they were tired and goin' to snooze."

"Wal, it's lucky I've raised plenty hell in my time," grumbled a driver as he picked up the reins and placed his cocked carbine beside him. "'Cause I figger this hyer play is a mighty pore one."

"It's all right for you," muttered a white-lipped younger man, "but me—I—I've got a wife back in Omaha."

"Cheer up, Tom," called the driver of another cart. "She'll make a mighty fetchin' widder before another hour's out."

Whips cracked, axles groaned and the six carts swung into a compact single line, the Pawnees and the two white hunters riding as flankers. For better or for worse the plan was under way. Burton's face was bleak as he cantered out to join Dog Soldier Nick at the head of the ambushed meat train. Harness rattled, heavily-laden wagons groaned. The powerful haunches of the heavy-footed draft horses quivered with effort as the train swung slowly toward the west wall of the valley.

"G-gawd, I'm s-s-scared," choked a moon-faced skinner. "Wisht I was back in Vermont."

Clouds of choking dust climbed lazily skyward while the column moved steadily toward the ominous line of buttes. It was not long before the meat party arrived at the foot of the bluffs and, apparently unconscious of its impending doom, began to crawl along toward the promontory which sheltered the scalp-hungry Cheyennes. It was a nerve-racking business and the sunburnt men on the driving seats were sweating from more than the June sun as they guided their four-horse teams along the line.

At a certain point the wagons, in following the line of the bluffs, dipped out of sight of the promontory, then advanced so close under the heights that anyone standing on them could see no details. Dust clouds, however, rose as densely as ever, marking a steady advance toward the ambush.

When the betraying column of dust had crawled directly under the foot of the promontory it appeared that the meat train had been given an alarm. Whips cracked like pistol shots, horses broke into a dead run and the wagons sheered away from the heights.

Still galloping, the lead team turned and swung back to form a circle as the drivers yelled and whooped. Shots began to spatter down from the heights. At a bellowed command from the head teamster the wagons halted and the teams swung to face in. This done, the drivers jumped down from their seats and secured their badly frightened teams with practised skill while some skinners opened fire with their carbines. The outriders galloped to shelter and, within two minutes of the forming of the ring, little could be seen of the defenders save for a hat here and there, showing above the wagon covers.

"Hell!" panted the young teamster who had spoken of his wife. "Look at them devils come!"

A concerted groan burst from the men crouched inside the improvised corral. Pouring out from a narrow *arroyo* near the head of the promontory came a screeching avalanche of mingled Sioux and Cheyennes. There were about seventy warriors in the band and they quirted their ponies straight at the wagon circle, brandishing lances, bows and rifles.

The head teamster, crouched behind a rampart of buffalo quarters, tried to obey Burton's final instruction to wait until the gaudy charge was within twenty yards. When the attackers reached the fifty-yard mark, however, the old man's nerves snapped and he yelled, "Let 'em have it!"

The inert buffalo meat shuddered under the recoil of his gun. At the roar of the teamsters' first volley, the horses snorted and began to rear dangerously. The blood-freezing clamour of the onrushing savages heightened as they continued their mad charge at the wagons. Now and then a pony or a hideously painted brave

fell, but all in the attacking band could see that the teamsters'
defence was ineffective.

"Gawd help us !" groaned the young teamster as he sent an
empty cartridge case spinning through the dazzling sunlight. "We
can't stop 'em !"

Since they now were firing at almost point-blank range, the
defenders' bullets began to tell more effectively, but the Cheyennes
swerved not a foot in their charge. The savages were not more
than ten yards from the corralled wagons. The younger braves,
eager to count a *coup*, were frantically drumming their ponies'
bellies with moccasined heels when it happened !

From halfway up the walls of an *arroyo* directly behind the
charging savages there burst out the snarling crackle of well-
controlled carbine fire. By twos and threes, painted and feathered
braves tumbled onto the sere buffalo grass.

Burton knelt among the dozen skinners he had taken with him.
They had slipped from under the wagon covers during that brief
moment when the train had been completely hidden from the
promontory.

With a thrill of grim satisfaction he threw his sights between
the shoulder blades of a towering Black Foot chief whose naked
body was daubed in grotesque designs in ochre and green. The
bullet's impact threw the Sioux over his pony's shoulder and tripped
the animal, sending rider and beast down together amid a cloud
of dust.

"Give it to 'em !" "Blast the red swines back to hell !" "Pour
it into 'em !"

The still air grew heavy with powder fumes by the time the
repeating Spencers had fired their third volley, and it was hard to
sight accurately. By that time the ambushers were disastrously
caught between two fires. They checked their charge and wavered
between flight and further fight.

Pausing, the braves presented easier targets. More garishly
caparisoned Cheyennes were stricken down. Then from another
arroyo came the howling wolf war cry of the Pawnees, age-old
enemies of the Cheyennes. It needed only the appearance of the
four scouts headed by Buffalo Caller and Dog Soldier Nick to
decide the issue.

Galled by fire directed from the beleaguered wagons and punished by Burton's men, the Indians suddenly lost heart and, scattering, went fleeing across the valley. Only forty or so were in the
retreating band that was pursued by long-range shooting on the part
of men who had learned marksmanship at Vicksburg and Antietam.

"Purty good," grinned a leather-featured skinner as he got up
and methodically reloaded. "Them Cheyennes are brave all right
but they sure hate a surprise."

"Hey, Roscoe ! See me wing that buck with the turkey feather headdress ?"

"Hell, that warn't nothin'. Mark that red brute out yonder with the green shield ? Picked him off at nigh onto two hundred yards."

"Good eye. Reckon his scalp will buy you plenty of red-eye in Julesburg."

Both Burton and Dog Soldier Nick were sure that the meat party was in no further danger. Indian philosophy held that when a war party was surprised and defeated it was due to a medicine too powerful to be denied.

Buffalo Caller came galloping up, leading Burton's buckskin on which a skinner had masqueraded as the ex-Confederate during the early stages of the counter-ambuscade.

"*Wagh*," called the chief. "Our brother Long Knife is a great war chief, a worthy *Pa-ni I-ra-ri*. Ho ! Cheyenne dogs will feed coyotes to-night."

Teamsters, skinners and hunters alike joined in the time-sanctioned rite of taking the scalps of the fallen Cheyennes. Of the twenty-seven fallen savages, the Pawnees claimed three trophies each. Dog Soldier Nick demanded four. He expertly scalped his first victim and tossed the dripping trophy up onto the seat where perched the young teamster from Omaha.

"Keep an eye on that napper, will ye, bub ?" he asked. "Hell, don't puke on it ! It's worth twenty bucks in Platte."

"Shucks, Tom," grunted the head teamster, "that ain't nawthin' to git sick over. Wait till ye've seed a man tortured by Sioux squaws. This here's no country for tender stomicks."

Burton took no part in the grisly ceremony. Instead, he rode over to inspect the warrior with the green shield who had fallen apart from most of the others. He looked down at the open eyes of the dead man and started. A blue-eyed Indian ! Quickly, he dismounted and examined the man more carefully. A moment's close inspection and he settled back on his heels, whistling softly.

"I'll be damned," he said. "A white man."

He beckoned to Nick.

"Take a look at this one," he invited as the frontiersman ambled over.

"A rennygade, b'Gawd !" Nick exploded, scratching his thin grey hair. "Seen him once, too, back in Willer Springs. Let's see, what's his name ? Fisher ? No-o. Farmer ? No—ha, the name's Fryer—Fred Fryer. Dirty rennygade ! Hyar, you might as well take this war pouch for a sooveneer, seein' you won't have no scalps."

In silence Burton accepted the dead man's beaded and fringed pouch and tied it to the pommel of his saddle. He left Nick to his grim work as he rode over to a pile of captured weapons in hopes of finding a decent rifle. He keenly felt the frontier disgrace of owning only a company-issued Spencer. But, as usual, the Sioux and Cheyenne guns proved to be crude single-shot muskets or antiquated muzzle-loaders. Many of them were bound with copper wire to keep their barrels from bursting.

Swearing with disappointment, Burton remounted and called to the others.

"Come on, boys," he yelled. "Shake a leg. It's a right smart way back to camp and if the flies get at that meat much longer we won't be cartin' in anything but bones."

One by one the teams and carts were untangled and the slow journey back to End o' Track began. He had ridden only a short distance when Burton felt the renegade's war pouch knocking at his knee. He hoisted it and loosened the pucker string, then gasped as he saw what the bag contained. There was a double handful of twenty-dollar gold pieces, some women's rings and a simple necklace, two or three watches and a square of paper.

Burton's eyes brightened. His share of the plunder had turned out well, after all. There were more than enough gold pieces to buy him a modern rifle and a complete outfit, as well.

'Maybe,' he told himself, 'my luck's turning.'

He unfolded the clean square of paper and stared wonderingly at the few lines of writing. They consisted of jumbled letters which made no sense to him. But at the top of the strange note was the address: J. Smiley, Esq., Julesburg.

He turned in his saddle and spoke hurriedly to Dog Soldier Nick.

"Listen," he said. "I've found something that ought to get to the railhead right away. Can you take the train in?"

"Shore," drawled Nick. "You go right along, Cap'n."

Whirling a good-bye over his shoulder, Burton jabbed his mustang with his heels and loped off toward the line of buttes behind which the Union Pacific was painfully lunging westward.

CHAPTER XIII

WHEN he reached camp, Burton found General Casement astride a powerful chestnut at the top of a small rise, accompanied by two men whose faces were instantly familiar to the ex-Confederate, even though he never had seen them before.

One of the horsemen was thin to the point of fragility, the deep lines of his face half hidden by a three days' growth of beard. Sight of that man's profile sent an electric spark coursing through Burton. There, wearing a black slouch hat and a dusty uniform coat, sat

Lieutenant-General William Tecumseh Sherman. The Sherman who had broken the back of the Confederacy. Although he had spilled the blood of fewer Southerners than any other great Northern General, it was Sherman who was the worst hated below the Mason-Dixon Line.

Robert Burton considered the paradox. Grant, the butcher, was esteemed by North and South alike. Sherman, who had destroyed replaceable property but not irreplaceable lives, would forever be the object of Southern hatred.

Long-bodied and ever alert, the Victor of Atlanta sat his horse easily while he studied the panorama below him, a long thin cigar jutting aggressively from his unshaven jaw.

At Sherman's right rode the red-bearded Contractor General of the Union Pacific and beyond him was the New Englander whose very soul had become that of this mighty project. Grenville H. Dodge, a Major-General at thirty-three, was short, square of shoulder and face and wore a sweeping moustache which just failed to conceal a wide mouth, now set in angry lines. As Burton approached, he could overhear Dodge saying:

"But, damn it, Casement, these men must be handled ! We can't slow up now with the opposition in Congress yelling bloody murder to hold up our subsidy."

The Irishman flung out an exasperated hand to indicate the surrounding hills.

"If yez will be tellin' me how one soldier can surround three Injuns," he roared, "I'll have yer track into Ogden before snow flies in '69. Faith, we've only a quarter o' the soldiers we're needin'."

Sherman spoke without removing his cigar from the slash of his mouth.

"Then, General," he asked, "your progress is much slower than you had anticipated ?"

"It is that," Casement admitted, his blue eyes agleam. "'Tis bad enough to have no timber, not a drop of fit water, and a chuckle-headed Board o' Directors tryin' to run things from New York; but 'tis worse havin' to build without decent protection. Thank Stanton and the rest that these damned redskins can cut off and murther"—in his heat Casement's brogue thickened a bit—"our survey parties like they did poor young Hill's last month and Percy Brown's not a week back."

Sherman tilted his hat further down over his eyes and puffed a cloud of rich blue smoke into the still air.

"We'll see what we can do, but, with the costs of the last war still to be paid, getting military appropriations from Congress is—well, like trying to draw blood from a stone," he said. "What's this I hear about a threatened strike ?"

Casement urged his powerful gelding forward a few paces.

"And true it is, sir. The hands are near the breakin' point. Poor food and these Injun attacks day and night are wearin' the bhoys down." He turned sharply in his saddle. "There, sir, listen to that !"

From a distance came the *tock-tock-tock* of rifle fire that swelled into a rattling volley and then died away to scattered reports.

"There's an advance party having a brush now," Casement explained. "'Tis trouble like that all the time. But the bhoys don't mind that so much. The real trouble is that their pay's three months overdue. Ye'll understand, sir, that men can't work like my poor divils do on tack and salt horse."

Dodge nodded vigorously.

"That's what I've been trying to tell Ames and the rest back East," he said. "We've *got* to have enough soldiers to protect our hunting parties. Furthermore, I——"

General Dodge wheeled his horse quickly, aware that an unnatural silence had fallen over the dust-veiled scene. Every man in sight was dropping his tools. Grader, track layer and teamster were quitting work. Axes, picks and shovels fell to the ground by the hundreds as a mass movement toward the camp began. Near at hand, Burton saw a bronze giant with a ragged beard shake a furious fist at the clump of horsemen on the knoll overlooking the railroad. In effect, it was the Body of the Railroad defying its Brain. The big man pointed to a pick he had flung to the ground.

"And there it stays, by God," he roared, "till I get decent food and the money I'm owed !"

"Ahhh, to hell with the damned railroad !" howled a teamster from the seat of his wagon. "I'm goin' back East, I am, while I've still got some hair to run a comb through."

"Down with the Protestant bloodsuckers what's starvin' us."

"Come on, Slave Driver Jack Casement ! We ain't scared of ye."

Burton spurred forward as Casement, a dull red flush staining his heavy face, began to ride down on the advancing strikers, one hand gripping the butt of a long-barrelled revolver. Simultaneously a half troop of cavalry which had been posted at the foot of the hill straightened in their saddles and, leaning forward, grimly loosened the long Chicopee sabres they had wielded with such telling effect against Stuart's and Wheeler's men.

"Squads l-e-ff-t," shouted a captain and buckles flashed as the cavalry wheeled into line.

Sherman remained motionless, a brooding dominant figure on the knoll top. General Dodge turned to a civilian aide and snapped out an order in an undertone.

"Get to the telegraph station as fast as you can. Wire Forts Sedgwick and McPherson to rush every man they can spare."

The aide looked at the sullen crowd that was gathering between him and the administration tents and turned pale beneath his tan.

"I'll try, sir."

"Try, hell!" roared Casement. "You get there!"

Like a river supplied by a score of feeder brooks, the unskilled workers of the Union Pacific came streaming in from their various tasks to roll up the sun-baked valley of the Lodge Pole toward the camp. Burton forced his horse to Casement's side and, raising his voice, cried:

"You can tell 'em, sir, that they'll have fresh meat to-night."

"How much?" demanded the Irishman.

"Six forage wagons full of prime buffalo meat. It'll be here inside of two hours."

"Can you get more?"

"I'll guarantee it." Burton promised recklessly.

"Good." Squaring his shoulders, Casement spurred forward, pausing on the way to rap out a command that held up the threatened charge of the thin, blue line of cavalry. Alone, the red-bearded Contractor General rode up to the foreman who had slammed down the pick. He methodically dismounted, letting the reins trail. Jaw set, Casement walked up to the ringleader who towered above the Irishman by at least three inches.

"Is it you who're questionin' my authority?" he demanded.

The big foreman snarled as he placed ham-like hands on his hips. "I am! I'm damned if we'll——"

Jack Casement leaped forward. For a few minutes there raged as vicious a fist fight as Burton ever had witnessed. It ended with the giant going over backwards, dropped by a terrific right to the jaw. Then with the calm confidence which is bestowed upon the few who are born to command, the Contractor General faced the ugly, dusty mob surging up before him.

"Get back to work, ye buildin' fools!" he shouted. "Get back, ye omadhauns! Ye'll be havin' buffalo meat for dinner And yer pay——"

A deep-throated gale of noise drowned out Casement's voice. Sherman's cigar shifted from one corner of his mouth to the other.

"Aye! What about our pay, Red Jack? What about our pay?"

"Yer pay, ivery cent of it, will be here in two days. Yez have Jack Casement's word for it."

"Lies! Goddam lies!" somebody shouted from the depths of the work-stained throng.

"*Nunca*," came the thin voice of a Mexican labourer. "Not again will we be fooled. *No somos tontos!*"

A huge orange-whiskered Irishman yelled:

"'Tis nivver a bit o' mate we'll be gettin' to-night. Yez have lied to us before about that, too ! Apache Ware is dead. We seen his corpse."

There was a hesitant surge forward. Casement snatched out his Colt. Murder and disaster hung over the scene and the handful of blue troopers bit their lips as they closed in together.

"Back ! Every blasted spalpeen of yez. I tell yez the meat's comin'."

It was then that Robert Burton decided it was time to take a hand. He spurred forward until his horse stood beside the dismounted Casement.

"The meat's really coming !" he yelled above the clamour. "It's comin'. I shot a lot of it myself." He stood in his stirrups and cupped one hand to his mouth. "Dog Soldier Nick and I have got six wagonloads on the way. Look !"

The fringes of his hunting shirt waved like wind-tossed reeds as he pointed off to the north. There, barely visible, was a line of white dots that marked the meat wagons toiling down the near slope of grey-yellow butte.

"There you are !" Burton cried. "Yonder comes your meat !"

The change in the spirit of the mob was immediate. From a growling, churning mass of malcontents, the workers were transformed into a cheering, whooping throng of hungry men who knew that they were going to get fresh meat. Then, with the skill of a trained diplomat, General Dodge spurred forward and addressed the crowd. He told the sweaty, foul-smelling railroad workers that he knew they had been patient beyond belief, that they had been unsparing of themselves, and that they had fought on where weaker men would have long since given up in despair.

While Dodge talked, Sherman sat silent, his narrow eyes studying the terrain. It was clear that he was far from convinced that trouble had been dispelled for good. Burton, as he watched the General, got the idea that Sherman was planning just where he would place his troop detachments when the inevitable catastrophe took place.

It was not long before Casement's bullying and Dodge's oratory carried the day and sent the gangs clumping back to their jobs. Soon picks were flashing in the sun again ; harness jingled and the railroad crept onward toward the forbidding reaches of the Black Hills.

Captain Burton turned his horse and headed the mount toward his quarters in Dog Soldier Nick's lodge. He reined in when General Dodge's voice summoned him.

"Come with me, sir," said the New Englander. "I've something to say to you."

Whatever he had to say, Dodge postponed it until Burton, Casement and Sherman were in Dodge's private car, a passenger coach fitted out as a headquarter on wheels.

"Captain Burton is the man I mentioned earlier, sir," Casement said, dealing the ex-Confederate a slap between the shoulders. "For this day's work——"

"Yes, yes," Dodge interrupted as his shrewd eyes took in every detail of Burton's face. "The captain's words went far to save the situation out there."

"You have a cavalry stride," Sherman remarked curtly over his glass of Bourbon and water. "First cavalryman I've met who had brains."

"You're right, suh. I was in cavalry."

"And, from the way you look at me," Sherman added with a wry smile, "you were on the other side during the late unpleasantness. Right ?"

"Yes, suh."

"I'm sorry," Sherman said quietly. "You saved an ugly situation. I'd be honoured if you'd drink with me. And have some cigars. Later, I'll see what can be done toward using your gifts more efficiently. You're too good a man to waste your time playing tag with bison."

"I—I'm satisfied with my job, suh. I like the prairie a lot better than most towns I've seen since the war."

The eyes of the other men in the railroad car office swung toward Burton with new interest. There was a brief silence. Sherman cleared his throat.

"Not an unusual thing, Captain," he remarked. "A good many men have found it hard to fit themselves back into civilian life after being demobilized."

"It's more than that," the ex-Confederate began. "I—I've seen some sterling demonstrations of civilization since I came out here. I——"

He broke off as the door of the car burst open and a tanned, wiry old man with grey hair and a tight-lipped countenance entered. The newcomer's face betrayed mixed emotions, all of them agitated.

Burton found the tall stranger's face vaguely familiar. He knew he had seen that face somewhere before, but where and under what conditions he could not recollect. Ornate spurs glinting, the newcomer hurried up to the council table.

"Well, Dodge," he said in deep tones. "I've got news—good and bad. The good comes first. Stock sales are booming and the money you were promised leaves Omaha to-night. Tom Durant has wired me his personal assurance of it."

"All of it, Valcour ?" Casement demanded, red eyebrows raised. "It'd be dangerous not to pay a red cent under what's owin' the men. I've never seen them so damned insistent on their pound of flesh. It's too unanimous to be natural. I—well, I'm wonderin' a bit about that."

D

"Every cent due will be paid—every cent, gentlemen !" boomed the man in dusty riding boots. "You have my word. We'll not let the Kansas Pacific or the Central Pacific get our labourers away again."

Senator Valcour—Jessica Valcour's father—broke off short to run a finger around the top of his low, wilted collar.

"And the bad news you mentioned, Senator Valcour ?" Dodge asked, settling heavily into a canvas armchair and savagely biting off the tip of a long cigar. "I suppose it has to do with our subsidies ? There have been rumours by the bushel floating around."

The quick-eyed promoter's austere features contracted and grew grave.

"Unfortunately, those rumours," he said, "are true. Political treachery and chicanery in Washington are responsible, of course."

"What's the bad news ?" snapped Sherman.

"Just this—unless our track is into Big Spring by the fifteenth of this month——" Valcour left the sentence unfinished and shrugged.

"Big Spring !" shouted Casement, his jaw sagging. "By the fifteenth ! Why not say Laramie or Salt Lake City and be done with it ? Have they gone clean crazy in Washington ?"

"It seems so," Valcour admitted gloomily. "Oakes Ames and I have used all possible influence. But the Secretary of the Interior and his advisers insist on the Big Springs date before they'll authorize fresh stock issues. Claim the public must have this proof of success."

Dodge, his face pale beneath its tan, sprang to his feet.

"I see," he grated. "They're clever enough to set the goal just beyond our reach. When did you learn all this ?"

Valcour's hand trembled slightly as he splashed Bourbon into a glass.

"I was just returning from an inspection ride when the wire came. At first I couldn't believe it. Friends, knowing that my whole fortune and that of my daughter as well is invested in this venture, slipped me advance information. I was assured in Saint Louis last week that more time would be granted." He sighed deeply in what was almost a groan and turned to Casement. "Is— is there any chance of reaching Big Spring on time ?"

"It's almost impossible," Dodge snapped. "Even if Casement could get enough decent ties it would still be a Herculean task. Good God, Senator, we're using Burnetized cottonwood as it is. Besides that, we're crippled for lack of timber and, to make it worse, the damned Indians keep burning our small bridges. To-day we're on the ragged edge of a strike. You'll have to telegraph Washington again. Explain to Stanton and the stockholders, persuade, threaten —anything—but get that goal changed. It's a dozen miles beyond possibility."

"I *have* telegraphed," heatedly replied the elderly politician. "Good heavens, man! you know I'll be a pauper if the road fails. I've used every bit of influence I own, but President Johnson still listens to fools and blackguards. Cost what it may, that track must reach Big Springs or"—he spread his thin hands in a helpless gesture —"or all we've hoped for will be lost—irrevocably lost. General Sherman, as Commander of this Department, can't you help us?"

"I've already stripped the forts of every man they can spare," growled Sherman. "I can't drain them of any more men at present."

The hot, stuffy atmosphere of the administration car became a well of silence. Sherman chewed silently on his cigar, Dodge stared in blank dismay at the bearer of ill tidings, and Casement stood speechless, his thick neck red with rage. Quite forgotten, the ex-Confederate stood in the shadows studying Sherman, the man who had brought a pleasure-loving, outmoded civilization crashing to ruin. Queer, he told himself, but he could not hate the Victor of Atlanta, much as he once had despised the man.

Everyone started nervously when a door handle rattled and there entered a young officer in uniform. Over his shoulder was visible a panache of emerald green ostrich feathers. As the officer stepped aside to face Sherman and salute, Burton's heart gave a great leap like a buck clearing a windfall. There, framed in the doorway, was the smiling face and incredibly beautiful figure of Jessica Valcour.

CHAPTER XIV

BITTERNESS speedily supplanted the curious elation that had filled Burton at sight of Jessica's heart-shaped face. The girl brought to the ex-Confederate a poignant reminder of what had happened during the past few days. She provided him with a link to the past he was trying to forget.

Clearly he remembered now the look of disgust in her eyes as she had watched him clutch the harlot, Lulu Jameson, to him during the saturnalia that had rioted through the streets of Julesburg. He shuddered at the recollection and felt unclean.

Senator Valcour's daughter was smiling her response to the bows of the men in the administration car. At her side the young officer in blue was making the introductions in an easy manner bespeaking experience in many a drawing-room.

"Faith," Casement was saying, "'tis a sad, savage spot your father has brought yez to, Miss Valcour." The Irishman turned and noticed Burton standing in the shadows. "But as a recompense I'll present Captain Burton."

"Captain Burton! Oh—I——" The girl turned sharply as

her hand shot up to touch the bosom of her grey dress. The gesture was the same as that she had used after the ex-Confederate had laid bare her breasts that night on the besieged knoll.

Burton bowed stiffly.

"I am honoured," he said. Then, without meeting her startled eyes, he stepped through the door and out into the drenching sunlight that flooded the car's platform. A voice hailed him from within the car but he jumped to the ground and pointed his swinging stride down the new right-of-way toward the small city of travel-stained tents over which hovered a haze of smells.

He cursed himself as he swung along. Why, he asked silently, should the sight of Jessica Valcour affect him like this? Was he afraid of the icy contempt she must hold for him or was it that he feared her nearness would break through the shell he had built around himself and throw him again into a miasma of doubt and longing? Why had his heart leaped at sight of her?

'You damn fool,' he said savagely, half aloud. 'You're in a fair way to lay yourself open to another stab in the back if you stay around her! You've got to get away.'

And, asked an inner voice, what about the U.P.? Was he going to run away now, when dark days were descending over the project, spelling ruin for the big Irishman he had come to admire, Jack Casement?

'To hell with the U.P.,' he told himself. 'You don't owe the road anything. You've settled your debt with Major North and Casement, too.'

Civilization, he decided, was not for him. Far better, he told himself, to ride away up to the north. According to Dog Soldier Nick, he should have no trouble joining up with a party of 'mountain men,' the professional trappers who buried themselves for a year at a stretch among the rugged confines of the Rockies. A year with the 'mountain men,' Burton thought, would rid him of the ideals that persisted despite everything that had happened.

He reached the lodge of Dog Soldier Nick and began throwing things into a haversack. Then footsteps sounded outside the tepee and a figure darkened the oval opening. Looking up, he recognized the handsome young officer who had escorted Jessica Valcour into General Dodge's car.

"Captain Burton?" demanded the intruder.

Uttering a mouse-like squeak, Nick's Sioux wife lifted a far edge of the tepee cover and scurried out of the lodge.

"What do you want?" Burton asked bluntly.

"Two things," smiled the officer. "First, I want to thank you for saving my—my cousin from Turkey Leg's Cheyennes. It was, sir, a splendid defence you organized on the knoll. As a soldier I can appreciate it. And your rescue of Jessica was heroic."

Squatted beside his half-filled haversack, Burton looked up and then away.

"You exaggerate, suh," he said. "It was only the obligation of being white." He winked at a pretty little half-breed girl who, hugging an incredibly dirty Indian doll, peeked in the door. "I'd have done the same for a squaw."

The young officer coloured to the brim of his black cavalry hat and bit his lip. Recovering himself, he went on.

"But Miss Valcour wishes to thank you herself. It seems she has corrected certain mistaken opinions she had about you and——"

"I'm not interested in the lady's opinion of me. And now, if you've given your message, I'm very busy."

"Look here," the other said in sharper tones. "Can't you be a bit more civil? Miss Valcour is being uncommonly kind."

"Indeed?" asked the man, carelessly toying with the long knife. "Well, I suppose there's kindness attached to speaking with a—a buffalo hunter—and a dirty one at that. Thank her most humbly."

"But you're wrong," the other insisted as he stepped into the sour-smelling gloom of the tepee. "My cousin Jessica *was* angry about the—the celebration, but she has changed."

"I'm honoured, suh," Burton said grimly. "But, as I said, I'm busy. In fact I'm leavin' camp as soon as I can get packed."

The young man's eyes widened and he took a step forward.

"But—but you can't do that!"

Silently, Burton continued counting out the gold pieces he had taken from Fryer, the renegade. A hundred dollars, he thought, would more than repay Dog Soldier Nick for the equipment he was taking.

"I say you can't do that," the officer repeated.

Burton looked up with cold eyes.

"Mistuh," he said. "I can do anything I damn please. Present my compliments to Miss Valcour and tell her that I'm savin' her the embarrassment of havin' to meet me again, for which I'm sure I deserve her thanks."

The lieutenant straightened with an incredulous expression.

"May I say, sir, that there are damned few men who'd dare send such a message to Miss Jessica Valcour. Why, my good man, half the beaux in New York and Boston would spend weeks to earn a single evening in her company. Young Astor himself followed her to Saint Louis."

"I'm not young Astor," Burton said, as he secured the haversack straps, "and I'm leavin' this place in a few minutes."

"Then, sir," burst out the caller, "all I can say is that you're a damned churlish boor. Miss Valcour's first impression of you must have been right."

He spoke so loudly that Dog Soldier Nick's youngest papoose, who had been peacefully sleeping in its voluminous swaddling clothes behind an old saddle, awoke. The baby howled and twenty mangy dogs just outside the tepee joined in enthusiastically.

"What you have to say is about as important as that kid's yowlin'," Burton drawled as he got to his feet. "Now, get out."

The lieutenant bent at the entrance and collided with Nick's third wife. Scarlet-faced and pursued by incredible profanity couched in Crow and broken English, he took himself away from the Pawnee camp.

Ten minutes later Captain Robert Burton was re-saddling the buskskin mustang he had ridden that morning on the buffalo hunt. His brain seething with contradictory emotions, he rode away among the smoky lodges out beyond the horse lines and away from the golden haze of dust that hovered over the whole area. He was deaf to the impatient screeches of the locomotive whistles, the clangour of engine bells and the rhythmic *clink-clink* of sledges driving spikes home into the misshapen ties at the rate of ten to the minute.

He paused for a moment to watch Dog Soldier Nick's meat wagons being unloaded at the big cook shack, surrounded by dozens of cheering, hat-waving labourers. Then he turned his pony's nose away. He was leaving all this confusion and worry behind with his memories. Perhaps, in the eternal silence of the mountains, he might recapture the love of living that had been his up to the time Enid Culver had crouched over her paramour, spitting curses at him.

It should have been pleasant to leave End o' Track, but somehow there was a certain reluctance that communicated itself from the pony to its rider. The buckskin was urged into a trot only to fall back into a walk, tossing its head now and then to look back at the picket line. For a time Burton fought the impulse to look back. Then, twisting in his saddle, he turned to throw one more glance at the turbulent scene he was leaving. Deserting? No, he told himself fiercely. He had sworn no pledge to serve the U.P. His life, such as it was, was his own.

The cavalry camps were deserted except for lame horses and disabled troopers. Apparently, all available men had been ordered out on a furious hunt for Apache Dick Ware's murderers. Two privates wearing bandages waved a friendly salute.

"Heyo Cap'n," they called. "Goin' out alone?"

Burton nodded briefly.

"Better keep your eyes peeled or you'll be kissin' your hair good-bye. The whole country's still alive with them red swine."

The sun had begun to sink amid a glorious welter of fire-hued clouds when the noise of the construction camp faded. The silence of the sand hills reached out to meet Burton like soothing and welcoming hands. Soon the ex-Confederate dismounted to water his horse at the trickle of a parched creek. He gazed about him, breathing deeply, revelling in the silence broken only by the murmur of the water and the occasional frantic dash of a jack-rabbit.

"Take a good drink, *caballo mio*," he advised the buckskin as he filled his spare canteen. "We'll be travellin' a long way to-night."

As Burton dried his hands on his shirt, his fingers encountered a hard little square in one pocket and, wonderingly, he pulled it out. Looking at the paper in his hand, he got up so suddenly that the mustang jumped and flung up his dripping muzzle.

"Damn !" Burton cursed deeply as he unfolded that enigmatic square of paper he had found on the renegade who had perished during the Indian attack on the meat train. Carefully the ex-Confederate studied the note's curious contents again. Across the surface of the paper crawled five lines of meaningless letters.

"To J. Smiley, Esq., Julesburg.

Dear Smiley:
XTJRBTMNLQRLRKLERTML
DTQLGLFCOTQBIOSMLALFQFNQLLC
OUFBLVSUUFRRFBH23QCFUUDTQBLE
EIMCKTMLXHSRDTWZSUUFNL
ALFZLQDTQHEFOOFBQSBH

NALMR."

To J. Smiley, Esq., Julesburg ! And coded. And found in the possession of a murdering renegade.

"Oh, Lord," groaned Burton. "I sure am a fool to have forgotten it. Reckon the girl's showin' up kind of upset me, eh, *caballo mio ?*" he addressed the china-eyed buckskin. "Yes, she sure has an upsettin' way with her."

He retightened the cinch and swung up into the saddle.

"Looks like we'll have to go back," he said aloud. "Any business Boot Hill Jack Smiley is mixed up in is our business."

"If you want to have a good time
A good time, a good time—jine the cavalree !"

He fell to humming Jeb Stuart's favourite song, a habit he had acquired during the war when things had begun to look up a bit.

The coyotes were lifting their first querulous plaints to the new stars as Captain Burton set off at a space-eating lope, back toward the dim glow that marked End o' Track.

CHAPTER XV

HE rode directly to General Dodge's private car and, dismounting, hitched the buckskin to a pile of rails. A sleepy-looking sentry challenged at once.

"I'm Captain Burton," the ex-Confederate explained. "I've got important business with either General Dodge or General Casement at once."

"Captain Burton? Oh, all right, sir." The boyish sentry motioned the tall figure of the soldier of fortune up onto the platform and on into the car. Inside, a clerk was toiling over a small snow-drift of papers. When he raised his tired, perspiring face Burton recognized the man as the aide General Dodge had sent to telegraph for troops during the trouble earlier that day.

"Oh, it's you, Captain." He shoved back the papers and arose. "This is a surprise. Gen'ral Casement couldn't understand your going off like that. He was mighty upset."

"Where is he?"

"He and General Dodge are escorting General Sherman to Fort Sedgwick. They'll be back most any time now. Guess you'll be more comfortable in the sitting-room." The clerk's glazed green eyeshade flashed as he nodded toward a passage-way connecting the office compartment with the living-quarters of the eighty-foot car. "I'll tell Carmody to fix up quarters for you. Gen'ral's orders. Funny, he said he thought you'd be coming back, even when the lieutenant said you were leaving for good."

"The lieutenant was right," Burton said, pausing at the doorway. "I'm leaving after I've talked with the General."

Because he was speaking over his shoulder, the tall ex-Confederate was well inside the next room before he heard the smothered gasp that made him spin on his heel. He stopped short as he saw Jessica Valcour sitting beside a lamp, very small and demure, an open book in her lap and—could he believe his eyes?—a slow smile of welcome curving her lips.

"Captain Burton, I believe?"

The ex-Confederate's Indian-like features were tinged with a dark red tide as he retreated toward the door.

"I—I beg your pardon, Miss Valcour," he stammered. "I really had no idea you were here."

As he spoke, his eyes betrayed him by glorying in the sheer beauty of the girl, revelling in the maddening glints that the lamp drew from her hair, fastening on the high-lights that painted her aristocratic features.

"Is my company so very distasteful, then?" There was faint mockery in the girl's voice and a subtle challenge in her eyes.

"Why, no. Far from it." He managed a jerky bow. "But I—I really must be goin'."

"I see," observed the girl as she looked straight at him. "It couldn't be, could it, that you're a—a coward, Captain?"

"Coward?" The taunt brought him to a standstill with one moccasined foot in the doorway. The lamplight gleamed on the wolf's head tang of the long knife.

"Yes, coward. For some reason you seem afraid of me."

She got up, full skirts swaying, and came toward him.

"Oh, please stay," she said. "I—I don't like to mention your personal affairs, but back in Julesburg I heard—everyone was talking about—about what happened. Please believe me, I was terribly sorry for you."

With a step as light as a ballerina's she had crossed the car and paused before him, dwarfed by his lean six feet, her eyes more deeply inscrutable than ever.

"I—I've really learned a lot since that horrible night at Plum Creek," she said in a low voice.

His tight face relaxed a trifle. So she had heard about the scene in the Julesburg House writing room, had she?

"I imagine," he said grimly, "that I supplied some of your education that night you saw me in the street——"

"Yes," she broke in, "and I'll confess at the time I despised you. I didn't understand. But I do now and"—impulsively a slim hand went out to touch the soft leather of his cuff—"I'm so sorry about your—your disappointment. Colonel Peyton told me all about it."

"Peyton?"

"Yes. He's to be the new Division Chief. A fine man, Daddy says, and one whom everybody in Julesburg trusts. Daddy says that without him the railroad could never get ahead. He's afraid of nobody, not even that horrible Jack Smiley. He's terrible, that Smiley! An utter beast! I heard about your—your Scotch friend."

Burton's deep-set eyes searched the face looking up into his.

"You'll do me a big favour, Miss Valcour," he said, "if you won't mention the—what happened in Julesburg—either affair."

The girl nodded silently and turned back to her chair.

"Come in," she invited in a lighter voice. "Please sit down. Papa is off on some business near Morrow's but the others should be back very soon. Perhaps we can find something to talk about until then."

He bent, the thrums of his shirt swaying, to lean his Spencer against a polished mahogany panel. Then he straightened, the long scar along his hair roots turning red as he gazed down at her. The girl, looking away, smoothed her skirt with deft, quick motions.

"You're taller than I'd imagined," she said. "It's funny, Captain, but I've never really had a chance to look at you when there wasn't something to distract me."

"Reckon there isn't so much to look at, ma'am," he drawled, "but you're welcome to see what there is."

They both laughed and then a brief silence fell.

"What brings you to End o' Track?" he asked. "It's mighty rough here. I'm surprised that they'd let a young lady come out here."

Miss Valcour's nose rose a trifle.

"They didn't 'let' me, I just came," she explained. "Papa was horrified at the thought but he couldn't get rid of me. I coaxed my cousin to escort me out here. Papa was here when I came in and"—she giggled—"you ran away."

"It's a soldier's privilege when in the face of superior forces," he grinned, toying with the wolf's head on the handle of his long knife.

"But if there is a good reason for staying and fighting?"

Her intent, ever-questioning look puzzled Burton as she raised her head.

"That—that's different."

Abruptly she became serious, almost pleading.

"There *is* something to fight for, Captain Burton. If this railroad fails it will ruin a great many people back East. Not only wealthy people like Daddy and Mr. Ames but thousands and thousands of little people who have bought Union Pacific securities. That's why General Dodge brought Colonel Peyton all the way from the Army of Occupation in Georgia. He's to handle the base camp at Julesburg."

The girl's plea interested Burton, despite himself. He always had thought of railroad investors as fat financiers with millions at their command. That there were countless small investors whose all was staked on the project never had entered his mind.

Somewhere in the lantern-lit camp a banjo began twanging away at 'The Arkansaw Traveller' and hoarse voices bawled out one ribald stanza after another. Far away, a locomotive whistle sounded faintly. Nearer at hand the clicking of a telegraph instrument cricketed incessantly. The night wind, drifting in through an open window beside Jessica, stirred a copy of the diminutive *Topeka Mail and Breeze* as it ushered in the familiar camp smells now modified by the scent of cooking food and the clean tang of wood smoke.

Jessica's voice recalled Burton to the present. She was still looking at him with that curiously intent expression, her bright head cocked a little to one side.

"I—I'm going to ask you a rather silly question," she announced. He wondered at the scarlet tide that suddenly flowed into her oval face. "I hope you'll answer it."

"I'll be glad to if I can."

"When you were bringing me into Willow Springs I—I fell asleep and ever since then I've wondered whether I dreamt that you kissed me or whether you——" She left the sentence unfinished.

"Why—why I reckon I did," he stuttered. "I'm sorry."

She bent forward a little.

"Why did you kiss me, Captain?" she inquired.

He hunched his shoulders uneasily.

"It—well, I don't rightly know," he said. "I mean—well, you're a right pretty girl. I was sorry for you—no, that ain't exactly right, either. But—well—I just did, that's all."

"And you're sorry?"

Burton looked at her and showed his white teeth in a grin. Hell, he told himself, this girl is just a woman, after all. No reason to be afraid of her just because her father was a Senator and a monied man.

"Sorry? No, I'm not sorry, Miss Jessica. Matter of fact, I've always been glad I sort of took advantage——"

He broke off as running feet thumped along the passage-way and a telegrapher, still wearing his eyeshade and black cuff guards, broke into the compartment.

"Where's General Casement?" he panted. "I've got to find him right away!"

"He's not back from Fort Sedgwick," Burton answered. "He's due here soon. What's wrong?"

"Plenty! Colonel Peyton was murdered in Julesburg not an hour ago!"

"Murdered!"

"Yeah, murdered. A gang of drunks picked a fight with him and shot him. That's a regular slaughterhouse. 'Hell on Wheels' is killin' off our men faster'n the Indians. Two assistant engineers last week and three section bosses the week before that. Here, take this. I've got to get back to my keys."

Jessica Valcour's fingers tightened on the arms of her chair.

"Colonel Peyton shot?" she asked in a quavering voice. "Oh, it can't be true. Why, I was talking to him only this morning."

"It takes only a few seconds for a man to die," Burton said briefly. "But I hope it's a mistake, too."

"But without Colonel Peyton, the railroad—it won't go on!" Jessica wailed.

The laboured panting of an approaching locomotive split the silence that followed the girl's plaintive cry. Soon the brazen clang of the engine's bell sounded near. Two minutes later General Casement, lines of weariness etched on his face, entered the car with Colonel Barry and a trio of railroad officials. Casement's red-bearded features lit up when he saw Burton standing opposite the door.

"Faith, Captain, so yez come back?" he called. "And I find yez keepin' company with the prettiest colleen in all the territory of Nebraska. I——"

Something in Jessica Valcour's expression made the big Irishman stop short.

"Oh, General!" the girl said. "You haven't heard the news?"

"What news, Miss?" asked Colonel Barry, his spare body stiffening.

Amid a dead silence, the ex-Confederate gave Casement the telegram. The Contractor General, contrary to Burton's expectations, did not go into a fiery rage. Instead, he heaved a slow, shuddering sigh.

"Poor Nat," he said. "What a death for a good soldier. Smiley's work—no doubt of that."

"But why can't the local authorities put a stop to these outrages?" demanded the grim old officer hotly. "They're killing more than a man a day in that sinkhole of iniquity. It's got to be stopped. We're being hamstrung by these murders."

A thin, bewhiskered supply superintendent who, Burton had been told, was named Conger, spoke up.

"There's a duly sworn sheriff in Julesburg, and some town marshals. Also there are troops there. I don't see why they can't keep order between them."

"Because," grunted Casement wearily, his big fingers tapping on a table, "troops have nary bit o' jurisdiction in such purely civil matters and the sheriff and all his deputies are either in Smiley's pay or are afraid of him."

"We ought to get hold of Judge Lynch and civilize Julesburg with rope and Springfields," rasped a small, thick-bodied man whom Burton knew as the Chief of Surveyors. "Those gamblers, toughs and whoremasters—beggin' your pardon, Miss—have buffaloed all the decent citizens."

"A good idea but it wouldn't work," Conger objected swiftly. "It would cost a lot of lives and stir up all kinds of trouble in Washington. It would be almost fatal. What proof have you that Peyton's death is aimed at the railroad?"

"Conger's right," Casement said dully. "That's the last resort. But one way or another, this killin' off of railroad men has got to stop! First McDermott, then Lyons, then Keagh, then Burgess and now Peyton. If we're to stand a chance of gettin' to Big Spring on time, we've got to stop it." He suddenly turned to confront Burton. "Look here, will yez work for me? Quite independent of Colonel Barry, of course?"

"Sorry, suh. I'm no engineer and I know nothin' about railroad buildin'."

"You don't have to. What I need is a man who's not afraid of

Smiley, who'll establish law and order along this stretch of track."

"Come, come, General," objected a man Burton did not know. "You can't ask a man to agree to his own death sentence."

Conger, the terrier-like supply superintendent, raised a protesting hand.

"He wouldn't last half a day in Julesburg," he said, "and besides, how could we be sure he wouldn't go over to Smiley? Smiley pays well and we know nothing about this man."

His face impassive, the ex-Confederate surveyed the earnest, grim men who argued over his fitness for a job he had not asked for. What, he asked himself, were they to him? Why should he risk his life for their success? Smiley he would kill some day, in his own time and fashion. Until then——

"Mr. Conger's right," he said calmly. "You don't know anything about me. I might steal everything in this section of the road, sell you out right and left."

"Nonsense," Casement cried and his red beard flared in the lamplight. "Ye've got nerve, Burton, and intelligence, which counts for a lot more. 'Twas you alone saved the situation this day. Yez brought in meat when everybody else failed. Right or wrong, Jack Casement is for trustin' yez!"

"I appreciate your trust, General," Burton said, "but I don't reckon I'd care to take on such a responsible job."

Casement forgot the girl's presence long enough to rap out a string of amazed oaths.

"What's the matter?" he demanded. "Are yez afraid? Afraid because I can't give yez any help?"

"I'm not afraid," Burton said. "I'm just not interested. I've made my own plans."

"But Captain," Casement pleaded, spreading his hands in a helpless gesture, "please consider——"

"I think, gentlemen, that you are proceeding too fast."

All eyes swung toward Jessica Valcour as she stepped forward, her cheeks bright.

"Perhaps I have an idea of what's holding Captain Burton back."

She turned to face the tall, gaunt soldier of fortune and gave him a smile that was appealingly pathetic.

"Please don't make a final decision, Captain," she asked, "until we have—talked."

She linked an arm through Burton's buckskin-covered elbow and led him toward the door. Unable to protest, the ex-Confederate found himself outside the car and, a few minutes later, on a hill overlooking the great encampment with Jessica Valcour beside him.

Dewy buffalo grass dampened their ankles and a soft wind, redolent of the warm, drowsy earth, stirred the silk of the girl's skirt into a soft whispering. Below, like fiery nails studding a black velvet cloth, blinked hundreds of camp fires. On a nearby siding the banked fires of three locomotives sent columns of smoke curling lazily downwind, as smoke drifts from the pipe of a man who rests after a hard day's toil.

"There," breathed the Senator's daughter, "is a sight which few people ever will be privileged to see."

Captain Robert Burton nodded silently. He recalled other great encampments—in Kentucky, in Tennessee and in Guanajuato. Those had been war encampments while this—well, he asked himself, was this so much different from the others?

Jessica Valcour suddenly stepped in front of him to look up into his face, the sheen of a million stars lending a silvery radiance to her face. That intent, searching look was in her eyes.

"Robert Burton," she cried in a low, thrilling voice. "I know I'm risking something that means more to me than almost anything in the world. I—I'm going to ask you—though it's brazen, I know —not to go away! For my sake!"

She flung out her hands in a gesture of appeal.

"Oh, don't you see?" she asked. "Are you blind?"

His aching loneliness transcendent, he gripped her wrists.

"What do you mean?" he asked. "Why should I stay for your sake? What am I to you? What could I mean to you?"

"You mean everything," she said. "I've always been taught to rule my heart, always to be mistress of myself, but—but from the first, even during that awful night there on the hill, I—oh, I've loved you! Even when I seemed to hate you most, I've loved you. Can't you understand?" Her eyes fixed his like two bright and lovely daggers. "Now do you see why you must not go away?"

When Burton said nothing, she relaxed and tried to take her wrists from his grip.

"I suppose I've acted the fool," she said, "but I—I couldn't see you ride away like that, turning your back on me, without your knowing."

Burton stood stock-still, clasping the girl's wrists. Within him, a chorus of elation struggled against a derisive shouting that clamoured within his brain.

'She loves you!' cried the angels' voices.

'Don't be a damn fool!' screeched the devils. 'She's saying this to make you stay and fight for her father's money!'

His hands relaxed their grip on Jessica Valcour's arms and the girl turned away, small head bent, dejection written in every line of her slim body.

"Wait!" Burton cried in a breathless undertone. "Don't go— please! I—I had to think. Your—your trust—what you've just said—I've got to stay now."

He reached for her and pulled her to him.

"For God's sake," he said wanly, "help me find a little happiness."

Jessica drew a deep breath and her perfect lips parted.

"I—I'll try, Bob," she breathed. "Oh, Bob—Bob!"

Her arms went about his neck and drew his face down to hers. There was fire in her kiss and her body arched up to meet Burton's in an embrace that left them both breathless. At length she tore her face away. The girl was panting a little then and her eyes were strangely hot. Gone was the veneer that her life in the East had applied. Now she was a woman and the night was soft and warm. About her pulsed the throbbing force of Life, stripped of its trappings, raw, ugly and yet beautiful at the same time.

Her mouth searched for Burton's again, her knees beneath the silken skirt pressed against the soldier of fortune's, her finger-nails bit deeply into the back of his neck and he could feel her teeth behind those demanding lips.

Brain reeling and hands pressed against her shoulders, he gently pushed her away. Her eyes blazed as she looked up at him and then her bright head dropped. She buried her face on his chest and clung to him, her shoulders heaving as her breath came deep and hurriedly. His hand patted her rounded shoulder.

"I know," he said gently. "I know."

CHAPTER XVI

"CAN'T make anything out of that note," said Supply Superintendent Conger, irritably tugging at his grizzled whiskers. "What about you, McCue?"

"Hell, I don't know anything about things like that," admitted the North Platte division's assistant traffic manager. "It's so much Greek to me."

General John Steven Casement passed powerful stubby fingers through his red beard and chewed on the splintered stub of a pencil as he studied the square of paper that Robert Burton had taken from the pouch of the slain renegade.

"I'd give a couple of fingers to know what this means," he growled. "'Tis a shame we've no cryptographer nearer than Saint Louis. Tell yez what, Lem, we'll telegraph a copy of this thing to Gin'ral Sherman's headquarters there."

"Right." Conger sat down and made two copies from the crumpled note. When he had finished Casement cast a glance at Burton, his eyebrows raised as the ex-Confederate carefully salvaged the grimy original from the trash basket into which the Supply Superintendent had tossed the paper.

"I've a feelin' in me left shin," said Casement, "that this code business is important. We'd better get that copy off right away. Call an orderly, Conger."

"If you think it's that important," said the terrier-like little man, "I'll take it over to the telegrapher myself. No use taking chances."

He slipped away. The other five men in the car, including the starched-face Colonel Barry, remained silent for a time.

Burton's eyes were narrowed as he began to talk in a low, level voice.

"Seems to me," he said, "that renegade's bein' with the Cheyennes with a message for Smiley might mean a heap of trouble, especially since those weren't Northern Cheyennes from above the Platte but Southern Red Shields and Dog Soldiers from down in Kansas. That's where most of the trouble's been comin' from."

"Mebbe we're barkin' at a knot," McCue pointed out. "It's most like jest some pers'nal message for Boot Hill Jack. But if it ain't, I agree that there's trouble ahead."

"Take a word of warnin', me boy," Casement said. "Boot Hill Jack Smiley's no common tough, even if he hasn't got any more conscience than a Black Foot. He's as smart as a barn full of owls and a dead shot with sixteen nicks in his guns. What's more, he's never a bit of a coward like some bad men are."

"And God knows how many plug-uglies, road agents and professional killers are on his pay roll," put in Lieutenant-Colonel Simpson of the Engineers Corps. "You'll be watched, Burton, as soon as you put foot in Julesburg."

"How are yez planning to work?" Casement asked. Burton sat frowning into space, toying idly with the wolf's head tang of his long knife.

He started at the question, was about to speak, and then closed his mouth for a second before he replied,

"If you don't mind, General, I reckon I'll keep my own counsel, exceptin' for you, of course."

Colonel Barry broke his hostile silence as he twisted in his chair.

"I can't tell you, General, how grave a mistake I think you're making," he said harshly. "I'm sorry my objections do not prevent you from practically putting the fate of this railroad into the hands of a man who knows no more about honour or loyalty than to wage war against his own country—a man who later sold his sword to a foreign tyrant."

As Burton clenched his fists, fighting for self-control, the Irishman's big body turned slowly in its chair.

"I know what I'm doin', Colonel," he said with exaggerated politeness. "And with all respect to your grey hair, sir, I've a funny idea that I know more about human nature than you. In fact, I'm near to stakin' my whole career on this one bet."

Barry arose, his thin hands grasping the back of his chair.

"Then, sir," he rapped out, "all I can say is that you're blind—a colossal opinionated fool!"

"Careful, Colonel," warned Simpson. "We want no disputes among us."

Barry, his thin face flushed, levelled a long forefinger at Burton.

"This paragon of Casement's was a sneaking guerrilla, one of Forrest's raiders!" he exclaimed. "Once a knave always a blackguard! Mark my words, General Casement, you'll live to wish you'd listened to me!"

The Irishman's red beard jutted belligerently.

"Faith and I don't recall havin' asked your advice, sir," he said. "This appointment isn't in your province, so, if yez have had your say, I suggest that we don't take up any more of your valuable time."

Barry wheeled and marched to the door. As he reached it, he turned. His precise tones suggested the grinding of steel on stone.

"All right, go ahead and wreck this railroad! But mark my words, sir, it is also my duty to protect this road. I'll have this damned Rebel watched. Let him make one false move"—the old man's voice rose to a shrill shout that resounded through the lamplit car—"and I'll have him hanged first and explain later—if necessary."

He shot Burton a furious glance.

"Do you hear that?" he demanded.

"I heard it," Burton said imperturbably, "and I'm not worryin'. To me you're a cross between Sumner and Silver Spoon Butler."

Speechless with fury, the Colonel stamped out, slamming the car door with such violence that the windows rattled.

"Colonel Barry," remarked Simpson, "is a fine officer but a mite prejudiced. You see, Captain Burton, he lost three of his sons in the war, one of them at Fort Pillow, so you see he hasn't any sympathy for those who fought on the other side. But a word of warning, sir. Be careful. He can do you a lot of harm."

"I ain't envyin' you," said McCue when Conger re-entered the car. "How're you fixin' to work."

Burton cast a questioning glance at the red-bearded Contractor General of the Union Pacific.

"Not intendin' any offence, sir," he said, "but I reckon I'd better keep my plans to myself."

Casement spat out a bit of the splintered pencil and looked up, his heavy eyebrows drawn down.

"Mr. Conger and Mr. McCue will have to be in on our plans," he said. "I'm not always around, you know, and they'll have authority to co-operate with yez."

Burton pondered the explanation and nodded his head. What Casement had said seemed sensible on second thought.

"All right," he smiled. "I'm right sorry to have appeared so secretive."

"Ye'll work alone?" Casement demanded.

Burton pulled at the cheroot that jutted from one corner of his mouth and watched the smoke drift over a lamp chimney.

"Not necessarily, suh," he replied. "Reckon I'll look around a bit to-morrow and see who I can pick up. I—it'd be a big help if you could make a guess as to where you expected trouble next."

"There'll be the gold shipment," Casement pointed out. The other men nodded. "Gold is always a temptation, but you know that it means more than its face value to us. No pay and we'd have a strike on our hands and the railroad would go to hell and gone."

Conger kept his eyes fixed on Burton as the ex-Confederate nodded.

"I'll think things over to-night, General," the soldier of fortune said, "and see you in the mornin'. I suppose you-all gentlemen are fairly convinced that all this trouble is more than bad luck—that there's an organized movement afoot to ruin the Union Pacific?"

Lieutenant-Colonel Simpson snorted.

"Colonel Peyton's murder proves it, doesn't it?" he asked. "Mark my words, from now until we hit Big Spring——"

"Holy Mother!" cried Casement. "What's that?"

Everyone turned in the direction that Casement was staring to see a throbbing orange glare rising on the horizon some distance away.

"A fire!" McCue shouted. "A prairie fire!"

"Prairie fire, hell!" exploded Casement as he reached for his hat. "That's the Buffalo Creek Bridge! Guards!"

Almost immediately a bugle's harsh, insistent voice began screaming 'Fire Call.' Half-dressed infantry and cavalrymen poured out of their Sibley tents.

"Where's your horse, Burton?" the Irishman rapped out. Then, as he turned to the man who had been at his elbow, he gaped. Burton had silently vanished.

As he headed for the door of the railway carriage, Casement's arm was caught in McCue's grasp.

"Just a word with you, sir," said the man in an undertone. "I thought you ought to know that your Rebel might bear watchin', at that. Just a few days ago, as I understand it, he was throwin' a fortune in jewels around the bars and whorehouses of Julesburg. Where would a soldier get things like that?"

Casement scowled threateningly and McCue drew back a step.

"With one of me bridges burnin' down," the General grated, "yez start askin' me riddles! What the hell do I care where he got the jewels?"

He reached the door and looked back over one burly shoulder. "But just the same, McCue," he added, "you and Conger'd better keep an eye on him. If he makes one false move you've authority to arrest him. If he resists, shoot him down !"

CHAPTER XVII

CAPTAIN ROBERT BURTON raced his big buckskin along the right-of-way. He was ahead of a long column of hard riding cavalry, ahead of the locomotive which spouted flame and sparks into the night as it pushed before it a gondola loaded with infantry.

Far down the tracks the flames roared higher. Sparks ascending from the burning bridge in clouds set fire to the buffalo grass and threatened to send a sheet of flame racing toward the U.P. camp, directly downwind.

Burton swore under his breath as he leaned over the muscled neck of his mount.

"Won't be a buffalo left south of the Platte soon's they see this glare," he muttered. "Nick will have to scout a long way to find the herds now."

The night wind whistled past his ears, tore at his hair, made the buckskin fringes on his sleeves rattle. Behind him, the camp exploded into activity and a locomotive's whistle began wailing the summons that brought the labourers tumbling out of their bunks.

As the buckskin thundered over the prairie, the site of the fire grew distinct. The flames, Burton saw, were eating away at a new bridge that had been thrown over a tributary of Lodgepole Creek. He carefully reconnoitred the firelit terrain, then rode up to the blazing bridge and dismounted. Shielding his face with his hat, he began a survey of the ground under the blazing span. The ruddy glare revealed every imprint in the muck.

Before the heat of the roaring flames, fed by the pitch-filled timbers, drove him back, Burton had scanned the hoof prints of several horses. He knew at a glance that no Indian ponies had made those marks. These horses had been shoed and their prints were deep enough to mark them as bigger mounts than the average Cheyenne rawhide. Two empty kerosene cans showed how the incendiaries had started the blaze. The fact that all telegraph wires not only had been ripped down but had been carried fifty yards away from their poles proved that this was no work of an Indian raiding party. The Cheyennes and Sioux, Burton told himself, would be content with merely breaking the wire, in their belief that to snap the cables was to 'choke the voice that spoke through the air.'

With the buckskin snorting and plunging in terror, Burton backed away from the withering heat.

'So,' he pondered silently, 'those cayuses were shod and there was one with a broken shoe. Better remember that broken shoe.'

He looked down at a footprint in the stream-moistened earth, then shook his head.

'Wore moccasins,' he said, 'but they were no Indians. Too big a foot and too high an arch. A white man wore those moccasins —a white man used to wearing boots.'

His thrusting eyes cast at the ground about him. With a muffled word he went down on one knee to pick up the object that had cast a gleam in the flickering light of the blazing bridge. Half buried in the sand he found a large spur boasting a sunburst rowel and some Mexican filigree work consisting of entwined cactus plants inlaid on the spur's shank.

Sparks showered on Burton and stung the buckskin. The animal reared, pawing the air and whinnying in fear. Thrusting the spur into a saddlebag, Burton swung into the saddle and rode out of the danger zone. Looking back down the track, the ex-Confederate saw the headlight of the locomotive bringing the fire fighters. He turned the buckskin and, bending low in his saddle, studied the marks on the ground which pointed out the trail that the incendiaries had taken after firing the bridge.

For some distance the tracks of the retreating raiders showed dark and distinct in the soft earth beside the right-of-way. Then it swung sharply east and Burton saw that one rider had separated from the others. He had struck out toward the south at a fast gallop. The soldier of fortune was tempted to follow that lone rider but he swung his buckskin's head about and kept on after the main group.

As he widened the distance from the burning bridge, Burton found it more difficult to follow the faint trail. Now and then he dismounted and felt the prairie floor with questing fingers, seeking the shallow marks left by the fleeing horses. He had learned tracking in Kansas and, later, with Jeb Stuart, and all his accumulated knowledge stood him in good stead now as he followed the trail across the prairie.

The trail headed east, then reversed itself and struck back toward the west, and Burton sent his buckskin splashing across a ford of the Lodgepole. On the far side of the stream the trail joined the old Overland State route and threaded a tortuous course among the buttes which loomed on either side, reflecting the glare of the bridge fire.

Burton guided the buckskin cautiously and silently over the sandy ground as the prints turned off the road to follow a raw cart track leading up from the Platte River crossing known as 'Mormon's Ford.'

"Reckon they'll follow this track a piece, *caballo mio*," Burton told his horse. "Let's make some time."

He quirted the buckskin and the big animal leaped forward, only to be dragged back on its haunches by the ex-Confederate's wrenching pull on the reins.

"I may be wrong," Burton half whispered, "but I'd swear I heard somebody talkin'."

As if in confirmation of Burton's words, the buckskin's ears shot forward. The rider's .44 slipped from its holster and he peered into the gloom ahead.

'Fine place for an ambush,' he told himself. 'Thank God this horse don't make any noise on this soft ground.'

With startling clarity a voice came from around the bend ahead of him.

"Plug his hoss first," the voice said.

So, Burton told himself, he had blundered into an ambush where waited at least six and possibly eight killers. He knew that he had not been sighted; otherwise he would have been shot down before now. Apparently they were waiting for him to round the bend in the track. He looked about him and picked out a gulch which might—just might—circle the bend and put him on the other side of the ambush. There he might stand a chance of attacking his enemies from the rear. Here he stood no chance of shooting it out with whoever waited beyond the bend.

He wheeled the buckskin carefully, holding his breath for fear that his mount might turn out to be a 'talking horse' that would nicker at the mounts of the men who had set fire to the bridge. His hand went out to gently clasp the buckskin's nostrils and the horse walked sedately back down along the cart track toward the gulch.

Burton's heart stopped its hammering when he heard the *click* of a cocked rifle lock. He fought down the impulse to lash the buckskin into a run and kept the horse at a silent walk. He had almost reached the dark haven of the gulch when the shots began thundering out behind him. He bent low and quirted the buckskin —and no bullets whined past him!

He reached the gulch and slid off his horse, his gun at ready, listening to the uproar behind him. There was a fusillade of shots, wild yells and then the voice of a pair of guns that were no rifles. That hollow crash identified the new guns as heavy revolvers, fanned expertly by somebody who knew how to use them.

'What the hell is this?' Burton asked himself. 'They're not shootin' at me! They're after somebody else!'

He twisted the buckskin about and raced the big horse back up along the cart track, recklessly taking the mount around the bend. He burst upon a scene of furious action. Brief jets of orange-gold flame raked the night. In front of him was swaying a dark pattern of mounted men who, reined in, were all shooting in the opposite direction from Burton.

A wounded horse began a blood-chilling scream. Another horse crumpled and sprawled as Burton went into action. He took a snap shot at a bulky man close to him; a man who was standing in his stirrups emptying a carbine at a solitary figure who stood astride a fallen horse, throwing lead from two long-barrelled revolvers. The big man with the carbine went over sideways, falling with a thump to the ground.

He picked another of the bridge-burners as a target and missed in the uncertain light. The raiders turned to meet this new enemy.

"What the hell?" one of the marauders yelled. "Behind us! Look out! Oh-h-h!"

Powder smoke and the dust raised by the stamping horses veiled the scene for a moment. Burton felt something pluck at his sleeve and knew it for a questing slug. He was throwing his sights on a half-seen rider when someone rode up beside him and lunged with a knife. Burton beat back the deadly strip of steel with his revolver barrel. The other man grabbed at him, trying to pull him backwards out of the saddle. The buckskin reared and Burton lost his stirrups. With his assailant clutched in his arms, he fell and the two went rolling along the ground.

A hot, foul breath fanned Burton's face as he grappled with his enemy. The ex-Confederate's gun had slipped from his grasp in the heavy fall from the buckskin but, the soldier of fortune soon found out, the other man's knife had been lost in the same fall.

A gouging thumb grazed the ex-Confederate's eyelid. The outlaw was as strong as a bull and an expert in rough-and-tumble fighting. Burton dug furiously with his heels to find purchase, then heaved and threw the other man away from him. His hand flashed back to snatch out the long knife. He went forward, the gleaming blade glittering in the reflected light from the burning bridge.

There were muffled curses, the stamp of horses' hoofs and the raiders burst into full retreat. Burton's assailant, watching his comrades desert him, stumbled over to a horse that stood motionless, its reins over its head. Panting heavily, his face coated with sandy dirt, Burton threw himself at the man who had dragged him from the saddle. He saw the other hurl himself into the saddle and rowel the horse frantically. Burton drew back his hand, trying to calculate the distance of the throw through the sand that half blinded him and the gloom that was descending. The knife flickered through the night.

"Missed him, by God!" Burton swore.

"No you hain't, Mister," said a new voice. "You got him plumb centre!"

There was the sound of bubbling gasps. The raider began to sway in the saddle, then suddenly tumbled into the crackling sagebrush with the lumpy stillness of a sack of potatoes. The broncho galloped on a few yards, then circled and came back to sniff at his fallen master.

"By Gawd, pardner, that was some throw !"

Burton rubbed the sand out of his eyes and looked about him. There were five still forms lying about on the prairie. He stared at the bow-legged man who was ambling toward him, a sombrero canted on one side of his head.

"You—you're pretty handy yourself, suh," Burton managed as he stooped to pick up the .44 he had dropped in his fall.

"No," said the stranger. "I weren't so brash. Only drilled three and winged a couple more. You got two with your gun and that feller there with your knife."

The newcomer wore wide leather *chivarros*, above which rose a tall, wiry frame of much the same stature as Burton's. He stumped toward the ex-Confederate, then turned to bend over a wounded man on the ground.

"Mercy !" choked the man on the ground. "Don't kill me !"

"Yeah," grunted the stranger. "I won't kill you like you wouldn't kill me if I was where you are !"

Burton watched, his face taut, as the newcomer placed one of his long-barrelled guns against the whimpering wretch on the ground and snapped the hammer, sending a bullet thundering through the heart of the outlaw. The stranger twirled the barrel of his gun and jammed in fresh cartridges. Then he walked up to the ex-Confederate, a hand outstretched.

"I'm shore thankin' you," he said. His voice was the soft drawl of a South Texan. "My name's Kildare—Curley Kildare."

"I'm Bob Burton," the soldier of fortune replied as he gripped the other's hand. The handshake proved that the second and third fingers of Kildare's right fist were missing.

"Glad to know you, Burton," said the Texan. "You shore sailed into the ruckus at jest the right time. That were as purty a *cuchillada* as ever I saw nawth o' the Rio. Must ha' been all o' forty yards."

Rolling on his high-heeled boots, the lanky apparition silently paced off the distance between the fallen body and the spot where Burton had stood when he had thrown the knife.

"About fifty paces when it hit or I'm a Digger Injun," the Texan said. "Stranger, you shore possesses a heap o' what goes to win my onqualified esteem !"

"Mostly luck," Burton replied. "Suppose you take that fellow's horse. Your own cayuse doesn't seem to be so healthy."

The Texan's eyes flickered toward Burton in an unspoken

expression of gratitude. By the rule of the prairie, a fallen man's horse and kit belonged to the man who had won.

"Thanks," he said briefly. "Some yaller dog plugged my hoss, Mike, the first shot out o' the box. I'll borrow this hoss from you, pardner, till I git one for myself."

He walked over to the drooping broncho which still seemed to mourn over its unworthy master, slipped up onto the saddle and trotted back to Burton.

"What is all this anyway?" the Texan asked. "They weren't no road agents, were they? Didn't act like 'em anyway."

"It's a long story," the ex-Confederate said. "They burned the railroad bridge and then came up here for some reason. I thought they were fixin' to ambush me."

The Texan reached into a pocket and bit off a chew of tobacco from the pulg that emerged.

"Never was more took aback in my life," he said, "than when them swines cut loose. I was ridin' at night on account of Injuns. First thing I knew pore Mike was goin' down and I was grabbin' for my guns. Unsettlin', those things are."

"Headin' north?" asked Burton.

"Headin' for the railroad. Down in Dodge City I heard tell of a sportin' gent in Julesburg who pays good *dinero* for *hombres* that's handy with a gun. Hyar's my testimonials *and* yore new friends—the Hierro Twins."

With a movement which Burton could not follow, the man who called himself Kildare thrust forward the butts of his two big guns. Each of the six-shooters, Burton saw, bore a row of deep nicks in their grips.

"And no Greasers counted," said the Texan. "And not one of 'em countin' for an *hombre* that didn't draw first. I ain't no killer but it seems like trouble rides pack horse to me."

Burton went up into the saddle of his buckskin.

"Look here," he said, "do you *sabe* the name of the man you're lookin' for in Julesburg?"

The Texan shook his head. He dismounted and began to cast loose the horsehair cinch of the dead rider's broncho. That done, he walked over to his own dead horse and loosened the elaborate silver-mounted saddle that the mount still wore. As he was throwing the new saddle over the broncho, he looked up at Burton and shook his head again.

"Beggin' yore pardon," he said quietly, "I don't ever remember things like that. Besides, I don't care what the feller's name is. Money's what I'm huntin'—money and enough action to keep the Twins from goin' hungry."

Burton laughed.

"Stranger," he said, "you've finished your travels. You don't have to look any further. I'll pay you good money, Kildare, and if it's action you want I'll promise you a bellyful."

The Texan eyed him and then chuckled as he adjusted his gear on the back of the dead raider's mount.

"Yo're shore a mighty satisfactory gent," he said. "You bought yoreself a rider, Mister."

The saddling up completed, Kildare joined Burton in a search of the slain raiders' pockets. Burton cast the money pouches aside after a quick inspection. His quest was another coded message or some other bit of evidence that would connect these night riders to Jack Smiley.

His hunt went unrewarded although Curley Kildare swore in amazement at the articles the pouches contained. There were odd bits of jewellery, rings, earrings and necklaces, wore thin and of no great value. Burton paused as he realized that the pounder taken from these men was almost identical with that taken from the loot found on the renegade, Fred Fryer—when had that been ? *That same morning!* Good God! How could twenty-four hours contain so much of a man's lifetime ?

"Funny lookin' *dinero*," Kildare remarked as he passed over a pair of heavy silver coins. "It ain't Mex. Mebbe Spanish."

"No," said Burton after examining the pieces. "That's German money. Maximilian's Austrian Hussars used that kind of coin. The rest of this jewellery looks foreign, too."

The two completed their search by the fading light of the distant fire, then collected the rifles and revolvers of the slain outlaws and hurled them into the turgid waters of the Lodgepole so that the guns would not be picked up by wandering Indians.

"Where we headin', pardner ?" the Texan asked.

"My job, and yours if you want to take my offer, is to find out some more about the men who burned the bridge."

"Right," said Kildare. "Let's find out where them ambushin' brutes are headed."

The fresh tracks showed the experienced eyes of the two men that the raiders first had scattered in headlong flight, then rejoined and after a while had stopped. Leaning low in their saddles, the two riders studied the trampled earth where several empty cartridge cases told of a consultation and the reloading of empty guns.

"Appears like there's four of them *chincheros* left," the Texan said.

"Only three," Burton argued. "There's one horse with no rider on him."

Kildare smiled slowly.

"You're right," he admitted. "I was jest curious to see how much of a tracker you was. What do you want to do, ride 'em down and polish off the rest ? I'm hankerin' to tangle with them low flung *hombres* who'll crack down on a gent without callin' him first."

"Not to-night," the ex-Confederate said. "I've got a lot of plannin' to do—reconnoitrin' as they say in the Service. Come along?"

Kildare heaved a regretful sigh.

"You're the doctor," he said. "Since I'm plenty in yore debt I reckon the Twins have finished work for to-night."

In silence the two horsemen headed back for the railroad. Pitch darkness had descended with the extinguishing of the bridge fire and only the scuttling of startled jack-rabbits broke the stillness.

Burton jogged along, his thoughts calling back the scene on the hill overlooking End o' Track, when Jessica Valcour's reserve had suddenly melted, revealing her as a passionate woman, as hungry for love as any smouldering Mexican beauty.

He straightened in his saddle as Kildare's soft voice broke in on his reverie.

"Camp fire over yonder," said the Texan. "Prob'ly some damn fool of an immigrant thinkin' he's campin' in Illinois or Michigan. Nobody else'd be loco enough to light a big fire like that in Injun country. Ain't far out of our way. Want to drop in and warn 'em?"

"Might as well," Burton agreed. "Too bad that most of them are so damn green. Half the scalps come from fools like those."

The two had ridden only a few rods further when the Texan quickly reined up and squinted at the twinkling blaze ahead of them.

"Say, pardner," he drawled. "That ain't no camp fire. Mebbe we'd better not stick our necks out right away. Let's see what's goin' on first."

CHAPTER XVIII

THE smell of wood smoke grew more pungent as the two riders cautiously approached the fire, their quick eyes scanning the shadows outside the reflection of the blaze on the alert for some movement in the darkness.

Burton's nostrils widened as he sniffed at the strange rank odour that mingled with the smoke, an odour that brought to mind the smell of a badly-scorched steak. The ex-Confederate's scalp tingled as he remembered the times when he had smelled that same stench.

"Injuns," the Texan breathed. "Don't see any, so the torturin' must be over."

The camp fire's glow played in the depths of a small gully about fifty yards off the old Mormon trail. The ground was torn up showing that several horses had entered and had left the gully, apparently within the past few hours. Wordlessly, Burton signalled to the Texan to dismount. While Kildare held the horses, the soldier of fortune squirmed forward, wriggling on his belly, until he reached the sagebrush clumps that topped the rise above the gully.

As he peered downward, Burton started with surprise to see two yoke of brown and white oxen browsing placidly on the buffalo grass, secured by their hobbles. Occasionally, the great beasts raised their long-horned heads to stare stupidly at a large heap of coals in the centre of the clearing. For several minutes, Burton looked down on the strange scene and then wormed his way back to Kildare.

"Don't see any Indians," he half whispered. "I don't know what the hell to make of this."

The two men divided and reconnoitred all sides of the gully. Then, failing to find any sign of life except for the oxen, they rode down into the gully.

"Immigrants," Burton grunted. "They didn't have a chance. Look over there."

His face an emotionless mask, he pointed at the bed of coals in the centre of the clearing. Scattered about in the dying embers was a litter of iron household implements, iron tyres and the charred spokes of several Conestoga wagon wheels. Half in the fire lay a shapeless object which might once have been a small boy.

The steers raised their heads, snuffling a little, as they watched the two riders. Burton swung down out of the saddle and began an examination of the charred wagon box. Scraps and the burnt-out remains of a cooking fire showed that a meal had been prepared and at least partially eaten by several persons before the raiders had struck.

In a hollow fringed with sagebrush Burton came upon one of the bodies. It was that of a woman, her clothes ripped from her big, handsome body. Like the tattered banner of a defeated army her long, pale hair streamed wildly over the rough horse blanket upon which she had suffered the ultimate outrage. One temple was blackened by a powder burn that told where the rapists, finally sated, had held a gun to the woman's head and ended her torture.

Cursing deep in his throat, Burton stooped to cover the woman's violated body.

"Cheyenne or Sioux?" asked Kildare in a low voice.

"Neither," replied Burton in a granite voice. "No Indians did that. She's not scalped. That"—and he spat disgustedly—"was the work of people who call themselves white men."

Fighting back the gorge that rose in his throat, the adventurer stalked back toward the smouldering wreck of the covered wagon to rake coals over the half-consumed body of the boy. He was finishing this grim task when a slight stir off to the right sounded. He dropped flat, motioning to Kildare to lie beside him. His lips close to the Texan's ear, he whispered:

"Somebody over in those willows near the creek. Stay here."

The ex-Confederate slowly edged toward the trees, out of the light from the burning wagon. When his eyes became accustomed to the darkness, he was able to make out an indistinct figure sprawled beside the brook. The figure stirred faintly, tried to raise itself and dropped back.

Gun in hand, Burton covered the distance to the side of the creek in a bound. He looked at the man on the ground and shoved his gun into its holster.

The man obviously was an immigrant. Blood dripped from a ragged furrow in his scalp streaked by a bullet which had come within a hair's breadth of blowing out his brains. The stranger's flat, snub-nosed face was blotched with an ugly scarlet pattern.

"Okay, Kildare," Burton called. "It's all right."

"*Ach Du lieber Gott !*" moaned the wounded man when Burton dipped his hat in the brook and poured it over his face. "*Schlachten sie uns nicht.* Don't kill us !" His voice rose to a blood-curdling wail of despair. "*No ! No !* Blease ! Ve haff done noddings wrong. *Ja !* Take—money—leave Anna alone ! *Ach Gott !* She is good vomans ! *Teufeln!* Blease leave her alone ! !"

The immigrant tried to struggle up to a sitting position as Burton's hands pressed him back.

"Easy, pardner," he said. "We're not the crowd that was here before. Got any whisky, Kildare ?"

The Texan was back in a moment with a flask. The dazed immigrant gulped a mouthful of the fiery liquor and raised a close-cropped blond head.

"My vife," he cried in a weak voice. "Vere iss Anna ? Anna ! Anna !"

Burton shook his head as he clapped a hand over the German's quivering mouth.

"Quiet !" he commanded. "This is Indian country. Your wife is—is resting."

"Resting ?" Wild, bloodshot blue eyes glared up into Burton's. "Resting ? *Ach,* that is not so ! I heard her screaming. I vas helpless. They shot me. I could not move but I heard. *Gott,* I heard, I tell you !" The big-boned frame shook with sobs. "*Ach, im Namen Gottes* don't lie to me."

"I'm not lying," Burton said gently. "Your wife is resting, my poor friend. Nobody can hurt her now. Nor the boy."

The German immigrant fell back on the damp ground, his fists clenching and unclenching, deep ripping sobs tearing at him. The two men looked down at him, the lines in their faces deepening, their lips tightening. The Texan cast one glance at Burton, then looked away hurriedly.

Gradually the moaning cries quieted. Then Burton crouched beside the wounded man, his voice persuasive, soothing.

"What happened ?" he asked. "If you'll try to keep hold of yourself, maybe we can make this up to you."

"Vot haff I done ?" asked the German brokenly. "Ve did not ask much, Anna, me and *der kleine Bruder*. Only to work. *Gott* and his Mormon prophet, Smith, promised us happiness in Utah."

Bit by bit, Burton learned the story of Paulus Stattler, the immigrant. Demobilized from the Union Army, Stattler had used the pay he had hoarded to send back to Saxony for his young brother and the blonde girl who now lay so still beneath the horse blanket. Paulus had married Anna in Saint Louis. Converted to Mormonism, Stattler and his little family had struck out for the promised land of the Latter Day Saints, Utah. Until the previous day they had travelled with a long, well-guarded wagon train, but, impatient at the bulky caravan's snail-like progress and afraid that all the good farming land might be grabbed up before the train arrived in Utah, the Stattlers had pushed on ahead.

"Early this night," the German said in a dreary monotone, "Anna vas de supper cooking ven seffen or eight men rode up."

Burton looked up at Kildare from the rude bandage he was fixing to the immigrant's head. Kildare, catching his glance, nodded slowly. Eight men—there had been eight men in the bunch which had tried to ambush the Texan, the gang which in all probability had set fire to the bridge at Buffalo Creek.

The ex-Confederate heard out the grisly remainder of the German's story and then rose abruptly to go back to the smouldering pyre of the Conestoga wagon. He selected a glowing wagon spoke, swung it until it burst into flame again and then used it as a torch to light his examination of the hoof prints that had dug up the ground at the entrance to the gully. He ranged forward and back for more than five minutes before he uttered a smothered grunt and stooped to examine more closely the imprint of a horseshoe which was broken across the left cleat.

"So," he said under his breath, "the bridge-burners *were* the crowd that staged this—this massacre; the crowd that tried to waylay Kildare! I hope to God that German can give me a description of some of them. With Kildare, I might be able to do something. Lord, I can use a cold killer like that Texas man now !"

He beckoned to Kildare and the gunman left the German to bear his grief alone as he joined Burton. Together the two went through the camp, gathering up what few articles the despoilers had not thrown into the flames. There was a spade among the recovered tools.

The towering yellow-grey buttes were throwing back the pre-dawn howling of the wolves and coyotes when Burton and the Texan finished digging the pit that the ex-Confederate had marked out.

As faint silvery tones on the butte tops proclaimed dawn's arrival, the two men carried the laden horse blanket to the side of the grave. Some inaudible voice roused Paulus Stattler and he staggered to his feet and came tottering to the side of the pit.

"Blease," he choked. "Vun last time I vish to see her."

His eyes burning, Burton steadied the big German as he bent over the blanket and pulled down the corner to look into his dead wife's face. Curley Kildare wiped his hand across his eyes and walked away to make a great fuss of tightening the cinches of the two horses. Burton fixed his gaze on the clean brightening skies whose colourful beauty looked down on this stark evidence of man's vileness.

Stattler muttered a few words in German and then turned away. Burton pulled the blanket into place. The immigrant tottered back to the edge of the creek and sat down, his head in his hands, while the soldier of fortune and the Texan gently lowered the girl's body into the grave and covered it with the soil of the prairies she had not had time to grow to love.

"God!" muttered Kildare, "it's bad enough fer Injuns to do things like this but fer whites——"

"They used to do things like this in Kansas during John Brown's day," Burton said. "We've got to get Dutchy to the railhead, *pronto*. They've got doctors there and he's creased pretty badly."

They took time to make a rude cross of two wagon spokes lashed together before they went back to Stattler and led him toward the lowing oxen.

"Better take those along," Burton counselled. "You'll be needing money when we get to where we're goin' and oxen are at a premium right now."

"Money!" said the immigrant heavily. "Who cares about money now?"

The three set off on foot, Burton leading the horses and steadying Stattler while Kildare herded the four slow-footed oxen ahead of him. As he walked, his eyes never ceased their casting about, Burton, patient, quietly insistent, fed questions to the German, undiscouraged by the dumb shaking of the big man's head.

An hour passed before Stattler looked at the soldier of fortune, a new light in the haunted blue eyes.

"*Ja*," he said, "I *do* remember somet'ings now. *Ja!*"

"What was that, Paulus?" Burton asked in quiet tones that belied the upsurge of his inner self. "Take it easy. If you don't want to talk, we can wait."

"No, I must talk now, before I forget," the big man mumbled. "After I vas shot and me they thought dead they talked among themselves vhile they laughed at Anna and whoever vas mit her. *Ja*, I heard them talk. I know vhere to find those *Schweine*—by a train near Lone Oak. Three o'clock—*ja*—*that* vas it ! *Ach, mein* Anna ! Anna *liebchen !*"

"Lone Oak ? What was to happen at Lone Oak ?"

"I must dry to t'ink," the immigrant said in a laboured voice. "*Ja* a train—Lone Oak. I heard them say to wreck a train, to pull spikes. Maybe it already hass happened."

"*It hasn't !*" Burton almost shouted. "Try to think ! Did the men say when they were going to wreck the train ? Think, Stattler ! Remember !"

As if each word were being hauled by his own oxen, the German immigrant began to speak.

"*Ja*—the bridge to-day—*ja* to-day, *und* to-morrow—let me think —*Freund, ich muss denken. Ja !* At t'ree o'clock to Lone Oak I am going !"

"To-morrow ? That was said last night."

Burton eyed the big German narrowly. He asked himself whether the immigrant was raving, gone mad with grief and the wound he had suffered. But Stattler had mentioned hearing the men speak of 'a bridge to-day.' That could have been the Buffalo Creek Bridge and 'to-morrow'—that could mean this day and a new outrage planned by the gang.

"And, by God," Burton told himself, "they'll probably go through with it ! They think everybody in Stattler's party was killed. It's a chance to call the showdown !"

Forcing his voice to be casual, Burton asked:

"You got a good look at those men ? Would you know them again ?"

The German's bandaged head lowered itself like that of a bull preparing to charge.

"*Ja !*" he growled. "Should I be a hundred years old I know effery vun of dose *Hürkinder !*"

Gradually life woke on the prairie. Far away, a bell-funnelled, labour-stained locomotive came toiling up from the direction of Julesburg, its freight cars bulging with supplies. Dawn brought new spirit to the tired horses and they shied playfully, unmindful of Burton's genial curses. Even the placid oxen broke into a lumbering trot as Kildare, hauling at the lines, hollered and screeched imprecations at the huge beasts. The big animals quieted when a freight train clattered by, its flat cars heaped with rails due to be in place before sunset. Another train puffed past behind the freight, carrying a small army of cheering, hat-waving labourers.

"'Pears like they ain't collectin' no moss yereabouts," the Texan commented, watching the two trains disappear down the track.

"Probably new construction gangs goin' up to End o' Track," said Burton. "The U.P.'s speedin' up these days. I forgot to tell you, and you didn't ask, but if you work with me you'll be workin' for the U.P."

Kildare shoved his sombrero back on his head and grinned over his shoulder at the soldier of fortune.

"You wasn't fixin' on havin' me halter one of them enjines, was you, pardner?" he asked.

"Not exactly," Burton grinned back. "You'll find out, in time."

It was a few minutes after the two trains had passed them that the oddly-assorted party overtook a bull train of fifty wagons, the shabby covers of the carts bearing the blue insignia: 'Majors, Russell, Wadell & Co.' The train boss, mounted on a thoroughbred Kentucky stallion, trotted up and down the length of the line, cajoling, cursing and wheedling the bullwhackers to get more speed out of the oxen that strained against their yokes.

The train boss glimpsed the four brown and white oxen heading the little party that drew alongside and immediately he swung his charger over to approach the newcomers.

"Heyo, pardner!" he called. "Want to sell them bulls? I'll give yuh top-notch prices. They ain't much to look at but I got ten pair down sick and I'll take almost anything that's standin' on four feet. You're lucky to meet up with this train. Otherwise, you'd have to take the skinflint prices they're offerin' down at Tod Welton's train. Tod would steal the pants offen a dead nigger."

"They're not my bulls," Burton said, "but I'll ask the owner."

It seemed that Stattler was rousing from a deep sleep when he responded to the quick words that the ex-Confederate spoke into his ear. The German looked dully at the oxen, then at the train boss and back at Burton.

"*Ja*," he said. "Sell dem if you wish. I neffer will need dem again."

The soldier of fortune drew the train boss aside and minutes passed while the two argued. When the four oxen had joined the train, the boss rode off, shaking his head and proclaiming to the early morning skies that "he'd rather a goddam sight do business with ten Philadelphia lawyers than one goddam Rebel."

Stattler only shrugged heavily when Burton handed him more than eight hundred dollars in greasy 'Lincoln greenbacks.'

"But vot difference does it make?" he asked. "Anna *und der Kleiner* are dead."

Burton's hand gripped the wounded immigrant's thick shoulder.

"It makes a lot of difference, Paulus," he urged. "It's enough for a new beginning."

"A new beginning? Vot for?"

"I—I felt the same way not so long ago," the ex-Confederate said. "And now—now I've got something to live for, where I thought that nothing would be worth livin' for again."

Something to live for! Jessica Valcour and her fragrance and softness and the fire that lay beneath the quiet perfection of her features, her manners. Yes, that *was* something to live for!

The construction camp was roaring with activity when Burton left his companions in front of Dog Soldier Nick's tepee and rode away to find the Contractor-General. Casement, already in shirt-sleeves, was personally supervising the laying of rails put down by a gang of new labourers. The big Irishman's language was of a richness that brought envy and awe to the assortment of former mule skinners, veterans of the army of the Potomac and Micks from the slums of Ireland's teeming cities.

"Ye green-livered, slab-sided, butter-fingered, low-pressure, single-cycle sons of Sassenach baboons!" roared the red-bearded man. "It took yez *three whole minutes* to bed that rail! Holy Mother! Must I send for the heathen Chinee from the Central Pacific to teach yez how to swing a maul? Hump yourselves, ye splay-footed brutes."

Whips cracked, horses and oxen strained and tie-laden wagons rumbled into place. By fives and tens the timbers tumbled off onto the road-bed. A fussy little switching engine pushed up a flat car heaped with rails.

"Unload!" roared Casement.

Fifty men swarmed onto the cars to send the long strips of iron clashing down onto the right-of-way. Track layers armed with carry-claws picked up the rails, went forward at a run and laid them in position across the Burnetized ties which went into place a split second before the rails came down on them. Another crew—the one that had attracted Casement's wrath—was equipped with spikes, sledges and fishplates. Under the red-bearded man's lashing tongue they went into action the moment after the gauger had trued the position of the rail. A deafening clatter split the skies as the brawny half-naked Irishmen swung their sledges to send the spikes thudding home. Bolters moved in, making their wrenches spin like miniature flywheels.

"Rails?" howled the section boss. "Give us rails!"

The whole operation was repeated again and again. The Union Pacific inched on toward the west toward Big Spring.

Burton moved up beside General Casement and touched the red-bearded man's arm. The Irishman swung to look at him and scowled fiercely.

"So there ye are!" he yelled. "Mother of God, what manner of man are yez to go sneakin' off like yez did last night? I'll have ye know that if ye want to work fer me ye'll play no more such ape's tricks!"

Burton spoke a few words and Casement's brow cleared.

"So yez scragged five of the sneakin' buzzards," he exclaimed when the soldier of fortune had finished. Roaring with satisfaction, he clapped a hand on Burton's shoulder, sending up a tiny cloud of dust. "Foine work! Foine work! By God, though I was half doubtin' ye meself, I swore to old Mealy-Mouth Barry that yez knew what we were about. So you and your friend sent five o' them omadhauns to hell, eh?"

"Yes, suh," Burton responded. "And if you'll hear some other news I have and detail me men enough this afternoon I reckon we can civilize some more of those om—om——"

"Omadhauns, Captain," Casement grinned. "Ye'll have the men, even before I hear your news. I'll listen to your story in a minute."

He turned to fling a string of commands at a sweating foreman who stood nearby, then put his arm through Burton's.

"Come along, Captain. I want Conger and McCue to listen to this!"

He walked to his long-legged chestnut, flung a leg over the saddle and joined Burton in a gallop back to the private car. There, the adventurer gave a detailed account of what Paulus Stattler had told him. Casement's oaths were sulphurous when he heard Burton's description of the outrage that had befallen Stattler's camp. Even the usually bland and impassive Conger looked impressed while McCue's shock showed plainly on his face.

"If we could only prove your theory, Captain," said General Casement savagely, "that the lawless element in Julesburg is at the bottom of our troubles, I'd wind up Smiley and Company's clock in a hurry, law or no law!"

"With luck," said Burton, "we may find our proof at Lone Oak."

He leaned back in his chair, envisioning the way Jessica's eyes would shine when he told her that the gang that threatened the very existence of the Union Pacific had been caught red-handed and crushed.

'Whoa,' he cautioned himself. 'There's a lot of work to be done before you can tell her anything like that.'

"Who knows about what this Dutchman told you?" Casement was asking.

"Nobody, suh," the adventurer replied. "That Texan I told you about was ahead of us when Stattler told me what he did."

"Good," grunted Casement. "Keep everything to yourselves, gentlemen, and they may walk into our trap. Now let's look at the map."

The creased chart was spread on the table and the four men grouped themselves around it. Conger pointed a tobacco-yellowed finger at the dot that was the Lone Oak stop.

"It's an ideal place for jerkin' out a few spikes," Conger said. "See, that dry gulch comes right up to the embankment. That culvert would be a fine place to hide in."

"Right on a tight curve too," added McCue, the Traffic Manager, rubbing his bristly chin raspingly. "Yes sir, that'd be a smart place to wreck a train, but"—and he grinned—"it ain't such a bad place to set an ambush for 'em either. It certainly ain't ! About twenty good shots ought to settle their hash plenty quick !"

Casement pushed a telegram blank pad over the scarred pine table.

"Here, Mac," he said. "Ship out a wire to Traffic Manager Denton and warn him in code. Tell him to put a full platoon of infantry on Number Eleven. Can't afford to take any chances. Rails due on that train, aren't there, Conger ?"

The Supply Superintendent consulted a clip file hanging from a nearby nail.

"Yes, Gen'ral," he said. "Two days' supply."

"Thought so," Casement remarked. "McCue, order that engineer to stop two hundred yards short of the Lone Oak curve. Tell him to take no chances. Two days' supply of rails lost and a bad wreck would finish what chance we have of getting to Big Spring on the fourteenth.

"Hold on, Gen'ral," snapped Conger. "Ye'd better not put any troops aboard Number Eleven."

"And why in hell not ?" asked the big Irishman.

"Think, man ! If you loaded a bunch of guards aboard that train there'd be sure to be a Julesburg spy who'd see it and get word to whoever is runnin' his outfit. That would spoil the Cap'n's chance to corral the wreckers and it would give those damn swine a chance to make another try at some other point of the line."

Casement's heavy head swung toward Burton and the ex-Confederate nodded slowly.

"Mr. Conger's right, General," he said.

The Contractor-General tugged at his beard and then crumpled the telegram he had given to McCue. His big hand dashed out a second message and he arose.

"Come on, Captain," he said to Burton. "We'll hand-pick our boys and get 'em all set and ready by noon just in case Boot Hill Jack Smiley's outfit shows up early."

CHAPTER XIX

LONE OAK, to Burton's mind, was about the dreariest country it ever had been his misfortune to see.

On all sides stretched dun-coloured plains, sparsely populated by a sprinkling of blizzard-killed poplars. One small building squatted at the eastern head of the great curve that the tracks made at that point. It was little more than a tumbledown shanty which once had served as a telegrapher's shack, back when End o' Track was further east.

The sun beat down unmercifully. It hammered at Captain Robert Burton, at Curley Kildare and McCue and Conger and the dozen sharpshooters who had been picked to break up the ambuscade of the Number Eleven freight from Julesburg to End o' Track.

The men lay on the parched ground, panting and cursing the heat as the leaden minutes trudged by.

"God!" Kildare gasped as he wiped a checkered sleeve over his dripping face. "I reckoned it was hot down Chihuahua way! It was cold compared with this!"

Viciously he blew a drop of sweat from the tip of his nose. The blob of moisture made a dark circle in the ground and, ten seconds later, was gone.

"Never mind, Tex," Burton said. "They'll be comin' along any time now. The freight is due here at three o'clock and they'll have to spend some time in gettin' those spikes loose. These *mal hombres* will have to be showin' up right after Number Seven goes back to Julesburg."

Conger swabbed his face with a red bandana handkerchief and groaned.

"Them scoundrels couldn't have picked a better place," he said. "That's a good four per cent grade down yonder, Cap'n, and that culvert's at the centre of the curve. Hope nothin' goes wrong."

The ex-Confederate wet his mouth with a few drops of warm water from his canteen.

"Don't see how many of 'em can get away," he told Conger. "We ought to catch 'em in a neat enfilade fire. But—well, I'm worried about Smiley. He's so damned smart, it may be he's caught on. If he puts a few men on those buttes back of us——"

He broke off and shrugged as Conger twisted to look at the lowering hills behind the ambush party. Burton spat a gob of saliva as thick as cotton into the dust. He swore again, mentally, as he remembered Colonel Barry's refusal to lend troops to this expedition. It had been Casement who had detailed twenty railroad guards to come along. That force would be enough if everything went according to plan. If not—Burton shut that possibility out of his mind.

"I'll bet a month's pay Smiley ain't caught on," McCue said as he kept his little red eyes fixed on the tracks below. "We'll have the laugh on that swine Barry when we cart in a wagonload of stiffs and prisoners."

"Them *hombres* had better hurry or we'll be gettin' sunstroke," Kildare rasped. The Texan tried to shade his eyes with an upflung hand to keep out the throbbing glare. The rails streaking along the right-of-way shimmered and danced in the nerve-torturing heat.

Burton sucked at the pebble in his mouth while his thoughts wandered. That niggling doubt that he had shunted aside before crept back into his heat-weakened brain.

'Sure, Jessica Valcour told you she loved you !' jeered the unspoken voice. 'She wants you around to help protect her father's money. What else does she want with a penniless hired gunman ?'

'Don't listen to that,' counselled another voice. 'Don't believe that Jessica Valcour's passion on that hill was forced, artificial. It was a sublimely big-hearted gesture—the girl surrendered because she loves you. She can't be anything but honest. You need somebody to share your laughs, your heartaches—somebody to work for. If you doubt this girl you're alone again.

'Yes, alone,' continued the voice. 'Alone, as you were when your family was massacred in the Kansas wars. Alone, as you were when Enid Culver showed what she was. This girl loves you and you listen to that other voice—you fool !'

He shook his head to clear it of the clamour that filled his brain. Gradually he came back to the present, vocal with the curses of the railroad guards as they lay broiling among the sagebrush. Number Seven went puffing on its way back to Julesburg, pushing a long string of empty cars ahead of it. Still, long after Number Seven had passed there was no sign of life at Lone Oak curve nor on the buttes surrounding the sharp bend. A momentary lapse in the tension was offered by the unexpected appearance of a special freight that panted and strained its way along with a cargo of ties. But when the freight had passed there remained only the unendurable heat and the nerve-twitching silence.

"Damned if I like the looks o' this layout," Kildare grunted. "Maybe that Dutchman was loco."

"How did you-all know what Stattler told me ?" Burton rapped out.

The Texan cast him an injured glance and fumbled with his rifle sights.

"He told me about it in that lodge of your friend, Nick," he admitted.

"And did you tell anybody ?" Burton demanded.

Kildare's face tautened.

"You ain't got any funny ideers, about what side I'm on, have you ?" he asked softly. "If you have, just tell me and I'll drag my ass out of here. I ain't aimin' to be where I'm not wanted. For your information, though, I didn't tell anybody."

The two men held each other's eyes for full twenty seconds. Then McCue's snarling voice broke the spell.

"I ain't standin' this much longer," said the North Platte Division Manager. "I'm about roasted."

Conger's thick nickel-plated watch showed a quarter past two and a frown deepened on Burton's forehead. When half-past two arrived, Conger turned toward Burton, his bristle-covered face darkened by a scowl.

"Say, Reb," he snapped. "I thought you were *sure* about this !"

"We're actin' on what Stattler overheard," replied the soldier of fortune. "It's not three o'clock yet."

McCue sat up and wiped the sweat from his dripping face. For the past four hours the temperature had hovered around 105 degrees and tempers had been frayed by the heat. McCue stared at Burton and then turned to Conger.

"Mebbe old Barry wasn't so wrong after all," he growled. "What d'you boys think ? Looks like a mighty cute sell-out to me."

"Walk easy, McCue," Kildare suggested in his soft voice. "Burton's a friend o' mine."

"Says you !" rasped the Traffic Manager. "We'll see whether Barry's right or not, at three o'clock !"

"Aw hell ! All that stewin' fer nothin' !"

"It's a trick of some kind."

"Let's get out of here. They ain't comin'."

Man after man began to sit up. There was the gleam of sunlight on steel and Burton's Colt flashed in his hand.

"Everybody stays here till Number 13 shows up," the ex-Confederate announced harshly. "First man who moves gets plugged, *sabe*? That goes for everybody !"

Conger and McCue glared at Burton, then Conger shifted his eyes to McCue.

"You heard him," he called over. "If he's foolin' us——"

He broke off. In the distance could be heard the hoarse panting of a locomotive toiling towards End o' Track. McCue grinned and spat.

"Where's these raiders of yourn ?" he asked contemptuously. "Here comes Eleven and I ain't seen nothin' of 'em."

"Get down and stay down !" Burton ordered. He crouched behind a boulder and peeped over its top to sweep the blue-black shadows of the gulch with his grey eyes. Tension gripped the watchers. Now, if ever, the train wreckers must appear ! But only the distant puffing of the locomotive broke the stillness and the yellow-brown right-of-way remained deserted.

"So it *was* a sell !" Conger snarled. "Most likely your pals are busy somewhere else. I shouldn't wonder——"

From somewhere not far away and behind a great butte around which the track curved came a heart-stilling, nerve-paralyzing crash that thundered out explosively. It was a mighty metallic roar that sounded like a million anvils crashing down on a bed of steel plate. The silence that followed was broken by the hiss of escaping steam and then the jangle of metal falling on metal.

"Great God !" yelled Burton as he sprang to his feet. "They changed places !"

"So I *was* right !" Conger shouted, his face pale with rage. "So you're a Smiley man, after all ! I—I'll——"

"You'll what ?" asked Kildare gently.

The gunman stood very still in the blazing sunlight, his feet a bit apart and his hands hanging loosely at his sides.

"Lone Oak *was* the place," Burton cried hoarsely. "I haven't lied. I'll prove it later. Let's get to those men in the wreck now."

He led the way down to the track and, with Kildare's help, trundled a handcar onto the rails. He turned as the others ran toward him, Conger and McCue in the van.

"You two comin' ?" he asked.

"Yep," Conger snapped. "There'll be people hurt in that wreck and their blood's on your shirt front, Burton. Later on, Jack Casement can decide about this—if McCue and me can get back to camp alive."

"You keep talkin' big," said the Texan in his soft voice, "and maybe neither of you will see the camp again. You do like Captain Burton says and you stay healthy."

It was upon a curve almost identical to the one at Lone Oak that the men panting at the bars of the handcar came on a scene of chaos. Rolled over on its back at the bottom of the curve's outer ditch lay a big Rogers locomotive, oozing white steam as a wounded man spills blood. Twenty or thirty flat cars lay heaped up in a gigantic cairn of destruction. Like the jackstraws of some giant's child, the ponderous rails jutted from the wreck at fantastic angles. Here a bunch bristled like the quills of a porcupine, there they assumed a fan-shaped design, still others had half buried themselves in the ground or had tumbled far out onto the prairie.

"Sixty thousand bucks' worth of rail ruined," said a trainman in an awed voice, "and it'll take days to clear this mess off the track."

"And I reckon that about settles the U.P.," snapped Conger as the handcar jolted to a stop. "Not even Red Jack Casement can ever get to Big Spring by the fourteenth. Reckon Smiley will be happy to hear that, *Mister* Burton !"

Of the ten-man train crew, only the engineer still breathed and he had been crudely disembowelled by the throttle shaft. Burton was sickened by the entirety of his defeat. Number Eleven's fireman evidently had been feeding logs into the firebox when the accident occurred. Now all that could be seen of him was a pair of legs protruding from the flaming maw of the dying locomotive.

The ex-Confederate turned away and ran up the right-of-way, his eyes on the track. Not far distant, he found where a whole section of rail had been loosened. He whirled and sought out a young man who carried a portable telegrapher's outfit straddling his shoulders.

"You," he ordered, "get up that pole and wire Julesburg and End o' Track. Tell General Casement he'd better stop all work—send everybody to clean up this mess right away."

"Right away?" said the telegrapher. "Hell, it'll take weeks."

As the man started toward the pole, McCue stepped forward, his eyes beady.

"Never mind takin' his orders," he grated. "I'm runnin' this outfit now. I'm callin' ye, Burton, ye goddam Smiley spy!"

McCue's hand flickered downwards with the speed of a snake's strike. Quick as he was, the drawn-faced Burton was quicker. His Colt seemed to spring into his hand and spit flame at the same instant. A yell burst from McCue. His revolver dropped from his hand and he staggered back, clutching at his shoulder. The fingers of his left hand dripped blood.

"Anybody else?" asked the ex-Confederate.

Two burly trainmen lurched forward but stopped when Kildare's guns leaped from their holsters. While those in the rear shouted threats and promises of what they would do to Burton, the men in front pushed back in their effort to get out of line with the three guns that confronted them.

"Get back to work!" Burton's voice cracked. "You telegrapher, send that message! Go on, send it!"

Sullenly, the sun-scorched train guards went back to their work. One of them called back over his shoulder.

"We'll get you if Jack Casement don't hang you!"

"*And Casement will!*" yelled Conger, his arm thrown around McCue to support the cursing Traffic Manager.

"I'll kill him for this!" McCue screeched, still holding his shattered arm. "I'll—I'll——"

"You'll choke on your spit if you don't shut up," remarked Kildare pleasantly. He turned to Burton and lowered his voice. "C'mon, pardner. Let's punch the breeze for Utah, *muy pronto*."

"No."

"Ain't no use buckin' bad luck with a deuce high hand," said the Texan. "Yo're in wrong all 'round. Come on. You can come back later and explain if you want to. These *hombres* will lynch you and, from the way things look, they got a case."

"Sorry. I'm stayin'. You can go."

Kildare made a final appeal.

"You forgotten about old Colonel Barry?" he asked. "This'll be meat fer him. Casement won't have a word to say, even if he wants to back yore hand. C'mon Burton, while thar's yet time !"

The gaunt soldier of fortune shook his head doggedly.

"Be damned if I do," he replied. "But I want you to go. Get back to camp as fast as you can and tell Casement the truth about what happened. Maybe he'll listen to you."

Kildare hesitated.

"You'd better go," he said, "and I'll stay——"

But Burton already had turned away to stalk over to the telegraph pole where the man he had sent aloft perched on a crossbar. Burton yelled up a few words and the story of the disaster began tapping its dire message to Julesburg and End o' Track.

He was standing there, the message sent, when the savage trainmen jumped him from behind. He made no effort to defend himself and there was a jubilant roar as they pinned his arms. Conger, his face flushed with savage glee, drove a punch into Burton's face and dropped back a step.

"That's just a sample, you damn Reb," he said. "Wait'll Jack Casement turns you over to the boys. Then you'll learn how we treat Smiley's spies !"

CHAPTER XX

"LYNCH him now !" yelled a trainman. "Why wait for a lot of goddam rigmarole ?"

There was a surging yell of approval from the others. A noosed rope appeared out of nowhere and Robert Burton felt the harsh strands of hemp burn his neck as it was snapped over his head. His eyes bleak, the soldier of fortune watched the free end of the rope thrown over the same crossbar that the telegrapher had used to send his message.

'This looks like it,' Burton told himself. 'Jessica—I hope you won't believe what you'll hear.'

A brawny trainman hauled at the rope and Burton felt the noose tighten about his neck. His heart pounded achingly but only in rage at the injustice being dealt him.

The rope pulled tighter and Burton's brain swirled close to the brink of unconsciousness. Involuntarily, he struggled, his tethered feet kicking and his bound wrists straining to get free. Then, just before blackness descended, the pressure of the rope loosened; hands were at his neck wrenching free the noose. Somebody was steadying him as he swayed to his feet.

His vision cleared and he saw the grim face of Major North, eyes squinted under the black cavalry hat. Beyond North, Burton could make out a dozen or more of the Major's Pawnee Scouts, their carbines pressing back the raging mob that had been cheated out of its kill.

"I—thanks, Major," Burton gasped.

North did not smile.

"Don't thank me," he said, coldly. "I had my orders from General Casement."

He turned his back on Burton and strode away to confront the trainmen.

His words cut the strange stillness that had fallen. "This man," he said, "has to go back to the camp. Anybody who tries to stop us from taking him there gets shot on the spot. Casement's orders. Get to work and don't worry about this man getting what's coming to him if he's guilty."

The crowd dispersed slowly. Burton half stumbled to a horse that a young Pawnee brave brought forward, lurched into the saddle. He looked about him. Buffalo Caller sat his pony close to him but the Pawnee chief did not look his way. Bleeding Fox and the others who had been on the buffalo hunt with him and Dog Soldier Nick turned their stolid faces away. He swayed in his saddle as he spoke in Pawnee.

"Do my brothers believe me unworthy?" he asked. "Do they think Long Knife should wear ashes in his hair and sit with the women?"

Buffalo Caller flashed a glance at Burton and then looked at Major North. The commander of the Pawnee Scouts shook his head.

"No talking, Burton," the Major warned. "Save your breath for Jack Casement."

The trip to the camp was a journey of misery for Burton. Numbed in body and spirit, he slid off the pony's back at the camp and trudged between the two lines of infantrymen to the guard tent. There he sank down on a rifle chest under the guard of four leather-featured privates who looked eager to use their bayoneted Springfields.

'Come on,' said a silent voice. 'Stop feeling sorry for yourself. Think, man, think!'

Reluctantly, Burton forced his brain to slide back over the events of that crowded day. He thought of the hatred that had raged through the crowd of trainmen with the speed of a prairie fire. He saw the antagonism of his guards. He remembered the stony faces of the Pawnees, North's coldness.

There had been suspicion and hatred everywhere, directed squarely at him. Yet the fact that he had misunderstood Stattler or that the German had mistaken the raiders' words was an understandable error. Then, he asked himself, why should the wreck be accepted by the whole camp as a piece of deliberate treachery?

There was only one answer to that in Burton's mind. Somebody was making every effort to put him in a black light and, finally, to have him killed.

Barry? No. No matter how bitter the Old Colonel might be against all men who had served the South, Barry was a West Pointer. He never would stoop to such tactics, no matter how deep his hatred.

Then who could it be? McCue, Conger or—or—no, it couldn't be General Casement, himself!

He shook his head, gave up his muddled pondering and listened to the sounds that filtered into the tent. From what he heard he learned that the railroad workers were toiling through the night, their work lighted up by the huge bonfires made of precious ties, clearing the track of the wreckage. From End o' Track, from Julesburg, from every nearby base station, panting specials were bringing every available pair of hands to the scene of the disaster.

Red Jack Casement was flinging the full force of the railroad into the job of clearing the track. Wires had rattled off to Omaha, to Saint Louis. Rails! Rails! More rails to replace those that had been ruined in the wreck. Spurs were ordered stripped, sidings, even old rails from across the Mississippi were called for.

Throughout the night three thousand men swarmed over the wreck to heave and sweat and pull until, unit by unit, they disentangled the jam of spilled rails. Those steel strips that were undamaged were loaded on flat cars and rushed back to End o' Track. The bent and twisted rails were piled at one side to be sent back to the smelters.

Burton overheard snatches of conversation between his guards that told him that a Cheyenne war party had struck at dawn, sniping at the weary labourers until they were driven away. One guard spat tobacco juice at the ex-Confederate's feet and said:

"Reckon yore boss planned that, too, didn't he? Ye goddam renegade—ye're no better'n George Bent. I hope I'm around to see ye swing."

From second-hand reports, Burton learned that Major North's Pawnees had managed to chase the Cheyennes away after bitter fighting; that the railroad men, their personal grievances forgotten in this new disaster, had managed to get the track cleared. And that he was probably the most hated man west of the Mississippi.

But despite his own predicament, Burton grinned happily when the first train puffed into End o' Track, less than twenty hours after the wreck. It was after only an hour's rest that Casement sent his construction gangs out to their jobs. By one o'clock that afternoon the rails were dropping into place again and the Union Pacific began creeping westward once more.

Burton was still sitting on the rifle case, the music of ringing sledges and thudding picks playing a symphony in his ears when a black-bearded sergeant entered the guard tent and ordered the ex-Confederate to his feet. Escorted by a squad of infantry in dusty blue, the soldier of fortune was marched toward the Contractor-General's tent. He walked with his head erect, looking straight ahead, trying not to hear the yells that greeted his appearance.

"There he is, the dirty dog !"

"Take the food out of our mouths, would he ?"

"Hang the swine now and get it over with !"

"Hang him !"

The guards closed in. Sticks, stones and hunks of mud flew through the air to splatter and sting Burton and his guards. The soldiers cursed and moved their guns menacingly. The ex-Confederate walked on, unmindful of the cut one stone had opened or the blob of mud that had struck his cheek. He still was straight-backed and impassive when the detail reached the headquarters tent.

"There's a council going on inside," said the Company clerk. "Keep him here until General Casement sends for him."

Burton, standing as stiff as he ever had when presenting himself to General Forrest, waited in the sunlit antechamber of the great tent. From beyond the canvas partition he could make out Colonel Barry's precise voice; Casement's deeply resonant words; Conger's exact tones and the curt, sharp speech of General Grenville Dodge.

"These things have got to stop !" Dodge was saying. "Another wreck like this will certainly mean the ruin of the U.P.—if this one hasn't done the trick. You'll have to go at the problem from a different angle, Casement. You've got to find the men who are stabbing us in the back."

"That's easy to say," growled Casement. "And who do yez figure would be most interested in seein' us go down—outside of the Injuns who don't want to see their huntin' ruined, I mean ?"

There was the murmur of Conger's voice, saying something that Burton could not catch. Then came General Dodge's statement.

"There are three groups of people who stand to lose a lot if we keep on," he said. "I'm not making accusations, gentlemen, but the facts still stand. First, of course, there are the Indians. Second, there are the Kansas Pacific people building parallel to our line in the south. Thirdly, there's the Central Pacific."

"The Central Pacific !" Casement burst out.

"Yes. Or, rather, speculators in C.P. stock. I don't believe for a minute that Leland Stanford or Huntington or Charles Crocker would have anything to do with dirty business like this, but some of their shareholders and promoters aren't above it."

Colonel Barry's acid voice cut in.

"But, General, I don't understand," the old Army officer said. "Why should the C.P. want to hinder you ? You're building to meet them and the sooner the completed line is finished the sooner everybody starts getting dividends."

Burton, standing among his bayoneted guard, heard Conger laugh harshly.

"It ain't easy to understand, Colonel," he said, "but it happens that Congress has decided to give each railroad subsidies and permanent control of the track it builds to the point where they meet."

"In other words," Dodge amplified, "if the U.P. builds two thousand miles of track before it joins the Central Pacific, we control and get all the profits from two thousand miles of railroad. But if we're delayed for any reason, then the Central Pacific has a chance to build further and get the income from five hundred miles of railroad we might have had. During the course of years, the revenue from each mile will be tremendous."

Involuntarily, Burton nodded as understanding of the situation penetrated his misery.

"I think I see it now," Barry was saying. "And this group, or groups, have hired somebody—perhaps Smiley—to hamper the U.P. in every possible way. Speaking of Smiley, gentlemen, the prisoner should be outside. Shall we see him now, General Casement ?"

Casement's voice sounded to Burton as ominous as the clang of a cell door.

"Yes," the big Irishman said. "Let's get this nasty piece of business over with."

Burton kept his face stiff and proud as he was conducted into the tented room dominated by a long paper-littered table around which sat a row of hostile faces.

"Well," asked the red-bearded Irishman, "what have yez got to say ?"

Unhurriedly choosing his words, Robert Burton gave his account. He told how he had acted on information given by the German settler, Stattler. The Mormon, he said, must have misunderstood what he had overheard or the train wreckers had changed their plans. He had done his best and he had failed.

"I admit failure, gentlemen," he said quietly, "but I do not confess to the charges that obviously have been put against me, of being a traitor and a spy. Most of you are military men. I don't think one of you who have been in command has escaped some reverse. I don't think you were court-martialled for a success over your command by the enemy."

He looked around the table. Their eyes met his, cold, unyielding, slightly contemptuous. His heart sank as he realized that his appeal had failed. He looked again at Major North, on whom he had depended once as a friend. The chief of the Pawnee Scouts met his stare with eyes that might have been carved out of blue crystal.

"A touching speech, Burton—or should I say, *Captain* Burton?" said Colonel Barry. "But, unfortunately, I don't believe a word of it."

"Aw, let's get on with it," burst out McCue. "We're wasting time. I tell you, the man's——"

Casement quieted the Traffic Manager with a blunt gesture.

"Come on, man," the red-bearded Irishman said. "I'll give yez another chance. Tell the truth this time. What really happened last night when yez sneaked out of the car?"

Burton's face tightened and his lips thinned.

"As I reported, sir, I rode after the men who burned the bridge and I——"

"Stop your bejeezus lyin'!" yelled Casement, bringing a fist down on the table. "'Twill do yez no good! We've got positive information that yez met them wreckers at the bridge and talked to 'em. Send in that trackwalker, Orderly!"

Burton gaped as the orderly brought in a shambling figure distinguished by a completely bald head and buck teeth. The ex-Confederate knew that he never had seen the man before. He switched his glance toward Colonel Barry as the elderly officer got to his feet, the silver eagles on his shoulder gleaming faintly in the lantern light.

"Simmons," said Colonel Barry. "Tell us what you saw last night."

The trackwalker shifted his feet and looked down at the shabby hat he fumbled in his hands.

"I'm runnin' up the line on account of the fire," he said. "Then I seen that feller standin' there ride up, git off and pick up somethin'."

"It was a spur," Burton said quickly. "One of the raiders lost t."

"Yez said nothin' of anny spur to me!" Casement rapped out.

"It wasn't anything that could be called conclusive evidence," Burton replied. "I wanted to investigate it further. Besides, I had a lot of things on my mind."

There was a brief silence. The ex-Confederate realized that his explanation of the spur sounded very weak. More cadaverous than ever, Colonel Barry leaned forward.

"You're sure, Simmons, that this is the man you saw?" he asked.

"Certain sure, sir. I saw him plain by the light of the fire."

"Very good. Go on, please."

Revolving his hat in his hands, the trackwalker went on.

"I seen that feller put the spur away—if it was a spur—and he kinda looked around, sneaky like, and then he rode off a piece to join a bunch of horsemen what was watchin' the bridge burn. I heard him holler out: 'Better git movin'! Casement fell for the idee fine but he's comin' here fast !' That's what he said, sir. Then they all rode off together."

Burton's lips were white as he gritted,

"You mother-murderin' blackguard ! I want to get my hands on your lyin' throat some day !"

The guards leaped for him and held him as the trackwalker scuttled out of reach. Burton's rage cooled and he straightened to face the council table again.

"All I can say, gentlemen, is that outside of my pickin' up the spur, that man has been lyin' through his teeth. Don't believe him."

"I'm afraid we must, *Captain*," General Dodge cut in icily. "The evidence bears out what Simmons testifies. Two of the railroad guards have sworn that they found that your horse's hoof-prints joined those of the raiders."

"Of course they did, sir," Burton said. "I followed their trail and——"

He stopped, overwhelmed by the realization that somebody— *somebody*—had cast a perfectly woven net over him. He turned on his heel and spoke directly at Major North.

"For God's sake, Major," he said, "send some of your men out to find Kildare ! He can clear me !"

North shook his head silently.

"Find Kildare !" Casement neighed. "Now, by God, that's a good one. Your pal, Kildare, can't be found though we're still lookin' for him. He cleared out a couple of minutes after he rode in here to try to tell me yez didn't have anything to do with the wreck ! Find Kildare, eh ?"

Burton shrugged. If the Texan had ridden out, bound for Utah, there was no hope for him. He heard the men at the table opposite him talking but he took no notice of the words. His fate was sealed. The only thing now was to keep his shoulders back and his face emotionless and take what was coming like a gentlemen and an officer.

"I suppose hangin' is the only thing ?" Casement was asking as he swung his head to look up and down the long table.

Hanging ! Burton shivered despite himself. It was not death but the manner of dying that appalled him.

"It's too damned good for the dirty spy !" Conger cried.

Colonel Barry sat back in his chair, a cold smile on his lips. Burton wondered if the old man imagined that he was getting satisfaction for the death of his sons.

"This isn't a legal court, gentlemen," Major North said. "Somebody might make trouble about a Judge Lynch trial later on. Of course this scoundrel deserves death and I've got a suggestion that'll guarantee death and still keep our hands clean—legally."

"What's that ?" asked Colonel Barry. "I—well, my superiors—General Sherman—I mean, what did you have in mind, Major ?"

Major North looked Burton squarely in the eyes and spoke slowly.

"We could order Burton out of camp and give him a mount—I'd suggest a slow mule—and send him in a given direction. There are certain neighbours of ours who would make short work of anybody. It might be that the squaws would make long work of this particular person."

Burton's brain reeled as the import of what Major North was saying sank in. Horrified, he bent over the table to stare at the man who once had saved him from death and now was consigning him to something infinitely worse than the quick oblivion of bullets.

"Major North !" he gasped. "You don't mean you're goin' to send me into Cheyenne country unarmed and on a mule !"

"That," said Major North, "is exactly what I mean—you goddam renegade !".

"But—but, Major," McCue protested. "If he works for Smiley, the Cheyennes will take him in !"

"Not him," said North grimly. "Not after that buffalo hunt where he killed a few Dog Soldiers."

"But them Pawnees like him," McCue persisted. "They're liable to sneak out and get him to safety !"

Major North turned his cold eyes on the Traffic Manager.

"My Pawnees do what I tell them, sir," he said. "They won't aid Captain Burton unless I tell them to."

For the first time, Robert Burton's shoulders slumped. For some reason, he had believed Major North to be his friend and yet this man had proved to be his most vindictive enemy. It was North who had suggested the idea of driving him into Cheyenne country where the squaws would have their orgies of bestiality over his prostrate body. He looked at the Major with disbelieving eyes.

"Ain't scared, are you, Captain ?" jeered Conger.

He straightened himself with an effort and looked at General Casement.

"I don't know who's back of all this," he said, "but among you-all you've managed to make me out a criminal, even though I've risked my life a half a dozen times to justify your faith in me. All right—so I'm killed !"—he pinned a withering look on the red-bearded Contractor-General—"I'm out of the way, like somebody wants me to be. But you'll regret this, every damn one of you !"

Casement leaped to his feet, quivering with rage.

"Take him out of here !" he bellowed. "Take him out before I shoot him where he stands !"

Rude hands hauled Captain Robert Burton out of the headquarters tent into the blazing sunlight. A detail of four infantry drummers stood there with Colonel Barry in the background. Burton was half thrown into the centre of a hollow square and the drummers took positions about ten feet behind him.

"March !" snapped a burly sergeant.

With the guard tramping about him and with a half platoon of infantry drawn up in column behind him, Burton marched through the camp while the snarling drums behind hammered out the 'Rogue's March.'

Never did Bedford Forrest's young captain forget the agony, the degradation of that half-mile march to the edge of camp. When they halted him, spattered with filth and dirt, his body ached from the blows of rocks and clubs. He found himself standing beside a gaunt, old mule, its fleabitten head drooping low and mangy ears tilted dejectedly.

Dimly, he heard the curses of his guards as they pushed him up astride the unsaddled animal. The big sergeant pointed to the open desert.

"Ride that way and keep on ridin'," he ordered. "We got orders to shoot you down if you try to come back."

Dully Captain Robert Burton shook the decrepit beast into movement. Soul-sickened and leaden-hearted, he bent over the mule's neck, grasping the frayed rope hackamore.

'To hell with it !' he told himself bitterly. 'Kildare ran out. North gave me this. Casement wanted to shoot me. To hell with it. Come on, you Cheyennes ! Only shoot me—don't capture me.'

The mule jogged on toward the hills where the Cheyennes waited. Burton neared a slope and, as he lifted his head, saw a clump of sagebrush move.

"There they are," he murmured. "Come on, mule. Let's get this over with."

CHAPTER XXI

AT a shuffling walk, the ribby mule shambled past a long windrow of sun-bleached buffalo skulls and bones which, from a distance, had seemed to be an impossible snowbank drifting across the burning prairie.

The ex-Confederate wiped a bit of particularly malodorous filth from his face and looked down at himself. He grimaced at the sight of his lean frame splatted with offal, horse manure and mud. Inside his skull his brain began to glow like a white-hot iron. Captain Robert Burton never had come so close to going mad as he did then, astride a mule, trudging toward almost certain death.

He began to laugh. Wild, breathless laughter. Gale on gale of strange, frantic merriment shook him. By God, it *was* funny !

Everything had gone wrong that could go wrong. There wasn't a man alive who could have had all this happen to him—except Robert Burton, Esquire. The tears of laughter coursed down his dirty cheeks, leaving narrow white channels in their wake.

Then the mule suddenly bucked and the soldier of fortune landed on his back, sending up a cloud of alkali dust.

The jar saved Burton's reason. The seething kettle of his brain died down to a simmer. He began to feel better—a great deal better. He was almost smiling when he recaptured his knobby-boned mule and remounted.

He knew that there was somebody waiting for him to ride into a trap; he was resigned to the fact that his plight was hopeless; yet he kept his smile as he dug his heels into the mule's ribs and rode toward his fate. Back at End o' Track they could think what they liked but he, Captain Robert Burton, C.S.A., had no apologies to make for himself. He nearly had been lynched, he had been spurned by the men he had thought his friends, he had been sent to a certain and horrible death. Still he had kept faith with Bob Burton.

The mule plodded around the corner of a towering bluff and ambled toward a small stream that crawled down to the Lodgepole. The animal stopped and its ears went forward inquiringly. Burton looked ahead to see two mounted horsemen in his path, half hidden by the incredibly blue shadows. At one side was a third horse, riderless.

One of the riders spurred his mount out of the shadows.

"Heyo!" Kildare called in low greeting. "I allow Frank North pulled off the idee all right."

"Idea! Why, goddam that——"

Burton stopped short. A light dawned. Now he knew why the Chief Pawnee Scout had put the proposal that he, Burton, be sent out to die at the hands of the Cheyennes. Now he knew why Casement had been so eager to accept that proposal. A warm tide swept over the ex-Confederate to thaw the ice that had formed over his heart. There still were men who held the bonds of friendship sacred.

Paulus Stattler rode up after Kildare and held out a huge, rough hand.

"*Ach!* I am glad to see you. I vass so frightened for you, *mein Freund*. I t'ought dey vould hang you."

"Not yet," Burton grinned. "I'm still in one piece. Just about. And don't shake hands with me, Paulus, until I have a chance to get into that creek. I'm no bunch of heliotrope right now."

As he stripped and squatted in the brook to wash the filth from him, Kildare kept up a drawling conversation that had to do with the plan that Major North and General Casement had concocted.

"Y'see," the cowboy explained, "everybody but them two was

all set to lynch you. So North, he says how about suggestin' somethin' worse than lynchin', like turnin' you loose in Cheyenne
country. Casement, he balked about that, wantin' to fight the whole
goddam camp fer you, but North, he pointed out that if you got
sent out into the prairie the *hombres* what are makin' all the trouble
would think you dead so they'd show their hand and you could
work in the dark and find out who they was. So Casement finally
said all right and they sent Paulus and me out here to watch
fer you. We been spottin' you almost ever since you left
camp."

He reached into his saddlebags and threw a fresh set of buckskins down on the creek bank.

"Leave them stinkin' things here," he said. "Casement knew
you'd be needin' clothes—and a gun. He shore did right by you
with the gun, too. One of the purtiest pearl-handled Colts I ever
seen."

Captain Robert Burton donned the new buckskins, strapped the
heavy Colt about his middle and walked over to the led horse
that Paulus was holding. The animal was the same well-trained
mustang that he had bought from Dog Soldier Nick. Strapped
to the mount's saddle were his rifle and bags that contained the
rest of his equipment. One of the saddlebags held the leather
pouch Burton had taken from the slain renegade, Fred Fryer, with
its small fortune in gold coins and the mysterious cypher message
still intact.

"That Major North," Kildare commented, "thinks of everything. Me, I'd never remember to bring your kit out to meet you,
but he did special to make sure you got everything that belonged
to you."

He glanced at Burton as the ex-Confederate vaulted into the
saddle.

"Where now, Cap'n?" he asked. "We headin' northwest to
Oregon or out Utah way whar' a man kin sport a whole passel of
wives—if he's fool enough?"

Burton shrugged.

"That's up to you, Tex," he said. "I'm lingerin' around these
parts a while longer. I reckon Julesburg has me under her magic
spell."

He bent at the task of loading his rifle. Kildare and Stattler
moved their horses closer.

"I know it ain't no use to argue with you," the Texan went on,
"but you got a good chance now to get to hell out of here while
yo're all in one part. It'll cost you yore neck to set a foot in
Julesburg, pardner!"

"I'm stayin'."

"*Aber nein!* Avay you must get. *Schnell!*"

"Listen," said Burton as he shoved the rifle back into its holder, "Major North and General Casement arranged all this so I'd be free to work on my own. They didn't expect me to run out and I don't intend to. You-all haven't got any reason to stay if you want to get out, but I've a debt to settle with Jack Smiley and everybody who's workin' with him. And I want to show Casement he didn't guess wrong when he decided to play his cards with me. And I've got to find out who the amiable person is who's workin' so hard to get me lynched."

His face tautened as he looked in the general direction of Julesburg.

"I'm goin' to balance the books with Boot Hill Jack. I'm goin' to——"

He broke off to laugh abruptly.

"Seems like I'm goin' to do a lot of things. But I'm holdin' you two up. You've done a heap more than repay me for any little help I've been to you. So, *amigos mios*, I reckon we'll roost here till sundown and then go rejoicin' on our separate ways."

Kildare swung a leg over his pony's back and dropped to the ground. The horse haltered, he walked over to the lee of a sage-brush and sank down, his long bowed legs stretched out before him. He tugged at a chew of tobacco with his white teeth. Wordlessly, Paulus Stattler lumbered down off his horse, secured the animal and walked over to sit down beside the Texan. Still silently, he accepted a chew from the proffered twist.

"I ain't taken back by what you say," Kildare explained. "I allowed 'way back that you wouldn't head west. Well, thar'll be three of us headin' fer Julesburg when we move."

The German bobbed his head.

"*Ja.* T'ree of us. Not yet haff I found dose devils dat—Ach, Anna !"

Burton looked at the two men, hands on his hips.

"You-all know what you want to do," he said quietly, "but 'Hell on Wheels' isn't goin' to be any picnic for anybody who throws his rope with me. Smiley's after me and every U.P. roustabout is after me. What I might get will be what you'd get, if they found out you're friends of mine. I'm not sayin' I don't appreciate what you're offerin' to do but I'm advisin' you not to do it just the same."

Kildare turned to the round-faced immigrant beside him.

"What's he talkin', Paulus ?" he asked innocently. "Sounds a little like Mex. I can't understand it at all."

Stattler frowned and shook his heavy head.

"Not me, neider."

"You two idiots," Burton said affectionately. "Can't you understand that the odds are heavy against us ?"

The Texan sank back and tilted the brim of his frayed brown sombrero low over his eyes.

"Now yo're makin' the proposition downright interestin'," he said idly. "I been hankerin' fer that kind of a situation ever since the Red River campaign."

Burton gave up with a shrug of resignation. He set about building the tiny fire over which the three cooked their evening meal. After they had eaten, Burton leaned back against a saddle and studied the sky.

"If you two *hombres* are determined to throw in with me, we might as well figure out the best way to work," he said. "We'll go at it like we're fightin' a war. We'll plan it like a regular campaign. The first thing, of course, is to conduct a reconnaissance.

"You try to get in with Smiley, Tex. Don't be too eager. Try to get him to suggest hirin' you. Maybe give him a little demonstration of your shootin'. But watch your temper, man, no matter what happens."

The Texan's face tightened a bit.

"I'll shore try, Bob," he promised, "but I can easier ride an outlaw mustang than keep from fightin' when somebody gets me riled. Anyhow, I'll meet you to-morrow night come sundown down by them cottonwoods you spoke of."

Burton turned to Stattler.

"You're to try for a job 'round the freight yards, Paulus. See what you can dig up by keepin' your eyes and ears open. I'm just goin' to mosey around. I reckon we'd all better show up at the post office at noon to-morrow. Something might come up."

The plan completed, the three turned in as the sun sank behind the buttes to the west. Tex and Stattler slept almost immediately but Robert Burton stared wide-eyed at the darkening sky. He thought of Jessica Valcour and his heart surged within him. The leap of his heart may not have been as tumultuous as the name Enid Culver once would have provoked but, Burton thought, that was just as well.

He wondered how Jessica had taken the news of his disgrace. Jessica, what a queer, determined sort of girl she was, unfathomable as an ocean. That night on the hilltop overlooking End o' Track she had wanted to give herself to him wildly. At other times she had been controlled, reserved to the point of coldness.

But she was beautiful—God, she was beautiful! When they were married he could claim and glory in the passion that had broken through her calm that night on the hill.

When they were married. Robert Burton found a strange ring in those words. . . .

CHAPTER XXII

IT was noon and Julesburg's tiny post office was jammed to over-flowing with an impatient crowd. A dark-skinned cowboy standing near the door tensed as he felt a hard object jabbed into his ribs. He turned his head to see the Texan, Kildare, grinning at him.

"Nother time," the Texan murmured, "stand against the wall."

He scanned Robert Burton's lean figure and nodded approvingly.

"Didn't hardly know you. You shore made some alterations."

The ex-Confederate had made drastic changes in his appearance. He had exchanged his slouch hat for a broad-brimmed sombrero with a band of rattlesnake skin. The buckskin shirt had been replaced by a sombre affair of black flannel. The buckskin breeches were now hidden behind wide leather *chivarros*, scarred and scratched by cactus. Stattler had clipped Burton's long hair to a short mop. The adventurer had thinned his heavy eyebrows and had stained his face to a deep mahogany hue.

"How'd you make out?' Burton asked. Tex Kildare paused to bite off a generous piece of 'nigger head' twist and rolled it into one cheek.

"Couldn't even get close to Smiley this mawnin'," he said, "but I'm goin' to see him after dinner. Git anywheres yourself?"

"Not far. Been loafin' around the telegraph office."

Kildare skilfully elbowed aside a smelly, half drunken immigrant who fought his way toward the door, clutching a handful of letters.

"Why hang around that?" asked the Texan. "Figger somethin' to be l'arned in that direction?"

Burton shrugged.

"Mostly a hunch. I was thinkin'——"

Burton's hand shot out and clutched Kildare's arm.

"Look! Here comes Smiley."

Without a change of expression, the Texan hitched his well-nicked guns a trifle forward and with narrowing black eyes surveyed the advance of Julesburg's dictator. Arrogant, self-assured, Jack Smiley came tramping up the muddied steps of the little post office, a quartet of hatchet-faced gunmen at his heels.

"Mornin', Jack!"

"Howdy, Honourable!"

"How are ye, Mr. Smiley?"

Voices called out greetings from all sides. A thin smile spread across Kildare's face as he subtly shifted his balance to his toes.

"We c'n take him easy, Bob," he murmured. "Them killers, too. All set?"

"No! Not now!" Burton's hand gripped Kildare's arm tighter. He drew back as Smiley, towering above the heads of the churning crowd, ploughed his way toward the small window at which the mail was handed out.

"Hey !" roared an elderly cattle dealer as he was shoved aside by the boss of Julesburg. "It ain't yore turn. Git back. I been waitin' half an hour."

"One side, you old fool," Smiley gritted. "My time's valuable."

As the old cattleman struggled forward, Smiley dealt him a cuff that sent him reeling across the room. The cattle dealer stumbled and fell at Burton's feet. Smiley's keen eyes followed the man's progress, then raised from the prostrate figure of the man he had hit to stare straight at the man who had sworn to kill him.

Every nerve in the ex-Confederate's body tightened as he returned Smiley's gaze. It seemed that the big man's piercing eyes were boring through his disguise, stripping it from him. He fought against moving his hands toward his guns and battled to keep his face emotionless. A moment that seemed an age ticked by before Smiley's eyes shifted to the cattleman who was struggling to his feet, cursing sulphurously.

For a second it appeared that the oldtimer was going for his guns. His gnarled hands hovered like hawks, poised to swoop, over the twin gun butts. Then, with the realization that to call Smiley, backed up by his gunmen, would be suicide, the cattleman turned and limped out of the post office.

Smiley gave a contemptuous laugh and raised his voice.

"Don't get excited, friends," he said. "It's all over. That stranger just needed a little lesson, that's all." He turned to the postmaster. "Here, Pop. Register this letter for me."

As Smiley turned from the window, his eyes reached out at Robert Burton again. Slowly he walked toward the ex-Confederate, his gaze pinned on the soldier of fortune. Burton kept his own eyes steady. Beside him, Kildare shifted his feet.

Smiley, a giant in his black frock coat, stopped directly in front of the man who had loved Enid Culver.

"New in town ?" he demanded.

"Sho' am," said Burton in an affected drawl. "Jest hit Julesburg this mornin'. Been lookin' fo' a job. Mebbe you could help me."

The big gambler's eyes deliberately ranged up and down Burton's body then returned to fix the ex-Confederate's eyes.

"Don't know about that," he said slowly. "What part of Texas you hail from ?"

"Pecos. Come up with a drove of cattle to Dodge City."

"Uh, Pecos, eh ?" Smiled asked. One of his big hands stroked the carefully barbered chin. "Well, see you later, stranger—mebbe."

"Sho' nuff," Burton replied. "This hyar seems like a right lively little town."

"It is," Smiley said with a tight smile. "Lively—and deadly for the wrong sort of people."

Burton nodded and turned aside. He saw Kildare standing a few paces distant, deeply interested in his study of a batch of 'Wanted, Dead or Alive' posters.

The ex-Confederate turned back again as Smiley and his entourage clumped toward the door. His eyes swept their spurs as they left. No luck. None of those dusty rowels even faintly resembled the elaborate steel and gold affair he had found under the bridge at Buffalo Creek. He wished that Stattler could have been there. It was possible that the German would have recognized some of Smiley's gunmen as the raiders who had killed the immigrant's wife. He edged over to Kildare and spoke quietly.

"So long, Tex," he said. "The cottonwoods at ten to-night."

"Okay. Keep yer eyes peeled, Bob, 'cause I got a funny little feelin' that that Smiley *hombre's* onto you."

Burton and the hawk-faced Texan had started for the door, watching Smiley's broad back as the gambler clattered down the board steps of the post office, when there was a screeching yell from outside. Burton turned to see the old cattle dealer whom Smiley had struck step out from behind the rear wheels of an ox cart. The grey-moustached man flourished a brace of old-fashioned, muzzle-loading revolvers. At the old man's side was a handsome, wild-looking youngster who clutched a double-barrelled shotgun.

Pandemonium reigned in the street and within the post office. Men and women scurried to shelter or dropped flat in the dusty street. Miraculously, the crowded board walk cleared, leaving Smiley and his gunmen standing some forty feet from the old man and the boy with no one between the two groups.

"Now, you son of a——" screamed the cattleman.

His archaic guns flashed up as Smiley's hands flickered down toward his own guns. Even as the gambler hurled himself to one side, Smiley fired. There were two reports, so close together that they might have been one. A split second later, the shotgun's deeper explosion boomed out and Burton could hear the buckshot going *tacot—tacot* against the front of the post office. Broken glass jangled. A man cried out hoarsely. Two of Smiley's bodyguards tumbled forward down the post office steps.

"Oh, God ! I—I——"

The old cattleman was sinking to his knees, coughing a bright spray onto the front of his shirt. With pain-racked effort, he managed to lift one of his guns as he collapsed.

"Tough old devil, ain't you ?" Smiley said. His guns spoke

again and the elderly man tumbled forward to twitch spasmodically amid the dust and dung of the street.

The boy, at the same time, raised his shotgun for another try at Smiley. The guns of the two surviving bodyguards bellowed to cut the young man down.

There was an appalling silence. Death had struck four times within as many seconds. Powder smoke drifted idly in the thin breeze. One of the gunmen began flopping hideously on the bottom step of the post office. His wheezing voice crescendoed to a squeal. The gunman's dirty hands clutched at his middle, apparently trying to cram protruding entrails back into a gaping wound that had opened his belly. The screams died down to a whimpering cry such as a hurt dog might make.

Smiley, unshaken and superbly arrogant, glared up and down the street, as callously indifferent to the cries of his own agonized henchman as he was to the twitching of the dying cattleman. He was shoving his guns back into their holsters when a thin wail sounded.

"Abner ! Oh, Abner !"

A grey-haired woman in a faded pink sunbonnet pushed her way through the crowd to break out into the open. She stared dazedly at the dead youth who had wielded the shotgun and then flung herself across the older man's slumped body. She crouched there for a moment and then raised her head to glare at Jack Smiley.

"Murderer !" she screamed. "Killer !"

Half mad, the old woman began babbling curses that made Burton's spine chill. He had taken a few steps toward the woman when, at a contemptuous signal from Smiley, one of the two surviving bodyguards stepped forward and dealt the woman a blow on the head with the barrel of his gun. The woman pitched forward over the body of her husband, knocked senseless.

"That ought to stop the old hen's squawking," Smiley laughed. "Lug Joe over to the Julesburg house. Give him plenty of liquor on me, so he'll slide over the Divide slick and easy.

"Come on, gents," Smiley continued. "Let's liquor up. All drinks on me. Everybody step forward to buck the tiger !"

He led a small parade of hangers-on toward the nearest saloon, ignoring the crumpled bodies he left behind him. Burton watched the gambler's broad back recede, fighting the temptation to call Smiley, to end the blackguard's evil career in a pitched duel, to avenge himself for all the wrongs this man had dealt him.

He shook his head. His first job, he reminded himself, was to solve the plot against the U.P. and vindicate himself in the eyes of those who mistrusted him. Smiley could wait.

Tight-lipped, he started across the porch of the post office. Up the street a buggy was wheeling in crazy circles, its horses wounded and threatening to bolt at any minute. A slight figure sawed at the reins, trying to hold the plunging mounts. He tensed as he saw the wounded horses gathering themselves for a dash down the street. He saw then that the driver of the buggy was a woman in an ostrich-trimmed poke bonnet. Her strength exhausted, she could no longer fight the maddened horses.

As the buggy thundered closer, Burton flung himself at the bits of the rearing animals. A hoof struck his thigh and sent an agonizing pain shooting through him but he managed to hold on until other onlookers ran out to help pull down the maddened animals.

It was not until the horses were quieted that Burton looked up to see Jessica Valcour in the driver's seat. When their eyes met he knew that she recognized him, despite his disguise. Her fear-whitened face flushed.

"Oh, Bob !" she gasped. "Why, I thought—they said——"

She stopped, one trembling hand creeping to her mouth.

"Glad to have helped you, ma'am," Burton drawled. He dropped his voice to little more than a whisper. "Must see you. Seven o'clock. Your back door."

"No, Bob !" she gasped. "You mustn't. I—it's too danger-ous !"

Burton tipped his sombrero and faded back into the crowd that had surged forward to stare at the stylish turnout, more uncommon on Julesburg's streets than the tableau of death that had been staged under the burning noonday sun.

The ex-Confederate slipped between two enormous warehouses, ignoring the ribby curs that yapped and snapped at his high, brass-spurred heels.

He asked himself what had been back of the frightened look Jessica Valcour had given him. Why, he wondered, had she told him to stay away ? Was it because she feared for his safety—or did she believe the story of his disgrace ?

He told himself that it must have been her fear for him.

"Of course that was it," he murmured. "She'd never believe that I was a traitor."

He halted in the shadow of the Wells Fargo Express office to gaze with unseeing eyes at the surging, restless panorama of Jules-burg. The brief glimpse of Jessica had started his heart pumping. He knew he must see her that night, hold the yielding softness of her body, taste the fiery fragrance of her mouth. No danger, real or imagined, could keep him from that.

CHAPTER XXIII

CAPTAIN Robert Burton, still in his role of a Texas cowboy, strolled along Julesburg's main street, conscious of the boring eyes of the half-breed he knew was watching him.

Twice during the afternoon Burton had noticed the half-breed, lounging in the saloons he had visited. The ex-Confederate had spent most of the day going from bar to bar, drinking sparingly and listening to the obscene jargon of the stage drivers and freighters in from their long journeys to Denver and the nascent cities along the upper Missouri.

'That breed,' he told himself, 'has been told to watch me. And that might mean that Smiley's wise—or just cautious of every stranger that hits this town.'

He deliberately turned and looked at the man who had been trailing him. The half-breed pulled his battered hat low over his eyes and dodged into a saloon. Burton turned and darted into an alley, cut back behind a row of buildings, and then made for the railroad station. He was confident that he had shaken off his shadow when he swung by a row of motionless Indians, huddled in their blankets on the station platform, and walked into the station's telegraph office.

The place was a maelstrom of noise. More than a dozen instruments were clicking off their messages as the operators flashed their pencils across the yellow and blue blanks without a pause. He paused at the message wicket. The chief operator put down a batch of blanks and came up to the window.

"What's yours, brother?" he demanded.

"My name's Jed Smith," Burton said. "I come up yere with a drove o' beef steers. My boss sent me a telegram but the kid what was bringin' it lost it."

The chief operator squinted suspiciously at the tall man in the black shirt, orange neckerchief and wide *chivarros*.

"What was the name?" he asked after a pause.

"Smith. Jed J. Smith."

"How long ago did this message come through?"

Burton rubbed a thumb over his chin thoughtfully.

"Lemme see," he drawled. "Mebbe it come only yesterday, mebbe two or three days back. The kid was too damn scairt to allow more than he'd lost it. Then he skedaddled before I could even boot his tail for him."

The telegrapher scowled.

"Smith, huh?" he asked. "Why in God's name would it have to be Smith? There's easy fifty people called Smith in this goddam hell hole of a town. Well, I can't help you. Mebbe your boss will wire again."

As he turned away, Burton raised his voice.

"Hey, listen, Boss," he protested. "That's a hell of an important telegram."

"Can I help it ?" demanded the clerk, his voice shrilling. "I can't go looking through them files for everybody. My God, cowboy, look at that ! "

His inky finger pointed to a mound of messages.

"All them wires have got to go out to-day and we're still sending out last night's."

"Listen, Boss," Burton said. He quietly peeled off a ten-dollar bill from the roll that had been supplied by the sale of Stattler's cattle. "That there telegram means a heap o' *buen dinero* to the boss and he'll shore skin me alive if I make a mistake. Suppose you lemme look through them old duplicates. Reckon I could find her myself and save you trouble."

The chief operator hesitated, hungrily eyeing the bill. He chewed furiously at his quid and spat into a spattered sawdust box set in the centre of the room.

"Sorry, cowboy," he said. "That's dead agin regulations."

Silently, Burton produced another bill and folded it in with the first.

"'Tain't goin' to hurt nobody," he urged. "I shore need that telegram powerful bad."

The clerk shrugged and reached for the bills.

"Come in quick and quiet," he said as he undid the catch of a swinging door. "The old telegrams are in them boxes yonder at the back of the room. Take a look but if the inspector comes around, you get out and get out quick, see ?"

"Sho' will," said Burton. "Thanks, Boss."

His heart was pounding with excitement as he walked to the back of the room and sat down at the stacks of telegram duplicates. Minutes slid smoothly by, the keys clacked on steadily and beneath Burton's flying fingers the heap of scanned telegrams grew higher. With the stub of a pencil he made a few brief notations. Jack Smiley, he noted, received numerous messages from someone in Saint Louis who signed his wires 'E.K.W.' The messages themselves appeared harmless but Burton suspected that they might have double meanings. He considered taking them with him for further study and then decided against the idea as too risky.

There were other telegrams with significant contents. Again and again, Burton saw familiar names on the duplicate blanks— Casement, Dodge, Valcour, Conger—but Smiley's name appeared more frequently than any other.

"Hey, cowboy, how you makin' out ?" the chief operator called.

"Ain't cut her trail yet, Boss. Reckon I'll find her soon, though."

"Well, shake a leg. You can't roost in here all day."

Burton worked faster, fearful that the telegrapher's dread of a visit by the inspector might mean his dismissal. It was when he was examining a pile of duplicates for the second previous day— a Wednesday—that the ex-Confederate felt his mouth go dry and his heart leap. Between fingers that trembled he held a telegram form addressed to Smiley—a form containing a long message *in a number cipher strongly reminiscent* of the coded message found on the slain renegade, Fred Fryer !

Burton's pencil flew over a telegraph form as he copied the message. He had barely finished the job when there was a soft step behind him and a shadow fell across the blanks in front of him. The adventurer automatically slid the copy under a sheaf of wires but there was no time to conceal the original when a drawling voice spoke.

"Think it makes interestin' readin', Stranger ?" asked Boot Hill Jack Smiley.

Burton forced himself to turn to look up at the boss of Julesburg. He managed a grin.

"Hell, Mister," he said, "only a Chinee could make any sense out o' that kind of stuff."

He turned back and put Smiley's telegram on the pile of those he had examined. Then he selected the next duplicate and scanned it, conscious of Smiley's eyes on him from above. He looked up again as the big man's hand touched his shoulder.

"What're you doin' here ?" Smiley rapped out.

"He's lookin' fer a telegram duplicate," the chief operator broke in hurriedly. "A telegram from his boss got lost a couple o' days back."

Smiley's eyes narrowed.

"That's funny, Stranger," he said. "Thought you told me a while back that you'd just come to town and was lookin' for a job."

Burton nodded.

"I did," he admitted.

"Then how come you're lookin' for a telegram from your boss that came two days back ?"

"My old job ends when the cows are sold," Burton explained. "I been out on the prairie the last two days."

His nerves as taut as overkeyed guitar strings, Burton watched Smiley. With the big man standing over him, he knew he had no chance to beat Boot Hill Jack to the draw should the gambler go for his gun.

"What was that telegram about ?" asked Smiley, scowling.

"Cattle, Mister," Burton replied. "My boss was tellin' me how many head to sell in this hyer market."

Smiley rubbed his chin, obviously only half convinced. His blue eyes hardened.

"It's a fancy story, Stranger," he said at length, "and I don't know as I like it. Anyway, you're goin' to quit moseyin' through these telegrams."

He turned to the cringing chief operator.

"Throw this cow-chaser out of here," he ordered bluntly, "and keep him out if you want to stay on the job."

"Yessir, Mr. Smiley," said the perspiring clerk. "Sorry, Mr. Smiley. You get out, cowboy ! You've looked long enough."

Smiley stood waiting, rocking a bit on the heels of his black, high-heeled boots. Burton stared straight at the boss of Julesburg.

"Sorry, pardner," he drawled, "but I aim to finish this hyer box. That telegram means a heap to me."

Smiley glared at Burton and then shrugged. Unexpectedly, the big man turned away.

"Let him stay," he told the chief operator. "I guess it's all right. See you later—Stranger."

Burton gazed after the big man as Smiley tramped out of the telegraph office. Then, before the amazed clerk could turn from his gaping after Boot Hill Jack, the ex-Confederate slipped the copy of the coded message into his pocket.

"Beat it !" snapped the operator when he had recovered from his astonishment. "Don't come back, neither. You've likely got me in a peck of trouble with Mr. Smiley already and I don't want to make it worse."

Burton reluctantly got to his feet.

"Damn it," he grumbled, "I'm liable to be fired if I don't find that telegram."

"To hell with your telegram and your job, too ! Now, git !"

Burton walked to the door of the office, casually easing his gun in its limber and well-oiled holster. At the doorway he scanned the crowd milling about the railroad station waiting for 'Nebraska Special.' There was the usual number of beery loafers drowsing amid the heaps of freight and baggage. At a gnawed hitching post stood a half dozen dejected-looking bronchos, lazily switching their tails at clouds of flies. Over the heads of the horses, Burton watched the arrival of an immigrant train just in from North Platte and on its way to camp at the edge of Julesburg. Tall, dusty wagons lumbered past, ungreased axles filling the hot air with their complaints.

Automatically, Burton checked the position of the sun, then moved over to the far side of the steps as he descended to the platform, putting the glare of the sun at his back. He had just reached the splintered platform when one of the loafers detached himself from a group and swaggered up, driving an elbow into the ex-Confederate's ribs.

"Where the hell you goin'?" he growled.

"Sorry, brother," Burton growled. "Didn't mean to jostle you."

His eyes darted about him, sizing up the situation. He did not recall ever having seen the red-shirted loafer before but he did recognize a man who lounged against the side of a boxcar, about thirty feet away. That man, he saw, was the half-breed who had followed him earlier that day.

'Huh!' the ex-Confederate told himself. 'Smiley didn't waste any time!'

The red-shirted gunman in front of Burton gave him a shove.

"Git out o' my way," he snarled, "before I throw you out!"

The ex-Confederate set his arm and wrist muscles on a perfect mental hair trigger. He looked at the man in front of him and grinned.

"I was just goin' for a drink," he drawled. "Have one with me?"

He knew that he would have to draw and he decided that he should be able to beat this lumpy-shouldered bravo to the first shot. The breed should not be too much trouble. Few half-breeds were really quick. He was coldly calm; as calm as he had been before that desperate charge at Chickamauga. His whole world at that moment included only the deadly pale brown eyes of the killer in front of him.

"Drink with you?" Smiley's hired hand uttered a raucous laugh. "I'd liefer drink with a polecat!"

Burton read the danger signal when it flickered in the gunman's eyes. His hand shot downward and up again. He looked into the killer's staring eyes, saw the red-shirted man's shoulders droop, half saw the flash of his own gun, heard the crash of the shot as the gunman disappeared momentarily in a dense cloud of smoke.

Before the concussion of his heavy Colt had finished its jumping wrench, Burton had dropped to one knee and whirled toward the half-breed. The breed's bullet ripped through the air over his head and pinged into a smoke-blackened bucket swinging from the side of a passing immigrant cart.

The ex-Confederate's foot slipped as he whirled and his first shot whined over the half-breed's head to bury itself in the side of the freight car with a vicious *smack*. Smiley's second henchman scurried around the boxcar and disappeared.

Slowly Burton got to his feet. He stood with his legs apart, the smoke still curling from his gun as he looked about him. The man in the red shirt lay in front of him, his fingers spasmodically digging at the ground, his wide hat crushed beneath him and a slowly spreading red stain dyeing the sandy ground under him.

"Any more?" rasped Burton as he scanned the crowd.

Those who had not scattered for shelter at the first intimation that a shooting was imminent gaped at Burton respectfully.

"God a'mighty," asked one man of his companion, "did yer see him draw ?"

"Sho' did," was the enthusiastic reply. "Chain lightnin' can't compare with it."

"Good fer you, Stranger," yelled a voice in the background. "That's one less murderer in Julesburg."

A man in shirt-sleeves, wearing a blacksmith's leather apron, strode up to Burton and spoke in an undertone.

"That was good shootin' and a good job," he said, "but take a chunk of well-meant advice and get the hell out of Julesburg as fast as a hoss can tote you !"

"Thanks, friend," the ex-Confederate said with a nod, "but I reckon I won't go till I'm ready—and I'm not ready just yet."

He reloaded his gun and turned his back on the still figure of the red-shirted killer. Then, with a long stride that set his *chivarros* to swinging, he set off among the vast heaps of supplies that were piled about the station, nourishment for the growing railroad.

"That was close," he muttered when he found himself alone. "It's open war now, anyway, and that's a help."

He knew that if he wanted to live a little longer he would have to get out of sight and stay out of sight until dark. With nightfall, he could carry on his campaign with less chance of being recognized. He paused in the shelter of a great timber yard composed of ties, bridge beams and telegraph poles, asking himself where he could find the hiding-place he needed within the next few minutes.

Smiley probably knew of the outcome of his frame-up by now and would be on the hunt for him. He briefly considered going to Jessica Valcour and then shook his head determinedly.

He edged out of the timber yard and looked down a street composed of stores, warehouses and dwellings, all uniformly crude and ugly. Was there something familiar about the façade of that warehouse marked 'L. M. Lytle. Grain and Hardware' ?

Knowing that every second was precious, Burton delved frantically into the recesses of his memory. Then he snapped his fingers. He remembered last having seen that warehouse on the morning of Colin MacKaye's death, when he had left the room of the girl—what was her name ? Jameson. Lulu Jameson. She had lived on the top floor of the building. He hesitated.

"Why in hell shouldn't she help me ?" he asked himself. "I gave her a necklace worth a fortune."

He wondered how the girl would receive him. If she were a common whore she probably would turn him over to Jack Smiley. He doubtless owned her as he did most of the other girls in town. Still, that was a chance that had to be taken. Behind him he heard a babble of voices that could mean only one thing—Smiley's men were on the hunt.

He drew a deep breath, glanced about him and saw that, except for a gang of negroes piling ties about fifty yards away, the scene was deserted. He darted across a stretch of dusty road, chickens clucking and squawking as they scuttled out of his way, and circled to the rear of the warehouse. He pushed open the back door.

Burton heard the sound of galloping hoofs and a deep voice bellowing, apparently addressing the negroes.

"Seen a cowboy in a black shirt?"

The ex-Confederate fairly threw himself up the narrow stairway that creaked dismally under his weight. On the top landing he rapped gently on the door in front of him.

CHAPTER XXIV

THERE was a moment of silence and then a quick light step sounded beyond the door. A bolt clacked as it slid into place.

"Who is it?" came the soft voice whose Southern accent told Burton that Lulu Jameson was on the other side of the crude pine plank door.

"This is Bob Burton," he called in a low tone. "Let me in quick, please. I'll explain——"

"Captain Burton! Oh!" the girl gasped. "Come in. Wait a minute."

The bolt slid back again and the door was flung open. The ex-Confederate slipped into the room and turned to close the door and throw the lock. Outside, he could hear the trampling of horses' hoofs and the approaching voices of riders. The horses thundered past and Burton straightened to look about him. He stared in surprise.

The room he had remembered had been a tawdry place. Now he saw that a remarkable alteration had been made during the four days since he had last been there. The walls were painted in a soft shade of grey-blue, and several prints, apparently cut from some old French book which had wandered to this crude outpost, were tacked on them. White curtains shaded the oiled paper windows and the room boasted a few new pieces of comfortable furniture.

The change in the room was insignificant compared with the change in Lulu Jameson, the dancehall girl. He looked down at her. She was clad in a simple dress of nile green silk with a small Paisley shawl gathered over her supple, white shoulders.

F

A quaint old cameo brooch secured the apex of the V formed
by her shawl. The girl's hair, as black as Burton's own, had been
drawn back in smooth, lustrous lines that framed her face perfectly.
What colour there was in Lulu's face was genuine now. No paint
marred features which, Burton realized, were singularly delicate.

"Why—why——" he cried. "You've sure changed, Miss
Jameson. I hardly know you."

"You've changed, too, Captain," the girl said breathlessly.
"But I—oh, I knew you'd come back even though Smiley's killers
bragged of hanging your friend and chasing you into the Cheyenne
country. And I'm glad you came back—I'm so very glad !"

"Mighty nice of you to say that," Burton said. Then, as he
realized that he still wore his sombrero, he whipped the wide-
brimmed hat from his head. "But I ought to warn you, ma'am.
I—well, I just killed one of Jack Smiley's men and they're after me.
Maybe I shouldn't have come here. I——"

"You can always come here," she said in a low voice. "I don't
care what you've done or who's after you !"

Before he could stop her, the girl caught up one of his big hands
and pressed it to her lips. Clinging to his fingers, she looked up
at Burton, tears glistening in her deep eyes.

"Oh, I've wanted so to thank you for—for delivering me from
—from——" her voice broke and she looked away.

"Forget it, ma'am," Burton said uncomfortably.

"I—I'll never forget it," the girl's voice was low but fierce.
"Never !"

She dabbed at her eyes with a scrap of muslin handkerchief and
attempted a smile as she looked up at him.

"That necklace you gave me—I—I tried to give it back to you
in the—the morning but you wouldn't listen."

He held up a hand to stop the flow of the girl's words, but she
rushed on.

"I—I used one of the emeralds t-to get a few little things for this
room and some clothes. And with what was left over I can live
for ever so long without going back to—to the Prairie Belle."

"I'm sure glad, ma'am," Burton said simply.

"The other jewels are here—hidden. I'll get them for you."

She started across the room and stopped at the ex-Confederate's
command.

"I'd be grateful," said Robert Burton, "if you'd keep the
emeralds. I've no use for them and if they've been a help to you
—well, it's probably the first time that necklace has helped anybody
instead of hurt them."

"I can't keep them," protested Lulu Jameson. "They're worth
a fortune."

"Well, then, suppose you just hold them for me," Burton

suggested. "No tellin' what'll happen to me and—well, I'd like for you to have 'em if something does happen."

She hesitated and then reluctantly agreed.

"But your ring," she said. "I found that on the floor. You'll want that."

"Yes, ma'am," Burton nodded. "I sure would like to have that back on my hand."

For some reason a comforting feeling flooded Burton as he slipped the heavy seal ring over his finger. Jessica Valcour's declaration of her love had stripped much of the bitter cynicism from the tall cavalry officer, and now this girl's revelation that she had kept his ring and necklace for him removed the last vestige.

"I sure thank you, Miss Jameson," he said. "It was mighty fine of you to safeguard these things for me."

Her eyes wavered under his gaze and she forced a wan smile.

"I reckon I'd better fix you something to eat," she said. "You —well, you look as if you've been having a pretty bad time."

He watched her as she donned a yellow gingham apron and vanished into a small room at the far end of her quarters. Burton walked over to peer into the cubicle and saw that a small coal-oil stove had been set into the tiny room. It was not long before the room was fragrant with the scent of coffee and frying ham.

Just how it happened, Burton never quite realized but, as the girl set about preparing the meal over his feeble protests, he found himself talking to her as though he had known her for years instead of having seen her just once before.

Swiftly, the ex-Confederate told the former dancehall girl of the furious procession of events that had followed his discovery of the tragedy in the cottonwood grove. He told her everything, sparing himself nothing—everything except of Jessica Valcour's declaration of love that night on the hill overlooking End o' Track.

The Jameson girl listened intently, offering a word of sympathy now and then and asking a few questions as she finished frying the ham, sliced a loaf and set two places for supper.

"How do you have your eggs, Captain?" she asked when the story reached its end.

"Over and over, Southern style," he grinned. For some reason, talking with this girl seemed to have lifted a weight from his shoulders. He was almost light-hearted as he stepped out of his flapping *chivarros* and slapped the dust from his shirt.

"'Pears like I've forgotten what soap and water smells like," he hinted as the Jameson girl emerged from the alcove carrying two smoking plates of ham and eggs.

"You'll find a washstand behind that curtain," she said. "There's all the soap and water you can use."

The soldier of fortune was puffing, blowing and splashing happily

when the quick tramp of heavy feet sounded on the stairs outside.
In an instant, Burton had whipped out his revolver and was wiping
the soapy water from his eyes with a towel as he turned toward the
door. Those negroes, then, had seen him cross the road and slip
into the warehouse.

"Stay where you are !" Lulu whispered. "Stay behind that
curtain !"

There was a thunderous knock on the door and a hoarse voice
called out.

"C'mon, Lulu !" a man yelled. "Open up !"

"What do you want ?" asked the girl, her voice shrill with
feigned annoyance.

"Open up !"

The pounding came again, making the door rattle. Burton
silently slid the long knife from its sheath.

"You can't come in," Lulu called.

"The hell you say ! This is Comanche Ted on Jack Smiley's
business !"

To Burton's ears came the sound of snapping clasps, the rustle
of silk. The girl's voice, when she spoke, was different than it
had been. It was insinuating with a voluptuous lilt to it.

"Oh, why didn't you say it was you, darlin' ?" Lulu called.
"What can I do for you, Ted ?"

"Open up. We're lookin' fer an *hombre* the boss wants to see."

"He's not here, Ted," Lulu called.

"Aw, make the goddam little tramp open up," somebody growled
from beyond the door. There was more pounding and Burton levelled
his Colt. He peered around the curtain and gaped at what he saw.

Lulu Jameson had slipped out of her dress. Now she stood in a
short white undergarment that came to the knees of her slender
immature legs. As he watched, he saw Lulu pull down one of the
shoulder straps of the low-necked garment so that her breasts were
all but bared. One hand reached up to disarrange her hair, tousling
it recklessly.

She turned, saw him watching her and made a furious gesture
that made him drop the curtain. He heard her footsteps cross to
the door and groaned as the bolt was snapped back. By the creak
of hinges, Burton could tell that she opened the door only a crack.

"Goodness' sake, Ted," he heard her say, "you sure don't care
how you come breakin' into a lady's privacy, do you ?"

"Lady, huh," Burton heard a man roar. "That's purty good."

"Say," another voice put in, "you look all right to me, Lulu.
How about me comin' in and settin' a spell with you, huh ?"

Lulu gave a low giggle and Burton, his teeth clamped over his
lower lip, heard the sound of a soft playful slap.

"You stop ticklin' me, Ted," the girl murmured. "I'm busy

right now with—with another gentleman. You come back later, if you've a mind to."

"Hell, no harm in havin' a quick feel is there ?" a man guffawed. "Your customer ain't that stingy, is he ?"

"Say, wait a minute," said one of the men on a sudden note. "I thought I heard tell over at the Prairie Belle that you'd quit the business, got religion or somethin'."

Lulu Jameson's laugh was hard and brittle.

"For the Lord's sake," she grated, "a girl's gotta eat, don't she ? There ain't no fun to starvin' to death with a prayer book in your hand."

There was a mumbling at the door and then Comanche Ted grumbled.

"Well, we got to find this *hombre*, that Jack wants and we won't do it standin' here gabbin' with this floozie. You seen a cowboy in a black shirt, Lulu ?"

She laughed that metallic laugh again.

"I've been busy lately," she said. "I haven't had any time to be lookin' for a cowboy in a black shirt. I had other things to do."

There was another guffaw from the men at the door, some more mumbling talk. Burton relaxed as he heard the door close and the bolt drive home. He stepped around the corner of the curtain to find Lulu Jameson leaning against the door, her head bowed on one arm and her bare shoulders trembling uncontrollably.

Softly he walked up behind her and put an arm about her.

"It was grand," he whispered. "I want you to know I realize what you did and—and I'm mighty grateful."

She looked up at him, tears staining her face.

"I—I was terrified that they'd break in," she whimpered. "That was the only way I could stop them."

Her eyes dropped and Burton became cognisant of the near nudity of the girl he held in his arm. His face flushed and he stepped quickly behind the curtain. Again he heard the whisper of silk and the snapping of clasps and catches. When she called he emerged and found her as she had been when the footsteps first had sounded on the stairs. She met his eyes with a faltering smile.

"I'm afraid our supper's cold," she managed. "I'll put the coffee back on."

Later, when not a scrap of food remained on his plate, the ex-Confederate leaned back in his chair and sighed gustily.

"You sure know how to fill a man up," he said. "That's the best meal I've had in years, seems like."

He dug into a shirt pocket and produced a pipe, then pulled out the long knife and began shredding tobacco from a plug. The golden wolf's head tang glowed like molten ore in the light from a kerosene lamp in the centre of the table.

"Where did you get that?" the girl asked, once the pipe was lit. Burton looked down at the knife affectionately.

"My Dad took it from a 'Pache he killed in Nevada, back in '44," he explained. "He was on Fremont's Expedition. I reckon it was Spanish made."

He handed the long blade to the girl and watched her turn the steel shaft in her small hands.

"This wolf must have seen some interesting sights," she said when she handed back the blade.

"I reckon so. Dad carried it down to Mexico City in '48 and then in Kansas until John Brown's men shot him in the back durin' the Wakarusa War in '56."

"That was a horrible business," Lulu said gravely. "Why must humans always kill each other? You carried it all through the war?"

Haloed with clouds of the blue smoke, Burton nodded reminiscently.

"Yep," he said. "It came in handy now and then. Dad taught me to throw it Mexican fashion. 'Long Knife' has been my Indian name for years."

He glanced curiously at her.

"Maybe it's none of my business, ma'am, and you don't have to answer unless you want to. But Lulu Jameson isn't your right name, is it?"

The girl's eyelids fluttered downward as she shook her head slowly.

"Nobody will ever know my family name, Captain. But I'll tell you my given name. It's Lucinda. Would you please call me that?"

"I'll never call you anything else," he replied smiling. "What do you plan to do, Lucinda?"

Her slim fingers suddenly busied themselves with the hem of a red and white checkered napkin.

"I—I haven't made up my mind," she faltered.

"Going back east, maybe?"

"No. Probably west to—to California where no one knows me."

The long-legged cavalry captain drew on his pipe, sending a series of fragrant, grey-blue cloudlets drifting lazily toward the ceiling.

"I suppose it was a question of the war with you, too?" he suggested.

Lucinda bent lower over the napkin and a flat quality tinged her voice.

"Yes. Back in '61 Father had a prosperous little plantation on the Mississippi. He grew cotton, like everybody else. Then the war came and—and our plantation was between the lines during three campaigns. First one side and then the other requisitioned or looted our property. My two brothers died at Shiloh and Father was killed a little later. My mother didn't wait long to follow the three of them."

The girl's slender shoulders rose in a half shrug.

"Of course by '64 there was nothing left on the plantation," she continued. "The slaves had gone and before they left they set fire to the gin and the barns. I tried to get in a little crop but I couldn't. Things went from bad to worse."

"But you must have had some relations," Burton put in.

"No," she said, shaking her head. "Father was English and he was the only one of his family to come over here. Mother had no relatives that I ever heard of. So, you see, I was all alone."

Burton glanced at the oiled paper windows and realized with a start that it was dark outside. He sprang from his chair and began pacing up and down the room. Then he turned to the girl.

"Lucinda," he said. "I'm in a predicament. I—I've got to meet a certain person as soon as possible and I can't go through town in these clothes."

"I—I could carry a message," the girl suggested. Burton shook his head.

"It's—it's something I have to do myself," he told her. "You see, the person I've got to meet is—is a girl."

"A girl!" It was almost a broken cry.

"Yes," Burton said, plunging on. "Her name is Valcour—Jessica Valcour."

So absorbed was he with his own problem that he did not see Lucinda's shoulders droop, weariness creep into her face. With an effort the girl straightened in her chair.

"I see," she said, her voice jerky. "I—I hope Miss Valcour is everything you want her to be."

"She is," Burton replied. "She—she's wonderful. And so you see why I've *got* to get to her house and see her to-night. She's got to realize that I'm not giving up the fight."

"But how can you get there? You can't go out like this. Smiley's killers wouldn't let you get a hundred yards."

"Reckon I'll just have to risk it or try to get hold of another disguise of some kind."

The room was silent for a while. It was Lucinda who spoke first, forcing a stiff smile.

"I've got an idea, Captain. A discharged soldier who lived next door got shot in a saloon fight last week. Maybe I could get some of his things for you."

Burton shook his head.

"You can't get mixed up any more in this business," he protested. "You've done enough already. I can't have you riskin'——"

"Oh, hush up!" Before Burton could move, the girl had thrown the bolt and darted out of the door.

CHAPTER XXV

LIGHTS were glowing in all of Julesburg's windows and a deep-chested song was roaring from the immigrant train corralled across the river when a tall corporal stepped out of the back door of L. M. Lytle's Grain and Hardware Warehouse.

The soldier swung his yellow-striped legs in the swaggering, slightly bow-legged stride of a veteran cavalryman. His black felt hat, showing at its front a brass device of crossed sabres, was pulled low over his eyes. Apparently, the corporal was suffering from a toothache. He wore a blue bandana handkerchief tied about his swollen jaws.

The 'corporal' was Captain Robert Burton, the uniform he wore was the one procured by Lucinda Jameson and the 'toothache' was produced by half an apple held in Burton's cheek.

Heart in his mouth and pistol hand tensed, the ex-Confederate swung along the rutted road leading to the railroad depot. The street was comparatively deserted at this, the supper hour, and Burton knew that he would make an easy target for any of Smiley's henchmen who might pierce his disguise.

His eyes picked out three sinister figures who stood among the shadows and carefully examined all passers-by. As Burton drew near the trio, a cowboy ahead of him, wearing leather *chivarros*, was halted by the three burly gunmen and, despite his sulphurous protests, was dragged over to a lighted window.

"Naw, it ain't him," growled the leader of the party. "Don't look nothin' like this here Jed Smith. But the *hombre* ain't left town, that's certain, and if he's in Julesburg we'll git him."

The trio looked across the road at Burton.

"Jest a minute, soljer!" the leader ordered. The three crossed the road and confronted the ex-Confederate.

"Wha's matter?" Burton mumbled. He braced himself for action as he recognized Comanche Ted, the yellow-shirted gunman who had led the searching party to Lucinda's room.

"Seen a cowpuncher in leather chaps and black shirt, Corp'ral?" the burly killer asked.

"Naw. Been nursin' this cursed tooth. On my way to git her yanked now. One side, for the luvva God before I go crazy with the pain!"

Boldly, he elbowed aside the searchers and tramped on, his heart thudding like a tom-tom. Curses followed him but that was all. The bluff had worked.

A drunken Indian was screeching like a plucked jay somewhere on the outskirts of Julesburg when Burton quietly entered the back yard of a house in the window of which stood Jessica Valcour.

The thought that he was going to see her again sent a tingling to his fingertips.

He grinned with satisfaction that the yard boasted a high board fence. The body of a broken down stagecoach, for some reason left in the corner of the yard, offered an ideal place for a rendezvous.

He marched to the back door, the bandana removed, and knocked.

"A note from the Fort for Miss Valcour," he snapped, his salute correctly jaunty to the delight of the freckled, pug-nosed Irish maid who had answered his knock. "I'm to wait for an answer."

"Faith, Miss Valcour's at dinner," the girl replied. "Yez'll have to wait a bit. Will yez come into the kitchen, Sarjunt? There's mince pie to-night."

"Thank ye kindly, dearie," Burton said, "but ye're to give her this note immejiately."

He pinched the servant girl's plump thigh in the best non-commissioned officer's manner and the girl shied away, giggling.

"Run along now, Norah—or is it Katie?—and give it to the lady," Burton said. "Another time and I won't be in such a hurry. I'll take yere pie then and mebbe somethin' else along with it—if ye've still got it."

He dodged the girl's playful slap and watched her walk into the house. He wondered if Jessica could keep her face emotionless when she read the brief message:

'Am outside. Must see you at once.

Devotedly,
Bob.'

It was some twenty minutes later when the back door opened to briefly flood the back yard with light, picking out the yellow chevrons of the tall corporal who stood in the shadow of the dismantled stagecoach.

She hurried across the yard to him and her hands clutched at his shoulders as he drew her close. For a moment both were silent as he inhaled the soft fragrance of her, glorying in her nearness.

"Bob, oh Bob!" she murmured. "You shouldn't have come here. I—I've been terrified for you ever since this morning. You know Smiley has sworn to kill you."

He laughed light-heartedly. With Jessica in his arms Boot Hill Jack Smiley seemed very far away.

"Swearin' is cheap, darlin'," he said. "Now hop into the coach there, out of sight."

He felt her trembling as he helped her into the musty coach and sat down on the creaking seat beside her. His mouth searched for hers in the darkness and his brain made a dizzy whirl as he felt the ardour of her kiss. When the embrace ended, she leaned back and looked up at him.

"Bob," she said softly, "why are you in Julesburg? You can't accomplish anything here—or can you?"

"With luck," Burton said fiercely, "I can. I've got to, Jessica!"

"But how?" she countered. "Smiley has ordered you shot on sight. Father despises you. General Casement thinks you turned traitor."

"And you?" he asked.

"I—I think you've made a brave fight—and lost, Bob," she said slowly. "It stands to reason you can't beat Smiley and all the others single-handed."

"But, Jessica," he insisted earnestly, "I'm going on. I've got a plan that stands a good chance of working right. I've found some code messages I'm going to have deciphered somehow. They're bound to help."

"Code messages?" she asked. "Don't count too much on them. They're quite common. Even Papa uses one for private business. But, Bob, how can you beat Smiley? He must have over a hundred men in his pay and you're alone."

He shrugged his shoulders in the gloom.

"If I can get Smiley," he said, "his gang will break up. And I've got to get Smiley. Nothin' can stop me from that."

He pulled her to him again and kissed her. When he let her go, her hands went up to her hair in little patting gestures.

"What is this plan of yours, Bob?" she asked.

"Can't tell you, darlin'," he said, "till every last detail is worked out."

He felt her stiffen in resentment for a second and then relax.

"I understand," she murmured. "Is there any way I can help? I'd have to be careful, though. Papa is very bitter against you. I can't understand just why he should feel so strongly."

"We'll soon be showin' your father he's wrong about me," Burton predicted confidently. "Your father is in General Casement's confidence. I'd like to know more about that pay shipment, if you know anything."

He saw the gleam of her eyes in the semi-darkness as she looked up at him.

"You mean the gold shipment?" she asked. "The money to pay the labourers?"

He nodded sharply.

"The whole struggle, dear, is going to hinge on that gold, if I'm reckonin' right. Around the railroad depot this morning I heard a lot of grumblin' about the overdue pay. Not ordinary grumblin', either, but dangerous talk about strikes and riots. The situation is a lot worse than even Dodge or Casement realize. If anything happened to that gold there'd be trouble—big trouble !"

"I see," Jessica Valcour said softly. "It so happens, Bob, that I can help you. This afternoon I rode with Papa to End o' Track and I heard General Casement say that the gold had already been shipped from Omaha."

"Already !"

"Yes. Casement said it's due to be in Julesburg around six to-morrow morning."

"Six ? Are you sure ? There's no train scheduled at that time."

"General Dodge has secretly arranged for a special train because he wants the money transported at night and to run through Julesburg about the time when there's nobody around. He thinks it's safer that way."

Her clenched hands beat her knees softly.

"I don't know why," she continued uncertainly, "but I'm afraid—I've a feeling that the money will never get there. It's silly, probably, but—oh ! why did Papa put all our money in a gamble like this awful railroad ?"

"Six o'clock, eh ?" Burton said slowly.

"Why do you say it like that ?" Jessica demanded abruptly. An indefinable chill seemed to pass through the old coach.

"I just wanted to be sure, dear."

Her hand clutched at his wrist.

"Oh, Bob, for heaven's sake don't make any mistakes this time," she implored. "Remember how much it means to me—to all of us. Papa actually telegraphed to Mr. Ames that the fate of the Union Pacific depended on that gold shipment. Oh, Bob, nothing must prevent it from getting to End o' Track to-morrow !"

"It'll get there," said Burton from between tight lips, "or I'll die tryin' to see it's delivered."

Her kiss came to him then, and Burton revelled in the satin warmth of the lips she raised. His arms grasped her so tightly that she cried out.

"Good-bye, Bob, dear," she whispered when he let her go. "I've got to go back to the house. Papa will be missing me. I'll see you again—soon ?"

"To-morrow, Jessica, when the gold is delivered and—and a certain other matter has been settled."

"Good-bye, dear."

She was gone with a silken whisper of skirts. Burton saw her briefly silhouetted against the light of the kitchen door and then all was dark again. Heaving a short sigh, the ex-Confederate put the half apple back in his mouth, retied the bandana about his jaws and jammed his black cavalry hat low on his head. When he quit the old coach his step was springy and his heart high with the realization that Jessica Valcour really loved him. Had not her trust in him been proved by her willingness to tell him about the gold?

Plunged deep in thought concerning his next moves, Burton made his way down the memory-haunted road that led to the cottonwoods. He wondered whether Tex Kildare and Paulus Stattler would show up, whether either had been recognized during Smiley's furious search of the town.

Absently, he glanced at the River Platte, so accurately described by Washington Irving as 'the most magnificent and the most useless of streams,' that same river which Bill Nye had epitomized as 'having a wide circulation but little influence.'

Out over the prairie rang the roar of Julesburg, the town's wild night-life now in full stride. Burton could hear the squeaking of fiddles, blasts of tinny piano music, shouts and, every once in a while, the exuberant shot of some bull-whacker on a spree. Almost before he realized it, tall cottonwoods loomed blackly ahead. A cold fist seemed to squeeze Robert Burton's heart as he remembered Colin MacKaye and the fate he had met amid those cottonwoods.

The soldier of fortune discovered the German Mormon, Stattler, sitting all unsuspecting on the bole of a fallen tree. Burton muttered a curse as he stole up behind the German. The big immigrant made an inviting target, sitting in the open like that, for any stray brave anxious to lift an easy scalp.

"*Ach*, Bob," said Stattler. "I am glad you haff come. It iss so *dunkel*, so lonely, here. Only Anna I can think of in her grave out there somewhere."

Burton dropped a hand to the big Mormon's shoulder.

"Cheer up," he counselled. "I reckon before long you'll have a chance to square accounts."

"So? Dot iss good news, *lieber Freund!*"

"Find out anything at the railroad yard?"

"*Ja*," Stattler said in a hoarse whisper as he leaned closer to Burton. "Two men all day the vorkers vere telling they vould never get paid, that they are fools to go on vorking for no'tings."

"Hear anything about a special train, Paulus?"

"A special train? *Nein.* But MacCue, the Traffic Manager, and some guards east on the six-thirty vent."

The muffled sound of a horse being ridden at a cautious walk sent Burton into the shadows, pulling Stattler after him. They crouched as the rider approached. Burton let out his breath as he recognized Kildare.

"Tex!" he called softly.

"Okay, Bob," the rider called back as he swung off his horse. "Seen you two minutes back. Got some news, *amigo*. Reckon it's good."

"Smiley take you on?"

The Texan chuckled grimly.

"Sho, nuff. He's payin' me a thousand pesos a month."

"A thousand !"

Kildare's teeth gleamed briefly.

"Sho'," he said. "He started lower but when I split the ace o' spades, edge on, with one o' the Twins and allowed his *hombres* hadn't done so good to-day, Boot Hill Jack ponied up *pronto*."

Excitement sent the blood pounding through Burton's head. Thus far his campaign had proceeded auspiciously—almost too well, he suspected.

"And say, Bob," Tex was saying, "it sho' burned up old Smiley when you drilled that feller he sent to cancel you—man by the name of Turkey Jones. Wish I could have seen you in action."

"It wasn't anythin'," Burton said abstractedly. "You could have beat him left-handed and rheumatic."

Crouched in the shadows of the cottonwoods, Burton told his two companions of what he had learned that day, of the code telegram and the secret of the gold special. When he had finished, Kildare slapped his hip and chuckled.

"So *that's* it !" he said.

"That's what ?" asked Burton.

In the starlight Kildare grinned widely.

"Nothin' much, pardner. Only Boot Hill Jack says fer me to git set fer some big doin' around three o'clock to-morrow mornin'. Later I heard he's been studyin' the fair face of nature around the old stage station at Diamond Springs. O'Gorman, his Number One man, allows to me it's to be a big hold-up."

"Is Diamond Springs on the railroad ?" snapped the soldier of fortune.

"*Ja*," Stattler put in. "Only twenty-nine miles from here it iss. By the roundhouse I vass at a map looking."

"Did Smiley say anythin' else ?" Burton demanded of the Texan.

"Not much. Jest that fifteen o' his toughest, hardest shootin' *malvados* is to be on hand with a spring cart and a pair of fast hosses. And—oh yes—he also allowed as how he'd personally drill whoever opened his yap about this little *pasear*."

"I wonder," said Burton slowly, "just how Smiley found out about that gold special ?"

"*Hombre*," drawled Kildare, "you shore got a gift fer askin' tough questions."

"Those code messages might tell us but I reckon they'll have to wait," Burton said, thinking aloud. "So it's a train hold-up. It's a neat idea. Plenty of gold for Boot Hill Jack and his boss—whoever he is—and an obituary notice for the U.P."

"What are you fixin' to do about it ?"

For a second, the man in the blue corporal's uniform hesitated, softly beating the knuckles of his right hand against the palm of his left. Then he snapped his fingers.

"Reckon I'll ride out to End o' Track and have a little confab with Frank North."

"No need to," Kildare said. He got up and walked to his horse to pull something from a saddle-bag. "I saw North in town jest as I was leavin'. Hyer. He gave me this fer you. Allowed you set a store by it."

Kildare passed over the ornate steel and gold spur Burton had first found beneath the burning bridge at Buffalo Creek. Eagerly Burton's fingers closed on the cold metal and he studied it in the semi-darkness.

"Where'd he find it?" he asked.

"Funny thing, Bob," drawled the Texan. "He found that in a pile o' ties near Jack Casement's car. One of the Pawnees saw it and turned it over to him."

"That's odd," mused Burton. "I thought General Dodge took that spur away with him. How late is North stayin' in town?"

"Till near midnight. He's interpretin' at an Injun trial over at the Fort. But you ain't goin' back to Julesburg to-night!"

"I am."

"Wal, don't!" urged the Texan. "Boot Hill Jack's sworn to wear yore ears on his watch chain on account o' you goin' through his telegrams. He's l'arned about that cypher message you found on the renegade, too. Every roughneck in Julesburg's got an eye out fer you. And remember, yore luck cain't hold ferever."

Silence descended and the noise of Kildare's broncho munching contentedly at the dewy grass came loudly to the ears of the three men. Then Burton drew himself erect, his dark eyes gleaming.

"I've got an idea," he announced, "and I've got to see North to-night. Tex, you'd better stick along with Smiley, but I'll need Stattler."

"What air you fixin' to do?" Kildare demanded.

"Plenty, if Smiley intends to do what I think he does. I'll tell you my idea on the way to town."

"Yo're a fool to go there," Kildare grumbled. "You'll last about as long as a quart o' likker at a Texas weddin' if anybody spots you."

CHAPTER XXVI

HER dirty yellow special flags snapping in the stiff, pre-dawn breeze, a locomotive came roaring up to a sharp curve at the end of a straight stretch some five miles east of Diamond Springs. Like bright, speed-crazed fireflies sparks whirled up out of the engine's funnel to go streaking out over the prairie or fall to oblivion in the turgid Platte.

Clanking rhythmically, Engine Number 54's six-foot driving wheels were taking hold of the beginning of the curve when a plume of steam shot skyward suddenly. The locomotive's whistle broke into a desperate, breathless screaming for brakes and Number 54 came to a groaning, chattering halt, her long and pointed cowcatcher not twenty feet from three ties firmly lashed across the right-of-way. From the top of the pile fluttered a bright red flag.

"Back her, Bill, for God's sake ! Back !" panted the fireman as he scrambled to his feet. "The goddam Injuns have blocked us !"

Cursing, the walrus-moustached engineer started to reverse, then dropped his hand from the throttle with a whistling gasp of surprise. From a gulch behind the train came half a dozen men in dark clothes, carrying more ties, their faces masked by blue handkerchiefs.

"So help me God !" yelled the engineer. "Them ain't no redskins at all. It's road agents !"

He reached for one of the two Remington rifles in the engine's cab.

"To hell with that," snapped the fireman. "They's plenty of guards in the wagon. Let them do the fightin'. They're paid fer it."

The two enginemen watched, wide-eyed, as the bandits flung more ties across the tracks.

"God, Bill, there's a raft of them. Fifty or a hundred, maybe."

"Yeah," said the engineer, "and we can't do nothin' more. It looks like there'll be some hot shootin' around here in a minute so it's me fer the timber."

Rifle in hand, the engineer crawled into the tender and burrowed down into the fuel logs. The fireman was not long in following suit. Number 54 was left untended to pant wearily, wasting her steam on the morning air.

On a ring of buttes almost completely surrounding the helpless train appeared a line of broad hats and gleaming rifle barrels. Sight of this small army brought a clamour of noise from the treasure car coupled on behind the engine.

"Funny them guards don't start shootin'," mumbled the engineer. "They ought to have cut loose by now."

"Yeah," the fireman agreed. "Damned funny they don't shoot. They can't hardly git hurt behind all them beams and sandbags."

Still the strange silence persisted. Then, an outlaw on the highest butte stood up to wave a white rag tied to a rifle barrel. Two more appeared, carrying small wooden barrels such as contain blasting powder. The noise in the treasure car grew louder.

"Fer Gawd's sake, don't shoot," McCue was urging the guards who were lined up at loopholes let through the car's double body.

"Why the hell not?" roared a guard. "This here car's bullet proof."

"Yeah," squealed McCue, "but it ain't powder proof! Look at them barrels! We're helpless. They can blow us to hell!"

"Why, you yellow dog," said the guard. "I believe you're——"

That was as far as he got. Another guard felled the belligerent one with a clubbed revolver, saying:

"I know when I'm licked, and I've got kids at home."

McCue grabbed up a handkerchief and waved it through a loophole as the guards crouched to peer out at the bandits.

"This shore is a reg'lar job," said one. "Wonder who's the big blackguard in the yaller shirt and the red wipe acrost his face?"

The yellow-shirted outlaw, obviously the leader of the gang, cupped his hands and shouted through his makeshift mask.

"We want that money!" he bawled. "We aim t'git it, too. Now do we blow you to hell or do you hand it over, sensible-like?"

He made a commanding figure, that yellow-shirted man with the scarlet handkerchief mask. He stood at the top of the butte, rifle in hand, directing the movements of men whose hats and heads peered up over the rim of the bluff.

"Come on down," yelled McCue. "We ain't goin' to fight when it ain't no use."

The outlaw chief and a group of bow-legged henchmen scrambled down the slope of the butte and approached the train.

"Open up that door," snapped the man in the yellow shirt, "or we'll cut loose with the blastin' powder."

Six gangling, masked outlaws, all carrying rifles, moved up to the door of the treasure car as it opened. Three of the bandits, led by the yellow-shirted man, swung up into the car. McCue gaped and stepped back.

"Hey, Ted!" he muttered in an undertone. "Don't come in here!"

His jaw dropped as he saw a .44 Colt's muzzle swing in his direction. He backed away, a puzzled expression on his face.

"Hands up and keep 'em up," snarled the yellow-shirted outlaw.

"Say, what *is* this?" McCue stuttered. "My God, fellers—say —what—who——"

"This hyer's a hold-up," grated Yellow Shirt. "It'll be a funeral if you don't stand still and shut up. Unlock that chain or we'll blow it loose and the bunch of you to hell with it!"

McCue, his hands shaking, his face chalk white, pulled out a key and, stooping, unlocked a heavy chain that held a large, iron-bound chest to the side of the car.

"By God," quavered the Traffic Manager as he watched the chest being trundled to the door, "you'll be sorry fer this. You'll hang for this, you goddam thieves. You'll wish you'd never been born!"

McCue kept his eyes fixed on the man in the yellow shirt as the bandits toppled the treasure chest out into the right-of-way. The weight of the chest half buried the strongbox in the sandy soil. All the weapons in the car followed. Yellow Shirt nodded and the bandits scrambled down out of the car. The leader turned to McCue, chuckling behind his mask.

"Well, McCue," he said, "you can tell your pals down the line that you were a great help. So long."

As Yellow Shirt turned toward the doorway, McCue, with a courage born of desperation, snatched at the outlaw's red bandana mask. His fingers caught it and jerked the cloth downward for a split second before the outlaw's fist lashed out and knocked the Traffic Manager spinning across the car.

McCue lay glaring up at the tall man in the yellow shirt.

"Burton, by God!" he gasped. "I always thought you was crooked. I'll shore fill yore hide full o' lead fer this."

Calmly, the ex-Confederate readjusted his mask.

"Stow that talk, you snivellin' pup," he said. "You had your chance to fight just a little while back. Funny you didn't take it up. Wouldn't have been any trick at all to have held out until Number 9 showed up."

"Just lemme get my gun!" snarled McCue.

"All full of fight now, aren't you?" mocked Burton. "Five minutes ago you were mighty scared. Certainly is funny. Or maybe it's not so funny, at that."

He turned his back on McCue and jumped down to the ground. His sharp commands sent some of his companions running up the track to tear away the ties that blocked the rails. That done, the masked men started toward the top of the butte. Burton walked up to the engine and looked up to see the engineer's grimy face peering at him from over the side of the tender.

"Get out of here," Burton ordered. "Make it fast."

"Yessir," said the engineer. "Come on, Hank."

The steam that had been jetting from the escape valve was closed off and a herd of buffaloes that had come down to the water on the far bank of the Platte snorted and galloped off as the engineer threw open the throttle. His yank was so violent that Number 54's driving wheels raced furiously for a time before, as the throttle was closed, the wheels caught and the little train began to move. It gathered speed swiftly and clattered away.

Just as the treasure train clanked through the western edge of the outlaw ring, someone in the looted car opened fire with a gun he must have hidden well. One of the raiders, halfway up the butte slope, pitched forward on the hard-baked earth. Instantly a howl of rage came from the butte tops and a furious volley crackled out. Splinters kicked out of the side of the treasure car and Burton saw the head and shoulders of a man pitch forward out of the open door. He breathed more easily when he saw the stricken man caught by his comrades and pulled back into the train as it rounded the curve toward Diamond Springs.

Burton bent over the wounded masked man. The handkerchief stripped from his face revealed a Pawnee in white man's clothing. The Indian was not badly hurt. A bullet had creased his scalp but, as Dog Soldier Nick pointed out, it "would still look good some day on a Cheyenne's lance."

"Buffalo Caller is glad," grunted the Pawnee, "that my brother is not hurt bad. *Pa-ni Leshar* would be angry if he was. Did all go well, oh Long Knife?"

"Very well," Burton replied. He grinned as he watched the six Pawnees hurriedly strip off the binding white man's clothes which Major North had miraculously produced from some mysterious source. On all sides, other brown-faced warriors who had remained half concealed on the butte tops were pulling off the felt hats which had disguised them as white bandits.

"My brothers did well," said the ex-Confederate, "but I wish that guard hadn't been hit."

"Hell," said Dog Soldier Nick, "ye cain't get the yolk outen an aig without breakin' the shell. Ye were right, Bob. The train guards didn't fight but I'm damned if I see why they didn't."

"It's a long story," Burton said. "Wish you could have seen McCue's face when he finally saw he'd surrendered to the wrong outfit. Come on. Let's get goin'."

"Buffalo Caller!" Nick hollered. "Jest you yelp up the ponies."

Buffalo Caller threw back his narrow head and sent out the long, wolf-like rallying call of the Pawnees. Immediately other scouts, gaudy in their regalia, appeared galloping out of an *arroyo*, leading a herd of horses. Lit by the newly risen sun, the warriors made an unforgettable picture as they thundered up to the detachment gathered about the treasure chest.

Some of the Indians wore buffalo horns and the skinned heads of animals for their headdresses. Others sported clumps of scarlet-tipped *coup* feathers twisted into their oily black locks. A few sub-chiefs boasted gorgeous war bonnets which sprouted as many as sixty nodding eagle feathers. Shaking their rifles over their heads and brandishing their lances, they pulled up at the railroad and began to raise a chant of victory.

"Let 'em celebrate later," Burton yelled. "We've got to get out of here quick. Every second counts."

Grunting and straining, half a dozen jet-eyed young braves lugged the treasure chest up the bluffs and across several gulches. Here a strong horse kicked and squealed between the shafts of a *travois*, that Indian carrier consisting of two long poles lashed to the pony on either side and connected at the far end by two strong crosspieces and a wide strip of rawhide.

"Get goin'," Dog Soldier Nick urged. "I got to get these bucks away from here. It'll cost North his commission if these doin's is found out."

"Sure the Pawnees won't talk ?" asked Burton.

"Hell, no. They'd liefer die at the stake. Orders mean orders in the Pawnee Scouts."

The soldier of fortune superintended the lashing of the chest on the *travois*, securing the heavy burden with rawhide thongs. By the time the chest was fixed, the Pawnee Scouts were forming up in a loose column behind Nick.

"So long, pardner !" yelled the frontiersman as he kicked his pony into action. "We're crossin' the Platte to lose our trail among the buffler herds. That *travois* will get ye to the waggin. *A Li-hit I-ra-ni !* Ride, my brothers !"

He waved a fringed arm and the whole Pawnee detachment raised a wild cry and raced away. It plunged down the bluff and, in a brief moment, was lost amid a whirling cloud of yellow dust that now and then yielded the flash of a painted shield or the glint of a long gun barrel.

Captain Robert Burton wasted no time in catching the lead rein of the *travois* pony and setting off in the opposite direction. Beyond that line of barren hills on the horizon, Paulus Stattler should be waiting to receive the precious cargo.

As the carrier moved off with the trailers scraping loudly, the bronzed man in the yellow shirt—the shirt that had been so faithfully patterned after Comanche Ted's—wondered what happened at Diamond Springs when Smiley's raiders stopped the gold special for the second time.

"I reckon," he said aloud, "that there was some plain and fancy cussin' there for a minute."

CHAPTER XXVII

PAULUS STATTLER grunted and slapped his reins loudly across the rumps of the team.

"Ve are now better time making. Dot iss goot."

"Yes," said Burton, "but keep those nags movin'. Our real danger is still ahead of us. Smiley will know what happened by now and he won't be sittin' still long. Damn shame that McCue recognized me."

"*Ja.* Dot vuss bad, *mein Freund.* But vunce de money iss at End o' Track he vill haff nodings to say."

The two men, dusty and thirsty, were jolting and swaying on the spring seat of a light, strong buckboard borrowed by Major North from a rancher by the name of Morrow. Drawing the wagon was a pair of spirited half-bred bays reputed to be stronger than the best team that ever had belonged to Ben Holladay's Overland Stage line. Morrow was not one to lend his prize team to everyone. It had been Frank North's quiet word that had brought instant permission.

Burton glanced over his shoulder to watch the black dots which represented the Pawnees who had waited with Stattler to help load the treasure chest and lead the *travois* pony to some hiding place nearby. As the ex-Confederate looked, the dots disappeared over a rise and the buckboard was alone, a tiny speck of life on the face of the vast, dun-coloured prairie.

The prairie was level at this point and the sun-baked earth slid easily under the narrow spoked wheels. At the end of two hours' travel, the sand hills to the north of Julesburg were visible, glimmering far off on the southern horizon.

Sitting on the swaying driver's seat under the warming sun, Robert Burton felt his worries fading. Judging by the position of the sun, he estimated the time at past noon. Another three hours should bring them to End o' Track.

He tried to picture the fury and consternation now raging in Casement's headquarters car. McCue, he knew, would be making a grand story of it, spitting lies as fast as he could move his lips. Senator Valcour would be trembling for his investments and Colonel Barry's cavalry would be combing the south banks of the Platte.

He knew there were bound to be some ticklish moments when he first drove into End o' Track and he knew, too, that the risk had to be run. He only hoped that some of Barry's troopers would not shoot first and ask questions later.

Automatically, he reined aside to avoid a prairie dog village. Stattler, beside him, was like a graven image, rifle across his knees, scanning the horizon.

Burton thought of Jessica Valcour. To-night he hoped to be able to go to her openly, vindicated in the eyes of the world as well as in her own lovely ones. He planned to hunt up Lucinda Jameson, too. There had been no time to thank her properly for what she had done for him.

Lucinda—that was a pretty name, he thought, and she had proved to be a fine friend. Yes, he would have to hunt her up and make certain that she was provided for. He would help her get to California, if that was where she wanted to go.

He touched up the bays for a quarter hour's trotting. The iron wheel tyres were rattling on some gravel when the German Mormon stiffened, clutched his rifle and pointed toward the south. Burton's eyes squinted as he looked. Still far away but plainly discernible were riders, quirting their horses as they galloped in the direction of the buckboard!

"The hell!" Burton swore. "Four of 'em and headin' out from Julesburg!"

He turned to look at the treasure chest and saw that the lashings still were tight. Then he gathered up the reins.

"Well, Paulus," he said calmly, "looks like we're in for a damned close race. Hang on and we'll see how fast these bays can travel to shelter of some kind."

Bracing his legs against the dashboard and brake lever, the ex-Confederate leaned forward and cracked his whip over the dusty backs of the half-breds. Startled, the bays hesitated an instant, then lunged forward into a gallop that sent the landscape careening dizzily past.

Alternately praying and cursing, Paulus Stattler clung to the side of the lurching wagon. Presently he turned a grey face toward Burton.

"Vere ve go?"

"If we can get to that dry river ahead," Burton shouted, "we can maybe ambush 'em."

He swung the bays toward the north, into Cheyenne country, toward the distant dry river bed. Bitterly he lamented the necessity of turning away from his destination but he had no choice. The riders behind him were hunching over their mounts' necks now and using whip and spur recklessly in the chase.

"*Ach Gott !* Stop—you kill us!" Stattler was chattering.

"Maybe, but those fellows will if I don't!"

His long body rocking to the buckboard's crazy plunges, hands rigid on the reins, Burton kept his eyes fixed some fifty yards ahead to pick out his course over the rolling prairie. The wind tore off his hat, roared in his ears and brought tears to his eyes but he managed to guide the buckboard around disastrous gullies, dense patches of sagebrush and piles of bleached buffalo bones. The New England builders of the buckboard had done their work well. The wagon held together, even though it was flung savagely to one side time after time, throwing the full weight of the burden on a single axle.

"Dey come up!" shouted the German. "Let us stand and fight."

"No! We'll make it!" Burton yelled jubilantly, his eyes darting now and then to the dark streak that marked the course of a dry river bed, not more than a mile ahead.

Black manes and tails flying, Morrow's half-breds kept up their surging gallop, leaving behind a cloud of dust which rose and hung motionless in the hot air of late midday. On over the prairie careened the buckboard behind its foam-flecked horses.

Burton risked a glance over his shoulder to see that the riders chasing him had strung out. Well in the van was a small man in a vivid green shirt. Behind him came a heavier rider on an enormous black horse. The other two were half hidden by the dust.

Taking a firmer grip on the reins, Burton used the whip for the first time. He hoped to open a longer lead on the two foremost riders so that he would have time to select his ground. Strangely, he felt superbly confident. Once amid the curves and bends of the old river bed, he told himself, they could turn suddenly and, with a little luck, knock off those first two riders. The other two, if they kept up the chase, would be easy.

The haven lay only a quarter of a mile ahead when, without warning, one of the off-horse's hoofs fouled in a small tangle of sagebrush and threw the animal off stride. Desperately the bay staggered. The near horse shied and the lunging off horse went down in a boiling cloud of dust. He pulled his mate down with him as he fell.

Miraculously, neither Burton nor Stattler was thrown from the buckboard. The horses had barely landed with sickening thuds before the ex-Confederate was off the seat to snatch at the bits of the foaming, snorting half-breds.

"Hold those men off!" he yelled to Stattler, his voice as staccato as a musket shot. "Near horse is over the trace."

Burton strained to unhitch the trace as the bays plunged furiously, trying to regain their feet. Ironically, it was the thoroughbred blood in the bays' veins that proved their undoing. Whereas cold bred horses would have quieted quickly, the Kentucky blood of Morrow's team brought frenzied buckings and kicking.

White-faced, risking a shattering kick, the desperate ex-Confederate struggled to free the entangled traces. Stattler's rifle cracked and Burton could hear two shots snap back their replies. As a bullet whined overhead, Burton snatched out his Colt, spun around and saw that the first rider was already within range. His eyes shifted and he groaned.

A second and larger party of riders had come into sight. This second group was still far away but Burton could see that they were coming fast.

"Get off that box," he yelled at Stattler. "Drop flat. Can't hit anything with the horses plungin' like this!"

Burton knew what the riders would do. Experience had taught him that the men from Julesburg would circle around, dismount and creep into deadly range, sniping at the buckboard until the second group came up. There was almost no chance that either he or Stattler would escape.

Bitterly, he cursed himself for trying to bring the gold to End o' Track on time. Much better to have followed Dog Soldier Nick's advice and circled far to the south. But that trip would have taken two or three days and the gold should be in Casement's hands by nightfall, if trouble with the labourers was to be avoided.

As Burton had foreseen, the men who had chased the buckboard scattered and formed a circle among the little hillocks rising on all sides. Bullets began to kick up the dry soil around the fugitives as the gunmen found the range. First, the riders shot the two bays, cutting off all chances of the men making their escape on those horses.

Neither Stattler nor Burton found much to shoot at. There were brief glimpses of crouching, dodging figures that moved from one spot to another. On the other hand, the hidden men were beginning to snipe with increasing accuracy. To make matters worse, Paulus Stattler, though brave enough, proved to be an execrable shot.

"Here, let me have your rifle," Burton snapped when the immigrant again missed an easy target.

"*Ja.* I cannot do much."

Stolidly, the German passed over his Wesson and accepted Burton's Colt in exchange.

"Try to kill dot man mit de red beard, blease," he said. "He vas vun of *mein* Anna's murderers."

"I'll do my best, Paulus. Now crawl up between the dead horses. They'll give us a little protection."

He sighted the rifle on the green shirt of the rider who had grown contemptuous of Stattler's marksmanship. The ex-Confederate's trigger finger squeezed and the green-shirted man whirled about and fell.

"One down," Burton grunted. "There may be a chance, after all."

A moment later, the soldier of fortune felt a sharp tap on his right shoulder. When he tried to raise the Wesson again, his right arm failed him.

"What the hell?"

Pressed against the warm belly of a dead horse, he twisted sidewise and looked down to see his shoulder drenched with bright new blood. A sickening chill swept through him. He shrank lower between the dusty carcasses.

"I can't manage the rifle any more," he panted.

Stattler's wide blue eyes met his. Between the two men passed a silent acknowledgement of defeat. Both knew that this was the end. Then Stattler shrugged his big shoulders and handed the Colt back to his companion while he clumsily took the rifle.

Burton shuddered with a chill, despite the burning heat of the prairie. With an effort he reached for the long knife and drew it from its scabbard, then drove it into the earth beside him. That, he knew, would be his last hope.

Hope? He almost laughed aloud. There was a frail chance that the second group of horsemen thundering toward them were not Smiley's riders, but, even so, where was there any reason to hope he would get better treatment from Colonel Barry or even Casement?

He sighted the Colt and snapped a shot that missed. Loss of blood make his aim waver and slowly, inexorably, the pursuers began to close in.

At length Stattler turned his face to Burton and said quietly, "Ve are finished. Good-bye, *lieber Freund.*"

Burton flipped aside a strand of mane that was blocking his view and saw that the larger group of horsemen now was almost upon them, a tall pillar of dust in their wake. He turned back toward Stattler.

"Hey, wait!" he croaked. "What're you doin'?"

The Mormon, muttering to himself in German, had sprung to full height and, rifle in hand, begun to run heavily toward the gunman with the red beard.

Bullets flicked into the ground around Stattler's clumsy cowhide boots, but the German, his blond head glinting in the fierce sunlight, kept on. A slug struck the big Mormon and Burton saw Paulus sway under the impact. The German stopped for a second and then began lumbering forward. Again he was hit. A red stain appeared on the back of his sweat-soaked blue shirt. He kept on, a terrible illusion of invulnerability.

Now the others were shooting frantically. Fascinated, Burton saw the German drop to one knee, raise the rifle and carefully sight at the red-bearded murderer. The bearded man half turned to run for a clump of sagebrush. There was a spurt of flame and a puff of white smoke clouded the muzzle of Stattler's rifle. The bearded man shrilled a thin scream, dropped his gun and fell forward on his face.

Stattler limped toward his fallen enemy. Then he stumbled, sank to his hands and knees and crawled on a few paces until he reached the other's side. He raised the slain gunman's head with a terrific effort and spat redly into the other's face.

That done, Paulus Stattler slumped down on the earth.

When a bullet whined by just over Burton's head he turned to fire back. Then blackness swept down over him.

CHAPTER XXVIII

THE ocean sounded rough and angry, its ceaseless roar thundered in Captain Robert Burton's ears as loudly as it had that time off the coast of Yucatan when his ship had come close to being wrecked.

Slowly, his tumultuous brain cleared a bit. Ocean? Why was he on the ocean? Where *was* he?

The roaring subsided a little. He drew a deep breath and made an effort to open his eyes. A wave of nausea swept over him. Sweat broke out on his forehead. His mouth filled with villainous-tasting bile.

He gave up the attempt to see and relaxed. Bit by bit, he recaptured scraps of memory. He knew he was Captain Robert Burton, C.S.A. That's who he was—*but where was he?*

He opened his eyes at the second try. He saw a dim light reflected on rough boards. He tried to lift his head but the searing pain that shot through his skull made him sink back, a wheezing groan bubbling from his mouth.

A deep voice spoke from the noise-filled darkness.

"So, ye'll oblige us and live to hang, huh?"

Hang? *Hang?* He rolled his head and peered dazedly about, his eyes focusing on the battered kerosene lantern set on a chair across the room. Standing beside the chair was a man in a blue uniform, a brass buckle and golden buttons gleaming. The man held a bayoneted Springfield rifle, his hands clasped over the muzzle. This stranger, moon-faced, impossibly tall in the distorted shadows, blinked owlishly at him.

Burton turned his head away, the better to shut out the noise, so like the surf. Gradually, the realization dawned on him that the roar was the horrible, bestial cry of a mob.

"Lynch him!" "String him up now!" "Let us have him!" "Hand him over, you goddam conscripts!"

Burton turned his head back toward the soldier.

"Where am I?" he demanded.

"Ye've just landed in the guardhouse at Fort Sedgwick," said the guard coldly. "Lucky fer your dirty neck ye did, too. Them railroad paddies would tear you apart right now."

Burton shifted miserably on his shuck pallet and tried to drive his memory back. His body pained in two places—his right shoulder and his head. Sluggishly, his mind brought him snatches of his talk with Jessica Valcour. His brain refused to go further. He raised a feeble hand to touch his head. How had he gotten these wounds?

"What happened?" he asked the soldier.

The guard seated himself with the musket resting across his

knees. He stared at Burton, then pushed his kepi back on his head and spat at a knothole in the floor.

"Some of the boys from Julesburg was set to fill you full of lead," he explained, "when a patrol of the Second Cavalry comes up. When they find out who you was they follered orders and took you away from them Julesburg boys. They was right peeved, too. We-all figger Colonel Barry aims to have the fun of hangin' you himself."

"How many Julesburg men were there?"

"About eight or ten," replied the guard stolidly. "Two more was kind of dead."

Memory flooded back into Burton's mind now with a rush.

"Is the pay chest safe?" he asked.

"Pay chest safe!" exclaimed the guard. He stared at the man on the pallet. "I should tell *you*! Why, you damn——"

His words were drowned out by a rising of the savage clamour outside. The sentry jumped up and ran to a small barred window, peering out. Two shots cracked and then came a deafening volley.

"By God, look at 'em run!" the guard chuckled. "The yaller civilians! Just fire over their heads and they run like rabbits. No, by God, a couple of our boys are down, and bad hurt, too. That mob must've fired first."

He whirled from the window and half lifted his gun, glaring at Burton.

"You dirty dog!" he spat out. "This is all on your goddam account! By God, I'd like to ram this bayonet into your stinkin' carcass!"

"But the treasure," Burton insisted. "*Didn't the cavalry find the treasure?*"

The guard's face blackened as he bent over the man on the bunk.

"You—you damned lying snake!" he growled. "You dast tell me you didn't hide the treasure yourself and—and——"

The bayonet's point twinkled in mid-air.

Burton closed his eyes and groaned. The treasure, then, had disappeared before the soldiers arrived. Good God! There was no hope for him now.

Outside, the din was quieting. A scattering of curses, groans, were audible and the approaching tramp of men that foretold the arrival of more troops. Then came the footsteps of another group advancing purposefully on the guardhouse.

"Judge Lynch comin'?" Burton croaked. The guard, without answering, sprang to the side of the door and stood at rigid attention. Burton closed his eyes again.

The scrape of boots told him that a large party had paused in the corridor outside his cell. He heard the heels of the guard click precisely and the slap of his musket strap as he presented arms.

"Isn't he conscious yet?"

Burton winced as he recognized Barry's cold voice.

"Yes, sir," said the guard. "He's shammin'. I was talkin' to him only a minute ago."

"Shake him then. Hard!"

Casement's voice broke in.

"Yez would do better, I'm thinkin', to send for some whisky and water," the Contractor General suggested. "This man's got to talk and he looks in bad shape."

Burton waited until the lukewarm mixture was poured into his mouth, dribbling down his chin as he gulped. He opened his eyes and saw the shadows of a group of men, made gigantic on the ceiling by the lantern on the chair. He picked out Casement's huge bulk, Barry's erect figure and then looked at McCue, marking the gleam of triumph that shone in the Traffic Manager's eyes. There was Conger, the terrier-like Supply Superintendent; Andrew Valcour and, close to the foreground, the big, hard-faced, domineering figure of the Honourable Jack Smiley.

"Mr. McCue," said Barry in a voice as cold and incisive as a surgeon's scalpel, "do you recognize this man?"

"Sure I do. It was him that led the bandits who took away the pay chest. All I hope is——"

"That will do!" snapped the fierce old officer in blue. He nodded his head toward a burly individual who stood at the side of Jack Smiley. Burton recognized him as the big man who had ridden the magnificent black in the chase after the buckboard.

"O'Gorman," asked Colonel Barry. "Is this the man you followed?"

"Sure," said the thickset thug gruffly. "It was him and a big Dutchman we filled full of slugs. We suspicioned 'em and when we went to investigate 'em, they started shootin'."

Barry turned to General Casement.

"You see, General?" he demanded. "There's absolutely no doubt of his guilt."

The big Irishman walked to the side of Burton's pallet and looked down at the ex-Confederate, a grieved frown contracting his thick eyebrows.

"Burton," he said slowly, "yez are the first man I've ever been bad mistaken in since I took this job. I still hope there's a decent streak in yez. Prove to me I ain't altogether wrong."

His voice took on a note that was almost imploring.

"Tell me where ye've hid the gold. Without it we're done. End o' Track is goin' crazy to-night. Come dawn and there'll be a terrible riot. The public and Congress will lose confidence and the work of years will go to hell! Think, man! Poor people will be ruined and thrown out of work by the thousands. Come on,

tell me ! I'm appealin' to anythin' that's decent and honourable
in ye."

"Decent and honourable !" snorted Colonel Barry. "That dirty
guerrilla !"

Jack Smiley's lips parted to emit a laugh as mirthless as grinding
steel.

The blood-splashed, half-dressed figure on the pallet struggled
up on one elbow and faced the agonized Contractor General.

"General Casement," he said, "I give you my word of honour
as an officer that I only took the gold to make sure it would get
to End o' Track. I learned beyond a doubt that he"—and he
levelled a trembling forefinger at Smiley—"was plannin' to hold
up the gold special at Diamond Springs. I wanted to get there first
and take the gold to you, General."

Smiley's derisive laugh made the sour-smelling cell resound.

"Hell, that's rich !" jeered the big man. "So *I* was going to
steal the Union Pacific's money, was I ? Me, the richest man in
Colorado !"

"You know you were !"

"All right, outlaw," said Smiley, his mouth twisted. "Prove it !
Who told you so ?"

Kildare's name leaped to Burton's lips and died there. The
Texan was God knew where. To mention his name would be to
seal his friend's death warrant. The cavalry captain shook his
head wearily.

"I can't tell you that," he said. "But it's true. For God's
sake, General Casement, believe me ! Wasn't the express *also* held
up at Diamond Springs ? I—oh !"

He knew then that the volley of rifle fire that thundered after the
treasure train as the Pawnees returned the shots from the pay car
would have given Smiley's men a warning that something had gone
wrong. He knew that there was little possibility that Boot Hill Jack's
gang would try a hold-up in the face of heavy firing just up the line.

"Of course there was no hold-up !" Colonel Barry thundered.

"There's really no use lying any more, Burton," cut in Andrew
Valcour in a softer tone. "General Casement has promised to
spare your life if you'll tell where you hid the gold."

"That gold was on the buckboard when I was knocked out,"
the prisoner stated in a tired voice. "If it wasn't there when the
troopers came it was because this man, O'Gorman, and the others
took it away and hid it."

The burly gunman lurched forward.

"If you wasn't set to hang anyhow," he bellowed, "I'd shore
drill yore dirty hide for you !"

Colonel Barry shrugged with distaste as O'Gorman brushed
against the Army man's immaculate uniform. It was evident that

the Colonel was none too pleased with Smiley's connection with the case.

"That'll do, O'Gorman," said the officer. "Since there is nothing to be learned here, we will proceed with a trial in half an hour. Come, gentlemen."

The straight-backed Colonel turned on his heel and stalked out, followed by Casement, Conger and McCue. Jack Smiley paused and looked down at Burton.

"You're a pretty smart one," he observed, with a shade of grudging admiration. "You damn near had me fooled with that 'Jed Smith' game. Well, when they fit that rope around your neck, remember that nobody can buck Jack Smiley and git away with it !"

He swaggered out, followed by the leering O'Gorman. Only Senator Valcour remained in the cell. His patrician face reflected his contempt as he looked at Robert Burton.

"To think," he grated, "that my own daughter should have wasted her affection on a cur like you ! I'll be glad to see you hang !"

"I can't exactly blame you for feelin' that way," Burton sighed, "but it so happens I'm tellin' the truth about that hold-up. Will you please tell your daughter——"

Andrew Valcour's narrow face stiffened.

"I'll tell her nothing," he snapped. "She's prepared to testify at the trial of how you lied to her and wangled railroad secrets out of her to set the stage for your crimes."

"She—she's heard, then ?" whispered the stricken prisoner.

"Of course she has. All Julesburg knows you were caught red-handed. Pray God the riots won't start in the morning until you've paid for what you've done."

The grey-haired promoter cast one more contemptuous look at the ex-Confederate and tramped out. Burton sank back on his shuck sack, dropping deeper into the maelstrom of despair. He had only one hope and he knew it was a forlorn one. If Kildare could take the witness stand to tell what he had learned from Smiley —but that was impossible. Tex would be killed before he ever could reach the court or if, by some miracle, he could get there, he would be shot down by one of Smiley's men before he could speak. No, there was no use hoping for Kildare's help.

It was a short time later when a young lieutenant, pink-faced and with fluffy yellow sideburns, came in. He was cold, correct and antagonistic.

"I am Lieutenant Hanson," he announced. "Colonel Barry has appointed me to defend you."

"Defend me ?" asked Burton. "But this so-called trial can't be a court-martial. I'm no longer in the Service."

"You're not going to get a military trial," answered the lieutenant stiffly. "To prevent disorder, the trial will be held here at Fort

Sedgwick. The judge is a fair and impartial man. Both he and the prosecutor will be civilians. Nobody could be found in Julesburg who was willing to take your case so Colonel Barry, who is a very just man, assigned me to that honour."

Captain Robert Burton smiled in wan resignation.

"How kind of Colonel Barry," he managed. "Of course Jack Smiley will co-operate in furnishing a fair and impartial judge."

The young lieutenant looked at him with cool disdain.

"Now then, my man," he said, "tell me what really happened. I can't help you, you know, unless you tell me the truth."

Burton stared up at the shadow-flecked ceiling despairingly.

"I've told the truth," he said.

Lieutenant Hanson coughed. There was a slight pause and then the lieutenant offered:

"Well, then, if you insist on sticking to that story, can you produce any witnesses?"

Burton thought of Kildare and then shook his head.

"No. I'm sorry, Lieutenant," he said. "The court will just have to take my word."

CHAPTER XXIX

THE trial began at nine o'clock that night. It was held in the mess hall of Fort Sedgwick and into that building jammed a dangerous crowd of smelly, pushing, cursing, eager men and women. The mob was swelled by the fact that this trial was a novelty, the first time in Julesburg's history that a man was to be condemned to death without Judge Lynch on the bench.

Fifty privates of the 30th Infantry in full equipment lined the walls, sweating in the stinking heat. Their bayonets glinted in the light of the kerosene lanterns when Burton came in, half dragged by a pair of corporals. Because his wounds had weakened him past standing, he was allowed to sit at the right end of a table that did duty as a legal bench. Stiff and silently implying that this enforced association with the prisoner was a personal disgrace, Lieutenant Hanson appeared and took his place.

More witnesses, clerks and other officials of the mushroom court appeared. Burton, ignoring the vicious glares that greeted his eyes, looked about the crowned room in vain for a friendly face. Jessica Valcour sat rigid in a chair at the left of the tribunal, beside her father. Her eyes were blank and her bright lips were pressed in a thin line.

In the outer fringe of the crowd stood another woman whose face reflected even less sympathy for Burton than did Jessica's.

Stamped on Lucinda Jameson's features were hard lines and her mouth was twisted in a sardonic smile as though witnessing the death of her last illusion.

"Order in the court !" bellowed a clerk. An enormously fat man with beery, bruised features waddled in and flung a sweat-stained black hat onto the table.

"That's Judge Downer," Hanson informed his client reluctantly.

"Pretty, isn't he," Burton drawled. "Maybe he'd look better if he wasn't quite so drunk."

"Shh-h-h."

"Ah, hell," Burton said. "What's the difference if he does hear me ? What chance have I got ?"

The prosecutor, a bantam rooster man with a surprisingly deep voice, began calling his witnesses. One after the other the men who took the stand added their contributions to what was an utterly damning case against Burton. A bitter smile overspread the ex-Confederate's lips while he heard McCue and O'Gorman and the rest tell their carefully rehearsed lies. The smile vanished when Jessica Valcour came forth to testify.

He listened intently as the girl told of Burton's appearance at her house on the previous night, of what she had told him regarding the gold special.

"You say, ma'am, that he particularly inquired as to the time the special was expected in Julesburg ?"

"Yes," replied Jessica Valcour faintly. "I remember distinctly. Of course I had no idea—I—I—trusted the Captain and I thought I was helping the railroad."

"Of *course* you did, ma'am," the prosecutor agreed heartily. "That will be all."

White and shaken, Jessica returned to her seat without a passing glance at the bandaged man in the prisoner's chair. He looked down at his hands and winced.

The dreary affair came swiftly to a close and a jury of gamblers, toughs and a few decent characters—railroad men who stood to lose everything if the U.P. failed—filed out. They returned almost immediately and a roar of excitement went up from the waiting crowd as the foreman handed the verdict to the Silenus who masqueraded as judge. Burton looked at the mob curiously, picking up snatches of conversation.

A whore with sullen lips which flamed crimson red scratched her nearly naked bosom with evident relish as she said,

"Gee, Gus, they sure uses swell words hyer. This shore beats a theayter."

"Yep. This shore is the legal-est trial I seen since I helped hang Hank Wlikens fer hoss stealin', back in Kansas."

"Hangin's too good fer this swine. I hear they's troops comin'."

"Won't do no good if the pay ain't found. I'm haulin' my ass back to North Platte before sun-up. There'll be hell to pay!"

After an interval, Judge Downer focused his liquor-hazed eyes on the jury's announcement sufficiently to learn that Captain Robert Burton had been found guilty of highway robbery. The immense judge wavered to his feet and hooked his thumbs in his suspenders as he addressed the court.

"Ahemm! Wal, boys *and* ladies, bein's how the jury has dooly found this here skunk guilty of robbery, murder and crim'nal conspiracy among other things, it's now my dooty *and* pleasure to instruct the Officers of the Law to take said skunk to some public place to-morrow mornin' and there increase the length of his neck with a hemp necktie. And the sooner the better, says I!"

"That's the boy, Wally!" shrilled a harlot in the back of the room. "Give him Julesburg justice, you old souse, you!"

The courtroom broke into a howl of cheers and laughter. There was a surge toward the prisoner, but the guards standing at the walls beat back the would-be lynchers with their gun butts, driving the crowd out of the mess hall. Among the last to leave was Lulu Jameson. She stood looking at the doomed man, her painted mouth twisted in a bitter grimace. Then her bedaubed eyes moved to watch Jessica Valcour sweep out of the hall, looking to neither right nor left. Lulu laughed aloud harshly.

"So that's his pretty lady, huh? Wonder how he likes her now that she put the rope around his neck?"

Burton sat in his chair, his shoulders sagging. He looked up wearily to see Colonel Barry standing in front of him.

"You should have been hanged after Fort Pillow," the old officer said, "but better late than never! It's a comfort to me that at least one of Forrest's cut-throats is going to pay for that massacre."

Burton lifted his chin.

"Old man," he said, slowly, "I might have expected something like that from you. It's a good thing for the North that her armies were officered by men different from you; men who didn't let personal grievances strip them of their honour."

Colonel Barry glowered and started to speak. Then he turned away, his face rigid.

"Come on, you," growled a corporal, clutching Burton's arm and sending a twinge through his wounded shoulder. "You'd better get some beauty sleep so's you can put on a good show at yer hangin'."

When he reached his cell, the ex-Confederate stopped dead in astonishment. There, muffled in a grey travelling coat, stood Jessica Valcour, waiting for him!

"Sorry, ma'am," said the sergeant of the guard, "but you can't stay here."

"I've got a pass signed by Colonel Barry," said Andrew Valcour's daughter, her voice even. "Here it is."

The N.C.O. took the slip and his lips moved as he read it. He saluted and tucked the pass in his belt.

"All right, ma'am. You can talk to the prisoner alone for ten minutes, but that's all."

There was a silence that lasted until the sergeant of the guard had withdrawn his men and had bolted the barred door on the outside. Then Bob stretched out his hands toward the girl.

"Jessica!" he said. "I hoped you'd see me. I've made a mess of things and I wanted so badly to——"

He stopped as she moved out of the way of his reaching hands.

"I know you've made a mess of things," she said. "I—I'm in trouble, too. Papa is furious with me. When he found out that I'd told you about the gold special, he nearly struck me. I—I was frightened."

"Oh, Jessica," he said. "If I could only make it up to you."

He looked at her. She was biting her lips with her small, perfect teeth.

"You can," she said finally. "You—you could tell the truth."

"The truth! *But I did tell the truth!*"

She grasped his hands quickly.

"Casement has powerful friends," she rushed on. "He'd see that you weren't hanged. And—and the railroad would be saved if you'd tell where you hid the gold. I—Papa wouldn't be ruined and he wouldn't be so angry with me any more. Please—oh, *please*, Bob, tell me where you hid the gold!"

He stared at her disbelievingly, his eyes going bleak. She looked up at him and then glanced away.

"You—you've no right to look at me like that," she faltered. "I've done nothing. It's you—you who have spoiled everything!"

"You—don't—believe—me."

She turned her back on him and spoke over one slender shoulder.

"How can I believe you?" she asked. "How can anybody believe you? You did ask about the gold special. You did hold up the train and the troopers didn't find the gold. You *must* have hidden it somewhere!"

She whirled about, her hands outstretched.

"Tell me where it is, Bob?" she pleaded. "I—maybe Papa and I can recover it and say it—it fell off the buckboard somewhere. I'll speak to General Casement. I'll do anything!"

His stony features did not change expression as he looked at her. She put her hands to her face and her shoulders jerked beneath her sobs.

"I—we'll be poor," she said. "I—I can't stand the thought! I've always had money and now—now we'll be ruined. I won't have any clothes, any jewels."

G

She looked up, her eyes swollen.

"You said you loved me once, Bob," she wailed. "If you did, tell me—tell me now where you hid the gold! It won't do you any good. You're going to die. For God's sake have some pity on me. Colonel Barry——"

She stopped and one hand went to her mouth as her eyes widened. Burton's lips made a slash across his grey face as he took one step toward her.

"Did Barry send you here?" he demanded. "Is that the game?"

She backed away from him until her shoulders pressed against the bars. Her voice was little more than a whimper.

"I—well, he thought you might tell me," she admitted. "He said——"

Her voice dribbled off into silence and she licked her lips nervously. Burton's eyes were piercing as he looked at this girl who had told him she loved him.

"That night, then," he said in a steely voice, "that night on the hill over End o' Track—The railroad wanted me to stay and I wanted to ride away. *You* begged me to stay because, God help you, you said you loved me. It wasn't that, was it? You thought that if I stayed I'd help the U.P. and your father's damned investments. That was it, wasn't it?"

She tried to meet his eyes and failed.

"That *was* it, wasn't it!" he thundered.

When she failed to answer, he barked a short, eerie laugh and turned away.

"I should have taken you that night on the hill," he said brutally. "Taken you for what you were, a woman selling her kisses for money. A pampered perfume house-cat without the honesty to love decently."

"How dare you! Sergeant! Sergeant!"

He laughed again in that inhuman manner.

"Don't worry," he said. "I won't hurt you. I wouldn't touch you, Jessica Valcour. You can go back to Colonel Barry and tell him that Captain Robert Burton of General Forrest's cavalry didn't fall for his little stunt. Tell him I couldn't fall for it, even if you had been better at your game than you were. Because what I've said all along is the truth and it will be the truth as long as I'm alive."

She was fairly hissing at him now, like the cat he had named her.

"That won't be long, Bob Burton," she spat. "And I hope I'm on hand to see you hang!"

The lock grated and the guard stood outside the open door. Head down, Jessica Valcour hurried out of the cell. After she had left, the towering guard looked curiously at Burton.

"What did a fine lady like that want to see a polecat like you about?" he asked bluntly.

"She wanted to find out where I hid the gold," Burton replied recklessly. "I told her that I'd buried it two miles outside of Saint Louis. If you hurry, maybe you can beat her to it—but you'll have to ride like hell, soldier!"

The trooper grunted and slammed the door. The key turned in the lock again and the ex-Confederate slumped to the husk pallet on the low bunk. He sat there with his head in his hands. For a time, his brain reeled under the impact of bitter realization. Then he straightened and shrugged his shoulders, oblivious of the pain his gesture cost him.

"What could you expect, Burton?" he asked aloud. "After Enid Culver, how could you think any woman could be honest? You asked for it and, by God, you got it. Now all you have to do is take it with your chin up."

The minutes slid by. The notes of a bugle sounding 'Call to Quarters' beat through the window bars. He stretched on the pallet, remembering the times when he and his mates had crouched above a Federal encampment listening to that same call, waiting to swoop down with his lean grey riders once the haunting notes of 'Taps' had sounded.

Gradually, the noises of Fort Sedgwick diminished. Only the crunch of a sentry's boots beneath his window broke the stillness. He dozed until a rattle at the door roused him. The light of a lantern gleamed through the bars and there came the sound of a woman's voice, strident, imperative.

"I tell you I've got to see him!"

"Sorry, sister. It's against orders."

"Don't be mean, Handsome." The voice of Lucinda Jameson was insinuatingly sweet. "Here's a pass signed by the adjutant. I've got a few words to say to the prisoner."

"All right, ma'am, but you can't stay more'n five minutes and I'm stayin' right here. It's orders."

"Go on and stay," snapped the girl. "What I've got to say to that swine anybody can hear!"

"Oh. I thought you was a friend of his."

"A friend of that man! Huh!"

There was the clang of the bolt; the door opened and Lulu Jameson stormed into the cell like a hungry tigress.

"So this is Captain Burton, the famous train robber!" she yapped. "Well, I've got something to tell you before they string you up!"

"Go ahead," he said quietly. "Nobody's going to stop you."

She placed her hands on the hips of her gaudy dress and leered at him through her blackened lashes, her painted mouth sneering.

"I'm just going to say I wish they could hang you twice," she grated, "because you're a double thief. You gave me a lot of bushwa about leadin' the *decent* life. You gave me some hope, something to live for, and now you've stolen it, like the dirty lying thief you are."

Her voice rose to a wail.

"Why did you do it?" she asked. "Why did you tease me that way?"

From the doorway, the whiskered jailer looked on amazed. As if to keep from hurling it into Burton's face, Lulu clutched the black reticule she carried tightly.

Robert Burton sank back on the bed rock.

"If you've finished, please go," he begged. "I'm—I'm very tired and morning will soon be here. I can't stand much more of this."

"You can't, huh?" she cried. "How do you think *I* feel? Answer me! Don't just sit there snivelling!"

She sprang at the ex-Confederate, bent low over him and dealt his cheek a ringing blow.

"Take that to remember me with on the gallows!"

The guard sergeant guffawed and called out as he turned toward the hall:

"Hey, Jake, come on in. This skirt's givin' Burton a goin' over!"

"Never mind. I'm going!" cried Lulu Jameson. As she turned toward the door she flung one last taunt at the man on the bunk. "When you swing, think of Lulu Jameson back at the Prairie Belle and be proud of yourself!"

Burton lay still, his wounded scalp stabbed by new pains and his head ringing from the blow.

'Poor child,' he thought. 'MacKaye, Stattler and now Lucinda Jameson. Everybody I touch seems doomed.'

In an effort to ease the throbbing ache in his shoulder, Burton turned onto his left side and winced as he felt a sharp lump in the miserable corn shuck bed sack. He reached down to move the protruding stalk, then tensed, his hand as motionless as though caught in a trap.

His fingers slowly pulled a cold, hard object from beneath his mattress. He looked down at a double-barrelled derringer, compact but deadly at short range. Projecting from one of the gun's barrels was a tiny scroll of paper. Cautiously, he pulled out the roll and, by the light of the stars, managed to decipher a message written in a neat, copperplate hand.

'Use this and try to reach my room.
I've arranged for a horse for you.'

Inhaling deep, head-clearing breaths, Robert Burton sank back on his pillow to plan and gain strength while he waited for the midnight change of guards. Soon the new relief appeared, repeated special orders concerning the prisoner and disposed themselves at their posts.

Burton called in a weak voice.

"Sergeant?"

"Whaddye want?"

"Water—please——"

"In a minute."

CHAPTER XXX

THE door to Lucinda Jameson's room creaked a little as the man in the uniform of an infantry sergeant wavered in. As he slipped inside the small room, hands caught at him and helped support him as he stumbled toward the bed.

"Oh, thank God!" Lucinda breathed as she lowered him to the white counterpane and pressed him back on the pillows.

Dimly Robert Burton saw that a stand beside the bed held bandages, disinfectants and a basin. On the tiny kerosene stove a kettle of water hissed comfortably.

"Thanks a lot——" he attempted and then lay panting, unable to talk.

He felt the girl's fingers at the buttons of his uniform blouse and opened his eyes. Lucinda was bent over him, the light from behind her framing her head with a halo.

"What was the noise and shootin' I heard a while back?" he asked.

"They're not after you—yet," the girl said. "Those were the rioters and guards fighting down by the depot. There'll be terrible things done before to-morrow's over."

"Irish stirred up yet?" he managed.

"Yes. Agitators have been talking all evening. They've convinced the men that they'll never be paid."

She looked down at him and saw his head sway as his weakness overcame him. Wordlessly, the girl crossed to a chest of drawers, pulled out a flask and poured a stiff tot.

"Drink this, Captain. You'll feel stronger. Now lie back and don't try to talk for a while."

He lay quiet while her deft fingers stripped the blouse from him and then unwound a blood-clotted bandage which had been roughly applied to the wounded shoulder. Gently, she washed the inflamed red hole of the wound with disinfectants and expertly she bound up the wound again.

"Evidently you've done that before," he observed, smiling wanly.

"You forget," she reminded him softly, "that I lived in the war zone for four years. I've had plenty of practice."

The whisky drove a tinge of colour back into Burton's sunken cheeks. Some of the feverishness of his shoulder wound left after the hurt had been washed and treated.

"How did you manage to get away?" she murmured as, with compressed lips, she clipped away the clotted hair about his scalp wound.

"Called for a drink as soon as the new guard came on. Shoved your derringer in his face. Tied him up and took his clothes. It was so easy I can hardly believe it's true."

"It *is* true," she said in a quivering voice. "Thank God you're going away from this dreadful town!"

"But surely you must see that I can't."

Her hands, now grimly stained, hesitated in mid-motion.

"What did you say?"

"I'm not goin'," he repeated gently. "You see, Lucinda, I've got to see this business through. I can't do anythin' else. Casement trusted me—Major North, too."

"Oh dear," she cried, tears starting to her eyes. "I—I was afraid you'd act like this! I—I——"

She began to weep softly.

"Why, Lucinda, what's the matter?"

"Oh, *please* go away!" she choked. "You can't do anything, at least not now. It's too late. Please go, Captain! I've got you a good horse and a friend of mine who'll ride with you—take care of you."

"No," he replied, his deep eyes soft. "I've got to stay in Julesburg."

The girl wiped her eyes and nodded as she completed Burton's head bandage.

"All right, then," she said almost briskly. "That's that. What do you plan to do?"

"I'm goin' to try to find out about those code messages. I know they've got a lot to do with this."

"But—but you can't read them—or have you found the key?"

He was silent as a gang of half-drunken labourers roared past the warehouse on their way to join the rioting by the railroad yards.

"No, I haven't found the key but I reckon it must be somewhere in Smiley's rooms. I'm goin' to hunt through his papers. If I get killed tryin'—well, it'll solve a lot of fool problems. If I don't, maybe I can save Casement yet."

"But you can't do that, Captain," Lucinda pleaded. "You aren't able to, don't you see? You can hardly walk and the streets are full of men who'd shoot you on sight."

Then, suddenly, the girl arose and hurried to the stove to stir a pot of broth that had been filling the room with its aroma.

"How long do you figure it will be before the new guards come on?" she asked over her shoulder.

"A guard usually has two hours on and four off duty," Burton said, as he sniffed the broth hungrily. "But with the rioting to-night they may be having four-hour shifts."

"Then they won't miss you until two o'clock at the earliest?"

"Maybe not, but I can't count on it. Why do you ask, Lucinda?"

"Tell you in a minute," she murmured, not turning toward Burton. He glanced toward the windows as a new burst of racket came from the street below. Occupied thus, he did not see the girl's hand flicker up to a small box lying on a shelf just above the stove. He did not see Lucinda dump the contents of a fold of paper into the cup of broth.

"Better drink this," she commanded while she slid a surprisingly strong arm beneath his shoulders. "You've got to get a lot of strength back if you're going over to Jack Smiley's."

He gulped thirstily and sank back with a deep sigh after he had drained the cup.

"These are your things," Lucinda said. He looked toward a row of clothes hooks and saw that the girl had cleaned up the cowboy clothes he had taken off to don the cavalry corporal's uniform for his visit to—he winced—to Jessica Valcour.

A Colt and a belt of cartridges hung from an adjoining hook but the long knife was gone. Burton wondered lazily about the knife and finally decided that one of O'Gorman's men must have taken it after the disastrous end of the battle by the buckboard.

As from a distance he could hear Lucinda talking.

"What's that?" he asked. "I didn't hear you."

"I said that since you're bound on seeing this thing through, I'm going to help you."

"Help me? How?"

It was queer, he thought, that he had become sleepy so suddenly. He yawned, then lazily shifted his gaze. His eyes widened a trifle when he saw her standing beside him, her face intent as she fumbled with some hooks at the back of her grey dress.

"Yes, Captain," came her soft voice. "You'll stay here and rest awhile. I'm going to find Tex Kildare. He must be around somewhere. I'll send him here."

Burton tried to form an objection but his buzzing brain refused to respond. Instead, he lay silent on the pillows, his eyes determined to close and stay shut. Sleep edged closer until, with an effort, he opened his eyes.

Dreamily, he saw Lucinda standing across the room, slipping the grey dress over her head, obviously confident that he had fallen asleep. Even the ex-Confederate's drugged senses stirred at the perfection of the girl's body, scarcely concealed by sheer underthings.

He lay there, dreamily admiring the lustrous sheen of her neck and arms, her shoulders. He was studying the girl through a haze of descending sleep when she turned and saw him watching her. Lucinda's face glowed as she darted behind the curtains in front of the washstand.

"What you doin'?" he mumbled.

"After I find Tex I'm goin' to talk to Smiley."

He struggled up to one elbow.

"What!" he exclaimed. "No! No! Mustn't——"

"Why not? You need the cypher key and I'm going to get it. It shouldn't be too hard. Jack always liked me." The old bitterness crept back into her voice. "——I think I could get invited to his rooms at the Julesburg House. He'll be busy to-night. I'll say I'll wait for him there."

"No. Mustn't. Won't let you! You—through—that sort of thing!"

"I thought I was," she sighed, "but some things are more important. You—and the railroad. Hundreds of poor, foolish men who'll be hurt or killed to-morrow if—well, if things go on the way they are."

She emerged from behind the curtain in a gaudy costume and sat down to strip off the grey stockings. He watched her as she drew on the flashy net and lace creations that she had worn the first night he had met her, in the bar of the Prairie Belle. Her voice sounded very far away. The sleeping draught inexorably closed his eyes.

"We can work out the messages," she said. "We can see what's to be done. You'll be rested when I come back—fit for travel."

"No—mustn't—nothing—worth—worth—wor——"

He fell asleep, his dark hair showing black against Lucinda's pillow. The girl sat still for a moment, one scarlet ribbon garter drawn halfway up the slender pillar of her leg.

"Dearest," she whispered. "Oh, my dear."

Five minutes later she inspected herself in the flawed mirror above the washstand and Lulu Jameson, handsome and tragic, looked back at her; Lulu of the bold black eyes, the flaming mouth and the pale breasts half exposed by the low bodice of the short-skirted yellow and red dress.

Lulu Jameson's high, rhinestone-studded heels twinkled as she crossed the room to pause by the bed. Suddenly she bent to kiss the sleeper. Her lips were close to Burton's gaunt, brown cheek when she shook her head and straightened.

"No, not like this," she murmured. "Never like this."

She blew down the lamp chimney and quietly made her way out of the room and down onto the churning streets.

CHAPTER XXXI

SIX years of hard campaigning had taught Robert Burton how to come out of a sleep, no matter how deep, at the first alarm. When the door handle of Lucinda Jameson's room clicked, he shook off the effects of the girl's light sedative at once and rolled over to the far side of the bed, dropping to the floor despite the pain the movement cost him.

He crouched behind the wide bed while the door swung open. Then Burton relaxed as Kildare's soft voice came from the doorway.

"Bob? Bob Burton. Where air you?"

"Inside, Tex. Close the door. There's a lamp on the table."

"Hope them blinds is drawn," the Texan drawled as he scratched a match. "They's hell an' repeat goin' on outside."

"So it's bad?"

"Damned bad, Bob. A bunch o' drunked-up section hands just lynched a section boss fer tryin' to stop their burnin' some bridge beams. Troops is bein' rushed from Omaha and points East but they'll shore git here a heap too late."

"My God! I didn't realize they'd got that far! Where have you been, Tex?"

"Boot Hill Jack sent me out to Alkali on a job. Had to go."

The lamp wick caught and the light spread through the room.

"Didn't know they'd caught you, *amigo*," Kildare went on, "or I'd never have gone. Only got back to town half an hour ago and was hearin' about your trial when a gal moseys up and tells me to come hyer. *Hombre*, they shore treated you rough, I see."

"I'm all right. Tell me what's happened."

Burton began pulling on his cowboy clothes. Because of his crippled arm he made slow work of it.

Kildare gave a swift account of how he and Smiley's raiders had ridden to Diamond Springs that morning. When the train was late and, subsequently, when the Pawnees had fired their volley at the treasure car, Smiley had known that something had gone wrong.

Accordingly Boot Hill Jack had abandoned his own trap, had split his men into groups of four and had ordered them to ride in all directions in an effort to find the successful train robbers' line of flight. Smiley's own group, Tex said, had run down and killed the Pawnee leading Burton's horse and the *travois* pony.

"They knew it was yore hoss," Kildare explained, "account of that spur in the saddlebag. Boot Hill Jack took it and he looked right upset about it. And say, pardner, speakin' of yore property. I took this off one of the gents who jumped you and Stattler."

A flush of pleasure lit the cheeks of the wounded man as Kildare produced Burton's wolf-headed knife from his shirt front.

"Thanks," said the ex-Confederate. "I'm mighty glad to have that back, Tex. Too bad about Stattler."

"Uh-huh, but that pore Dutchman wouldn't have lasted long out here, nohow. He couldn't shoot and he was always a-settin' out in the open, makin' a target. Reckon he was glad to go, though."

He regarded Burton speculatively.

"Say," he asked, "jest who's this hyer wench who hunted me up?"

"Lucinda's no wench," Burton objected sharply. "She saved my life; brought a derringer to my cell. Where did you see her?"

"At the King o' the Hills. There was big doin's jest then. Some gal who was locoed over Boot Hill Jack drank poison on the dance floor."

"*What was that?*"

"Yep. Some feller told me she done it account o' Jack's sendin' her out to hustle like the rest. Shore was a waste o' good looks. The gal was prettier'n a speckled pup. Ha'r like corn silk, face like one o' them valentines and her eyes was big and blue."

"What did Smiley do?" asked Burton, his voice metallic.

"Him? He jest looks at her layin' there and hoists a drink and says to Comanche Ted: 'Too bad. I meant her fer you.' Let's see, the gal's name was—was——"

"Enid."

"Shore enough," Kildare said, staring. "You mean you knew this gal?"

"I did know her," Burton said. "I knew her a long time ago."

Wooden-faced and wincing a little, Burton buckled on his revolver and knife, shifting both weapons to the left side.

"Now where's the girl you talked to?" he asked. "Lucinda Jameson's her name."

"Lemme see. Jest before the other gal kills herself, this Lucinda person was drinkin' champagne and kiddin' with Boot Hill Jack. Yep. I remember now. Jack kisses her and says somethin'. Then the Jameson gal nods and pretty pronto she teeters out, headed fer the Julesburg House."

"Come on," Burton ordered. "That's where we're headin'."

"But you're loco! That's Boot Hill Jack's *own hangout!*"

His mouth a taut slash, the ex-Confederate nodded.

"I know it," he said. "That's why we're headin' that way. That girl's goin' to try to search Smiley's room. We've got to hurry. He'll kill her if he finds what she's up to."

With his sombrero pulled low over his face and with Tex Kildare still protesting behind him, Burton stepped out into the night. For several moments the two stood silently surveying a street jammed with hot, excited citizens. Then they set off.

"So you're set on a showdown with Smiley to-night?" Kildare asked.

"If there's no other way to get that money back."

"You're in fine shape to fight Boot Hill Jack," Kildare grunted as he hitched the Twins higher on his hips. "Wal, I can mebbe help you some. I got a room upstairs right handy to Jack's. I'll mosey in and open up a window in back o' the hotel and then you can come in, pardner, and we'll see what's what."

Burton nodded grimly.

"We'll do just that," he said. "We'll see what's what."

It was apparent that hundreds of labourers already had deserted the camp at End o' Track. The streets between the raw pine shacks and shanties were thronged with sun-bronzed graders, teamsters, gaugers and track layers. On some street corners loud-voiced rabble-rousers were haranguing the mob.

"Them Eastern leeches are bleedin' us!" howled one. "They're cheatin' us. They've lied to us before and they'll lie to us agin if we listen. What are we, mice or men? Are we goin' to take their double crossin' like a lot of greasers? Let's git after 'em! Show 'em we can hit back! Stop the trains! Kill the slave-drivers!"

A grumbling roar came from the listeners. The labourers were still sluggish but they were gradually quickening with hate.

"Aye, we'll show 'em," somebody shouted. "We've had enough of gettin' starved and shot and sunstroked!"

"Sure, we'll show 'em we mean business!" yelled another. "We'll quit work, burn ties, rip down wires till they pay!"

The speaker's hoarse voice kept up its chant, flinging itself out over a street so crowded that it might have been midday instead of past midnight. Here and there frightened merchants armed with shotguns were loading their most valuable wares into carts. Elsewhere, groups of men, women and children, terrified by the mounting violence, were driving or riding out to camp on the prairie, preferring to brave Indians rather than the white men who threatened to go berserk.

The agitator shifted his attack.

"Let's get Casement," he screamed. "He's the worst of the railroad's flock of vultures. Let's get Red Jack, take him hostage, and we'll hang the dirty hound if he won't give us our money!"

There was the crash of shattering glass. Half the listeners, shouting incoherently, turned to dash across the street where a U.P. storehouse was being broken into.

"Look out! Here come the goddam soljers!"

A platoon of hot, sweaty infantry came up on the double, bayonets gleaming in the lights from the windows. Sullenly, the would-be looters scattered to reform a few blocks away.

"And this hyer's jest a sample o' what's comin'," Kildare muttered.

Further on, the two men met another orator inflaming a sizeable crowd. The speaker was none other than Comanche Ted, his yellow shirt glowing bright in the glare of a lamp-lit window. Burton's spirits fell. All over town could be heard the roar of the mob and scattered shots. Somewhere near the depot a big fire was raging.

Up to the entrance of Julesburg's biggest hotel ploughed Kildare, using elbows, fists and curses to carve a path for his weakened companion. Panting a little, Burton paused in the lee of a wagon that had been left abandoned in the centre of the street. He wiped his perspiring brow with a shaking hand.

"I'm headin' in now," Tex said softly, "so you jest mosey 'round to the back and when I open a window you come and come a-runnin'. *Sabe?*"

The Texan slipped away, leaving Burton to stare at the hotel which, it appeared, was destined to witness the two most important events of his life. It had been there that his grim reunion with Enid Culver had taken place. Enid who now lay dead beneath the roof of the roaring King of the Hills, a discarded mistress who had chosen suicide to life without the unworthy man she loved.

Carefully he surveyed the porch on which, for once, there strutted no swaggering Smiley gunman. Doubtless, he told himself, they were all too busy that night, making speeches to their 'fellow workers.' The hotel's windows glowed in even rows. There was no sleep in Julesburg to-night. Behind one of those windows, Burton told himself, must be Lucinda Jameson.

He tensed, his blood running cold, as two men lurched past him, their voices loud.

"Yeah," said one. "Jack Smiley jest went into the hotel. I seen him. Heard tell he's got a new gal."

Sheltering his wounded arm, Burton circled to the rear of the hotel and dodged into a dark corner. He waited there, his heart pounding with impatience, until he saw a window cautiously raised in what must have been the darkened dining-room. He ran forward, crouching, until he reached the side of the hotel. Kildare's lanky arms reached downward and hauled him up over the sill into the Julesburg House. Both men waited motionless for an instant, listening to the raucous voices, strident laughter and the incessant shallow-toned banging of a piano drifting in from the crowded bar.

"This way. Walk easy," said Kildare as he led the way to a back passageway.

"Seen anything of the girl?"

"Nope."

"Where's Smiley's room?"

"Second floor," the Texan replied. "Acrosst the hall and two beyond mine. Better unlimber yore gun, Bob, 'cause ye'd shore git recognized if you was to meet any of the boys in the hall."

His heart in his mouth and his aching body tensed for action, Burton followed Kildare's rangy, bow-legged figure into the dangerous passageway. They met nobody and had just slipped into Kildare's dark room when the thud of a fist smacking into bare flesh, a wailing cry of pain, made the hairs lift on Burton's neck.

"Oh, Jack, for God's sake ! Jack ! Don't hit me again ! Honest, I was only lookin' around. Just waitin' for you, Honey ! Oh-h-h ! Stop ! Please I—I——"

There came the sound of more savage blows followed by gasps of anguish.

"Git up, you thievin' wench ! No use dodgin'. I'll teach you to pry into my bureau !"

The crash of punches and the dull thump of a piece of furniture falling sounded from the room down the hall.

"Don't ! Don't ! Stop Jack ! I didn't take anything ! Stop ! You're killing me !"

His face a mask of hate, Captain Robert Burton started for the door.

CHAPTER XXXII

BURTON moved fast, but Tex Kildare moved like a panther, flinging himself squarely in front of the ex-Confederate and grappling with the taller man to keep him from the door.

"Keep quiet," he hissed. "You've gotta stay here !"

"Let me by ! Can't you hear ? Smiley's killin' her !"

"No ! Ye'd only get yourself killed and——"

"Damn you ! Stand aside !"

As he grappled with Kildare, the clear realization came to Burton that he loved Lucinda Jameson, loved her deeply. This was no hot, confused emotion such as he had suffered with Enid Culver and Jessica Valcour. He knew *why* he loved this slight girl— for her loyalty and courage and innate unselfishness.

He struggled with the Texan until Kildare, desperate, jerked out one of his guns and held it clubbed above the ex-Confederate's head.

"Shut up now," Kildare warned, "or I'll put out yore light. If Jack was fixin' to kill the girl he'd have done it long ago."

Burton's strength, born of his rage, deserted him abruptly and he staggered back toward the bed, forced to listen to the pitiful cries from across the hall. Soon a door slammed open and there was the sound of a body falling into the hall.

"Git out you goddam light-fingered thief !" Smiley roared. "And clear out of Julesburg before sun-up or I'll have you stripped bare, painted red and rid out of town on a rail !"

The door banged shut again leaving only the sound of dreary, uncontrolled sobbing. Then there was the scuffling of someone rising. Uncertain, halting steps approached the door of Kildare's room.

In a red mist of rage, Burton started forward again. The Texan made a fierce, restraining gesture. As the beaten girl's steps sounded just outside, Kildare, with the litheness of a cat, wrenched open the door, clapped a hand over Lucinda's mouth and swept her into the room.

The girl struggled weakly until light filtering in from the streets revealed Burton's face.

"*You !*" she choked. "You here?"

The ex-Confederate winced as he looked at the girl who had risked death to help him. A deep red welt marred one cheek. A strap of her red and yellow dancehall dress was torn off and the marks of fingernails showed on the girl's bosom. The knee was torn out of one stocking and Lucinda's midnight hair fell in a disorderly cascade across quirt-marked white shoulders.

"You hurt badly?" he managed to ask.

"Keep your voice down," Kildare warned. "You find anything, Miss?"

Lucinda nodded dazedly.

"Yes. I found and copied a c-code telegram. I—I put it in a w-weighted box and dropped it out of the window just as Jack came in. He saw——he saw the drawer open and knew I'd been l-looking and—oh——"

Burton supported the girl's light body across the room to the bed.

"Did you find the cypher key?" Burton asked.

Lucinda's lips quivered and her fingers ran through her hair as she shook her head.

"N-no. I couldn't find it anywhere. Oh, C-Captain, what—what can we do now?"

"You stay right hyer," said Kildare. "Both of you. I'm goin' down and fetch up that box."

When the door quickly opened and shut, Captain Robert Burton sank onto the bed beside the girl and gently put his good arm about her.

"Ah, 'Cinda—'Cinda darling," he whispered.

His lips sought her hot forehead as she clung to him with a desperate hunger, her whole body shaking from the violence of her weeping. Then she raised her trembling lips to his.

As their mouths parted, Lucinda began crying again.

"I—I wanted to help," she said, "and I failed. Y-you were mighty good to me and I did want to help you."

"You have, 'Cinda," he told her. "More than you'll ever realize. I—I wish I——"

Tex Kildare slipped into the room noiselessly for all his high heels and spurs. He handed Burton a small box, looking uneasily over his shoulder as he did.

"Hyer she be," he whispered. "But we've got to punch the breeze out o' hyer right quick. Smiley's been lookin' fer me. What's the weight in this box, Miss?"

"I d-don't know. I just took the f-first thing I found."

Burton held out a shadowy hand.

"Let me see the code telegram."

He lifted the box cover and, by the dim light from outside, looked down on a slip of paper covered by the familiar numeral code. Below the message was a pair of spurs wrapped in a grimy handkerchief. Snatching one out, the ex-Confederate held it to the light.

"Look," he said, his brain whirling. "Look—this spur. And the other, by God! They're the same design as the one I found by the burned bridge!"

"You shore?" asked Kildare.

"Certain sure. Look, see the cactus design on the shank? Look at those cougar heads on the bosses. I'd know them anywhere."

He eyed Kildare.

"Where did *the other one* come from?" he asked.

"I've been figgerin' on the same question, ever since North gave me that spur fer you. Somehow I'd a hunch that one wasn't the one you found by the bridge."

"I get it," Burton cried. "Then one spur *did* disappear at End o' Track and it was the other that was found later on in a pile of ties beside Casement's car!"

He held out his own good hand.

"Let me see that box cover," he said. "I thought I saw some writin' on it."

A shaky, illiterate hand had written on the box: "For Senator Valcour."

The words fell like heavy stones from Burton's lips as he read the inscription. A silence fell as the three in the darkened room eyed each other in amazement.

"Say," Kildare began, "they's somethin' *loco* about all this. Valcour wouldn't——"

Burton shook his bandaged head.

"I'd need a hell of a lot more proof than this before I'd believe he was mixed up in any way with that bridge affair," he said. Then his voice slowed to a slow drawl. "Just the same, Valcour *did* speak out against reinforcing the railroad guards. He *was* one of the four men who knew about that gold shipment. And he *was* away from End o' Track the time the Buffalo Creek bridge was burned!"

He whirled toward the Texan, charged with excitement.

"Tex," he said in a guarded tone, "maybe we can get the proof we need and perhaps the cypher key, too, if you'll try what I've got in mind. You're one of Smiley's men so you could take these spurs to Valcour's home and give them to him. Watch him closely when you tell him Smiley wants him to come right up here for an important talk."

Kildare shoved his hat back and scratched his sparsely-haired head.

"I reckon you're barkin' at a knot," he said glumly, "but I'll try to fetch him up hyer, if you want me to."

"Thanks, pardner," Burton said. "If he comes I'll try to get the cypher key or make him tell where the money's hidden, somehow. If that doesn't work, I'm goin' for a showdown with Boot Hill Jack."

He waited until a trio of clumping boots went down the hall toward Smiley's room. The Texan stretched his arms and flexed his hands as he turned toward the door.

"Now you keep quiet," Kildare urged. "Don't answer nohow or unlock the door till I give three double knocks. Then open up and cover Valcour mighty quick—if I've got Valcour with me."

The bow-legged Texan slipped out of the door, the spurs dangling from his belt and his hands hovering over the notched butts of the deadly Twins. Burton relocked the door and joined Lucinda, small and looking frightened, on the edge of Kildare's bed.

"Sorry you're in on this," he apologized, "but it wouldn't be safe for you to leave now. If it comes to shootin', which seems likely, you'd better lie on the floor, under the bed."

"I'm not sorry I'm here," the girl said defiantly. "Do you really think Senator Valcour is mixed up in this? Everybody says he'll lose his fortune if the U.P. fails."

"I don't know," Burton admitted. "But before I lock horns with Smiley I want to know why he had those spurs that were addressed to Valcour."

He moved closer to Lucinda and the girl looked up at him.

"I want to tell you, 'Cinda," he said in a whisper, "that no matter what happens in a little while I—well—I know the real thing now. I love you, 'Cinda."

"Don't!" she begged. "You mustn't, Bob. You—you know what I've been."

"All I know, darling, is that the real you never was inside the Prairie Belle. Not the real Lucinda."

"Ah, Bob," she cried. "You're hurt and tired and you don't know what you're saying. I——"

A heavy tramping of feet outside made the two stiffen and fall silent. A large and noisy contingent of Smiley's men tramped past on their way to Boot Hill Jack's room.

"Say, Ted," a hoarse voice said, "that goddam Irishman Casement is still keepin' End o' Track quiet."

"How come?"

"Oh, a few of his shanty Irish are stickin', helpin' him guard the enjines and rollin' stock."

"To hell with Casement! To-morrow he won't be guardin' nothin' but six feet of Colorado dirt. It's all fixed. O'Gorman's got the job."

The footsteps went on except for those of two men who paused before Kildare's door. Burton's heart sank as the door knob rattled.

"That tough Texas guy ought to have a chair in there," hiccoughed a voice outside. "Damn if I want to stand up."

"Kildare's out. Ye can't git in, Joe. It's locked."

"The hell with that. Half the rooms in this damn place open with the same key."

"Well, I'm goin' on. Bring me a chair if there's two."

An agonized look flashed from Lucinda to the ex-Confederate when the man named Joe began fumbling at the door lock. Noiselessly Burton crossed the floor, his gaunt features taut, his clubbed revolver poised in his good hand.

Kildare's key fell to the floor with a clink as the other's key pushed into the lock. Joe's key turned and there was a click. Yellow light flooded the room from the hall as a smallish man, clad in the black frock coat and string tie of a professional gambler, entered.

"Say, what're you doin' in here?" he demanded when he saw Lucinda. "Who——"

Burton's revolver butt crashed down on the back of the gambler's head and Joe pitched forward with a jarring thud. The ex-Confederate closed and locked the door, hoping against hope that the sound of the man's fall had not reached the ears of Smiley's men.

While he stood listening, Lucinda snatched towels from a rack over the washstand and tied the unconscious gambler's hands and ankles. Another towel served as a gag. She had just finished her swift task when a guttural voice roared down the corridor.

"Joe! Hey, Joe! Where the hell has that damned soak gone?"

"For another drink, most likely," growled Smiley's deep voice. "Come back here, Hank. We won't need Renault for a while. I'm goin' over those figures again."

"All right. I'll hunt him up later."

In the silence that followed there floated up the clamour of the tinny piano downstairs. Drunken voices began roaring out an obscene version of 'Oh, Susannah!' Burton leaned over the unconscious gambler and listened to his breathing.

"I didn't kill him, anyway," he said. "I was afraid I had, hittin' that way with my left hand. It's hard to gauge a blow that way."

"No great loss if you had killed him," said Lucinda bitterly.

"Joe Renault's responsible for plenty of graves on Boot Hill. I wonder where Tex is ? Oh, I wish he'd come."

"Easy does it," said Burton soothingly. "It's bound to take a little while."

Endless, nerve-racking minutes dragged by, each one longer than its predecessor, before footsteps could be heard on the stairs. Because of the raucous singing in the bar, Burton could make out no voices but, he told himself, that singing also served to keep Jack Smiley from hearing the footsteps. He crossed to the door. The double knock came and he unholstered his Colt. Would Kildare be alone ?

He jerked open the door and levelled his gun full into the startled face of Senator Valcour.

"My God, it's Burton !" the promoter cried. "You got away——"

"Shut up !" hissed Kildare from behind the Senator. "Git in thar, and quick !"

Valcour, his hands rising slowly, stepped into the room. Kildare turned in the hall, motioned to Burton to close the door and walked toward Smiley's room. Burton jammed shut the door, his gun jabbed into Valcour's ribs, and turned the lock. He listened to the voices outside.

"Hi, Tex !" somebody said. "Been lookin' all over fer you."

"Sho' now ?" drawled the Texan. "I jest come in. Renault ? Shore I saw him. He was over to the Blue Star, gettin' slopped."

"He is, is he ?" asked a voice Burton recognized as Comanche Ted's. "Jack'll shore frale him plenty fervent when he catches him. C'mon, Tex. The boss wants to see you mighty bad."

CHAPTER XXXIII

PRODDED by Burton's gun, Senator Valcour advanced to the centre of the room, stepping over Renault's bound and gagged body. The promoter's face was stiff, impassive, but his eyes glowed with— what ? Burton asked himself. Fear ? Anger ? *How much did this man know?*

Lucinda suddenly moved from the bed, stooped and took a brace of derringers from Renault's gaudy waistcoat. Then she returned to the bed, one of the tiny pistols aimed waveringly at Valcour.

Burton stepped close to the chalk-faced Senator and spoke in a low, strained voice.

"I need the key to your cypher, Valcour," he said. "Speak up but keep your voice low."

The promoter seemed surprised.

"Cypher ? What cypher ?"

"That cypher you use for sending some of your telegrams."

"Don't be absurd," Valcour snorted. "I use no cypher !"

The Senator looked tall and distinguished as he stood in the centre of the room, dusty boots a little apart and his hands at shoulder height. Burton knew that, now that the first shock was over, the Union Pacific's principal promoter was thinking fast.

"Don't lie, Valcour," rapped the ex-Confederate. "I know you've got a cypher. I saw coded telegrams of yours at the telegraph office."

Valcour smiled coldly.

"That's a private cypher," he admitted. "The nature of my business often requires a certain amount of secrecy. Even you must see that."

"I've got to have that key. Do I get it ?"

Burton's revolver rose in line with Senator Valcour's impassive features. The promoter's forehead suddenly became beaded with drops of sweat.

"Don't be a fool !" Valcour said disdainfully. "I don't carry the key around with me."

"Search him, Lucinda !"

The girl's quick fingers went over the contemptuous Senator's spare frame. She looked at Burton and shook her head. Burton bit his lip, then started under the impact of a sudden realization. Granted that Valcour and Smiley did use the same cypher, a code that could be used by an ignorant renegade must be a simple one that could be carried in the mind.

"You're lyin'," he snarled in pretended rage. "I've got nothin' to lose and a lot to gain. I'll certainly kill you if you don't come across with that key before I count five !"

"You wouldn't dare," stormed the Senator. "I tell you I know nothing of all this ! You've seen I haven't got my cypher key on me and if I had it wouldn't help you !"

"One !" said Robert Burton. Over the gunsights he saw the promoter's grey eyes harden. "Better talk !"

"This is outrageous—insane !"

"Two !"

"You gain nothing by murdering me ! Let me go and I'll promise not to prosecute——"

"Three ! Keep your damned voice down !"

Valcour was silent, staring at the gun.

"Four !"

Senator Valcour's shoulders rose sharply as he shuddered.

"Hold on !" he cried weakly. "I—I'll give you what you want. There's no use being murdered by a madman. After all, you'll never get out of here alive, Burton !"

"Give me the cypher key—and it had better decode the telegram I found at the office. Quick ! 'Cinda."

Silently, the round-eyed girl crossed the floor.

"The messages I got before to-night are in my right shirt pocket," Burton told her. "Take them out."

The tension was telling on the ex-Confederate. Men were constantly passing up and down the corridor outside. He began to sweat when Lucinda Jameson pulled out the renegade's note and his own copies of Smiley's code telegrams. In the same pocket the girl found paper and the stub of a pencil. Her skirts rustling, Lucinda stepped over Renault's body and dropped onto a chair near the bureau, where faint light beat in to let her see.

"Remember," warned Burton. "If that cypher doesn't work, I shoot, whether it's your fault or not."

"Write out J-U-L-E-S in capital letters," said Valcour in a low and tremulous voice. "Now put an l in front of the J and under each letter fill in the rest of the alphabet in groups of five."

The weight of the big Colt was dragging cruelly at Burton's left arm by the time Lucinda had created the following square:

```
IJ U L E S
A  B C D F
G  H K M N
O  P Q R T
V  W X Y Z
```

"There you are," Valcour grunted. His eyes ranged restlessly. "Can't you move that gun lower. Your finger might slip."

"Try the renegade's message first," Burton directed. "No, Valcour, there's no use tryin' to jump me. I'm a fast shot."

"How does this key work ?"

The promoter hesitated a moment, blinking as drops of sweat trickled down his forehead into his eyes.

"Take the first letter in the message," he directed finally, "and locate it on the key. But write down the letter which appears to the *right* of the one on the key."

'Dear Smiley:

XTJQKFMBTMNLQKLRKL
ERTMLDTJGLCOTQPOJML
ALQFRLQKETHVSUU
DTQBLEBLMCKLMLXHSRDTW
ZSUFNLALFZLQDTQHEFSBE
BQLLH

NAMLR.'

"The first letter is X, and the letter on its right is Y," said Lucinda, looking up. "What do I do if the letter I'm looking for is on the end of the line? The next is T."

Silence.

"Go on!" grated Burton.

"Look at the other end of the same key line."

Rigid muscles were standing out along Andrew Valcour's massive jaw and he seemed to be bracing himself for action. Lucinda wrote swiftly.

"*It's right*, Bob!" she breathed. "Here's the word 'your.' Shall I go on?"

"Yes. Better learn what we can. We can't get out now anyway. Work as fast as you can."

The three presented a dramatic tableau in the little hotel bedroom. There was Valcour, standing tensed and desperate; Burton, fighting pain and fatigue; the garishly-dressed girl bent over a corner of the bureau. Every now and then a breathless gasp of surprise burst from the girl's swollen lips but her pencil kept flying over the paper. Outside came the roar of the mob.

"Money!" howled a rioter beneath the window. "We want our pay! To hell with the U.P. slave-drivers."

"I've got two of the notes deciphered," Lucinda announced. "Shall I do the third?"

"No," Burton ordered. "Read what you've got. It may tell us what to do."

"This was the renegade's note. There were a lot of misspellings:

'Dear Smiley:
Your man Conger met me, Stone Forhed, Porqpine Bare. Terms o.k. Will atack 23rd with all forces. cend money Kit Fox vilage, Beaver Fork, Sappa Crick.
                                                                        G. Bent.'"

Conger! The floor seemed to heave under Burton's booted heels. Great God, Casement's right hand man was a traitor! Now the ex-Confederate knew why his ambush above the curve at Lone Oak had failed. Smiley had been warned in plenty of time.

Valcour, his thin face gone grey, remained rigid.

"The other note," he directed fiercely. "The copy you made of Smiley's telegram."

"It's to a man in Saint Louis called E. K. Wilson.

'Tricked by Burton, but have seized him and pay money. Plans succeeding. Labourers rioting. Sioux and Cheyenne gathering. Valcour suggests killing Casement. I think it risky. Advise concerning U.P. stock. Forward my money right away.'"

Burton stared at the taut-faced promoter.

"So you *were* in on it !" he grated. "Why ?"

"To make money, you fool !" Valcour said easily. "I'm heavily interested in Central Pacific, along with certain friends. The U.P. will smash to-morrow and they won't be able to give away its stock. And I'll have made a million."

"So you hired Smiley !"

"Surely. Conger, too."

"Where's that pay chest ?" demanded Burton.

"I don't know," the promoter said. "I had no part in that. Perhaps you can persuade Smiley to tell you where it is."

"Quiet !"

"Where the hell is Joe Renault ?" Jack Smiley was thundering down the hall. "Jim, you beat it out and find him. And say, Tex, Fenton and Wells are tuckered out. They can use your bed. No spare rooms left. You'll be busy till sun-up, anyway."

"Ain't nobody sleepin' in my bed," Kildare drawled.

"The hell they're not !" Smiley snapped. "*I'm* givin' orders here ! Luke, Bud, Terry ! Open up that room."

"Okay, Jack," said Kildare in a sullen voice. "Have it your way. But I'll clear my dunnage out myself. I'll sleep in the barn."

"You're goddam fussy about who you sleep with, ain't you ?" Smiley sneered. "I'll give you five minutes. Now git !"

Feet tramped down the corridor and Valcour nervously licked his lips when they halted just outside the door. The lock clicked and the gunman's bow-legged figure was briefly silhouetted in the door.

"Quick !" Tex snapped. "Knock that old polecat over the head and we'll try to get out."

The door of Smiley's room opened, forcing the four breathless figures in the bedroom to be so quiet that the measured tramp of troops marching somewhere in the street below sounded distinctly in the room.

"You damn fools," came Valcour's supercilious tones. "You've never stood a chance !"

His foot shot out and a washstand fell over with a resounding crash. Valcour darted for the door.

One of Kildare's Twins shot down Valcour before he had taken a full stride.

"Come on !" the Texan yelled. He flung open the door and then slammed it shut. Burton caught an instant's glance of Smiley's men, crowding the hallway outside.

"Valcour ?" called Smiley. "That your voice ? Tex ! What the hell's goin' on ?"

In desperation, Burton's eyes darted about the room. He saw a door connecting with a room to the right. It proved to be locked. The windows offered only a long and dangerous drop to the ground. Immediately below was a jumbled heap of boxes and barrels that spelled broken legs and arms for anyone who tried the jump.

"Open up !" Smiley was thundering.

Pistol butts clattered furiously against the door panels as Kildare began to shove the bureau out from the wall. Burton led Lucinda back across the room and flipped over the mattress to form some kind of a barricade.

"Soon's the shootin' starts, honey," he said, "I'll try to shoot the lock off that connectin' door. Crawl into the next room and get away, the first chance you get."

"I'm staying, Bob. I'm glad——"

Her voice was drowned out by the blows clattering on the door.

"So long, Burton," Kildare called. "You promised me action and you shore kept yore word."

He jerked several cartridges from his belt and dropped them to the floor beside his right knee.

"Hear that ? " Smiley bellowed outside. "Burton's in there ! Come on, boys. This time we'll get him for sure, and it's five hundred dollars to the first man who lays hands on him. O'Gorman, tell the men downstairs to cover the windows. We got him cornered like a rat."

Now a panel flew in and the whole door tottered on its hinges. Kildare kneeled behind the bureau, grinning like a hungry wolf, a Twin in each hand.

"Come on ! What's keepin' you-all. I thought you were hard *hombres* !"

Lucinda, disobeying Burton's orders, joined the ex-Confederate behind the mattress with one of Renault's derringers in her hand. She looked up at him and managed a smile.

"Whatever happens," she said, "I'm glad I'm with you, dear."

When the door swung open wider, Burton and Kildare fired in unison. Splinters flew and men shouted but the door went down, burying Renault beneath it. Deadly cool, the ex-Confederate fired one more shot at a mass of figures struggling in the doorway. Then he turned and shot the lock off the connecting door. Bits of metal flew and the door swung open. Burton groaned. Smiley had foreseen that kind of a move and the adjoining room was occupied by crouching gunmen.

The room became a fantastic and deadly realistic nightmare. Billows of grey-white powder smoke filled it with strangling, eye-stinging fumes lit by the glare of pistol flashes. Burton never had seen such shooting as Kildare's. Again and again the Texas gunman shot and he never seemed to miss. Only vaguely did Burton hear the mirror of the bureau shatter into a thousand jangling pieces. Window-panes crashed and shivered and the heavy, bitter smoke eddied in the draught.

Several of Smiley's men had been crippled and at least two more killers were stretched on the bedroom floor. Burton snapped a shot at a dim outline looking in from the side door. A strangled cough and the clatter of a fallen gun told him he had scored.

"Here, 'Cinda."

The girl's nimble fingers fed fresh cartridges into Burton's hot-barrelled Colt.

"I'm coverin' the side door," he called to Kildare during a brief lull.

"Pretty little ruckus, ain't she, pardner? Hi-yah! The Twins is gettin' warmed up."

The ex-Confederate risked a glance toward the hallway door. There he saw a small, tangled pile of men. One of them was groaning loudly, incessantly. Menacing shadows wavered on the corridor's bullet-scarred wall. A welter of yelping voices filled the Julesburg House. Outside, a noisy crowd had gathered.

"Hell's roaring bells!" howled Smiley. "What's wrong with you yellow bellies? Get downstairs some of you, They're lying low so fire up through the floor. Sure you can! Those boards ain't but half-inch pine. Rest of you come this way. A thousand bucks to the first man to bring either of 'em in!"

Burton's brain raced as heavy feet outside clattered off to obey Smiley's orders. He slithered over to Kildare in a crabwise crawl and placed his mouth close to the other's ear.

"Pretend you're badly hurt. If they come in to collect that thousand, jump up close to the wall and start shootin'."

"I don't get you, but I'll do it," whispered the Texan. "*Hombre*, all my life I been huntin' a scrap like this! Ain't she a *honey*?"

"A funeral, you mean. Smiley *can't* quit till we're dead. He must know Valcour spilled the beans. Good luck."

By filling his mouth with saliva, Burton began to imitate the wheezing, bubbling gasps of a man shot through the lungs. Actually, he found little room for hope. The trick *might* work but, in the end, he, Kildare and the girl at his side must die. He winced at the realization that he must die without proving himself to Casement and the others.

"Gee, Gus, hear that?" came Comanche Ted's voice. "Guess I plugged that Texas lobo after all!"

"The other one's hit too, sounds like. Listen to him bubble!"

"Naw, it's a trick," said O'Gorman. "Hold back, you *hombres*. Damn you, hold back!"

"And let you collect that thousand? Like hell!"

"One side. I'm a-goin' in!"

"Stay back, you fools!"

In a concerted rush half a dozen killers surged forward. Twice Burton shot from the floor then, when the gunmen dropped flat, he yelled: "Up!" and leaped to his feet, flattening himself against the wall. His two companions did likewise.

Then, suddenly, Smiley's men on the floor began to wilt in odd positions. As Burton had hoped, the killers downstairs had, at the first crack of the defenders' guns, begun to fire up through the floor. Splinters flew madly. Two of Smiley's men in Kildare's room were killed immediately while a third was badly hurt. The others scrambled out of the room, cursing wildly.

"Stop it down there, you goddam idiots!" screamed Smiley. "Stop shooting! God damn you, Burton, I'll have your ears for that stunt!"

There was another lull and Burton, checking his belt and gun, found he had but two shots left. This, then, was the end.

"So long, pardner," Kildare shouted. "Hope you and the gal hit it off!"

Before Burton could prevent it, Kildare began a *sortie*.

"Hi yah! Yah!" he yelped and, with his Hierro Twins flaming, the killer from Texas went limping towards the hall door. Guns spat back at him but the thunder of the Twins spoke louder. A man screamed hoarsely. Running shadows were seen on the bullet-pitted corridor wall. Then Kildare staggered, recovered and, shooting precisely, unhurriedly, he gained the doorway and drove the howling gangsters down the hall. His guns cracked spasmodically a little longer. Then came the sound of a heavy fall and the Twins were silent.

Out from the adjoining room bounded Jack Smiley and O'Gorman.. Burton snapped a shot at Boot Hill Jack—missed—and dropped O'Gorman! It was then that Lucinda's derringer added its tiny bark to the uproar. Smiley reeled and clutched at his right shoulder before shifting his gun to the left hand.

Lucinda quietly fainted.

A sudden, stunning silence ruled over the hotel as Burton and Smiley advanced from opposite sides of the room. Smiley, smoke-blackened, his tangled hair fallen over his eyes, gave no sign of fear. Burton, his right arm crippled, came on, a deadly gleam in his eyes.

"Well, Burton—it's come——" panted the big man. "You been hard to get—but now——"

"Get set, Boot Hill Jack! I'm callin' you!"

The two shots clanged as one. Captain Robert Burton heard Smiley's bullet hiss past his ear. He looked at Smiley. Boot Hill Jack was crumpling forward, clawing at the air in a wild effort to recover his balance. He dropped on his knees, then turned over on his side.

Burton's old hatred boiled over as he jerked out the long knife and flung himself upon the struggling figure of Jack Smiley.

"Lie still!"

One all-important thing remained to be done. With the other's hot breath fanning his face, Burton held the knife's point against Smiley's throat. The big man seemed entirely conscious.

"Where's the pay chest?" Burton grated. He bent low as there was the thunder of steps ascending the stairs. "Answer me, damn you! Answer me or I'll stick you like the pig you are!"

Smiley's eyes glared up at him.

"Where is that gold?" The knife dipped to prick Jack Smiley's throat.

"Under cottonwood stump—fifty yards from north of Dry Creek—left side."

Burton relaxed. Somehow, he knew Smiley was telling the truth. Now he must manage to get out—to get to North or Casement or somebody!

Too late! The clatter of many feet resounded in the hallway outside. Burton turned to face Death, then gasped.

Long bayonets gleamed in the hall lights. In the van of a detachment of red-faced infantry stood Major Frank North.

CHAPTER XXXIV

It was night again and peace reigned over bullet-scarred Julesburg—peace, because on Boot Hill a dozen and a half new graves marked the passing of Smiley's power. Peace, because the railroad throbbed with activity again. Peace, because the labourers, their pockets heavy with pay, were sleeping off the effects of their riotous spree, faced with the prospect of bitter toil on the morrow.

In General John Stevens Casement's private car sat three people drinking from tinkling glasses and viewing the town through bullet-punctured windows.

"So your Texas friend will pull through?" Casement was asking.

"Yes," Captain Robert Burton nodded his bandaged head. "I reckon Tex is too tough to die, even with six bullet wounds. Great God, General, you should have seen him! Both guns goin' and walkin' right out into the hall to meet that mob."

"Yez did a bit o' shootin' on your own account, I hear," was Casement's dry comment. "By the by, we're to be cheated out of a fine hangin'."

"Then Smiley's dead?" asked Lucinda Jameson in a hushed voice.

"Yes. He was a fighter to the end, but the bleedin' couldn't be stopped."

A short silence fell. Casement went on, his eyes lowered.

"Those omadhauns, Conger and McCue, are goin' east to-night for trial, on the same train as—as the third traitor." The red-bearded man sighed and drummed absently on his glass. "I can't help bein' sorry for Jessica Valcour. She near to died when she found out what her father had done. She had no idea, of course."

Burton nodded.

"Life will be hard for her now, I reckon," he said. "As hard for her as it's goin' to be easy for me."

A smile lit up his face as he put his good arm around the waist of the girl at his side. She glanced up at him, her black eyes eloquent of things too deep and beautiful for speech.

"And where will yez be going once you're married?" asked Casement, tugging at his flaming beard. "I'd like to show—to help, if I can."

"We've decided to stay on here, General," Burton said. "We've taken a—well, almost a family interest in the U.P., and we think we'll stay to watch it grow."

The Irishman roared in high delight.

"I hoped yez would," he said, lifting his glass. "There'll be a fine job for yez, Bob, and here's hopin' 'twill not be only the railroad yez will watch grow!"

THE END